Abdul Wajib Timee

*Bla.*

Along with

## *OhSo NeCessary*

Presents

X
X

# Pretty PoiSIN

An URBAN EXPERIENCE

By

Abdul Wajib Timeer Aziz

This is a work of fiction. Names, characters, some

places and incidents are the product of the author's

imagination or are used fictitiously, and any

resemblance to the real people or incidents is purely

coincidental.

## SPECIAL THANKS

To ALLAH, THE BEST OF PLANNERS, THE

BEST of GUIDANCE and THE OVERALL

SOURCE of ALL of CREATION.

I thank ALLAH for sending Prophet

Muhammad (Peace be upon him) as a

mercy to mankind. And I thank ALLAH for

choosing me as one of HIS Slaves.

### To The Muslim Mafia:

Shakiel, Amir, Timeer, Gibriel, Kareem

Akram, Kareem Lock and Muhammad (Spiritual

Advisor).

## DEDICATIONS

To MS. EMMA JEAN STACKS CARROTHERS (RIP). Your memory will forever live on thru me, your children and grands. LOVE YOU thru ETERNITY. Raymond Carrothers (Pop), Andrea "All Purpose" Pegues (Duh 1), Porchia, Lil Tim, Imari.... Sherry, Shayla, Man, Ty, Tracy, Lil Raymond, Var, Damon, Daryl, Hope, Yummy (Norgee), Louis (Spooky), Tori Stacks, Tameka, Colonda, Rhonda, Tiny, Buddy, Omari, Wayne, and Amia.  My aunts... Aunt Sis, Linda, Coline, Del, Iris, Lene....... To my Unlce Doc... (The Coolest) Y'all helped save my Life.The sky is the limit. I got'chall.

## REST IN PEACE

Francis Carrothers  (Granny)

Stephen Benard Stacks (Uncle/Brother)
(The Original Sleezy B)

Sammie Stacks (Daddy)

Queen Esther Stacks (Mother)

Louis Stacks  (Uncle/Pops)

## My future lies in my Lineage:

London 'Lucci' Hunt and Layla 'Neek Neek' Bethea

T-Daddy Do it All  fuh Y'all

## SPECIAL ACKNOWLEDGEMENTS:

Jacquis, Wondra, Beverly, Kay, Shawntia, Javaris &
The Pegues/Springs Family…..

Kimyon (Big Cuz) you have always inspired me to
be great.

Beverly Crowder and Sunshine Anderson are the
two greatest singers I have ever known…….

## SUPPORTING CAST:

Manager- Jamaal Griggs (Nlightenmental
Productions), Business Consultant – Tillman
Cowan (ON1Nation.com), Magagement Team -
Booklyn (4 Ever Ink), CEA - Rod (SkiBo Live)
Johnson, CEA – The incredible (Deejay Polo),
Avertisement WPEG- Najiyyah (Gia) Mateen,
Angela Marshall (Dash Studios), Taha Jabaar,
Richard Hovis Jr. (NCNG), Traci Tingle (Spiritual
Advisor),Toshia The Model(ME/ Timpt'n Ladies
Apparel Spokesperson), Cedric Brooks & Tonia
(Raw Cutz Entertainment), Power 98 -WPEG,
The STREETZ 103.3 and 92.7 The BLOCK.  Wade
Mosley, Dickie Davis, Dawn Davis, Terry Bradley,
Brian Springs, Patrick Cannon (The Mayor),
Marcellas Jackson, Netta Jackson, Darby, Pravis
(Pee) Jackson, Shannon Wortham, Vickie
Hernandez, Rita, Shannon (Dub C),

## INSPIRED BY:

Stephanie Stroud, Richard "Kato" Dayson, Ronald "Manifest" Winchester, Vicki Stringer, Blake Karrington, Edwina Brooks, Michelle Davis, TBRS (TEAM BANK ROLL SQUAD).

## SPECIAL THANKS TO:

### NeXt CoaSt NetworK'N Group Family

Fat Daddy, Cat- X, IQ, Dwayne"BIGGZ" McLaurin, James "J-MELODY" McQueen, Rash, Joanne Spruill (My Attorney), Eureka Wiggins, Alan Smith, Ash, Christina Johnson, Tiffany Huggins, CMC: Dump Truck aka Versace Black, Teezy Montana, CJ, T-Lay. Alias Mogul Brand, Aveion "Rent Due" Jones, Bay Boy"Krowntown King." Karolina Kings: LaQuan, A1, Dizzy, Mark Sparks, Davour, Finatic, Will Skee, D-Mac, Nyborn, Omniscience, Toz Torchuh, N-Tyce, Toshia (The Model), L-A-F: Afghan Can aka Guala, Bandana Bondz aka Marcus Darby. POP: Tony Sloan (Python & Power Of Pain Gang).

Oh Yeah…….. Author/Filmaker Marcus Massey (Game recognize Game) but we ain't Play'n, Grown Folk handle Business, children play games. I Salute and Thank you Brutha. Most gone hate, but I'm uh Salute a Legend. We some helluva dudes Flaws and All (Lmao). GARGANTUAM FILMS / C.E.A. fuh LIFE.

"Thank Y'all for EVERYTHING"!!!!  Y'all are the best….. THE BOSSES that NEVA SLEEP.  That's how my business gets handled.

## THANKS TO:

Temothye I LOVE U Darlin, Dana, Tina, Joey, Trippy, Layfette , Tanesha Martin, Donald (Shaft), Donqua, Pratt, Rod, Clarence McSwain, Ronnie McCree, Kobie, Hatari, Datari, Turk, Jim Grier, Larry Ray, Paul Williamson, Boogie (Electric), Fox, Jen, Tight, Obar, Big Terrance, Amp, Shack, Shanetta, Mimi, TC, Que, Lahari, Jatana, Nivia, Vanita, Tania, Kim, Odell (OD) Alexander, Tish, Crystal, Alethea, Jocelyn, Lashonda, Rosita, Star, Nikki (Nanette), Nikki Branch, Christy, Carna, Jinx and Muhammad.

## SHOUT OUTS:

To All My Family Behind The Iron Gate

Eric Ledwell (730), Jeremy "Murder" Moore Irongate Publishing …..Coming Soon.

"Charlotte gave me Life, Greensboro gave me Game and ISLAM branded me a Man".

## Chapter 1: The Start

From the beginning, I was never a big people person but for some strange reason people were always drawn to me (especially women of all sorts). Coming up as a kid, I know that I was different from most kids my age. Hell, they had both their mother and father in their home and lives. I had neither. It was just my little sister and me.

My father left my mom before I was old enough to walk but he found his way back to tap dat ass here and there. Which is the process that brought my little sister 2 years later. We would see our father's mother (Granny) quite often, along with our aunt Linda and 3 uncles (Anthony, Wayne, and Leon) before we were at the ages of 8 & 6. After that, it was ever so often. Mind you, I didn't say we seen our father, I said his family. Every once in a while he would pass through during one of our visits.

Being that my father was never around and never gave us any type of support that meant, my mom was the bread winner. She worked all the time. She was almost never at home and when she was, she would sleep until maybe an hour and a half before her shift started. That was time enough to bathe, grab something to eat and get to work on time.

She had to work regardless and we barely ever had sitters. From the time I was 9 and my sister was 7, we were staying at home alone-day or night and sometimes both depending on her overtime.   My mom had no support from her family members when it came to watching us so we watched ourselves.

My mom was very religious early in our lives. She attended an Apostolic Church in Northwest Charlotte called Progressive Church of our Lord Jesus Christ. They were very strict. The women were not allowed to wear pants, jewelry, or makeup. They didn't celebrate no holidays and the things that the normal children did to experience life and childhood eras were totally forbidden. No sleep overs, amusement parks, or parties. Their motto was "Evil communication corrupts good manners," so we were only allowed to experience the company of the other members of the Church. That was somewhat easy considering we were in Church 5 out of 7 days a week. The thing that attracted me to Church was the music. At the age of 5 I had mastered the tambourine and I was pursuing my interest in percussion instruments. Between the ages of 5 and 9 I would play the tambourine, bongos, and drums.

At any given service the "Holy Spirit" would take over and the whole church would be jump'n and shout'n while the musicians play gospel R&B. Not to down play the actual service but the music was what captivated me. Due to my mom's work schedule, by the time I was 9 or 10 we barely attended church which resulted in an early life of sex, drugs, and mischievous acts. By the age of 10, I had skills in cooking, cleaning, getting high and by far my favorite, having sex. It all started in 1979, I was 8 years old and on one of those rare occasions my mom found us a sitter. We lived in a 2 bedroom apartment in a complex called Tryon Forest.

My mom had met this little girl in the neighborhood named Tonya. Tonya had pecan brown skin with a slim frame. Her hair was right at shoulder length and she kept it in a ponytail. Tonya was 14 and she aroused my young ass with her sexy eyes and lips. At such a young age I was always fascinated by the female anatomy.

On this particular evening, Tonya was there with her little sister Tara who was a year younger than me. Most of the time Tonya really never paid us any attention, she was only there to make the money and talk on the phone. As usual, she was down stairs on the phone with her best friend Missy, my sister Shan was in here watching TV, and I was in my room closet playing with Tara. Shan must have realized Tara had been missing for a while because she came looking for her after she ran down stairs asking Tonya had she seen us. My fast ass and Tara was in the closet kiss'n and smooch'n like we were 16-17. Here comes Shan, "Teddy, Tara, where yall at?"

A finger over my lip, "shhh, she'll go away."

"Tara, where yall at? I know yall tryin to scare me". Shan assumed, not know'n we were in the closet experimenting.

I just looked at Tara and giggled, knowing Shan wouldn't dare open that closet door due to her fear of us scaring her. We continued our little freak show. Ten minutes had passed and I had just pulled Tara's pants and panties down when all of a sudden the closet door opened. There we were sitting in the corner of the closet, Tara's pants down, I'm on top of her, and we're busted. Tonya screamed, "Teddy what are you doing? Get off of her! Tara, what are your panties doing down? Yall in trouble! Git out of there, NOW! Tara and I both were scared to death. We both knew we were in a world of trouble. My mom didn't play, I was scared to death of that woman.

It was obvious from the way Tonya was yell'n that there was no way out of the trouble I was in. "Shan, Tara, go to Shan's room and git in the bed now. Teddy, you stay right here, I'm gone call your mom."

I sat there sick to my stomach thinking about how bad my mom was going to kill me. It was already hard enough for her to find someone to sit with us while she worked 3rd shift, I knew she would definitely crush my whole existence. As I sat there on the side of my bed in the dark with my stomach in knot's, about 25 minutes had passed when my door flew open. Tonya cut on my light and looked over at me with my head down playing with my fingers and said, "Oh, so you not sleep?"

I replied in the lowest, most pitiful voice, "No." Then she responded, "Don't be trying to look all pitiful now. You know better. What were you and Tara think'n?" In a low tone I said," We were just play'n."

Play'n! Yall were doing a little more than play'n." She closed the door behind her as she came all the way in my room and said, "In fact, I want you to show me what yall was play'n."

Look'n real stupid I said, "We was play'n house." She said, "I didn't ask you to tell me, I told you to show me."

She's standing there with this blue jean skirt on and a t-shirt barefooted staring at me.

All I could say is," I'm already in trouble."


"Teddy, do you want me to tell Ms. Queen on you?"

Ms. Queen was my mom. Which was short for Queen Ruth.

I looked up at her, "NO".

"Then come over here and show me how to play house."

"What chu want me to do?"

"Do to me what you was doing to Tara."

"Oh." Right then I walked over to her and stuck my hands up her skirt and grabbed her panties and pulled them down to her ankles. Once she stepped out of them, she laid on my twin bed and pulled her skirt up. This was unfamiliar grounds. I was use to smooch'n and kiss'n on little girls my age. This was different, she had hair on her cooty. So now I'm standing there looking at this beautiful playground between her legs when she tells me to take off my pants. Somewhat hesitant, I pull'd down my pants leaving my draws on. All you could see is my premature joy stick aimed straight ahead. "Take them off and come here."

At this point I'm real nervous because I never done the oochie coochie with my clothes off before. After I took off my draws, I was standing there with a t-shirt on and my little joy stick stickin out from under it. "Now what?"

"Come here."

As I climbed up on the bed she opened her legs wider as if she was guiding me to the playground. So I crawled all the way between her legs until my little joystick was close to the playground. Now I'm looking down in her face and all of a sudden I feel her hand grab me below.

"Come here," she said real softly.

Her handing guiding me, I slid up a little further until my little joystick was gliding into a warm, wet, sticky place. I couldn't believe what I was feeling. Tonya just began to roll her hips in a circular motion while she held me in place by my little butt cheeks.

"Ummm, yeah, that feel good."

I'm thinking to myself, it sho do.

"Teddy, you alright?"

"Ummm Hmm."

At this point, I'm so amazed. I'm just looking at her enjoy herself while I'm experiencing something I've never felt before that feels so good. I remember thinking to myself, "This has to be wrong."

Tonya aroused herself with me for a long time and right before she stopped I asked her, "You not gone tell on me, is you?"

As she smiled at me she said, "No, but from now on when I keep you and Shan, we gone do this before you go to bed, ok?"

"OK."

Once we was finished, she grabbed her panties, covered me up and went to the bathroom. She was gone for maybe 15 minutes. While she was gone I remember the strange smell from touching my joystick and smelling it. I also noticed the sticky stuff that was on me. It felt nasty but it was good. The smell didn't stank, it was just different.

Tonya came back in the room with a towel and wash cloth. She pulled my covers back and began to wipe me off. After she washed me off she dried me off and told me to put on my pj's.

"Did you like it?" She asked.

"Yeah, what was it?"

"It was sex, don't tell nobody. That's between us."

"OK.'

She kissed me in my mouth and walked out and closed my door. I made up the bed we had been in and got in my other twin bed because the other one had wet spots in it. It didn't take me no time to fall asleep and that night I dreamed I was having sex with Tonya. I woke up and ran to the bathroom to pee and I was just staring at myself. Looking down at my joystick, thinking to myself "something is wrong with me. I'm gone get in trouble."

It was real hard to sleep that night. Every time I thought about what had happened earlier that night my little joystick would get real hard. Little did I know, my life had been totally changed from that night.....on.

Finally I fell asleep just to be woke up only what seemed like a few hours later.

"Teddy, Teddy, git up and git ready for church, yall's ride is gonna be here in 15 minutes."

Looking up at my mom yawning, "Do I have to go?"

"What do you mean do you have to go? Go brush your teeth and start your shower, Shan been dressed. What time did you go to bed last night and why didn't you lay out your church clothes last night? Teddy, you know better!"

Sitting on the edge of my bed feeling real drowsy.

"Answer me boy!"

Whinning like my moma's baby, "Maa, do I gotta go? I don't feel like it."

"Whus wrong with you?"

"I just don't feel like going. I couldn't sleep last night."

"From now on when Tonya stays with yall, I'm gone make sure she put you to bed early."

Walking to the bathroom whinning and about to cry, "I don't wanna go. You ain't goin."

"Boy, I just got off from work and I got to get some rest before I gotta go back."

"I gotta headache." I explained.

"Well, soon as you get your shower and get dressed, You can get to church and go up for prayer."

NO matter how much I whined and slow poked around my mom meant what she said. Even if she couldn't make it to church she was sending us.

Just like clockwork, "Bomp, Bomp, Bommmp."

Teddy git down here. Mother and Daddy's out here"

Here I come moping down the stairs.

"Baby, you gone be alright. Gimmie some sugah."

"Ma...' I whined, wanting to refuse her kiss.

"Boy gimmie some sugah!"

I kissed her cheek and walked out the door.

"Don't forget to go up for prayer."

I kept walking towards the car. As I got to the car door my grandparents and my uncle was waiving at my mom. My grandma yelled back, "Queen send them some money. We going to Morrison's after church."

"Mother, I haven't cashed my check yet, bring them home first."

"No, you just pay me back when you cash your check."

"That's fine mother."

"We'll see you later. " My grandma rolled up the window and my grandpa drove off. My grand pop turned up the radio blasting the gospel music. I'm sitting in the middle of Shan and my uncle Steve.

Steve is my mom's baby brother. He is 13 years old and we were a helluva combination together. Before, I was born he got all the attention. I'm the oldest grandson and he's the baby brother out of 5 children, my mom being the oldest. She is 18 years older than Steve, so he was basically her child until I came along. For a long time he and I use to fight like dogs until one day we just bonded and now it's like he's my older brother instead of my uncle. The whole family hates for us to be together because they knew that there's gonna be trouble.

I was sitting in the back with my head leaned against the seat with my eyes closed thinking about Tonya and what we did the night before, when I feel my right arm get bumped by Steve's elbow. "Whus wrong wit'chu?" He asked.

Still whinning," My head hurtin and I don't feel like comin to church and moma made me."

My grandma said," You need to go up for prayer. Teddy, are you playing the tambourine this morning? Cause you know you and Steve can't sit together."

Still whinning please mother, I don't feel like playing today."

"That's all you and Steve gone do if yall sit together."

"No we won't mother, I promise"

My grand pops jumped up in the conversation. "Let'm sit together. If they start play'n, just send for me and I'll take them both out and take my belt off."

I looked at Steve and he looked at me and we both giggled because we knew we had'm. My granddad was the head deacon of the church and well respected. Once he spoke we knew we were getting ready to have plenty of fun in church laugh'n at all the old folks and watch'n all the same people fake the "Holy Ghost" and shout'n everywhere. No matter what we do, my grandma won't call Daddy (my grand pop) on us because she won't let him whoop Steve too fast. He had sickle cell and she was scared it would trigger a crisis. Needless to say, we had a ball in church. I reached over and whispered to Steve, "I got something to tell you after church."

"Tell me now."

"No, we'll git in trouble. I'm gone tell you just wait."

"Don't forget."

"I won't."

I just had to tell him about last night. He always tell me about his girlfriend. He let's me talk to them on the phone and set me up with his girl's sister or cousin. So I was anxious to tell him.

I thought church wasn't going to ever let out. I fell asleep soon as the preacher began to speak. All of a sudden I'm being shook to death by my grandma.

"Baby, go up for prayer."

Mad that she woke me up. I began to whine.

"Mother I don't want to go up there, I'm alright."

"Teddy, go up the aisle to the front of the church. Our pastor Elder Jenkins put some prayer oil on my forehead then grabbed the top of my head and began to pray. Finally, it was over and church had let out. At this point I am ready to go.

Through all the commotion of everybody shaking hands and greeting each other I finally found my uncle.

"Steve, git da keys and let's go sit in the car."

"Aa-ight, go to the car I'll be there in a minute."

While I'm waiting on him at the car our church girlfriends walk over. Steve went with Dee-Dee and I was going with her lil sister Mona. Steve and Dee-Dee were the same age and Mona was two years older than me. Simultaneously they spoke with smirky smiles on their faces.

"Hey Teddy."

"Hey Mona, hey Dee-Dee."

Mona came and stood beside me as I leaned on the car.

Dee-Dee stood front and center.

Where's Stevie?" Dee-Dee asked.

"He gone to git da keys to da car."

"Where yall goin out to eat at?"

"I don't know."

She went on to tell me that she overheard my granddad making plans with her dad for us all to eat at the same restaurant. Then Steve walked up. He spoke to Dee-Dee and Mona as he unlocked the car doors. Steve and Dee-Dee got in the front seat Mona and I got in the back. Mona was checking on me to see why I went up for prayer. Midway through our conversation Steve told them we would see them at the restaurant he needed to talk to me. Dee-Dee kissed Steve in the mouth, Mona kissed my cheek and they got out the car.

"Git up here."

I got out the back seat and into the front.

"What you gotta tell me?" He asked.

"I had sex with Tonya last night."

"No you didn't! What happened?"

I began to tell'm in detail when my grandparents and my sister came to the car for us to go. We left church and went to the designated restaurant (Morrison's in Eastland Mall). Every free moment we had he was waiting on more details. Finally, when we got back to my grandparent's house I finished telling him everything, answering all questions in between.

From then on he always tried to spend the night every weekend. Somewhere in his mind he felt that Tonya was going to eventually give in to him. Every time Steve stayed over, Tonya acted mean and strict. Then on the flip side, through the week and other times, she was giving me all I could handle. Looking back, it's hard to believe how often we would go at it like wild dogs. Every episode she showed me something new. I found out later on that she also had told someone about our little secret when she brought her best friend Missy. I remember it like it was yesterday.

Tonya called my mom one Friday night a hour before Moma had to be at work and told her that she was bringing Missy with her because Missy was spending the weekend with her to finish up a project for school.  Even though my moma didn't approve, she didn't have enough time to make any other arrangements. You best believe she laid the law down before she left.

"Tonya please don't keep my line tied up all night. I like to speak to my kids before they go to bed."

In her best most adult but immature voice, "Ms. Queen, I be talking to Missy and she's here with me."

"Yeah I know so now it will be some little boys."

What Moma didn't know was, that I was that boy!

"Tonya, I'm runnin late. Jus call me if you need me. Teddy, Shan, yall be in the bed by 11. Teddy come here let me have a one on one with you."

I was known to git into a lot a trouble when company was around so everybody was under the impression that she was getting ready to put the fear of GOD in me. When I walked into the room Moma closed the door and said, "Listen, you can stay up a little later if you want to and let Moma know if they have anything going on that you don't approve of. This is your house and you the man of this house. Here's my # at work, call Moma if you feel anything wrong or they have anybody else over here.

"Ok Moma."

She walked out of the room talking as she left, "Shan give moma some sugah. Teddy git my pocketbook. I gotta go, I'm late."

As she walked out the door she yelled," I love yall. Tonya yelled be good."

Once she was gone, I went to my room to watch this freaky movie comin on HBO call "Emanuelle." I only left my room once to go to the bathroom.

When I did Shan was in her room play'n, Tonya and Missy were in the living room talk'n and laugh'n. It was just like Steve was there, Tonya basically ignored us. I went back to watch my freaky movie.

Eventually I fell asleep. All of a sudden I'm being woke up. Gently shakin my back and whispering," Teddy, Teddy git up."

I roll over on my back and look up at Tonya. She looks at me and whispers, "you want to do it?"

Still half sleep I realize what she's talking about and began to sit up. I was rubbing my eyes and I notice Missy sleep in the other bed. At least I thought she was. When I stood up Tonya laid in my bed and pulled down her sweat pants under the covers. I pulled off my shorts noticing that my joystick was super hard, then I crawled into the bed straight in between Tonya's legs. Soon as I slid into her playground she started moaning like clockwork. I'm thinkin she is going to wake Missy up so while I'm going in and out I look to see if she was woke.

Strangely enough, she was lay'n on her stomach with her arms folded and her chin on her forearms watching us. I stopped and tried to slide out of Tonya and under the covers. Tonya grabbed me by my waist and asked me where I was going? I whispered, "Missy is looking at us."

She said, "So, she knows already. Come here."

I slowly slid back in her and after about 10 minutes Missy says, "Is he gone do it?"

Tonya said, "Yeah hold on."

We continued for like forever until it looked like Missy was sleep again. Tonya tells me that she has to use the bathroom.   As I slide out of her she asked, "Will you do it to Missy?"

I looked at her with this real stupid childish look and said, "When? She sleep."

All of a sudden Missy's head pop's up and she says "No I'm not."

Tonya grabbed her sweat pants and walked out of the room. Once she walked out Missy got up out of my other bed. Missy was somewhat opposite of Tonya. She was short, with the prettiest, smoothest brown skin. She got up and anxiously walked over to my bed pulling down her shorts and panties. Missy was 15 already and she let me know what she was doing. Her playground was different. Her hairs were very thin and barely there.

After being with Tonya, this was very different. Missy's playground was much larger than Tonya's and Missy knew how to make hers move on the inside. In the middle of Missy and I doing it, Tonya walked in telling us to hurry up. Now at this time in my life I never knew what a nut was. As I'm rapidly going in and out of Missy this strong sensation runs straight through my little body and comes out of my joystick. To this day, I've never felt anything that felt so good. It left me shakin and so was Missy. That was the first time I had felt a cootie move on the inside.

A couple of years later I found out she was contracting her vaginal muscles. Once I was able to move again, I slide out of Missy as she slid from underneath me and out of the bed. She went into the bathroom and Tonya got up and followed her. I laid on my back dodging the wet spots in my bed as Tonya came back in the door with a wet rag. She wiped me off and told me not to tell nobody about what happened. She also apologized and said it would never happen again.

Knowing what I know now, Missy was the ring leader in the whole scenario from beginning to end. She coaxed Tonya into having sex with me. At least it seemed that way and every once in a while Missy would come with Tonya and I knew what was going on.

I never said anything else to Steve about Tonya and I having sex because he didn't believe me since I had no proof. Tonya and I got away with our little secret for close to a year, until we got caught.

We were in the living room. On this particular night, Moma had been gone long enough for Shan to be sleep and me and Tonya to be play'n. All I remember is hearing the key in the door. We were both so young and dumb we froze. By the time we began to move, Moma was walking in the door. The look on my moma's face told the story. I knew I was in a world of trouble. She closed the front door and sat in the chair near the door watching Tonya and I squirm for our clothes. She looked at me and said, "Since you fuck'n, you don't need a baby sitter."

Then she rest'd her head on the back of the chair looking at the ceiling and says, "I lose my job and come home to my 9 year old doing GOD knows what in my living room." I thought she was going to beat me to death. She cussed me and Tonya out, fired Tonya, put me on punishment and called my granny so she could tell my pop's on me. I don't know why she called to tell him, he wasn't gone do nothing. By the time he got back in contact with her about this, we had moved to the projects and I had picked several new bad habits.

## Chapter 2:  The Projects

As a result of my mom losing her job, we ended up in one of the most notorious housing projects in North Carolina let alone Charlotte. We were residence of Earle Village (Da Ville to da ole hoods). My life as I had known, was on its way to being a best seller.

Moma took some time off before she decided to go back to work. There were no more fancy clothes, baby sitters, and going out to eat every Sunday after Church. Instead, she got a check once a month, we barely ever went to Church and she would never let us come off of the porch.

In the beginning everyday was a test. I got in a fight every day after school. This was nothing I was use to. My mom always taught me not to put my hands on no girls, but they were the biggest bullies. At this time in my life I wasn't trying to do no whole bunch of fighting, especially not with no girls. I knew what they had between their legs and that's all I wanted.

A year had passed and I had become a 10 year old problem on the low. My aunt would come to spend the week, sometimes months with us and my mom only allowed it because of my little cousin Rashawn. At this point, my mom is back working and I watch after me, my sister and Rashawn whose 3. After watching my aunt and her friends, I began to pick up little habits, like smoking cigarettes. Aunt Jean would leave cartons of Kool cigarettes at the house with us with a pack already opened. Being curious, I attempted to smoke. Not knowing how to inhale I would just puff on them until one day auntie came in and erupted. "Teddy, Shan! Come here now!"

We came running up the stairs. When we got to the door of Shan's room (that's where auntie would stay and Shan would sleep in my other twin bed), auntie was standing there dangling an almost empty pack of Kool's. "Whose been in my things"

Shan quickly replied, "Not me Auntie!"

Auntie looked at me, "Teddy, yo fast ass been in my cigarettes?"

Being a little dumb ass I reply, "What cigarettes?"

Immediately she knew that I was guilty. She told me to sit on the bed and she sent Shan back down stairs. My auntie was my favorite out of my mom's two sisters. I was like her child before Rashawn came. She lit up a cigarette and talked real calm to me,

"Baby, you smoke?"

I'm thinking I'm in the clear so I answer, "Sometimes".

She said, "You been smoking auntie's cigarettes?" with a real calm demeanor and smile on her face.

I said, "Yeah".

She reached me the cigarette and told me to show her how I smoke. I grabbed the cigarette and started puff'n. She stopped me, "No baby, you wasting cigarettes. Auntie gone show you how to smoke. Now take a pull on the cigarette and keep the smoke in your mouth".

I'm doing everything she says. "Open your mouth."

Once I opened my mouth and she saw the smoke she told me to take a deep breath. When I took that deep breath, I began to cough so hard that I was slobbering and seeing stars and she began cursing and yelling at me. "That's what you git witcho stupid ass! You ain't grown! I bet not ever catch you in my shit! Git out, little fucka!"

As I'm walking out, my chest is burning and my head is spinning. I was so dizzy I had to sit on the floor outside the room.

What did she do that for?

It's the summer of 1982. My cousin Messiah had moved to North Carolina from

Brooklyn, NY. Messiah and my uncle Steve went to the same high school. These two individuals single handedly raised me into a mini man. Steve gave me my first joint and Messiah made sure I had sex with a multitude of chics from their school and age bracket. I was 11 years old with a reputation of an 18 year old.

Being that my mom worked all the time (she was a nurse at Hawthorne Nursing Center), I did basically whatever I wanted to do. I was so wild, I stay'd back in the fourth grade. School was the least thing on my mind. I was smoking weed, fuck'n and hangin with the older crowd. They loved me because they couldn't believe how wild I was at such a young age. All of my friends were in high school and I was a 6th grader. Messiah and Steve breeded me like that. See in New York it was the norm for the young dudes to be ahead of their time because everything is moving so fast up there but out here, it was never heard of.

Messiah had a breakdance group called the "B-Boys". He made sure they were the hottest group in Charlotte. That Christmas one of our best friends was having a major party at his parent's house. His name was Donnie. We all had hung together throughout the whole year. My mom knew Donnie's mom real well and he made sure I was going to be at the party.

Donnie also went to school with Steve and Messiah. That's how I met him. Donnie's parent's house was like a mansion. It had two kitchens (one upstairs and one downstairs), two living rooms (one upstairs one downstairs), 7 bedrooms, 4 bathrooms, a lounge room and a disco room with the pool on the outside.

Messiah and his crew was DJ'n the party. Not only did he dance, he was also an MC. If you were having a party, you wanted Messiah's man Tiger DJ'n and Messiah on the mic.

I had been at Donnie's house all day waiting on the main event. Donnie's sister Vera loved me because she was dating Messiah and she knew that I was her ticket to him throughout the night. It's about 6:30pm and most of their family is upstairs and I'm in the disco room helping Donnie set up when Vera called me outside. "Teddy, come here. I want to show you something."

I followed her down the driveway to the back of their house. Sitting in the driveway was a camper. She opened the door and motioned for me to come on. I stepped up inside the mini home and was amazed. Vera began to show me a cooler with nothing but beer and wine coolers in it.

She said, "This is where you wanna smoke a joint with me?"

Anxiously I asked, "Where's it at?"

She fired it up. We smoke and tripped out. By the time we got back to the house, people were starting to pile in. The first person I saw when we walked back in was my uncle Steve. We gave each other five and I asked him, "When did you get here?"

He said, "About 15 minutes ago. Where you been?"

"In the camper with Vera."

With his eyes wide open he said "Boy, Messiah gone kill you!"

"She smoked a joint with me. She ain't given that pussy to nobody but Messiah."

We both laughed and he told me he had these chics meeting him here and when they arrived we were going to take them to the camper to smoke with us. See, Steve already knew about the camper from many past experiences.

Meanwhile, the party had started. They were just playing tapes since Tiger and Messiah hadn't arrived yet. Everybody was tipsy and enjoying the holiday. Second by second new cars was pulling up. Finally, I saw my Aunt Lillian's New Yorker pull up. I walked outside and my cousin Messiah got out the car with this bang'n ass Tripple Fat Goose jacket on. With his New York accent he yelled, "Yo! Come grab something!"

We all hurried out to the car grabbing crates of records, speakers, and other things. Before my Aunt Lillian left she told us to be good and she pulled off. The party was already at a high intensity level but as we were setting up the DJ equipment, you could tell that this was going to be a night to remember for years to come.

"Testing, Testing – Testing 1, 2."

And the crowd went crazy at the mere sound of Messiah's voice as he was checking the mic. A few minutes later, the dance floor was completely full.

I was dancing with Donnie's cousin Regina. She was older than Donnie which put her about 7 years older than me but I knew she had a little thing for me.  Even though I was experienced in having sex, I wasn't aggressive. I would let the girls initiate the proceedings and believe me, they would. Regina and I were walking from the dance floor to the bar to get something to drink, it was crowded and very hot. That room held 100 people and it was standing room only, elbow to elbow. As I was making my way to the bar I bumped into Steve.

"You ready? He asked.

"Yeah, let's go."

I immediately headed to the door. Once I was outside and maybe 30 feet away from the door, Steve came out with these two girls. Cars were everywhere and being that it was so crowded inside, there was a mini party outside.

Steve and the girls caught up with me. While they were walking towards me several girls and guys were speaking to Steve and the two girls.

When he approached me he asked, "Is anybody back there?"

I responded, "I don't know, let's go check. I want a beer anyway."

One of the girls asked, "Who is this cute little boy?"
Steve replied, "Glenda, Tracy, this is my nephew Teddy."

Tracy said, "He's the one that is always with Messiah, Tony and the rest of the B-Boys but mostly with you Donnie, and Juan."

Steve answered braggingly, "Yeeeh."

"Whussup Ted"? Glenda asked.

You could tell Glenda was the spark out of the two.

"Nothing much" I replied. "Yall c'mon."

As I'm leading the way to the camper, Glenda asked Steve where was the good (speaking of the weed)?

Steve replied, "That's where we're goin."

When we got to the camper Donnie and this ugly chic was leaving.

We all bust out laugh'n.

Donnie asked, "What's so funny?"

Nobody responded. We continued laugh'n and stepped into the camper. Donnie left lil ugly cuz outside and stepped back into the camper and said, "Yall bet not say nothing. Tracy, you know Tony don't know you back here." He let the door slam behind him as he left.

I looked at Tracy as I was rollin a joint and said, "That's where I know you from! You go with Tony."

She replied, "We broke up yesterday."

Steve asked, "Yall want a beer, a cooler or something."

Tracy responded, "Give me a cooler."

Glenda said, "Let me sit beside Teddy."

I'm thinkin she's going to give me some cooty but she wanted to smoke with me. It was Steve she was giving the cooty to. We smoke and drank and next thing you know Glenda jumped on top of Steve in the little bunk bed and they started kiss'n. I'm still smoke'n. Tracy asked,

"You just gone sit there?"

I answered, "C'mon over here".

I was already sitting on one of the little sleeper beds. She came, we started kiss'n and she blurts out, "Unt-ugh, girl he can kiss!"

Glenda being fully aroused by whatever Steve is doing to her said in an enticing and sexy voice, "Well kiss him and shut up".

Shortly after that, Steve and I had began to handle business.

For the next fifteen to twenty minutes it sounded like a moaning contest. "Oh Teddy this, Oh Steve that. Oooo, Ahh." Back and forth.

Now the funny thing was this, Steve had a girlfriend name Tammy that went to school with them. I mentioned earlier that Tracy was dating Tony. When we finished and got back to the party, Tammy was there looking for Steve and Tony was looking for Tracy. It was obvious that word had got to their partners that they were seen together earlier because both couples were to the side arguing.

Steve look'd like he was explaining and Tracy looked like she was cursin Tony out with her hand all in his face. Glenda and I hit the dance floor immediately. After about two songs, here comes Tracy dancing behind me and whispering in my ear let's go back to the hideout. Sandwiched in between her and Glenda, I turned around to face Tracy. By her being taller than me and it being so crowded, as I turned around her big ole bitties hit me in the face. We both laughed and I asked her about Tony. She pulled me close and yelled in my ear, "IT'S OVER!"

Glenda came in even closer, making me the meat in their sandwich, "Wha'chall talk'n bout?"

Tracy responded, "We goin back to the trailer."

"Where's Steve? Still arguing with Tammy?" Glenda ask'd

"Naah, look."

We all looked to the corner where Steve and Tammy were embraced in a kiss that let you know they were in love. Glenda was hip to the game she only asked me to save her some weed.

As we attempted to make our way to the door all hell breaks loose.

Tony came out of nowhere snatching Tracy by the arm, "Where the fuck you goin?" he ask'd, furious.

She snatched away from him and yelled "Don't be grabbing on me. Leave me alone!

"C'mon Teddy!"

Dude pushes me out the way and attacks Tracy. Being from the projects I'm now trained for combat but before I could get to him the music had stopped and Steve was on Tony's ass.

"Yo! Yo! Yall fuck'n up a good thing!" Messiah said over the microphone.

"When I find out who it is I'ma kick they ass, Myself!"

Someone yelled out, "It's Tony and Teddy!"

All you heard on the mic was, "Oh shit!"

The mic dropped and immediately Messiah moved towards the maylay. As he arrived at the eye of the action, Donnie and others were separating us. It was more of a wrestling match than anything because of the crowd. There was only one punch thrown and that came from Steve.

"What da fuck yall doin?" Messiah yelled. You could tell he was pissed. "What da fuck? I know yall niggaz ain't fight'n ova no bitch!"

He was yell'n at Steve and Tony. Neither one of us (Steve, Tony, or myself) were saying anything because we were out of breath from the wrestlin match. Tammy said, "Tony was about to jump on

Ted and Steve jumped on Tony. Tracy know Teddy too young for her. Gittin all this shit started!"

"Shut up BITCH!" Tracy snarled.

Before Tracy could get it all the way out Tammy was charging at her. She was stopped before contact was made. Tammy was known for beat'n a broad down.

Needless to say, the party ended and my name began to ring.

"Messiah's cousin, Steve's nephew, dat little young nigga that always be with Donnie and Juan – Teddy. He always got weed and he will fuck your girl."

At the age of 11 a ladies legend was born.

## Chapter 3: Junior High School

It's the summer of '83', the 4$^{th}$ of July. There has been rumors of several cookouts and parties float'n around for the past few days. I had no idea how this day was going to end up but I was positive the firecrackers was gone fly.

"Teddy, git da phone."

"Who is it Ma?"

"Boy git da phone, it's Steve."

I ran in the living room to the phone. It was Steve telling me he was coming to pick me up and he had this chic he wanted me to meet. What he meant was he wanted me to fuck dis new chic.

"Who is she?" I asked.

"It's Michelle's best friend. You'll like her. If I wasn't with Michelle, I'd fuck'er."

Michelle was Steve's new girlfriend. He hired and fired girls as if he was running a temporary agency. Her parents were out of town for a couple of weeks and they were turning their home into an all out hotel room for the day.

"Michelle told her about you. She just left and told me to have you here when she gets back."

"Where did she go?"

"She had to go to a cookout with her boyfriend but she said she'll be back by 4:30 or 5:00."

"You trying to get me killed. What's her name?"

"Her name is Angie and ain't nobody gone kill you. Boy, she ask'd about you."

"Alright den, what time you comin?"

"I'll be there by 3."

"Steve, I ain't try'n ta be sitt'n there while you and Michelle fuck'n. Don't set me up."

Just be ready when I get there."

We hung up and I began to get prepared. Here I am, a 12 year old with more prospects than the average college student. I hope this is worth it. I thought to myself. Just happy to be getting out, I got up and started getting ready to leave.


It was 2:45 and Steve got here early.

"You said three o'clock."

"I know what I said but we gotta go to the licca house and slide by Messiah's for some good.

Jus c'mon."

"I'm ready."

"Well les go."

"Michelle was sitt'n in the car wait'n.

"Hey Michelle."

"Hey Teddy." She smiled as I climbed in the back seat.

"Why do you always have on shades?"

"That's jus me." I told her.

"Yo liddle bad ass thank you so cool witcho cute self." She said jokingly.

We made all the necessary stops and made it back to Michelle's. As we entered the house, you could smell the scent of weed still lingering in the air. They also had the grill ready to be set up.

"T-Rock, get that charcoal and bring it outside. We gone go ahead and start cook'n while we wait on Angee."

T-Rock was a nickname Messiah gave me and it stuck.

"Ah-ight."

We cook'd, drank, and smoked. It was pass time for Angee to be there. "Man, where this girl at?" She comin, chill."

"Ah-ight, if she ain't here by six, I'm call'n Juan to come git me."

"That'll be you miss'n out on some pussy."

"Teddy, I promise she's comin." Michelle said. "Jus listen for the door, we goin upstairs."

"Man, fuck dat! Yall wait til she git here."

"She comin, fix you a drink and watch dat flick."

"Steve said as he walked up the stairs kiss'n and suck'n Michelle's lips.

"Shortly after they got upstairs, I'm smoking, drank'n and watch'n a fuck flick when I heard a lite knock, "doom, doom, doom, doom, doom." I stop the flick and went to the door. "Who is it?"

"Angee"

"I peep'd thru the curtain to see this thick, chocolate complected chic with nice juicy lips standing there. I open'd the door.

"Hey", she said "Is Michelle here?"

"Yeah, she's up stairs, You can come in."

As she entered, I noticed the car in the driveway didn't budge. I closed the door.

"You must be Teddy." She said with this smirk on her face.

"Yee uh, dat's me."

"Whus dat smell? Y'all smoking?"

"Somethin like dat."

"Tell Michelle, I'll be right back."

"Ah-ight."

And don't smoke everything. Give me fifteen minutes."

She ran back outside and jumped in the car. I went back to what I was doing.

"Who was that?" Michelle yell'd.

"Angee, she said she'll back in fifteen minutes."

"Oh! Ok."

Like clockwork, she was back at the door in exactly fifteen minutes. I let her in, offer'd her a drink and some food. Between her hollering back and forth with Steve and Michelle, she found time to tell me she wanted rum and coke. I fix'd her drink, got me a bull and went back down stairs. A few seconds later, she joined me. I was sipp'n, my beer, smoking and watch'n Vanessa Del Rio deep throat Ron Jeremy.

"Eww, what do we have here, Cutey?"

"You see it."

"Yeah, I see it but I ain't into watch'n, I'm into doin."

I smiled, as I exhaled the smoke from the joint.

"You wanna hit this?" I said holding it in her direction.

"I'll try it, but I've never done it before. That's why Michelle and Steve invited me, so I could try it." She said as she grabbed it with her thumb and index finger." You make it look like it's nothing."

"It ain't, it jus relax you."

She put it to her lips and took a pull. I could tell she took in too much because she immediately began to choke. She cough'd for about five minutes after I took the joint from her. She took a sip of the rum and coke to wet her throat. Tears were rolling down her face and I was laugh'n uncontrollably. As she gain'd her composure, she hit me and began to laugh,

"That's not funny."

"You alright?" I ask'd still giggling."

"I will be." She said as she took another sip of the rum and coke. "Eww, it's hot in here. I got to come outta this shit."

She had on a blue jean mini skirt, a pink tee shirt and some all white caper tennis shoes. She took off the pink tee shirt and fell back on the couch. Angee didn't wear no bra. She had the perfect titties. Although I want'd to jump right in, I let her initiate the proceedings so I continued smoking and watch'n the flick. She laid there with her eyes closed adjusting to the high, then she leaned over on my lap." I like this. And, I like you."

By that time, Ron and Vanessa were doggy style." Can you do me like that?" She ask'd as she unzipped my shorts.

"I can do whatever you want."

She pulled out my wood and complimented me by a simple" Alright now, "as she became friendly with my best friend". I was experienced in fuck'n but that was my first blow job and it blew my mind.

"Ssss...that shit feels good."

"You like dat?"

"Hell yeah." I said as I began to reach between her legs to get to her playground. As I pulled her skirt up, she turned her body to a frontward position so that she could open her legs. Once we were ready, I slid her panties to the side and began to slide my index finger and middle finger into the wet warmth of her soppin wet pussy."

Umm hmm" she moan'd and slirp'd on my wood. "I got to feel this in me, your fingers ain't gittin it. Come here."

We both stood up. I dropp'd my shorts and pulled down her panties. She bent over the couch and I plunged in. "Damn Boy! Come out a little bit." I started to pull out some "ssssshiiit, that's enough. Umm Hmm, right there." As I stroked, she went crazy. A few times she warned me about going too deep. Angee wasn't like Tracy. Tracy loved it deep but that last time I went deep, I must have touch'd something, " Yeah, hit it! Umm Teddy, that's it! Hit it, yes, hit it! That's it!" Now I'm bang'n her out. "Oh my GOD! Fuck this pussy!" She began to shake like she had the chills and she began to slowly jus roll on my wood ask'n me could I feel her wet pussy nutt'n on me.

"Damn Angee," Michelle said, standing at the top of the stairs with Steve." Teddy aint nothing but twelve and you going crazy like that?"

"Umph, Umph, Umph. Tell that to my pussy. Chris ain't never done nothing like that." I'm standing there, still knee deep in this broad while Michelle and Steve stand there like nothing's goin on.
"That's how he got the name T-Rock busy," Angee respond'd. They left we switch'd positions and continued. At 12, I had stamina outta this world. I know we fuck'd for at least another hour and a half. Being so young, I hadn't began to spray yet so I never came.

From that day on, I was Angee's dude. She still saw Chris until she left for college the next month but when she came home on the weekends, the first stop she made was to the projects-643 East 6th and I gladly fucked her stupid and sent her on her way.

Meanwhile, I had just started Jr. High. My mom sent me to Ranson which was a culture shock because even though I had very few friends in my hood, we were familiar. At Ranson I knew no one, but several ninth graders knew of me from their older brothers or sisters due to the fact that Steve, Messiah, Donnie and Tim went there. It was definitely something new. On lunch breaks, I'd be outside sneak'n a cigarette or a few pulls from a joint. Day by day, my popularity rose. I was known as "that boy form Earle Village." Earle Village's reputation held so much weight, I never had to fight there like I did in elementary school. Now, I simply concentrated on the girls.

I was real cool with this dude named Spencer from Tangle wood. He was probably the most gangsta out of all these squares. I hung out with him until I began to formulate my own little crew but Spencer was my dude.

Little chics in the seventh and eighth grade had their crushes but none were on my level. I flirted with a few of them but hell, if they couldn't fuck me like Angee did, then what was the purpose.

One day during lunch period, I was walk'n thru the plaza when this chic grabbed me by my arm.

"Where you goin in a rush?"

"Outside, why, you wanna come?"

"What-chu going outside for?"

"I gotta meet somebody."

"Come talk to me when you git back."

"Whuss ya name?"

"Sharon."

"Ah-ight. I'm Teddy."

"I know who you are."

"I'll be back." I said as I took off outside. I had to meet Messiah, he was bring'n me some weed. We had varsity football game and I was staying after school. Messiah met me with my pack and told me he would be back later to pick me up.

When I got back in the building Sharon was sitting on a bench waiting for me. I sat down beside her.
"You doin ok?" I ask'd.

"I am now." She said look'n over at me.

"So how do you know me?"

"I ask'd Spencer about you and he told me to talk to you, so I did. I know you in the seventh grade but you don't act like them."

"How they act?"

"Like them." She said as a group of guys wrestled with each other on the bench next to us.

"The only way I'm wrestling anybody is if it's you."

"With or without our clothes?" She ask'd.

"Your choice."

"I take that as an invitation to your house."

"You can come over."

"She gave me the biggest smile showing off her dimples.
"When?"

`"Whatchu doin Saturday?" I couldn't say Friday because Angee will be home.

"Saturday is cool. I'll see if my dad will watch my daughter."

"You got a baby?"

"Yeap, a one year old."

"I thought to myself, at least she fuck'n.

"I bet she's just as pretty as you."

Sharon was brown skin, about five-five, petite with real long hair and a sexy gap in her teeth, topp'd off with them dimples.

"Of course she is. Can I have your number? I'll call you tonight and let you tell me what you're going to do to me SATURDAY." She said with a devilish grin.

I told her yes and wrote my number down and she gave me hers before I took off. I walk'd away think'n, I like this school.

Friday couldn't arrive fast enough. Me and Angee had a crazy night. She arrived at 10:45 pm Friday night. Fifteen minutes later than normal. When she got there, she seemed a little distant.

"Whus wrong wit-chu?"

"I'm alright. You got something to smoke?"

"Nah, but we can take a ride."

"Where to?"

"Tanglewood," I said, then thought for a moment.

"My neighbor may have some. I'll be right back."

"I'm goin to your room."

I told her that was cool and walk'd out the back door. As I approach'd my neighbor's apartment, this dude walks up to me ask'n me did I know the chic driving the Escort parked in front of my apartment. The Escort belonged to Angee.

"Who wants to know?" I ask'd

"I'm Chris. That's my fiancée's car."

"My aunt's next door neighbor Bug came to the door. Bug was about 29 or 30. He was a functioning crack addict that kept weed and he would hit me off when Messiah wasn't around.

"T, whussup?" Bug ask'd, look'n pass me to Chris stand'n there look'n like a square or maybe an undercover.

"Who da fuck is that wit-chu?"

"I don't know him. He ask'd bout that Escort."

Bug know'n that the car belonged to Angee and she was seein me, he became real aggressive, "I know this muthafucka ain't knock'n on doors look'n for no broad?"

"He walk'd up on me as I was comin ova here."

"Teddy, come in here." Bug said when dude "immediately yelled," That is her car and she's here to see you."

"I tell you what faggot, be here when I get back."

Me and Bug walk'd into his apartment where he lived with his three sisters and two nephews.

"T, whatchu want'd?"

"I nud a nick."

"I'll be back."

Bug ran upstairs only to return 2, maybe 3 minutes later. "That bitch know dis faggot out here?" He ask'd as he passed me a bag and tuck'd his 38 snub nose in his waist.

"I-on know, she in my room."

"C'mon."

Bug open'd the door for us to go outside and dude was walk'n around Angee's car.

"Ay Yo!" Bug call'd out, "Come here."

Dude walk'd over to us. He was about to find out that his bold act was permitted in his middle class neighborhoods but not in muthafuck'n Earle Village.

"Whussup?" He ask'd as he walk'd up on me and Bug.

"Do you know anybody that lives over here?" Bug ask'd.

"Nah, I followed my fiancée over here and I know she here see'n money right here because I found his number in her car."

"Man, if you don't git cho ass from over here, you gone git the shit beat outta you."

I just stood there while Bug did all the talk'n.

"I ain't goin nowhere until I see my fiance'."

"I'm done talk'n. Go home dude."

"You don't know me! Fuck You-"

Before he could complete his rage, Bug had took out the 38 and smack'd Chris with it while letting off a shot at the same time. I thought buddy was dead when I saw him drop and lay in a puddle of blood but he had only been knok'd out from the impact of the blow Bug had issued, and in no time everybody was outside including Angee. She ran to me, "Are you alright?" She ask'd as she looked and saw lil buddy lay'n in the blood. "OH MY GOD! Is he dead?" She ask'd. Bugs sister was check'n his pulse and answered, "No, he just got a cut over his eye."

"If he wanna live, he betta git da fuck from ova here, DUMB Mu-Fucka!" Bug threaten'd.

Angee walked over to him as he regained his composure I thought she was going to help dude but instead, she cursed him out tell'n him how stupid he was. Finally all the drama came to an end and dude got the message and left.  Me and Angee went to do what we normally do Friday nights. As we smoked, she began tell'n me what had happened before she got there. We went on to release tension, enjoying each others body to the fullest. The majority of the night was spent exploring each other's sex game with very intimate conversations during intermissions.  This lasted thru the night and Angee got up and left as usual about 6:30 am before my mom got off from work.

"Are you going shopping with me Sunday before I leave?"

"What time?" I ask'd.

"It will be after church, so about 2 or 3. My dad just paid off all of my credit card bills and we're going to run them back up." She said with this look of satisfaction in her eyes.
"I just want some shoes."

"Shoes it is. I'll see you Sunday." She said as she winked her eye and walk'd out of my bedroom door.

Periodically thru the night, Angee kept say'n she hope Chris was alright but in some sick, twist'd kind of way, I could tell that she was turned on by the events that had taken place. Angee was 18 and I was 12, Chris was 20. I guess it excited her to see this young buck maneuver as an adult. Whatever it was, she kept comin back.

It was Saturday afternoon. I had slept all morning and my mom was the clock that woke me up. Standing in the doorway of my room, she stood there sarcastically talk'n shit.

"Teddy, Teddy!"

Very groggy and still exhausted from last night events, "Maah" I whined.

"I don't know what you be doin while I'm at work all night but I'm the only one that deserves to lay up in this house sleep'n all day. Git-cho ass up and go to the barbershop."

"What time is it?" I ask'd

"Goin on 1. Thank you for cleaning up last night. I cooked yall some breakfast, salmon patties but you need to get up and get to the barbershop."

"Ah-ight." That's all she want'd to here. She closed my door and I laid there a few minutes before I got up.

It was a sunny late August day. I hated going to the barbershop late because it meant I would sit there for 2-3 hours. I got back home around 3. My mom was in her room watch'n Rambo. "Boy, that phone has rung non-stop since you left. Some girl named Sharon has call'd every 30 minutes" her voice immediately changed to an aggressive yell, "and what the hell happened here last night with you and some girl's boyfriend?"

Where my sister Shan and my mom's boyfriend Ella left off, I filled in the blanks.

"Teddy, how many times I have to tell you? You not grown! You ain't even a teenager yet and you got bullshit follow'n you. As much as I tell you not to because of these projects, the more I'm seeing it in you."

"Ma, it wasn't my fault."

"Teddy, if you would just be a kid, you wouldn't be hear'n this but you got shit goin on that half the adults I know ain't never heard of." She lectured, "I tell ya what, you gone start carry'n yo but back to church. You done got out of hand."

I just listen'd until the storm was over think'n to myself. "I ain't been to church in a while."

That thought was interrupt'd by the telephone.

"It's for you, grown ass!" My mom yell'd.

"Hello?"

"Hey Teddy. I been call'n you all day. What time you want me to come over?"

"Sharon, whussup?" After hearing moma lecture me for the past 20 minutes. I want'd to postpone but I was young and think'n with my head in my pants. "Shiiit, whenever." I answer'd.

"Can Renee come? She drivin and have somebody for her."

"Ah-ight, so what time?"

"We'll be there inna-bout-a- hour."

"Ah-ight."

Before I could get off the phone, I was think'n of who would come keep Renee company. I called everybody Messiah, Steve, Juan, and Donnie and nobody was home. But like clockwork, they all popp'd up about 30 minutes later. We started drink'n, smoking and gambling. Doin what we do and then a knock came to the door.

"Whussup? Yall come on in." Messiah ask'd, inviting them in. It wasn't just Renee and Sharon, they had Camille and Tameka with them. Camille was older. She went to school with Messiah and Steve. She was bad as fuck! Hazel eyes, light skin with a big ole country girl ass. Renee was a cute mid complexioned, big boned chic wit mad attitude but she was in love with Steve. Tameka was the overseer. She was older than all of us but cool. Nothing really spectacular but if she was the only thing left, you'd probably fuck.

Everybody was introduced and we continued the festivities. Me and Juan was partners against Steve and Donnie play'n spades while Messiah entertain'd the chics. Sharon sat by my side at the kitchen table grabbing my dick under the table ask'n me what would I rather be doin? I tried to continue until I had, had enough. Then Tameka took my place and I took Sharon to my room. Luckily Moma was sleep, she would have flipp'd. She allow'd me to have company in my room but she had just given me the all out lecture earlier. As we entered my room, I noticed Sharon look'n around like. "This little guy is nasty." On every wall were naked women from Playboy and Penthouse, also my favorite Jet centerfolds were posted. There were mirrors on my ceil'n over my twin beds with a net hang'n from the ceil'n in between the mirrors with a blow up sex doll trapp'd in the net.

"OH LORD, what have I gotten myself into?" Sharon ask'd as she sat on the bed.

"Nothing yet." I retorted as I cut my radio on and laid back on my bed beside her.

She leaned over on top of me look'n in my eyes and gently rubb'n the side of my face. "For you to be so young, you act like a grown man."

"Whatchu mean?"

"You're so laid back, like I don't even phase you."

"I'm just me." I told her.

"My daughter's dad is 19 y'all two are like night and day. By now, I would have been naked, fuck'd and through."

"Shiiit, git naked so you can git fuck'd and we can git through." I said in a calm comedic way.

She lightly hit me in my chest say'n, "You know what I mean."

We both laugh'd. She began to kiss me. We kiss'd and grind'd in our clothes for about 15 minutes before we began to undress. While kiss'n and undress'n, I ask'd "Where is your daughter's dad?"

"He's in college in Virginia. We not together no more, he just takes care of Tia."

That was the end of all talk and we began to fuck like wild dogs. From position to position, it was like a dance battle and I was try'n ta win. All of a sudden, my body started to tense up and it felt like some kind of energy raced from my head and my toes to my dick. This was something I had never experienced before. I began to release fluids from my dick. Sharon was goin crazy and then I collapsed in her arms. She laid there rubb'n the back of my head. Once I get enough energy up, I slid my dick out of her, noticing this snotty lookin, bleach smell'n substance all in my private area. I jumped up, grab my shorts and told Sharon I'd be back. I closed the door behind me, slipp'd into my shorts and went down stairs. I stood at the bottom of the stairs and called out to Messiah by his nickname, "KATO!"

"Whut up?" He responded.

Scared to death, I said "C'mere. I need you for a minute."

He ran to the stairs, "What's wrong?"

I whispered, "I'm burn'n!"

He whispered back, "How you know? Come to the bathroom."

We ran up stairs to the bathroom and closed the door.

"Yo, you leak'n yellow shit and burn'n when you piss?"

"Nah, look." I pull'd my shorts down to show him the mess in my pubic hairs.

"Nigga, that ain't no VD, that's nut you nasty mu'fucka!"

He said laugh'n. Then he got real serious. "Yo, tell me you didn't bust in that bitch."

"I didn't know what was happen'n."

"Oh shit! All the fuck'n you doin and you just now nutt'n?"

"I guess so." I answer'd glad to know I wasn't burn'n.

"How'd it feel?"

"It felt toooo good!"

"Yep! That was your first nut. I swear I thought you was nutt'n. What did you do with them rubbers we give you?"

"They in my drawer."

"You better start using them shits now or it won't be VD you worry'n about, it will be babies wit'cho hot ass. Clean that shit up and put on some clothes."

He left out and I wash'd up. When I walk'd back into my room, Sharon was still lay'n naked in my bed. As soon as I saw her naked body, my best friend alerted me that I wasn't done with her.

"That's all I git? One round and you through?"

"Hell no, can't you tell?" I ask'd as I look'd down at 'Yung Teddy' then back at her.

Not think'n, I plunged back in without a rubber, totally disregarding the conversation with Messiah. For some odd reason, I felt very confident stroking Sharon until I began to experience the same feel'n as before. Once again, I sprayed all in her but this time, I stay'd in her until "Yung Teddy" was ready to party again less than a minute later. We were both sweat'n and breathin hard. Sharon had a very sexy moan and when I touch'd her special spot, she began to pant and dig her nails into my back. Before long, I was spray'n again.

"Damn, where you git that energy from? I done nutt'd several times, what about you?"

Feel'n like the man, I answer'd, "I got off 3."

"You only nutt'd 3 times? I thought it was more. You betta hope my birth control is work'n."

We laugh'd it off like a joke then got clean'd up, dress'd and went back down stairs. Soon as we got to the kitchen, the jokes began from both sides. Like the kids we were, we just blush'd.

It was going on 7 o'clock and Sharon had to pick up Tia and word was that we were hang'n out at Queens Park Movie Theater. That was the spot. Especially the game room where Messiah and the B-Boyz normally won dance contests.

Sharon and I said our goodbyes and they left.

## Chapter 4: Young Grown Ass

Teddy and Sharon wasn't a couple, they saw each other every day at school but Sharon knew about Angee so within the past two months, they only hook'd up three times. It was Halloween, Donnie had pick'd Teddy up from school because they were going to a party but Teddy wasn't his usual self.

"Whussup T?"

Donnie ask'd as he and Teddy gave each other a pound.

"Ain't shit!" Teddy said slamm'n Donnie's door.

"Nigga, take it easy on the door."

"My fault."

"Tracy told us to make sure you come to the Halloween party at Glenda's spot, Yo hot ass!"

Donnie said with a chuckle.

"That's the problem now." Teddy said with fear in his voice." Sharon ain't been to school in 2 weeks and Renee said she's pregnant."

"By who?" Donnie ask'd grabbing his mouth.

"Man, I'm too young to be a dad, Moma gone kill me."

"Oh shit! Queen gone kill yo ass.  Nigga, you ain't even a teenager yet. Have you talked to Sharon?"

"No, she ain't been at school."

"Well don't worry about it if she hasn't said anything."

"Yeah, you right." Teddy said.

"Have you spoke to Angee?"

"Yeah but she won't be home this weekend, it's Livingstone's Homecoming.  What Tracy been up to?"

"We bout to see tonight."

Donnie took Teddy home to change clothes and let his mom know their plans for the night and that's when Teddy's worst fear came to life. As soon as he walk'd thru the door,

"Teddy! That you?"

"Yeah."

"C'mere!"

Teddy walk'd into Queen's room

"Huh?"

"You been stick'n yo thang in that Sharon girl that use to call here?"

"What-chu mean moma?" He ask'd try'n to keep a straight face.

"Boy, don't play wit me! You know what I mean. That's a damn shame, here I am 34 and my 12 year old fuck'n more than me.

That girl say she's pregnant by you. Yo little ass got something comin outta that little pistol of yours?"

"Maaa-ma."

Teddy whinned standing there embarrassed by Queen's question. She was fairly calm compared to what Teddy expected.

"Tell Moma who gone take care of that baby?"

Teddy just stood there quiet while Queen answered her own question.

"Me! You're too young to get a job so that puts your child on me."

"When did she call?" Teddy ask'd.

"A little while ago. She was cry'n, and I just told her we would be here for her."

Queen meant every word of it. She wasn't going to let Teddy be like his dad. At that early age, she was going to see to it that Teddy accepted his responsibility. The best she knew how, she insisted on raising him into a real man. After all, she felt mostly responsible for his careless sexual behavior. She knew he had been experimenting since she caught him and Tonya and she still didn't bother to sit him down and talk to him.

"Teddy, you have to be more careful. You run around with Donnie, Steve, Kato and Juan screw'n like you in a marathon.

"Do you know what rubbers are?"

"Yeah, I got some. I use them now."

"Now?" She ask'd exasperatedly.

"Every since the last time I was with Angee."

"What about Sharon?"

"Nope. That's when I found out I need'd them."

"She's due June 12th. We'll see then. I can't believe yo young grown ass." She uttered.

"Ma, can I go to this party with Donnie?"

"Where?"

"In Greenville."

"With who?" Queen inquired.

"Donnie down stairs."

"Tell him to come here."

"Don-nay! Moma won-chu." Teddy yell'd down the stairs.

"Whussup Queen?" Donnie spoke entering Queen's room.

"Hey Donnie. You know this boy got a baby on the way?" She inquired with a smidget of pride and alotta disgust.

"I just heard." Donnie said look'n at Teddy about to bust out laugh'n. He knew Teddy's worst fears had come to life before his face." He'll be alright. We got'em."

"I hope so cause, I'm gone need some help.

"Whussup with this party?"

"It's just a little Halloween party with a few friends."

"Ok, little Halloween party". Just make sure to git the little freak some rubbers." Queen said.

Donnie let it go. He bust'd out laugh'n." I got'em, trust me.

"Trust you? You fuckaz got me bout ta be a grandma before I'm 35. Trust You! Y'all git out my face!"

Donnie really down play'd the Halloween party. It was an all out orgy.

From that moment on, Teddy fuck'd like he was a porn star. Word got around about him, and Messiah made sure he touch'd as much ass as he did, and Messiah was a chic magnet.

Donnie and Teddy arrived at Glenda's and the festivities had already begun. Couples were pair'd up in corners, on couches and damn near on every stair leading up to the bedrooms. Soon as Teddy and Donnie walk'd thru the door, the greetings began. It was as though everybody was actually waiting for this young ass dude.

"Donnie where y'all been? You know Tracy worry'n everybody, think'n Teddy's lil ass wasn't come'n." Glenda stated.

"Long story, but we here now." Donnie explain'd taking a deep breath.

"Teddy, whus wrong Sugah?"

"Nutt'n. I thought this was a party. Look like mufuckas need to git hotel rooms."

"Shiiid, this is a party!" Juan yell'd over the music as he came up for air eat'n Glenda's cousin Felecia's pussy," You brought dat whit'chu?" He ask'd, talk'n about the weed. "Tracy, Steve and Kato'nem been bitch'n."

"Where dey at?" Teddy ask'd.

"Up stairs." Glenda and Juan answer'd in unison, "bro, roll me a joint before you head up."

Juan request'd.

"Teddy made his way to the kitchen table where Glenda was hugg'd up with some new dude. "Who Steve upstairs with?" Teddy ask'd Glenda try'n to be funny-know'n that Steve and Glenda were no more than fuck buddies.

"He wit his crazy ass girl" Glenda respond'd with a smirk on her face.

Teddy and Donnie chuckled while Teddy pull'd out a twenty sack-a refah and starts roll'n joints. This was totally new to Teddy. He had been to several parties and fuck'd several chics but this was different. As he was roll'n up, he noticed a chic jack'n two dudes off while another dude was bang'n her from the back. Nobody had no shame in their game.

Enough was enough, Donnie was even in on the wide open action, eat'n out this chic name Michelle. Teddy had just roll'd 4 joints and got up to go after Tracy think'n I WONDER IS K UPSTAIRS FUCK'N TRACY.  It wasn't that he cared, he just didn't know what to expect after what he was seeing downstairs. Soon as he toss'd Juan a joint, lit his own and turned to go upstairs, he found his face in Tracy's bosom.

"Hey shorty, Where you been?" Tracy inquired with a huge smile on your face.

"We just got here-whut'chu been doing?" Teddy ask'd.

"Me, Steve, Tammy, K and Vera were up in Glenda's Mom's room wait'n on you. C'mon." She said grabb'n Teddy by the hard leading him up stairs to Glenda's room to get her freak on. They stepp'd into Glenda's Mom's room long enough for Teddy to speak and pass out joints, then they retreat'd to Glenda's room for the rest of the night.

At 13, Teddy had more issues than the average adult.  It was the summer of 84', school had only been out a week. Angee hadn't been home from school since the beginning of May. When she wasn't at work and Teddy wasn't in school, they were together. They weren't on no boyfriend girlfriend shit, Angee just enjoy'd being around. When she found out Teddy had a child on the way soon, she informed him that she had abort'd their child that was conceived Valentine's night nine weeks ago. He was so young, he didn't know how to feel. Angee want'd her child but she knew that her parents would have had a child of their own, had they known that she had jeopardized her college career having unprotected sex with a 13 year old project dude.

It was 2:40 AM, Thursday morning June 16th when Angee dropp'd Teddy off. Queen was startled when Teddy came thru the back door. He walk'd thru the kitchen to the living room noticing Queen laid out on the sofa still in her work uniform. "Go to bed Moma-git'chu some rest "Teddy said, kiss'n his mom on the forehead.

"I jus got in. Sharon had your child last night. "She began to explain in a groggy tone. Filling in all the details, she also told him that they want'd him at the hospital by 9:00 for the blood test and to name the baby.

By 7:00, Teddy was up and had call'd everybody. Steve was the first to arrive. Everybody else came later. Sharon's father and Teddy took turns passing Tedra back and forth. They named her Tedra after Sharon's deceased Mom. So many of Sharon's friends and family members had come thru with gifts. Then Kato came in with balloons, flowers and several outfits. He was like that. He wouldn't stand to be out done.

"How you doin little lady?" Kato ask'd Sharon.

"I'm fine just a little sore."

"That's my little cousin, you make sure if she needs anything. You let us know."

Steve, Juan and Donnie agree'd.

"I will." Sharon said with a smile.

Teddy took the blood test and they left. To be as young as he was, he was a good dad. Even before the test confirmed that he was 99.5%.

His daughter filled that void his granny left when she pass'd.

Teddy was already more mature than most 18 year olds but having a child put him in a different category. At 13, he want'd to provide for his daughter at all cost, so he started an in house candy store. Sell'n all sorts of candy, cakes and icees to the neighborhood kids. Also fillin his book bag daily with candy and serving at school along with his weed customers.

For the next 3 years. Teddy had flourish'd as a dad, a dealer and also with the ladies. Every area in his life had come full circle except his education. The only education he accept'd in his life was the ISLAMIC teachings his cousin Kato provided.

Kato was a name Messiah got because of his combat skills. Those skills were inherited by his father who was a FOI (Fruit of Islam) for The Nation of Islam. Kato, growing up in the streetz of Brooklyn strayed away from the NOI teachings and pick'd up on The Nation of Gods and Earths (a spin off of the NOI). He taught Teddy everything he knew and Teddy learn'd quickly, but Kato also want'd Teddy to complete high school.

Teddy had failed the 8th and 9th grade due to lack of attendance. The actual school work was easy to him but Teddy had adult issues and concerns and school at that moment didn't fit into his schedule.

At the age of 15, his grandpop's took him to Lancaster, SC to get his driver's license. He work'd 2 jobs. Bojangles on the weekends and help'n his grandpop's at his garage when need'd, along with his weed hustle. Teddy had a black Escort GT and all of his younger homeboys look'd up to him. They came from good neighbors such as Hidden Valley, Tanglewood, Garden Park and Hampshire Hills but they all were fascinated by the life Teddy lived in Earl Village.

Several of his buddies would come hang out for the weekend not believing the freedom Teddy possessed.

His persona spoke volumes, his maturity was unconceivable and his life was in full motion.

## Chapter 5: First Heart Break

Life was going all Teddy's way. Even though he wasn't seein Tedra as much as he want'd due to his work schedule, he was still doing for her as a dad should. On several occasions, Sharon attempt'd to get a relationship start'd with Teddy but he was content with what they had. He was still seeing Angee and several other chics.

Teddy was 16 and had got back in school. He attended Harding High, they had a night school program that would allow him to pick up the credits he need'd to graduate by 89'. Between regular class, night school and work, Teddy rarely had time for Tedra. Not to mention, he was livin with this 32 year old chic named Sasha Norris. She was a computer programmer from New Jersey working at IBM. He met Sasha at Side Effects night club one night, he was with Juan and Donnie. Sasha was a classy lady. She drove a BMW and lived in Pear Tree apartments alone. At 5'3 1/2, light skin, long jet black shoulder length hair, 132'lb petite frame with a bubble ass, Chinese eyes and sexy full lips, Sasha had Teddy's attention and everybody knew it.

Every now and then Teddy and Sharon would hook up for a rendezvous, but since Sasha came along, everybody was on hold including Angee and whoever else thought they had value in his life.

Everybody took a backseat to Sasha.

Three months after his 16th birthday, he moved in with her. Sasha spoiled Teddy. At first, she didn't know his age. After he had put her under the spell of his sex game, she became very possessive to the point Teddy couldn't hide the fact that he was still in high school.

Once he informed her she was upset for bout 30 minutes before inviting him into her home to live. Sasha open'd her whole existence to Teddy. Her work schedule was Monday thru Thursday 7am to 7pm. Daily, he drove her to work and went to school, picking her up from work and having some of the most intimate and romantic evenings ever known to a couple.

Although she had problems dealing with Teddy's age in the beginning, she immediately dismiss'd all doubts that existed because he treated her like ROYALTY. As Sasha walk'd Teddy into manhood, she also secluded him from all outsiders such as his family, his daughter and friends.

They took turns cook'n for each other. She couldn't believe the skills Teddy possessed in domestic affairs at his age. He was more mature than the guys she had dated her own age and older. Sasha found herself listen'n and learn'n from Teddy.

In return, she made sure his daughter was completely taken care of but he rarely spent time with her. She did everything in her power to keep Teddy to herself.

They would smoke weed, have a few drinks and create some of the freakiest and epic love makin scenes. Everything Teddy learned in the romance department came from Sasha. She allow'd Teddy to freak her stupid without limitations.

Their relationship took a turn for the worst when Teddy's mom called one day and requested that Teddy come by asap to discuss an urgent issue about his daughter. Sasha wanted to go with him but Queen request'd her son's presence alone.

Sasha didn't like that so it took him a week later to finally get by his mom's.

Queen was piss'd when he walk'd in. "That baby could be dead by now. Why are you just now comin by here Teddy?" she ask'd.

"Ma, I be busy."

"Busy doin what, that's so important that you neglect your child?"

Agitated at her accusations of neglect, he responded, "Tedra don't want for nothing. She has everything that she needs."

"Except her dad in her life physically. There's more to being a dad than buying clothes and dropp'n off money. For the past 2 months, that baby has spent every weekend I've been off right here with me and you never show'd your face.      That's irresponsible," Teddy listen'd as Queen continued scold'n him. "Do you love your child?"

"What kinda question is that?" Teddy ask'd

"One that I expect an answer to."

"Ma, you know I love Tedra."

"Teddy, I want you to listen and listen good. Sharon left town 3 days ago with Tia's daddy moving to Virginia for good. She said that she had to make the best decisions for both of her children. She needed stability for her girls and even though you were doing right by Tedra, she was hoping that you and her could have tried to be a couple but you were too busy up Angee's ass and then when Sasha came along, you distanced yourself from everybody. Here, she passed him a letter.

Teddy sat down and unfolded the letter;

*"Dear Teddy,*

*Once you read this letter, I hope you can*

*find it in your heart to understand my decision and*

*not hate me.   Teddy, I know you were very young when Tedra was born but I thought I had a chance to be that only woman in your life. I know you love your daughter, but I love my daughter's father (You) and you never gave me a chance. I always had to compete with Angee, and Sasha made sure nobody could compete with her. Well Tia's dad ask'd me to marry him and move to Virginia. I want'd to ask you should I do it, but you didn't care enough to meet me at your mom's to discuss it so that was my answer.*

*As much as I love you, I don't ever want to see you again and I want you to forget you ever had a daughter by me.  She'll be fine, Ant is a good man and father. Just focus on yourself, Tedra will be fine.*

*Please don't hate me. I Love You.*

*Sharon"*


Teddy just got up and left not tell'n his mom bye or anything. Queen knew that this was a lesson her son was going to have to go thru alone and learn from his mistake. She hurt to see him go thru it.

From that day forward, Teddy and Sasha grew apart until they finally went their separate ways. When he moved out, he didn't go back to his mom because he partly blamed her and partly blamed Sasha. He moved to Dalton Village with his Aunt Jean.

A broken heart can blind you into blaming everybody involved instead of placing blame where it belongs.

## Chapter 6: School Dayz

For such a young man, Teddy had experienced some severe let downs in life. A year ago, he had to accept the fact that he would possibly never see his daughter again. After some self-evaluation, he made a conscious effort to finish school. He attend'd Harding night school and was able to catch up on most of his credits to get him caught up.

It was the summer before the 88'-89' school year. Teddy had a meeting with his counselors and was told that if he took a full load in day school along with a semester of night school, he could graduate on time with his class next spring.

He was fully committed.

One of his electives was band. The band director Mr. Silden sent Teddy an invitation to try out for the marching band. Teddy was a helluva drummer so he took him up on the invite.

After his break up with Sasha, Teddy didn't have a steady chic in his life. He continued hang'n out with Angee occasionally and Sasha popp'd in and out ever so often but he didn't have anything consistent and he was content focusing on his educational goals.

Teddy's sister Shan was dating this dude name Derrick who was transferring to Harding from Myers Park, he played football. Teddy's grandpop's took his car years ago when Teddy dropp'd out of school and from that moment on, he used whoever car he could get his hands on. The Sunday before band tryouts, Teddy was at his mom's house for dinner and met Derrick. They became cool and Derrick offered to pick Teddy up for practice the next day.

Arriving at the school at 7:15 AM, football practice start'd at 7:30 and band practice started at 8.

"Yo T, I don't know what time practice is over so just meet back here when y'all done."

"Dat's cool."

They dapp'd each other and went their separate ways. Teddy went into the building to go to the band room. When he enter'd the building walk'n toward the classroom, he noticed this short brown skin chic standing against the lockers. She was cute with a very curvaceous body. Teddy didn't waste no time walk'n over to introduce himself. He walk'd up to her until he was close enough that if he pucker'd his lips, he would be kiss'n her.

"Whus yo name?" he ask'd

"Shanta" she said with a smile.

"I'm Teddy," He replied as his hands began to explore the curves of her body. She didn't seem to be phased by his aggressive approach.

"You got a dude?"

"Would it matter?" She ask'd in a very flirtatious tone.

"At this point, NO." They both laugh'd. Grabbing her breast to top it off, Teddy eased up and they engaged in a full conversation getting to know each other. Teddy enjoyed their conversation and realized that he was extremely attracted to Shanta. She was the first chic he had ever found interest in that was his age.

Other students start'd to arrive for practice so Teddy concluded their conversation with a wink and stepp'd off. Being the new guy, everybody was looking and whispering, wondering who he was, what instrument he play'd etc... Teddy noticed Shanta and several of her what appeared to be girlfriends engrossed in a chat that consisted of occasional glances and giggles his way. He stood alone accepting all the scrutiny that came his way.

Once they all load'd into the classroom, Mr. Silden introduced himself, the drum majors, section leaders and all newcomers (Teddy being the last). "Stand, state your name and instrument."

Teddy   stood   and   stated,   "Teddy, percussion." The guys on the drumline mock'd him and   various   chics   in   other   sections   looked whisper'd and giggled.

"Alright   guys,   quiet   down."   Mr.   Silden stated," We're   about   to   section   off   into   our individual   sections.   Each   section   leader   has   the material we'll be work'n on, we'll all meet back in two hours to start work'n on formations. You guys get to work."

"Whussup, I'm Rob, drum capt'n."

"I'm T-Rock."

"Whatchu play?"

"Whateva."

"We need another bass play'r so we'll try you there."

"That's cool."

Teddy   and   Rob   approach'd   the   other drummers, "This T-Rock," we gone put him on the bass line.    Y'all strap up."

Everybody grabb'd their drums and began to   work   on   the   cadences.   In   the   middle   of   the session,   the   tuba   line   walk'd   up   and   observed while   the   drummers   rock'd.   Once   Rob   cut   them off, this young skinny dude name Fly from the tuba line began to clown Teddy. "Yo, why Dad so serious? Check'm out." He said as everybody laugh'd.

Teddy didn't know how to handle being clown'd by this pee wee little dude. He had the mindset that none of the high school population was on his level. Instead of over reactin, he simply stared at Fly and if looks could kill, the little guy would have instantly dropped dead. Fly felt the tension so he slow'd his roll. "I'm jus kidd'n Dad." He said as he walk'd over to Teddy, "What'd you say yo name was?"

"Jus call me T-Rock."

"Dat's cool, I'm Fly. They call me Fly cause I'm small and always git'n on peoples nerves." That broke the ice and Teddy smiled. "Man, don't be nervous. You can play. Jus feel the music and you'll look more natural than uptight when you play."

Teddy took his advice and that lead to an immediate friendship between the two. Throughout practice, Teddy realized that Fly had a way with the chics there. He was so silly that he was a personal favorite with all the chics.

Once practice ended, Teddy sat on Derrick's car smoking a joint as everybody left the park'n lot.

All of a sudden, a 83' Celica pull'd up, it was Shanta, wit two more chics and two dudes from the drumline.

"Who are you wait'n on?" Shanta ask'd.

"What is he smoking?" The chic in the passenger seat ask'd.

"I'm wait'n on my boy. He's on the football team."

"You want me to wait with you?"

"I'm ah-ight, it may be too hot for you out here."

Shanta turn'd around and said something to the passengers in her car, then she park'd the car and they all got out. Everybody migrated to Teddy's direction.

"Teddy, this is Stephanie, Ebony, Tony, and Avery."

"Jus call me T-Rock."

They all shook hands and Stephanie ask'd could she hit the joint Teddy was smoking. He pass'd her the roach and pull'd out a Newport.

"Why do you smoke?" Shanta ask'd.

"Cause I like to." Teddy answer'd. They hung out with Teddy until Derrick came. He and

Shanta exchanged numbers and went their separate ways.

Shanta wasn't nothing that Teddy was use to and vice versa. Throughout the school year she tried to string Teddy along but when she saw him interest'd in another chic or heard a rumor of him and another chic, she appeared to be sincere about him until Teddy got tired of her games and stop'd return'n her phone calls. His stock was high at the school, he became extremely popular with his peers with little effort.

It was the spring of 89', late March. Teddy and his crew were due to appear in the talent show to sing "Can You Stand The Rain" by New Edition. Teddy pulled out in the end because the Nissan dealership called and told him to pick up his new car that evening by 7.

Since Sharon had taken his daughter, Teddy continued to work, hustle and save his money. His cousin Kato told him if he came up with half, he'd give him the other half for a car. Kato was simply proud that Teddy always listen'd to him and he was about to graduate.

Teddy saved up $9,000 for a brand new 89', 4 door Nissan Sentra. Since Teddy had more than enough for the actual car, Kato, Steve and Teddy's brother Juan purchased him some five star rims, a helluva stereo system, a rag top and tinted windows. It was one of a kind and even though

Teddy didn't participate in the talent show, he ended up being the star of the talent show.

When the talent show was over, Teddy was parked up front in the student parking lot with his system bang'n "How Deep Is Your Love" by Keith Sweat. Teddy and his main man Maverick post'd up in the park'n lot for about 10 minutes before the talent show was over. Once they saw people dispersin, they got out and lean'd on the hood of the car as admirer's walk'd pass in awe of what appear'd to be a drug dealer's car.

Teddy's crew GOG came in first place and runner up. Soon as word got to GOG that Teddy was in the park'n lot swell'n, they all came to see what all the talk was about. Teddy never told them why he back'd out of the talent show at the last minute so they were all surprised to see his new ride. Fly, E, Tippy and D-Nice were all crowded around Teddy within the crowd that had gather'd around to be notice'd by a hood celeb. As they laugh'd, slapped five and eyed all the new prospects, yours truly (Shanta) made her way thru the crowd to Teddy's side. "Is this yours?"

"Yeah.      Why?"    Teddy    anwser'd sarcastically.

"I like it."

"Whatever Shanta."

"Why you act'n like that?" She ask'd with that sparkle in her eye but Teddy wasn't bite'n.

"I ain't fuck'n wit-chu. You some bullshit!"

"No I'm not. Can I have your pager #?"

"Fuck No! What'chu want?"

Shanta lean'd into Teddy and whisper'd, "I thought you want'd this pussy?"

"I'm not going thru that with you."

"Let's skip school tomorrow." She suggest'd.

"Oh so you serious?" Teddy ask'd skeptically.

"Give me your pager # and I'll call you in the morning before I leave and we'll meet here in the park'n lot."

"You got a pen?"

"Yeah, go ahead." She instruct'd.

"It's 356-Fuck."

"Fuck you Teddy, What's the #?"

"That's it. I promise."

She took the # and said," You better not be play'n me."

"Just call the # and see."

Shanta took the # and turned to walk away, look'n back behind her sending Teddy a seductive wink.

"T-Rock, you thank you da shit." Fly yelled over the music.

"Nah, 'yall do." Teddy said as he and Fly dapp'd each other, "I see y'all won dat shit Dad."

Teddy congratulated.

"You know can't nobody see me rapp'n shit." Fly said and he check'd Teddy's new ride out, "Dat Keith Sweat is kill'n'm. Boy, dis shit is sweet. I'm rid'n wit-chu right?"

"You gone ride wit me to go drop Maverick off and shoot by Sasha's?"

"Nigga, I live right down the street. I ain't grown, we got school in da morn'n. My moma will kick my ass. It's already 9'o clock, by the time we git back it will be 11 or later. I ain't fuck'n wit-chu."

"Yo scary ass."

"Jus take me home."

Teddy and his crew basked in their glory for a few more minutes sett'n up prospects for the weekend and they left.

"T-Rock, turn dat shit down, its' kill'n my ears. We ain't outside the car nomo.

"Nigga, you complain more than a bitch."

"Speak'n of complain'n and bitch, I see you gave Shanta yo pager #. Know'n she ain't doin no fuck'n," Fly specified.

"We'll see. She betta hope she don't let me in dat ass cause that's as far as it's going to go. She only gets one shot, hit or miss."

"All y'all Niggaz talk about is stupid bitches. T-Rock, you thank you MACK'n these dumb bitches but who pay'n fo da room?" Maverick interjected.

"Nigga, all you wanna do is rob. And for what? Da bitches scared of you." Teddy replied.

"FA'VREAL!" Fly concurred.

"Man, fuck y'all!"

Maverick stated.

Teddy went on to drop Fly and Maverick off, then went to Sasha's place to let her see his ride. She was expecting him and glad to see him. Teddy was now 18 and Sasha loved watch'n him unfold into the man he was becoming. She offered to take him out to dinner. They ate at Athen's on Independence Blvd., pick'd up a porno tape and shot back to her place. The older Sasha got, the freakier she got. She started masturbating in front of him and using sex toys. They rarely saw each other but when they did, she made sure to make it memorable.

After stay'n up til four something, Teddy was woke up by Sasha at 7:25 handing him his loud pager. It read 469-411-911. WHO THE HELL IS 469? Teddy wondered. Then it hit him, SHANTA. He jump'd up, shower'd and brush'd his teeth, kiss'n Sasha on her forehead and told her to come let him out. She got up and follow'd him to the door in the nude. Still exhausted from a few hours earlier she fell into his arm and ask'd, "When can I see you again?"

"I'll call you later." He respond'd.

"You do dat. I'll be home all weekend."

"Be good lady." Teddy said as he kiss'd her lips. Sasha accept'd the peck and back'd away, self-conscious of her breathe and said, "Be careful and have a good day."

Teddy smiled and left.

Arriving at the school parking lot about 8:30, he found Shanta sitting in her car wait'n. Teddy pull'd up to her car and she jump'd out into his car. He rush'd out of the park'n lot.

"I thought you had stood me up. I was gett'n ready to go to class."

"Yeah, I was runn'n a little late. Actually, I thought you were bullshit'n as usual."

She look'd at the all white interior and caught eye contact with Teddy and smiled say'n "Naah, you deserve a shodah dis. Your car is really nice, I like it."

Teddy smiled think'n, I BET I DO DESERVE A SHOT, WIT MY NICE CAR. He turn'd up the radio and allowed Aaron Hall and Guy to tell her that she could have a piece of my love, "dumb bitch." AND THE PUSSY BETTA BE GOOD, he thought.

He drove across town to the Comfort Inn off of Sugar Creek on I-85 Access Rd.

"I'll be back." Teddy said as he park'd and ran in to get the room. Return'n 10 minutes later, he jump'd back into the car to Shanta rest'n her head on the head rest look'n relaxed and sexy as fuck. He pull'd around to the park'n space in front of the side door. They grabbed their belongings and made their way to the room. "What's in the bag?" Teddy ask'd.

"Girl stuff. You'll see."

They entered the room and Teddy noticed she look'd like she had never been to a room with a guy before. Teddy flopp'd down on the King size bed and cut on the T.V. He found HBO and got up to get a towel that he wet and put under the door so the herbal incense wouldn't pass thru to the other side. Shanta was in the bathroom. Teddy took off his jacket to his Flight 23 sweatsuit and his Jordan's.

He grabbed the ash tray and sat on the bed leaning on the head board, pull'n out his lighter and a joint. As he began to light it and take a toke, Shanta enter'd the room wearn'n only a green match'n bra and bikini panties. Observing every inch of Shanta's curvaceous body as she walked toward the bed, Teddy thought to himself, DAMN, SHE THICK! It's about time!

Shanta approach'd Teddy and reach'd for the joint, shocking Teddy. She grabbed it and seductively crawled over his lap. "Why are you still fully dressed?" She ask'd.

Teddy silently took off his t-shirt and pulled down his sweat pants exposing his erection held in his boxers. He got back into the bed and Shanta pass'd the joint back and ask'd, "You thought you wasn't gone ever git dis pussy didn't you?"

"After you kept play'n games, I didn't give a fuck. Git'n pussy ain't a problem. Shiid, I turn down more pussy than I actually fuck." He said non chalantly.

"Well, the wait is over and I don't see you turn'n this pussy down." She said as she grabb'd Teddy's wood. "Damn it's hard!  Come here."

Teddy slid the ash tray onto the night stand and turnt back to Shanta. They started kiss'n and caress'n each other. Teddy's hand slid down between her legs as she parted them accepting his warm and gentle touch. "Mmmm" she moan'd.

Her playground was warm and inviting. Teddy's fingers slid thru the side of the seat of her panties to be welcomed by her silky wetness that lead to her pleasure pot. "Be gentle." She said as Teddy removed her bra and panties. He began lick'n and suck'n her fully erect nipples. "Take off your boxers and c'mon." He paid her no attention and continue to explore her body. Shanta was so caught up, she began moaning as if they were already in the act until Teddy started push'n the tip of his head thru her frame "Oh! Hold up!" He immediately came to a hault with the tip of his head still squeezing thru.

"Whus wrong?" He ask'd.

"That shit hurt. Jus go slow."

Her body was severely tensed up. "Relax." Teddy said in a gentle tone, think'n. I KNOW THIS AIN'T HER FIRST TIME. She laid back with her eyes closed and Teddy continued to enter her frame. The deeper he pushed, the tighter she seemed. On the out stroke, she lift'd her head and look'd between her legs at the log coming out as Teddy drove back inside of her quickly, she scream'd "OH! I can't do dis."

"You want me to stop?" He ask'd.

With pain all in her face, she said "Ye-ahh- No. Jus go slow."

She pant'd.

Teddy came all the way out just leaving his head inside. Slowly stroking in and out, she began to get use to it and she started ask'n for more and with pleasure Teddy added inch by inch until she was filled thoroughly. She began to gyrate and accept the pleasure with the pain. Before long, he bent her over doggy style. To see Shanta's nice round ass up in the air, was definitely worth the price of admission. Teddy literally assult'd this girls body.

Teddy relieved himself inside of Shanta as she gripp'd the bed and hollar'd she couldn't take no more. Between the thought of the night before and Shanta makin Teddy wait play'n her games, Teddy show'd her no mercy. Once he was through, blood was everywhere. That was the second time he had experienced something like that. Shanta rolled over in pain and Teddy ask'd her, "You on yo period?"

"No, you done popp'd something." She said grabb'n her stomach.

"You gone be alright?" Teddy ask'd lay'n up against her.

"Yeah, jus get me a warm rag."

"I'll be back." Teddy started the shower, wet a rag and took it to Shanta before he got into the shower. Moments after, he was under the steam'n hot runn'n water, Shanta came to join him. She was affectionate. Teddy almost felt bad about how he was plann'n to treat her but he just enjoyed the moment.

They got out of the shower, dried off and laid back in the bed. It was 11:40, he would have her back at her car by 2:30 when school let out. His plan was to have room service come thru and replenish the King size bed with new sheets and have the room prepared for the weekend festivities.

Teddy thought he had tortured Shanta but after a few minutes of cuddling, she grabb'd his wood and massaged it until it was ready to ride. She straddled Teddy and slid up and down like she was on a see saw. The experience was far better than the first round.

"How is this pussy?" She ask'd look'n down at Teddy.

"Shiiid, it's straight."

"Mmmm, it's yours. I'm so wet. This shit

feels good. Ssss.Umph."

Teddy laid there enjoy'n the ride think'n, IT'S REALLY TOO BAD I CAN'T KEEP THIS BITCH ON FOR SERVICE.

They both reach'd climax and Shanta collapsed on Teddy's chest. She laid there whisper'n in his ear with her face in the crease of his neck. "That was, UMPH! I ain't never felt nothing like that.

Ain't nobody else git'n none-a-dis."

"Yeah, right" Teddy chuckled. He would have loved to have made Shanta his little tender if she hadn't tried to play him-but little did she know, this episode was the first and last.

"Seriously" she said, "You felt so warm inside of me. At first that shit hurt but then it felt like... nothin I ever experienced."

They dozed off for a few. When they woke up, it was ten til two. They shower'd again, got dress'd and Teddy dropp'd her off at her car right when school let out. Shanta's girlfriends were wait'n at her car when Teddy pulled up play'n 2 LIVE CREWS "THROW DAT DICK." When Shanta got out of the car, Teddy drove up front to wait on Fly. As he wait'd, Shanta walk'd pass going into school walk'n with an extra twist compliments of your truly. Her girls trailed behind her look'n into Teddy's windshield giggling.

Ten minutes later, Fly walk'd up while Teddy was giving this JV cheerleader name Ny'osha his pager #. Fly got in the car. "What up Dad?"

"Ain't shit."

"You do know that everybody know that you fuck'd dat bitch today. She walk'd in the school switch'n her ass like dat shit was broke. Then we noticed she couldn't help it. What did you do to dat bitch Dad?"  Fly ask'd "I put my foot in her ass." Teddy said as they laugh'd so hard.

"Whussup wit Ny'osha?"

"She got next. I got a room. She wants to hang out tonight."

"You know she fuck wit Tony on the football team?"
"I ask'd her about that, she said that's old news."
"Shanta is makin claims on you and makin sure it's known that you are responsible for that extra twitch in her ass."

"Ain't nothing like a spokesperson. Shanta won't never ride in this car again or ride this dick again. I'm changing my pager # Monday. She want'd to play games and I win."

## Chapter 7: Crime Pays

Hustlin was a part of Teddy's genetic heritage. He was a fool for high end fashion which lead to constant hustle antics. Any kind of new hustle that brought in a substantial amount of currency, Teddy had his hands in it.

Tip was younger than Teddy but his big city roots kept his mind bring'n forth new hustles. Tip was from Detroit. He and Teddy bonded naturally in school. They fuck'd best friends, worked the same jobs and had dreams of conquering the music industry.

In 89', Charlotte had a surge of new Check Cash'n spots. Tip had an idea of how to forge payrolls checks and cash them at the Check Cash spots instead of banks. Teddy was his cohort. At the time, they were work'n for Hardee's.  All it took was success with the first check and they never look'd back.

Workin at Hardee's was so easy because they would only work 6-8 hours a week just to say that they actually work'd. When they were there, one or both would work the cash register walk'n out with at least $50-$100.00. That was small change, they got paid every week and they would take a $19.00 check and instantly turn it into $1,900.00. Throughout the spring and summer, they made close to $60,000 within six months. The sky was the limit for the two of them.

Week nights were spent at the high end hotels downtown Charlotte. If it wasn't the Marriott, it was the Radisson Plaza. Teddy had a shoe fettish that consist'd of every color of Bally's that was made. When their senior year began, they made it seem as though Harding was the audience for their fashion show.

Everybody had their assumptions of what they were doing but no one ever knew what their actual hustle consist'd of, all currency. A rumor surfaced that they had taken over a block in Dalton Village where Teddy was supposed to be living with his Aunt Jean.

Being young and naive, the inevitable was destined to happen. It was a chilly fall morning in September, Teddy and Tip were call'd to the front office after homeroom and greet'd by the Queen City's finest. They were both arrested and taken downtown.

This was all new to Teddy being his first of many run-ins with authorities. Tip on the other hand had just completed a year's probation for B&E.

Once they arrived downtown, they separated the two of them in two different interrogation rooms for questioning. After hours of waiting alone in the little trashy room, a detective entered and sat across from Teddy offering him a cigarette, which was a relief because between his nicotine fit and his nerves, he was about to lose it. As Teddy began to fill his lungs with cigarette  smoke, the detective began to tell Teddy what he knew of their operation. Afterwards, he told Teddy it wasn't him and Tip that they want'd, it was whoever was behind them and who else was work'n with them. Teddy laugh'd and told the anxious white detective that he didn't know what he was talk'n about. The detective then left the room and came back almost an hour later with the evidence that they had against them and began to threaten Teddy with all kinds of years in the federal penitentiary. Teddy express'd to the detective that it was his personal operation, giving the detective the details of how he went about the business.  Once again the detective left out mad that Teddy hadn't given more than he had. In the opposite room, Tip had given the identical story implicating himself as the head of the operation.

Hours later, they were both given $10,000 bonds. Teddy's mom had been there at the police station since the school had called her that morning around 9:30. It was now 10:30 pm as Queen sat there with her good friend Alton Martin a bondsman wait'n to post her son's bond.

Meanwhile, after Teddy saw the magistrate, he want'd his phone call. Right when the officer was about to put Teddy in the cell, another officer called out "TEDDY MASSEY one way."

Teddy didn't know what was going on. All he knew was, they were about to put him in a cell with Tip and a phone. He argued with the officer, "Nah, put me in the cell with my brother." Speak'n of Tip.

Everybody in ear distance laugh'd, "T-Rock, you made bond! Git da fuck outta here and make mine!" Tip yell'd.

"I got you bru, soon as I get out, I got chu." Teddy express'd not wanting to leave his friend behind.

"I know you do, just git da fuck on." Tip yell'd.

The officer gave Teddy his property and lead him thru the door to release him to Alton.

Alton passed off a cashier's check to the officer and sign'd Teddy out.

Queen rush'd over to embrace Teddy express'n how she wasn't goin to rest until he was out. She introduced Teddy to Alton and Teddy immediately ask'd what did he have to do to get Tip out. Alton ask'd what did he have to do to get Tip out. Alton ask'd for Tip's whole name, then called the officer and ask'd for Tip's charges and bond. "He needs someone to bring me $1500 and sign for him."

"I got the $1500. It's in my car."

"Oh you do? "Queen ask'd with a skeptical look on her face." I pick'd your car up from the school after they called me."

"Moma, will you sign for him, I can't leave him in there?" Teddy express'd to Queen.

Knowing how close Teddy and Tip was, she agreed to sign for him.  Alton went into his brief case and pull'd out another check and alerted the officer to bring Tipton Williams out. Less than fifteen minutes later, Tip was walk'n thru the door smile'n at his friend in relief knowing that Teddy wouldn't leave him.

Tip dus Alton, Alton was a slim 6ft'-2', 40 year old, cool ass black dude. He drove a 88' burgundy Jaguar. Alton appreciated Teddy's loyalty towards Tip.

Once they all met back at Alton's office, Teddy and Tip walk'd in to take their pictures for

Al's records, Teddy pass'd him fifteen crispy hundred dollar bills. Alton count'd out with a smile and pass'd five hundred dollars back.

"Here you go young blood, $500 on me. Call me if you ever need me again. I don't care if you got money or not, I won't let you sit there but stay out of trouble cause I don't want you worry'n your mom."

"Preciate it." Teddy said as he shook his hand.

"Yeah, thanks man." Tip said as they walk'd out the door.

Queen was amazed that Teddy immediately reimbursed her money for his bond. She knew he was into some serious criminal activities when she watch'd him count out a thousand dollars to give her and still had a large stack of hundred dollar bills. Teddy couldn't see taking from his mom because she support'd his sixteen year old sister Shan and her two year old daughter.

After such an experience, Teddy took the twenty thousand he had and put it up to help him support his child that was on the way. His main focus was to complete his school credits by the Christmas holiday break which was the end of the fall semester.

## Chapter 8: Expect The Unexpected

Life for Teddy was everything you could want as a senior. Ny'osha was the main attraction in his life and had been for the past month. That didn't stop Teddy from putt'n a dent in the female population at the school. Ny'osha just consumed the majority of his time outside of work'n and hustling. Everybody knew they were an item including Shanta who was now scared to death to even look at Teddy when Ny'osha was in the vicinity. Teddy stuck to his word and stay'd away from Shanta since he broke her in. He also changed his pager # from 356-FUCK to 356-LICK after Shanta page'd him relentlessly the whole weekend afterwards. That Monday morning, Teddy skipp'd first period to be the first customer in Dial Page. Now, she could only reminisce of Teddy and their rendezvous.

The crazy thing about the whole scenario was that Shanta's mom and Ny'osha's grandma were best friends. Ny'osha was fiesty and didn't care what nobody had to say. She had it in her mind that she was going to have Teddy before he had his car and before she left Tony, so she wasn't allowing nothing and nobody to come between them.

Teddy really liked Ny'osha. She was 5'- 2', 122lbs. bowlegged with the deepest dimples. She was caramel complect'd with a fat ass and the perkiest titts. Ny'osha reminded Teddy of Sasha in the bed, she knew how to execute her muscles in her pussy, that drove Teddy crazy.

Teddy had been sneak'n around on Ny'osha with this chic named Keisha, Keisha knew about Teddy and Ny'osha but she was a hood chic from Small Wood. Plus, she ran with a clic of broads that was known to start shit and jump other broads.

This particular day, Teddy was late to school due to hang'n out with Angee. He arrived in time to make it to homeroom right after first period. That's where the drama began.

"Pssst Pssst."

"T-Rock," E whisper'd," Tippy want you."

Teddy turn'd around to notice Tippy motioning for him to come to the back of the classroom with him. He grabb'd his book bag and join'd him.

They gave each other their hand shake and Teddy sat beside him as their teacher ran thru the roll. "What up Dad?"

"Ain't shit, runn'n late." Teddy answer'd, noticing several people look'n his way whisper'n and smile'n.

"Yo you see Keisha, Toni, Karen and Bria?" Tip ask'd him.

"Nah, why."

Tip began to giggle. "Yo Dad, they got on these t-shirts that say "BOOM I GOT YO BOYFRIEND, I GOT YO MAN" on the back and on the front going across the heart, it has the nigga'z name on it.

Keisha got T-Rock on hers."

"Git da fuck outta here. Ny'osha seen her?" Teddy inquired.

"I don't know but that ain't shit, Shanta is pregnant and guess…. who's the daddy?"

"Bullshit! Where you hear that from?" Teddy ask'd with his eyes wide as balls.

"I heard Reaford talk'n bout it in first period." Tip answered.

Reaford is Shanta's first cousin. He play'd on the football team and was huge for a high schooler.

"I gotta git outta here before anybody sees me. Ny'osha gone kill me if she sees Keisha. I ain't worried about Shanta, if she is pregnant it ain't mine."

"You sure, word is that she was a virgin. That's why she play'd you in the beginning, everybody that tried to fuck labeled her a tease. You the first person that has been confirm'd to touch that."

"Don't say that." Teddy said reflecting back to the day he and Shanta fuck'd.

The bell rang to dismiss them from homeroom. "I'm gone Dad." Teddy said to Tip as they moved toward the door.

"Before you go, look who's at your locker."

Across from the classroom, there stood Ny'osha at Teddy's locker. He put on his poker face and walk'd up to her and they began to kiss. "Why was you late?" Ny ask'd as they separated.

"I overslept. I was out late with Kato." That was his permanent alibi.

"You know Shanta is tell'n everybody she's pregnant by you?"

"Where did you hear that at?"

"My Nanna told me last night. She told my Nanna to tell me but she begged her not to tell her mom. So you need to check that out."

"Have you seen her today?"

"Not yet, but when I do, I'll make sure we talk to her."

"You not mad?"

"About what? You had just fuck'd her earlier that day before you took me to the room that night. She's the stupid ass, her mom and Nanna took us to get birth control the same day. You haven't fucked her since, I know for a fact because her mom is makin a big deal about me seein you."

"Good!"

"Teddy Massey, report to the counselor's office immediately."

"What they want with you?" Ny ask'd.

"Who knows? It's probably about my cap and gown.  I'll see you after second period."

"Alright." She agreed as they kiss'd and parted ways.

This day was filled with surprises. When he got to his counselor's office, she sat him down and told him that she was sorry but he wouldn't be graduating with the class of 89 because he needed a semester of 10th grade English and two elective courses. She hated dropp'n the news on him. She gave him the option of walk'n across the stage with the class of 89 and return back to school fall semester to complete the credit or complete his credit next semester by attending half a day, and walk the stage with the class of 90. He chose the latter.

Teddy was so upset, he just want'd to leave school and burn one. He stay'd at school thru second period to see if Ny want'd to leave with him but nothing prepared him for the next hour.

After second period, Teddy, Ny, Tip and Fly was at Teddy's locker listen'n to him tell them that he wasn't graduating this year. Ny'osha and Fly were two years younger than Teddy, and Tip was a year younger. Tip made light of the situation due to the fact that he and Teddy would walk the following year together. While they were talk'n, all of a sudden, Ny'osha call'd out to Keisha and by command, Keisha and her whole crew walk'd over to Ny'osha and Teddy. Now Keisha stood 5'-6' and was stripper thick.

"Those shirts are cute- "Ny said, inquiring," What T=Rock are you referring to?" Keisha look'd over to Toni. Teddy and Tip look'd at each other and Keisha respond'd in a arrogant tone "I only know one."

Without hesitation, Ny was all over Keisha and by the time Teddy and his crew pull'd the girls apart, Keisha was without a shirt and stood there in her bra. "Bitch, you got my man! I gotcho ass! Fuck you and them bitches you hang wit! And fuck you too Teddy." She said a she snatch'd away from him.

Teddy had had enough. He grabb'd his book bag and headed for the student park'n lot. Once he got into his car, he noticed his mom had paged him with a 911. He raced to her place in Earle Village and arrived in less than 10 minutes. When he walked in, he call'd out to his mom lay'n pass'd out sleep in her bed.

Kiss'n her on her forehead waking her up, "Hey Baby." She said half sleep noticing Teddy's presence.

"I raced over here when I noticed your page and the emergency code."

Baby, moma alright. I was check'n on you. I got a call from this girl this morn'n tell'n me that she's pregnant by you."

"Shanta." Teddy called out.

"So it's true?"

"I don't know Ma. I jus heard about it at school this morn'n."

"I called Jean, she said you didn't stay there last night."

"I was wit Angee."

"That don't make any sense Teddy. Where's Ny?"

"At school. We broke up. She got into a fight over me."
"What happen'd?"

Teddy explain'd his whole morning. He told her the situation about his graduation. She comforted him and gave him some sound advice, letting him know she was proud of him.

Before he left, he called Shanta to see if he could come talk to her. She agreed. He went to pick her up. She told him that she didn't know for sure but she was two months late for her cycle. Teddy took her to Planned Parenthood that afternoon and it was true. The whole ordeal with Tedra had left Teddy's heart tender-even though he felt like Shanta was some bullshit, he vow'd to be there for her day for day and he never left her side until she gave birth to his second daughter Timia NaShay Massey. He wasn't the same kid he was when Tedra was born five years ago, he had a keen sense of responsibility. Come to find out, Shanta was a virgin after all and Teddy was her first.

Timia was born November 13th 1989. By February 19th 1990, Teddy had completed high school and was preparing to attend FAMU in the fall. He and Shanta had attempt'd to have a relationship for the sake of Timia and it ended this

day. Teddy caught her cheatin and that was all he
need'd to leave her and not look back.

## Chapter 9: Next Episode

The year 1990 had arrived. Teddy had successfully completed all high school credits to graduate, escaped the long arm of the law with a year's probation and had fathered a beautiful baby girl.

Life at this point was somewhat calm. Play'n with the law was one thing before Timia was born but as a loving father he knew that any kind of prison time would leave his daughter without her dad.

Upon completing school, Mr. Silden, Teddy's band director offer'd him an opportunity to play in a college band on a 50/50 scholarship ride down in Florida at FAMU. Teddy accept'd the offer for the opportunity to explore another state and city. As far as college in general, he never saw it in his future. Even after taking the SAT'S and scoring better than average, college just wasn't in the plans. After sitting and speak'n with his counselor, he had decided to attend CPCC part time for Business but now he was head'd to a prominent black college.

Right after the beginning of the year, Teddy submitted applications to FAMU. Howard and NC A&T as his band director instructed. His next mission was to find a few jobs so that he could add to the money he already had. He want'd to make sure Timia was financially stable when he left.

Around the end of January, he was in train'n to drive a school bus, work'n part time at Burger King and working weekends at a club call'd Party Zone.

Teddy rarely had time for Timia, let alone Shanta. When Shanta gave birth to Mia, Teddy remember'd all too clearly how Sharon snatch'd up Tedra and moved to Virginia with her older daughter's father. To prevent having Mia snatch'd away, he sign'd the birth certificate, took out child support on himself and began a so call serious relationship with Shanta.

Being with Shanta was Teddy's first real boyfriend-girlfriend relationship. All the others before her were flings and situations. This was all too new. Check'n in, calls every other hour and constant questions about other chics.

Their relationship was what it was. Shanta didn't excite Teddy's sexual interest as Sasha, Angee, Tracy, Ny'osha or many others did but she was his child's mother. He made sure that Shanta and Timia was taken care of. Actually, this relationship was more business than a family in the makin.

After Timia was born, Teddy and Shanta had all of three sexual encounters, which constituted Shanta getting caught cheating.

It was Teddy's 19th born day. Shanta's parents were in Atlantic City. They left on the 13th of February going up North to Philly for Valentine's Day. They were originally from Philly and moved to Charlotte when Shanta was 10. From Philly, they went to Atlantic City and was due back home on the 23rd.

Before they left town, they gave Teddy a key and told him to watch after their daughter and granddaughter. Her pop's was a police officer and her mom as was a principle at Wilson Middle School. They trust'd Teddy because he was responsible.

Shanta thought Teddy was at work but he was off celebrating with his uncle Steve down the street in Dalton Village. Steve was on the phone talk'n to Deanna.

Deanna was Shanta's neighbor. She was older and want'd to give Teddy a taste of what she had to offer. Teddy refused because they lived too close. So instead of fuck'n Teddy, she fuck'd his brother Juan and being that the pussy was all that, Juan left room for Steve. Deanna would catch Teddy comin thru and sneak and tell him that Shanta was cheat'n. He never took her serious, he felt like she was just try'n to git him in her bed.

While Steve and Deanna held an intimate conversation on the phone, she heard Steve tell

Teddy something and she immediately inquired about Teddy being off from work.

"What's Teddy doin home?"

"Today his birthday so he took off." Steve answer'd.

"Put him on the phone."

"Hold on."

Steve call'd Teddy to the phone.

"T, Dee want you on the phone."

Passing Teddy the phone.

"What up Dee?"

"Happy Birthday boy." She said in a intense sexy voice.

"Preciate that."

"You gone let me bless you for your day?" She ask'd as Teddy blush'd and they shared a laugh.

"Stop play'n Dee. You already know."

"You may as well, Yo woman up here gitt'n it off."

"Dee, You don't never stop. Do you?"

"I wish I was play'n. I'm look'n at her and ya boy right now. You know I can see thru her room from mine."

"Stop play'n man."

"Ok, well don't say I didn't tell you."

"So you serious?"

"Boy, just come see?"

With a sense of urgency he says, "We on the way. We'll be there in less than 10 minutes."

"Don't come to the circle, park in my driveway."

"Ah-ight. Peace."

Teddy and Steve grabbed their guns. Steve a .357 and Teddy a Mossburg pistol grip 12 gauge. They left immediately, arriving at Dee's in 4 minutes flat.

Dee met them at the back door underdress'd wear'n a thigh length silk house coat with nothing underneath. Teddy walk'd pass her check'n her from head to toe. Dee was short, light skin with a short blonde cut, nose ring and very sexy. Once Steve enter'd behind Teddy, warming his middle finger in Deanna's vaginal cavity, she walk'd pass Teddy lead'n him to her bedroom to witness his woman git her freak on. She look'd over her shoulder to be sure Teddy was takin in the whole show she was providing as she switch'd to her room.

He walk'd straight to the window and as described, he could see Shanta and some male figure slow dragg'n. Being that he really didn't have any feelings for Shanta, it really didn't bother him, he just want'd his daughter.

Teddy told Steve that they weren't going to disturb their groove, they were simply going to use the key Shanta's parents left him to sneak in, get his four month old daughter and leave.

Upon entering the house, Teddy noticed they were listening to his Isley Bro's "Spend the Night" tape. Their plan took a drastic turn once Teddy come to realize Mia wasn't in any of the other rooms. WHERE IS MY BABY? He thought while look'n at Shanta's closed bedroom door.

"I know this bitch ain't got Mia up in this room with them." Teddy said whisper'n to Steve.

"If she do, let's just get Mia and leave as plann'd. Don't shoot dis nigga!" Steve instructed.

"I might not." Teddy said as he slowly turn'd the door knob. To his surprise, it was unlock'd. As he slowly push'd the door open, his mind was racing a mile a minute think'n. I KNOW THIS AIN'T HAPPEN'N. Self-talk kick'd in. SHE AIN'T WORTH IT.

Immediately when he enter'd the room, his evil thoughts became his reality.

Some strange dude ly'n naked in Shanta's king size bed on top of the comforter, little as baby dick exposed, fully erect wait'n to get his baby freak on. While Teddy's infant daughter ly sleep'n at the head of the bed under a white and pink blanket.

"Shanta! Who is that?" The strange dude ask'd when he noticed Teddy and Steve stand'n in the doorway with what seem'd to be heavy artillery.

Steve moved towards the stereo system, stopp'n the Isley Bro's tape from play'n.

"Shut-cho bitch ass up! I'm doin all the question ask'n!" Teddy shout'd, notice'n Shanta's titties hang'n towards the ground as she was caught bend'n down taken off her panties, expose'n her thick curvy ass. "Yo, git'cho shit and git the fuck out, NOW!"

Shanta stood nude, fully revealed and caught in what was about to be the act. She quickly grab'd her house coat when she grasp'd the concept that this fiasco was actually taking place.

Meanwhile! You don't comprehend very well." CLACK-CLACK. Teddy said as he put a bullet in the chamber of the 12 gauge." If you don't want to die where you stand, grab yo shit and run! Don't look back, run! And if you even look like you try'n ta put on some clothes before you reach yo ride, I promise I'm gone shoot you in the back." Teddy threaten'd in a furious tone.

"Yo man, jus git dat shit and c'mon." Steve said wave'n the .357 at'm.

The rush overtook him. He was grabb'n and dropp'n, grabb'n and dropp'n as his nerves ruled his existence. Gathering everything he could, ass out, Teddy turns and kicks him dead in the shittah "Muthafucka! You was gone jus disrespect my daughter like that!" Teddy shout'd in anger. Attempt'n to go ahead and beat'm with the barrel of the 12 gauge.

"Go head Rock! Let'm go. Git Mia and les git outta here." Steve said jump'n in between dude and Teddy.
"Make sure that nigga run his little dick, naked ass across the circle" Teddy said starin at Shanta whose head was down look'n to the floor as she sat on the edge of her bed embarrassed, hurt and confused.

The room became silent as Teddy grabb'd Mia's diaper bag, filling it with clothes, pampers, bottles and other necessities. Shanta sat totally quiet, scared and motionless while watch'n her child's father gather their child, and some clothes and left.

Teddy kept Mia with him for the next 3 weeks with no physical contact with Shanta. He spoke with Mr. & Mrs. Curtis (Shanta's parents) on several occasions in between, out of respect but he really didn't feel that he owed them an explanation. They were very caring and concern'd after they received the report from one of their nosey neighbors that some guy ran from their home naked across the circle a few days before they return'd from their vacation.

Several of Teddy's friend girls and distant cousins help'd him out with babysitt'n while he work'd. Instead of the strenuous work hours he had work'd throughout the month of February, he had now began call'n and hurry'n home to be with his child. Teddy was a dedicated father and he loved Mia with his whole existence. As a father, he just want'd to do right by her.

It was the second weekend in March, Big Daddy Kane was perform'n at Party Zone Friday night. Charlie, the club owner had already told Teddy that he definitely would need him for the whole weekend. All of Teddy's usual assistants had plans and he had exhausted his last option, his grandparents. After having an in depth conversation with his grandfather about decisions, being that Teddy would be going out of town the following weekend to visit FAMU College, he decided to take Mia back to Shanta.

Their bond had became so close, when Teddy tried to reach his 4 ½ month child off to her mother, she cried with such a painful scream as if someone had secretly pinch'd her. Teddy's heart fell.

He grabb'd her up and sat on their couch console'n her. Rock'n back and forth, patt'n and baby talk'n to his child, she immediately surrender'd in peace and quiet, lay'n her head on Teddy's chest. He began to pull her out of her little lite spring jacket.

Mrs. Curtis reach'd for her grandchild and Mia ignored her by try'n to crawl up Teddy's neck to get away.

"Lord have mercy Teddy! You done spoiled her rotten and now you're dropp'n her off. You gone have to stay until you bathe her and put her to bed. Have you kept her hours?"

"Yeah, 7:30 she's out. She got a ton of clothes out there." Teddy said as he look'd over at Shanta who couldn't believe that he was return'n her daughter.

Shanta and her parents knew that they had to let this whole situation boil over because Teddy could have sought complete child custody at Shanta's negligence and won.

It was about 4:30 that Thursday even'n so Teddy made himself at home while allow'n Mia to somewhat get back adjust'd to what use to be her home. For the first hour, Mia just sat there in Teddy's arms as Shanta and her family attempt'd to play with her. All they received was head turns and Mia push'n their hand away. Mia constantly look'd at Teddy with her hypnotic gorgeous eyes as if to say, "Daddy, let's go." The only time she smiled was when her Daddy held her up to his face kiss'n and dazzling her.

A few hours later while Teddy and Mr. Curtis was sittin there make'n small talk about the Tyson loss to Douglas a month ago, Mia began to come a little receptive to Shanta when it was time for her to eat. She allow'd Shanta to feed her but takin her out of her Daddy's sight wasn't about to happen. The whole time, Shanta and Teddy didn't share two words with each other. Shanta barely said anything the whole time Teddy was there.

7:00 PM rolled around and Teddy gave Mia her bath, lotion'd her down and dress'd her. He then ly beside her in the same bed she ly in when this whole situation began. Mia suck'd on a small bottle of Gerber apple juice while Teddy ly beside her caress'n her smooth caramel skin in her face. Minutes later, she was asleep.

Teddy gave Mrs. Curtis his schedule for the next two weeks, lett'n it be known that he had nothing to say to Shanta. Then he left.

## Chapter 10: Party Zone

It's Friday night, Teddy arrived at the club late try'n to find Kato for some weed. When he arrived, the park'n lot was pack'd. The line was down the side walk. As he walk'd to the entrance, you could hear and feel the systems from the cars driving by vibrating the concrete. TREAT'M LIKE THEY WAAANNA BEE TREEEAT'D, YOU SHOULD TREEEAT'M RIII-IIIIGHT. Jodeci sang on the hook of FATHER MC'S song "TREAT'M LIKE THEY WANNA BE TREAT'D" rang out from a car filled with chics hollar'n out the window as Teddy pass'd.

"Hey Daddy! We comin in!" Teddy look'd back to put a face with the voice. He smiled and wink'd at the driver of a red 89' Honda Prelude. A chocolate sister with shoulder length hair and a slim face. IT'S GONE BE A GOOD NIGHT. Teddy thought to himself.

Since things had went south between Teddy and Shanta, work'n at the club was a good look being that every night he work'd, he left with a different chic, cause of Tiger. Tiger was the DJ and Teddy was his assistant.

Kato got the whole team on staff there. Donnie was the first one to have a job there as a bouncer. Then one night Kato and Teddy were there hang'n out when the DJ quit. The owner Charlie, almost lost his Italian mind. "Does anybody know a DJ that can save my ass tonight?" He ask'd in a panic as the pack'd club stood around wonder'n and anticipate'n when the party would start back.

"You got a phone?"  Kato ask'd Charlie as he and Teddy stood sipp'n on Heinekens.

"Sure C'm-on!" He said in his Italian accent'd voice.

Kato call'd Tiger, he agree'd to come and the take over began. Tiger's roommate Jamal became the bartender. Juan, Teddy's brother got a bouncer job and Teddy became Tiger's assistant. Kato and Steve were the only two that didn't work at the club out of their whole crew. And just like Teddy's school bus job, he was the youngest employee there.

Teddy loved work'n at the club. He made $70 a night to control some lights that mostly ran on auto. Charlie allow'd each employee to have four-five guests a night. Teddy used his guest list to lure chics when Fly, Tip and E his classmates) didn't show up.

As he approach'd the door to enter the club, he noticed one of the other bouncers (Big Pin), talk'n to some chics to the side.

"Whussup Baby Boy?" Pin yell'd out with a wave.

"Ain't shit. Whus goin on in here?" Teddy ask'd point'n toward the club.

"Shit is crazy! Mocha and her home girl is inside ask'n for you."

"Ah-ight, I'mma catch you later!" Teddy said as he chunk the deuce and head'd inside.

"Mocha was Alton's daughter. Teddy met her when he went to the bonding company to get his bond money refund'd. She was cool. Nothing freaky, they were just cool with each other. Mocha was a big block, high red with no ass and plenty stomach. She hung with some of the finest tenders the Queen City had to offer so he was real eager to see who she had with her tonight.

Teddy enter'd the door and walk'd toward the counter greeting everybody with a whussup here, a peace sign there. As he approach'd the counter he noticed the cashier Nina smile'n wait'n for him to give her his normal charming," Heey Neeenah." He said with a smile.

"Hi you doin Teddy?" She respond'd as she gave the guy in front of her his change and stamp'd his hand.

Nina was gorgeous! She had a beige-tannish complexion with the most exotic light brown eyes you ever want'd to see. Her hair was sandy red in a bob.

Teddy and Nina possess some-what of a history together.

Nina's boyfriend is Angee's ex-boyfriend Chris. Normally, Chris is at the club by Nina's side when she works, but not tonight.

Teddy always had an attraction to Nina and tonight, it was quite evident the way she look'd and smiled at him. For some odd reason, Teddy knew Chris had given Nina the rundown on him and it was possibly the reason Nina garner'd the crush she possess'd for him.

"Teddy, Mocha is in there look'n for you."

"Preciate it Neeenah, see ya lateh Neenah" Teddy said as he gave his signature wink and proceed'd to maneuver thru the club.

Teddy was feel'n himself as he turn'd the corner and exposed his presence to the crowd on the other side of the wall. He saunter'd thru in a pair of Ralph Lauren jeans with a red-blue stripe Polo pull over, set off with a pair of red suede Bally's, a red Kango, and some gold EK shades.

Immediately on sight, he was greet'd with handshakes, whussups, smiles, point'n fingers and a few finger signals to come here. Most aggressive was Mocha stand'n in a crowd with Donnie, Juan, Kato (who Teddy had been search'n for), and a few other bouncers, Not to mention this little thick, beige tender.

She stood 5ft 2', long straight hair, wear'n some of the tightest jeans look'n pasted on. She had very inviting features and she never took her eyes off Teddy from the moment Mocha call'd his name, til the moment he was up close greet'n everybody.

"Whussup Lil Sexy Cuz?" Mocha ask'd as Teddy hugg'd her.

Lil Sexy is a nickname Mocha gave Teddy because she says he's too damn sexy.

"Mocha. Whut up Lil Freaky Cuz?" Teddy ask'd as he released her from his embrace.

Lil Freaky Cuz is Teddy's pet name for Mocha because she talks freakier than a phone sex line.

"Teddy, this my cousin Porchia."

"Hi you Ms. Porchia?" Teddy ask'd as he held out his hand to greet her.

"I'm fine and you?" Ms. Porchia replied as she shook his hand and shot him a sincere smile.

"I'm ahh-ight." Teddy said as he went from shake'n her hand to kiss'n her soft, sexy knuckles.

Release'n her hand from his grip, Teddy immediately embraced Kato. "K, what da fuck?"

I'm late because I slid thru yo spot try'n to git at-chu."

"Whut up son?" Here I am in the flesh Cuzo." Kato said as he dapp'd his lil cuz'n.

"Big Bru!" Teddy shout'd to his older brother Juan.

"Nigga, you always got ta make a grand entrance." He said slapp'n five with his lil brother.

"Dat's Lil SEXY CUZ!" Mocha said as everybody in ear shot chuckled, laugh'd and/or agree'd.

"Teddy, your whores are showing." Donnie said, emmulatin a Morris Day scene in Purple Rain.

"Fuck You! Whut up?"

"Ain't shit, Jus wait'n to bus a nigga's ass tonight." Donnie replied," but seriously, bout five broads done ask'd about you."

"Umph, Its' like that?" Ms. Porchia intervened in the sexiest softest tone.

"Porchia I told ja, that's lil SEXY CUZ." Mocha reiterated.

"Yall trippin, les get some drinks so I can go to the booth."

"Who's buy'n?" Mocha ask.

"I hope you are, ain't I worth it?" Teddy shot arrogantly.

"Hell yeah 'Lil Sexy' but you ain't my man."

"I'll buy." Ms. Porchia stated.

Teddy look'd her dead in the eyes think'n to himself, DAMN SHE'S GOT SOME OF THE PRETTIEST LIGHT BROWN EYES.

"Damn all-a-y'all, first round on me but y'all betta come brang me a drank latah to da booth. K, you got me?"

"I'll see you in the booth son."

"Word!"

Teddy gave Jamal $35 for everybody to order drinks and ask'd for a Guiness Stout then hurried to the booth.

"My nigga, it's about time you got-cho ass here. You got dat?" Tiger ask'd referr'n to the weed.

"K on his way to the booth wit it."

Teddy was Tiger's little side kick. If Tiger bagg'd a bad bitch, his rule was,

"You got ta have a chic for my lil man."

The chics loved Tiger, he and Teddy both had a honey tan complexion. Tiger had green eyes like a cat. He made the chics moisten on themselves when he look'd at them. The two together was a problem. Every night, chics would flock to the DJ booth look'n to advance past the club and permanently into their lives, but after meet'n Ms. Porchia, little did Teddy know that his life would be change forever.

## Chapter 11:  What's Love Got To Do With It

After Tiger took over DJ'n at Party Zone, the club became the premier party spot for the 18 to 25 year old crowd, nothing else in the city was competing. There was Side Effects, they were already establish'd years before. St. Marks was alright for a change of pace every now and then, and The Jaguar which was a small spot on Camp Green where the nearby hooligans hung out. But if you were apart of the hip hop movement in 1990, Party Zone was the place to be every Friday and Saturday nights and some Sundays after leaving Freedom Park.

This particular Friday night in latter March, the club was severely pack'd to capacity with the line down the sidewalk. Everybody was in full swing. It was 12:30 and the party was reaching its' climax. Tiger had just mix'd in WRECKS-N-EFFECTS "Club Head" with BBD'S "Poison". The club was crazy! There were dance crews front and center on the stage going head up in friendly competition. Attractive young tenders, dress'd in little to nothing dance'd on top of speakers in all four corners of the club while the dance floor was so pack'd that it look'd like everybody was dance'n with everybody.

Fifteen minutes earlier, Teddy had put the lights on auto and hit the dance floor with one of his many admirers. Teddy was a helluva dancer. He and his homeboy E were dancers for Fly. Whenever they perform'd, they emulated their favorite rapper, Big Daddy Kane, Scoop & Scrap.

Many thought that they would go far with their talents because not only could Fly rap (battling and winn'n with major artist), he could also dance, fitting right into every routine Teddy and E had. Their success included, open'n up for Guy, Creto Boyz, Redhead Kingpin and the list goes on, and they never lost a contest that they enter'd.

This particular night, they were all on the dance floor, freak'n the chics that set out to dance with them. Fly and E was on each side of Teddy, Mocha dance'd with Big Pin (the bouncer) behind the chic Teddy was freak'n. Next to Mocha was Ms. Porchia, dance'n with Lou, one of the other bouncer's. They call'd him Lou because he could have been twins to bowlegged Lou from Full Force.

Not only was Ms. Porchia dance'n, she was seriously freak'n Lou's big muscular cut up ass. His jheri curl was dripp'n, intertwine'n with the sweat that dripp'd from his eybrow as Ms. Pochia grind'd her perfect round, petite derriere into his now stiff dick. That whole corner of the dance floor wreak'd of a scene from the movie "Dirty Dance'n." Lust was the scent that plagued the atmosphere.

Teddy had been gone long enough. He told the little tender that he was dance'n with that he'd holler at her later and went back to the DJ booth. Tiger had just finished kill'n the club with the Ed Lover theme by 45 KING ("Dunt! Dunna nu nunna nuh nuh." Yall know the rest) and was slow'n the club down with Lisa Stansfield's "Been Around The World."

As Tiger was giv'n Teddy instructions before he went on break, a fight broke out.

Tiger always went on break when it was time for the slow songs because he knew Teddy could handle that. Right in the middle of their conversation, Teddy says, "Oh shit! That's Mocha!"

"You know what to do! Stay here, I'll be back! Tiger said as he rush'd from the DJ booth.

Teddy stopp'd the music and yell'd thru the mic, 'It you ain't in the fight, git the fuck out the way so we can git this shit clear'd up and continue with da party! Niggaz always gotta fuck shit up!"

He sat wait'n on the commotion to clear. The DJ booth sat up 2 ½ ft above the ground and had a plexi glass window that allow them to see the whole dance floor. Teddy watch'd as some 280 somethin pound dude smack'd Ms. Porchia and Mocha before Donnie, Juan, Big Pin, Tiger and several other bouncers annihilated this idiot that disturbed what had been a festive even'n.

Once they beat dude's ass and put him in the care of the local authority, everything went back to party mode. Teddy put on "Smile Again" by BBD and start'd the slow jam session. Ten minutes later, Tiger return'd. Teddy was burn'n a joint.

"Let me hit dat." Tiger requst'd reach'n for the joint.

Teddy pass'd him the joint release'n the ganja smoke thru his flarin nostrils, "What da fuck? Whewwww......" He ask'd as he continued to exhale the left over smoke thru his pucker'd lips.

"Is Mocha ahh-ight? Who was dat nigga?"

"Ssssp, ssssp" Was the sound of Tiger inhale'n the smoke from the joint, Sssp, she ah-ight He said, try'n to hold the smoke in his lungs. "That was Porchia's boyfriend, whewwww......" He said as he let out a thick cloud of smoke. The two of them stoop'd down in a corner, hidin from the public view, start'd giggling. "But we beat his ass!" Tiger said before they both bust out laugh'n.

Every since that first night Teddy met Ms. Porchia, the first week in March on the 9th two weeks ago, Ms. Porchia had been in the club every weekend flirt'n and git'n her freak-on, on the dance floor. Her boyfriend was in college at Delaware State. He play'd football.  A 280 somethin pound line backer. Ms. Porchia never seen him comin. He was home for the weekend to surprise her. He was a freshman in college and she was a senior at Olympic High where they met and began their relationship.

Ms. Porchia wasn't available when her dude attempt'd to reach her when he got in town so some of his hometown buddies convinced him to go to the club. Once he was there, one of his friends noticed his partner's girl freak'n out on the dance floor with Bowlegged Lou and point'd her out.

Instead of an immediate reaction, he post'd up to the side and wait'd til Ms. Porchia and Mocha left the floor. Things probably wouldn't have gotten out of hand if he hadn't watch'd Lou kiss Ms. Porchia on the neck.

Her dude grabb'd her by the arm very aggressively from behind "What the fuck-" Ms. Porchia scream'd as she turn'd wondering who had her by the arm. When she noticed who it was, she was stunn'd, left with her mouth hung open, "Oh...Hey." She said with the fear of GOD in her face. Buddy turn't into Ike Turner in the restaurant shoving cake in Anna Mae's face and slapp'd the shit out of her back up singer. He literally Fuck'd Ms. Porchia and Mocha up before being apprehended and destroy'd by the bouncers.

The price you pay to love and play.

## Chapter 12: Single Life

For the past few weeks, Teddy's life had become somewhat fast pace. Between his three jobs he held down, he had began to court four different chics and a lady. Working at Party Zone brought about most of these acquaintances, such as: Sparkle, the little twelfth grade cheerleader from West Charlotte; Tonya, a little tender that show'd up at the club weekly to claim her spot as an exotic dancer on the speaker; Cherese was from Chicago, Kitty Kat was from Statesville and they both were sophomores at Barber Scotia College in Concord. Teddy did an excellent job jugglin the four of them for fun but then there was Ms. Rita. He met Ms. Rita at his first job, driving a school bus. She was a 35 year old teacher's assistant. Pecan tan, 5ft 6', petite with all the right curves and very sophisticated. Teddy called her Ms. because she represent'd the presence of a lady.

Most evenings when Teddy wasn't feed'n his heavy appetite for many different chics, he would accompany Ms. Rita to all types of new restaurants throughout the area. Teddy was a breath of fresh air for Ms. Rita, he was her first interest since leaving her daughters father after 10 years. They enjoy'd one anothers company on another level, sex wasn't involved. For her, Teddy was young, ambitious and driven to meet his goals in life. In Teddy's eyes, Ms. Rita was a more mature Sasha, settled and extremely classy.

This particular weekend, Teddy was attending a kosher cookout at Donnie's mom's. At the club, Kato A-K-A Messiah, and Tiger A-K-A Malik X had establish'd a Islamic Community consisting of 5 bouncers; Jamal, the bartender; Teddy and a few sisters that the brothers were enlightening. Their strive was within the lessons of THE NATION OF ISLAM.

Donnie's mom agreed to allow them the run of her home for this particular Saturday afternoon. With such a beautiful home and plenty of land, she always felt it an honor to entertain. She was every bit of a chef's cook. Her menu for their Kosher cookout was: black pot fried flounder, barbecue grill'd boneless chicken breast, slaw, baked beans, mac-n-cheese, fried sweet potato turnovers, homemade ice cream, and a Russian iced tea with assorted imported beers. Inside the disco room was a fully stock'd club bar with every type of liquor you could think of and some you never heard of.

It's 9:30 AM Saturday morn'n, Teddy was rest'n, recuperating from the late night after the club with Kitty Kat. BOOM-BOOM-BOOM-BOOM....Was the knock at Teddy's room door.

"Teddy git da phone!" His Aunt Jean yell'd.
"Who is it?" He yell'd back still groggy.

"Git da phone boy!"

Teddy roll'd over and grabb'd the receiver, "Yeah" He answer'd, agitated at being woke up.

"Wake up sleepy head," Ms. Rita said in a vibrant sexy voice.

"Goodmorn'n ta you too Ms. Lady." Teddy responded in his raspy morn'n voice.

"How would you like to join two lovely ladies for breakfast and a morn'n of shopping?"

"What time you talk'n?"

"How long will it take you to get up and get dress'd?"

"Give me a hour."

"That's cool, You wanna bring Mia? Iyana wants her to come."

"Nah, cause we goin to a cookout this afternoon."

"Who?"

"Us! You, me and Iyana."

"Sweetie I'm sorry." Ms. Rita said with remorse in her voice." I have to be in Durham by 4:00 PM for my girlfriend's baby shower and I'm stay'n the night. That's why I want'd to spend the morn'n shopp'n with my two favorite people."

"That's cool, You can drop me off on your way out."

"Cool, I'll see you in a few."

"Ah-ight den. ONE."

Teddy got up and began his procedure of getting dress. And to say it was a procedure, that's and understatement. He start'd with lay'n out his clothes. Being a Polo fanatic, he pull'd out a brand new red, white and blue, Polo sweatsuit with a Polo t-shirt, socks, boxers and a fresh pair of polo tennis shoes. Now it was off to the bathroom, when the phone rang. Stepp'n back into his room, he grabb'd the receiver at the begin'n of the second ring.

"Yeah!"

"Don't be answer'n my phone like that!" His Aunt Jean yell'd from the other side of her bedroom door.

"Donnie sat laugh'n on the other end of the phone. "Whussup?"

"Whut da fuck you want to be up? "Teddy said, piss'd off at being interrupt'd and yell'd at by his aunt.

"Yo, whut time you gone git here today. I need you.

"Whut-chu mean you need me?" Teddy ask'd.

Donnie began to explain, "You know Trina gone be here." Trina was this chic Donnie was see'n," and Anna and Porchia."

"Whut dat got ta do wit me?"

"You know if Trina thinks one of them are try'n to git wit me, it's gone be trouble. I jus need you to kind-a-be a diversion."

Donnie had a way of try'n to make it seem like he was this Don Juan character, when in fact, most chics play'd him cause they knew he came from a lot of money. Since he began work'n at the club, his stock had rose. If for nothing else, he'd get them in free. Donnie stood 6ft 5' and literally resembled a gorilla. Being Teddys' senior of 5 years, as a youth, Donnie couldn't stand next to Teddy in the arena of catch'n chics. When Teddy was in elementary school, he sex'd more chics at the high school Donnie attend'd than Donnie did the whole time he was there. So at this point, Teddy felt that Donnie was waste'n his time. "Since you real close with Mocha, You can keep her and Porchia company. "Donnie continued.

"You some bullshit-" Teddy said unamused, "How da fuck you know I ain't bring'n Ms. Rita?"

"Oh! My bad. That is right."

"Yeah, that is right. I gotta go, we bout ta go shopp'n." Teddy said as he finish'd roll'n a joint he start'd at the begin'n of this bullshit ass conversation.

"Ah-ight den. PEACE."

Donnie conclude'd. "Yeah."

Teddy was off to shower and change. Less than 45 minute later, Ms.Rita was at the door look'n exceptional in a tight fit'n Versace sundress with her toes finely pedicured in some open toe Nina West slip ins, smell'n like exotic fruits. Her hair was pull'd back in a bun, accentuated with a pair of Versace sunglasses on the top of her head.

"Hey Mr.Polo, you ready?" Ms. Rita ask'd with a radiant smile.

"Yeah, let me grab my things."

Teddy grabb'd his Ralph Lauren shades to keep his chinky red eyes from being exposed and giving off the fact that he was high. He grabb'd his keys, told his aunt bye and left hand in hand with Ms. Rita.

"You feel like drivin?" Ms. Rita ask'd.

"I'll drive." Teddy said as he walk'd her to the passenger side of her gold 1990 Honda Accord. He open'd the passenger door where Iyana was sitting. Iyana jump'd out of the passenger seat and into Teddy's arms. 'Hey Teddy." She said as they embraced.

"Hey Yana, whut-chu up to?"

"Nothin-You smell goooood."

"Thank You." Teddy said as he open'd the back door for her.
                    "Are we going to get Mia?"

"Not today baby. Maybe next week." He answer'd, closing her door with a smile.

They were off for a morning of splurging and shopp'n.

They ate at Cracker Barrel on I-85 Access Rd. off of Billy Graham Parkway. That was one of Ms. Rita's favorite restaurants. She loved their turkey sausage and pancakes with the crispy edges.

They enjoyed their way to South Park Mall.

The shopping began in HECHT'S, one of the premiere department stores in the mall. Teddy and

Iyana joked and play'd while Ms. Rita pick'd out different pieces and outfits for Iyana and Timia. They stop and shopp'd at several different spots before ending their spree at CHAMP'S Athletic Footwear. Ms. Rita and Teddy had spent close to a $1,000 together on their daughters. Ms. Rita runn'n up her charge cards and Teddy spend'n cash.

Teddy had purchased Timia and Iyana several pairs of sandals and shoes but he want'd to get them both some Jordan's.

"Sweetie, kinda hurry. We are on a schedule. I still gotta drop Iyana by her father's before we go."

"No problem, I'm getting her and Mia some Jordan's and we can go."

"Ewww, Teddy, You gitt'n me some Jordan's?"

Before Teddy could answer, Ms. Rita interjected, "No! You've already bought her so much stuff."

"And you've bought Mia a lot of stuff. Stop tripp'n."

"Teddy Mia is 5 ½ months old, buy'n for her is nothing. Yana is ten- "Ms.Rita lower'd her voice to a whisper near Teddy's ear so that Iyana couldn't hear her, "You're buying her stuff that her dad has never purchased her." She said behind clinch'd teeth. "Teddy, you brought her a gold necklace and I didn't say nothing but I think the Jordan's may be a little too much. Plus, where are you getting all that money from? I know you don't make that kind of money driving the school bus."

"Ms. Rita, first of all, I work three jobs and I have money saved froma accident I was in years ago." Hiding the fact of his past and present illegal activities. "Listen, I already told her I was going to get'm, I ain't into disappoint'n the babies. She's old enough, jus tell her not to tell her dad I bought'm."

Rita took a deep breath and exhaled as her thoughts came together. "Yana, Teddy can purchase these shoes on one condition. "She paused, going against her better judgement. "Don't tell your daddy Teddy bought them for you."

Before she could finish her sentence good, Iyana respond'd "I won't!" She said as she grabb'd and hugg'd Teddy." Thank You Teddy."

"It's nothing." He respond'd "You just be sure You do as your mom tells you."

"I will."

"You're spoil'n her Teddy. She already gets the majority of what she wants."

"My fault. I'll try ta do better "He said send'n her a wink and a smile.

## Chapter 13: The Chase

Ms. Rita and Teddy completed their shopping extravaganza and went on to drop Iyana off at her dad's. Leaving his place, Ms. Rita began to share her true feelings to Teddy. She express'd that she appreciated how attentive he was with Iyana and how much fun she always had in his presence. Teddy in turn exposed a little of his inner self. Express'n to her why he felt it was so important that he made sure Iyana knew she was loved. They bond'd heavily on the way to Donnie's house, enjoy'n the ride in the beautiful 80° spring weather.

"Let me ask you something?" Ms. Rita ask'd, "Do you find me attractive?"

"What kinda question is that? "Teddy ask'd with a crazy inquisitive look on his face.

"I know I'm not as attractive as the girls perhaps your age-"

Teddy cut her off "Are you serious? What makes you say that? You are gorgeous and I love your style."

"So why haven't you ever try'd or attempt'd to make love to me?" Teddy bust'd out laugh'n, "Git da fuck outta here!"

"I'm serious." She said look'n over at him with this playful baby look on her face.

"It damn sho ain't because you ain't attractive!
            You sexy as fuck!"

"So what is it then?"

"Ms. Rita, to me, You are a lady. I've been around the block a few times and I see something different in you. I didn't want to rush nothing. I felt like, since you and I both had just come out of our situations, that it would be cool to take a different approach by just hang'n out and enjoy'n each others company."

Ms. Rita look'd over grabb'd Teddy's hand, "You are so sweet and baby, I really appreciate your conscious effort to be accommodating mentally, but a woman at my age is not just horny, I'm freaky and horny. I need to be touch'd and explored sexually, daily."

Teddy sat listen'n and notice'n the erection she had given him by her sharp, sexy and explicit tone. "Well we gone have to see about gett'n you touch'd and explored sexually as soon as possible." They look'd at each other, given each other that look of seduction.

Teddy was satisfied with the way things were between him and Ms. Rita. Not to mention, his flock of chics that kept his sex game tight but now he had to prepare to bring pure satisfaction to this classy lady, not the normal run of the mill he was use to with his other chics.

They pull'd into Donnie's parents driveway. Ms. Rita immediately began to adore the mini mansion and the nice cars surround'n it. A few conscious sisters were walk'n toward the house in three forths along with a few hoochies following. "Baby, you be good. "Ms. Rita said as she lean'd over the console to capture some tongue play. "I'll see you tomorrow afternoon."

"You sure you don't want to come in for a minute?" Teddy ask'd.

"A few minutes won't hurt. I'll let you show me off while, I let it be known that you my Teddy.

"She said as they began to kiss.

"C'mon."

Teddy got out of the car and went around to the driver's side to open her car door.  He held her hand and escort'd her to the door that lead to the disco room. They walk'd straight in without knock'n, Teddy was family like that. He had hoped everybody was out back near the pool instead of sitt'n in the disco room because contrary to what they thought, Teddy never liked being the center of attention, it just always happen'd that way.

And today was no different. Soon as they enter'd the scene, it was like clock work. Mocha had to be the first to make it known that she saw Teddy," Whssup Lil Sexy Cuz? You stay fresh!"

"T-Rock! Whut up?"

"T-Rock, Donnie look'n for you."

All at once, everybody shout'd Teddy out. Speak'n, wave'n and point'n like the star had arrived.
"Whut up y'all? I want-chall to meet my lil peoples. This is Ms. Rita, Ms. Rita this is everybody." Teddy said waving his free hand across the whole room.

In unison, everybody said, "Heeyy Ms. Rita." and bust out laugh'n

"Hello everybody." Ms. Rita said in a bashful tone sorta hiding behind Teddy's shoulder.

"Make yaself at home honey." Donnie's mom said "Teddy, make her a drank and quit stand'n at the doh look'n crazy." Everybody laugh'd.

"Ms. Rita, that's Moma Davis."

"Nice to meet you Moma Davis but I can't stay. I'm going to my girlfriend's baby shower in Durham, I jus came in to speak."

"You sho is pretty chil."

"Thank you" Ms. Rita said blush'n.

"You be careful goin up dat ole highway."

"Yes ma'am, I will."

While Ms. Rita was exchanging pleasantries with Moma Davis, Ms. Porchia walk'd over and ask'd Teddy, "You leavin too Lil Sexy Cuz?" And smiled.

"Nah, I'm stay'n," Teddy respond'd notice'n Ms. Porchia's curvaceous body and bubble ass in those pink fit'n nylon Nike sweat pants she had on with the Nike t-shirt and tennis shoes to match. He still wasn't impressed.

Ms. Rita never gave a clue that she heard Ms. Porchia's inquiry but she took it all in, noticing Ms. Porchia's whole disposition.

"It was nice to meet you all. Y'all enjoy yourselves." She said turn'n to Teddy and giving him the most unexpected sensual kiss imaginable for show.

Taken by her open show of affection, Teddy didn't want to let her go. She look'd up into his eyes and said in the softest tone, "Prepare to ly in my arms tomorrow night."

"Let me walk you to the car." Teddy said feel'n intensely connect'd to her.

"No, you stay, I'm not going to take you away from your fans." She said with a smile and a wink, given him another peck on the lips as she turn'd and open'd the door to leave. Teddy follow'd.

"Be careful and page me when you get there."

"I will,"

"ONE."

"ONE, Lil Sexy Cuz." She said mimick'n Mocha with a smile as she enter'd the driver's seat of her car.

Teddy laugh'd at her sarcasm as he waved and sent her a wink. Meanwhile, the whole disco room watch'd as Teddy charm'd the sexy lady that he brought to meet everyone. The chics envied her and the dudes observin look'd on, proud that their influence was seen in the moves Teddy made.

"Damn Teddy, You ain't that same young nigga I use to get drunk in the camper. She's older than me ain't she?" Vera, Donnie's sister inquired.

"Teddy, I like her. That's whut-chu need. You betta do right by her." Moma Davis said.

"I-own-no moma, I might want his lil young grown ass myself." Vera said.

"I know that right V." Another chic add'd.

Teddy's stand'n at the bar blush'n, try'n to fix him a shot of Johnnie Walker red label, while being scrutinized by the 15 to 20 chics sitt'n in the disco room.

"Where's K and Donnie'nem?" Teddy ask'd.

They outside set'n up the DJ equipment with Tiger." Moma Davis answer'd.

Teddy grabb'd his drink and turn'd to leave.

"Y'all hot in da legs broads done ran dat baby off." Moma Davis said laugh'n at how fast Teddy was try'n ta git away.

"We'll just have to chase him then." Ms. Porchia said as everybody laugh'd, including Teddy.

Teddy wasn't shy or bashful by a long shot but he didn't like being the center of attention either.

Walk'n thru the day room pass the Jacuzzi, Teddy spoke to a few chics sitt'n around as he walked outside.

"T-Rock! Whut up son?" Kato yell'd.

"Peace LORD. Whut'z da science?" Teddy ask as they dapp'd each other.

"Yo, I heard about the little piece you came thru wit." Kato said in his heavy NY accent. "Dat's no surprise though son, I taught you well." He said as he gripp'd his neck.

"T-Rock, whut up money?" Big Pin ask'd.

"Dat nigga betta have something to smoke." Tiger add'd.

"You know I got-chu."

"Well roll something up." Tiger demanded as he continue'd to hook up wires to turntables and cross faders.

Teddy threw a plastic bag fill'd with herbal essence to Donnie with a box of Swisher Sweet cigars and told him to roll up, then told Kato they needed to talk.

Kato wrap'd his arm around his lil cousin's neck and they walk'd toward the camper. "Whut'z da deal son?"
                    "I need to reup."

"Word son, You ready?" Kato ask'd bein silly as he always was. Kato was the most serious and the comedian at the same time.

Teddy pull'd out a knot of money and began to count it out.

"I know you got currency. I'm fuck'n wit-chu. You need it now?"

"Long as I get straight before we go to the club tonight. I'm good."

"I got-chu straight." He said in a proud tone. "Yo shorty with Mocha? She's been ask'n about you every since they got to this joint."

"Yo, she step to me in front of Ms. Rita."

"Whut-chu expect son? It's ya pedigree. You can handle it."

"Yo, I'm straight. Dat bitch got drama. She got a dude. He beat dat ass in da club a couple weeks back."

"Word son!?! She's a batter'd spouse?" Kato ask'd in his comedic disposition.

"Word!" Teddy said as they both crack'd up laugh'n.

"Word up son, let's go around here and enjoy ourselves. It's plenty food, drinks, chics and smoke, You a "HO BOSS" so let da ho's choose a boss."

They finish'd there one on one and return'd to the festivities. Tiger was just begin'n to get the sounds right as he test'd the turntables with "ROCK DIS FUNKY JOINT" by Poor Righteous Teacher. Mostly everybody had began to migrate to the backyard and around the pool area. It was more people than expect'd. What was supposed to be like a 25-30 people gathering had turnt into something like 75-80.

Donnie had roll'd the whole pack of Swisher's for Teddy so when Teddy and Kato return'd, Donnie gave him four roll'd cigars and the rest of his herbals. Teddy socialized with a few people he knew and then made his way to a lounge chair near the pool off to the side, alone smoking and fantasize'n about Ms. Rita. His serenity was interrupt'd by Mocha and Ms. Porchia.

"Lil Sexy Cuz, why you bein ALL ANTI?" Mocha ask'd.
                    "ANTI?"

        "Yeah anti-nigga... antisocial."

"Go head on Mocha. Ain't nobody bein 'ANTI'. I just had to take care of some shit. I'm chill'n now. Hi yall doing?"

"We fine? Where's that sexy brotha of yours?" Mocha ask'd.

"Now that's a good question, he suppose ta be here."

"You gotta work tonight?" Ms. Porchia ask'd.

"Yeeh, I ain't seen you there in a few weeks. Since yo little altercation. You ah-ight?" Teddy inquired try'n to run them off.

"I'm alright? Was that your girlfriend who drop'd you off?"

Mocha intervened, "Y'all, I'll be back. I'm goin ta get me a drank."

WHY IS MOCHA LEAVE'N THIS NOSEY GIRL OVER HERE WITH ME? Teddy thought to himself.

As Mocha walk'd away, Ms. Porchia continued to inquire as Teddy smoked his herb.

"Nah, she's a good friend. Why does it matter?" Caught off guard Ms. Porchia said, "I was just ask'n cause y'all look good together."

"I look good regardless." Teddy said, allow'n his cocky side out the bag.

"You definitely do that." Ms. Porchia said, cosign'n Teddy's self compliment as Mocha return'd.

"Sexy Cuz, Vera want-chu in the disco room."

"Ah-ight. I'll be back." Teddy said, glad that Vera rescued him.

When Teddy got into the house, he noticed that this cookout had turn'd into a full blown party and he wasn't prepared for the surprise Vera had in store for him as he enter'd the disco room.

"Whussup V?" Teddy ask'd, as he step'd to the bar where Vera was mix'n drinks for two females that look'd familiar but Teddy couldn't put no face to them.

"That's all you see?" The short brown skin sexy chic ask'd." I gave you this pussy before you was old enough to be fuck'n."

Teddy notice'd the voice "Tra-cy?" He said unsure.

"You betta know it!" She said as she jump'd into Teddy arms, "If you don't look and smell good, I don't know what do!"

"Hi you been?" Teddy ask'd, as he held her close. Release'n Tracy and reach'n out to Glenda "Whussup wit-chu Glenda?" He ask'd, hugg'n her as she sat on the bar stool.

"Boy, we been ask'n about you. Teddy you really look good. How long has it been?" Tracy ask'd.

"It's been about 7 years." Glenda answer'd" and where is Steve."

Teddy answer'd in a somber spirit, "He in the hospital."

"Is he still suffer'n with sickle cell?" Glenda ask.

"Yeea."

"What hospital is he in?" Tracy ask'd.

"Presbyterian."

"We gone go by to see him as soon as we leave here." Tracy said.

"Teddy, it is really good to see you. When V call'd and told us you were here we had to see you, we hurry up and rush'd over here." Tracy continued.

"Y'all talk'n bout me, Y'all look'n like y'all just fell out the JET beauty of the week."

"Thank you baby, we try." Glenda said as everybody laugh'd enjoy'n the reunion.

"So what are y'all doin now, Glenda I heard you was in the service?"

"I was, but now I'm work'n at the Post Office over on I-85 Access Rd."

"And I'm married with two girls and work'n at IBM. But you know, you can always dig this out."

The whole team of chics enjoy'd a good laugh as Tracy put that out there.

"I was a pee-wee then, I don't mess with other dudes women nomo. In fact, Tracy you molest'd me." Teddy said jokingly and a roar of laughs went thru the room.

"Teddy, you so full of shit! As young as you were, you knew more than me. If anybody was molest'd, it was me." Tracy retort'd reminiscin of the old days." So what are you doin now?"  She ask'd.

"I finally graduated. I'm going to FAMU in the fall on a band scholarship major'n in Business and minor in Psychology."

"I heard dat." Tracy said.

As Teddy, Glenda and Tracy were catch'n up on old times, Ms. Porchia came and stood right beside Teddy at the end of the bar leaving Teddy very uncomfortable. He kindly offer'd her a drink. She accept'd, then Teddy excused himself tell'n Tracy and Glenda not to leave before say'n bye.

Teddy went about socialize'n and build'n with GOD's every step he took, either Ms. Porchia was alone on his trail or her and Mocha were right there. Fix'n his plate, there's Ms. Porchia. In the middle of a cipher, there's Mocha and Ms. Porchia. Kick'n it with Donnie and Trina, there's Ms. Porchia.

Eventually, he just stop run'n and sat there thru her third degree. It was evident that Ms. Porchia had a intense crush on Teddy but his mind at that moment was on bigger fish. However, after sitt'n and talk'n to her, Teddy ended up take'n a likin to her. She was a very pretty and shapely girl. Who knows what fate might turn up in the future?

## Chapter 14: Touch'n & Exploring Sexually

It was the first weekend in April, Teddy and Ms. Rita had plann'd one of their outings but April Showers were rain'n on their parade this Saturday. Teddy had yet to touch and explore Ms. Rita the way her tender frame desired, but there was no better time then the present. He made a reservation at the Embassy Suites, check'd in at 2 pm and called Ms. Rita and invited her to come over.

Her phone rung 2 times before she answer'd.

"Hello?" in a relax'd tone.

"Whus happen'n Ms. Lady?"

"Hi Teddy, I was just ly'n here think'n about you. I really want'd to go shopp'n today but it's really messy out. What are you doin?"

"I'm at the Embassy Suites laid back. I just need'd some me time before I go to work tonight."

"Sounds relax'n. Am I invited?"

"You ain't here yet."

"Give me 30-45 minutes." She said in a very exciting tone. "I got something for your ass.

Do I need an overnight bag or do I have to leave when you go to work?"

"If you check in, You check out wit me."

"I'm on my way."

Teddy laid in the front room of the suite in some Rio swim trunks, a wife beater and a pair of Polo shower slippers, smoking some weed and sipp'n on a Guiness. He went to the Harris Teeter's and got some Moet, pineapple juice, strawberries, green grapes and pineapples along with his beer of choice for entertainment purposes. There he sat burn'n sandlewood incense in the front room and in the bedroom of the suite. The stage was set. Teddy was prepared to take her there.

Ms. Rita arrived on schedule. Teddy answer'd the door to Ms. Rita standing there with a thigh length raincoat on, some black high heel sandals and a black and gold Versace scarf covering her head with her night bag on her shoulder.

She greet'd him with a hug and kiss as he took her night bag.

"Teddy, what are you doin? It smells good in here." She said as she stroll'd thru observing Teddy's setup.

"Oh, that's Sandlewood incense." He explain'd.

"No, I'm talk'n bout the smell that's mix'd in. You been smok'n marijuana?" She ask'd with a smirk on her face.

"Why? Is that a problem?"

"No Honey. I don't smoke but I like the smell and a lite contact. The aroma is exotic and seductive, especially mix'd in with those incense."

"Take off this coat and get comfortable." Teddy said as he grabb'd and pull'd her close attempt'n to help her come out of the raincoat.

"Stop Teddy," She said in a playful flirtatious voice, "I'm going to take it off in due time. Let me look around." She kiss'd him, Teddy let her go, spark'd up a joint and continued to play the Nintendo boxing game he start'd before she arrived.

Ms. Rita walk'd thru the suite, marvel'n at Teddy's style. When she walk'd into the bedroom of the suite, Teddy had taken some red roses he purchased from the gift shop and peel'd the rose pedals off makin a trail from the door to the bed, with more on the bed and 6 long stem yellow roses on the pillows.

"Teddy this is nice!" She yell'd from the bedroom while munch'n on a few grapes and strawberries.

Teddy never respond'd, as he continued to play the game, smile'n on the inside while fill'n the air with ganja smoke. Ms. Rita appear'd in the doorway of the bedroom, stand'n with the raincoat open and her perfectly shaped body and skin complexion glow'n.  Exposed, ready to be touch'd and explored sexually.

"If you want my coat off, come take if off." She said, rubb'n her right hand down the middle of her stomach past her navel to her freshly shaved vaginal area, taking her middle finger caress'n her clit and enter'n her ever so wet pussy, then lick'n the same finger.

OH MY GOD! Teddy thought as he look'd up.  SHE REALLY IS HORNY AND FREAKY.

"C'mere." Teddy said as he dropp'd the controller.

"No...You come here." She said as she stood there masterbate'n.

This was something new to Teddy, a serious turn-on. Stand'n to go join Ms. Rita, she noticed Teddy's full fledge erection.

"Umm, looks like I got somebody's attention."

Teddy grabb'd Ms. Rita by the waist and they began to tongue wrestle while Teddy back'd her up into the room, ly'n her on the king size bed. Dropp'n her rain coat to the floor, Teddy grabb'd the tray of fruit and join'd her on the bed. Still dress'd in his shorts and wife beater, Teddy crawl'd up between her legs to serve Ms. Rita the strawberries and grapes allow'n the juice from the pineapple to drip into her belly button before feed'n them to her. She found herself in ecstasy while Teddy feast'd on her upper body parts, wondering to herself, THIS FEEL SO GOOD!

IF ONLY HE WOULD TAKE THIS TOUR DOWNTOWN. He took his time, while lick'n, suck'n and nibbling on her nipples, he play'd a song with her clitoris as if it was a string on a guitar, gently enter'n her warm, super wet flesh with his fingers.

"It's been-sss-solong. Make Ms. Rita cum Teddy." She plead'd and moan'd as she enjoy'd the pleasurable sensations Teddy was providin.

Ms. Rita could tell that Teddy was going to meet her every expectation in pleas'n her sexually but she want'd him to also taste her orally.

"Ummm…" She purr'd, "Teddy-taste Ms. Rita." She said in the heat of the moment.

Teddy was experienced in providing pure pleasure sexually but orally he was green. Even though he want'd to try pleasing her in that fashion, he didn't want to turn her off by experiment'n on her for their first time. Lick'n around her neck and about to bring her to her second orgasm with his finger alone, Teddy softly explain. "I've never done that before," he whisper'd softly, but, You are definitely worth the try."

"Thank you sweetie for letting me know. Maybe I can let you experiment one day, or even later but right now isn't that time.

"Come here."

She demand'd, switch'n places with Teddy, assist'n him out of his wife beater, while passionately kiss'n, lick'n and suck'n his chest, nipples, neck and ears. "Now it's time for me to introduce you to the freaky side of Ms. Rita." She said as she grab'd the bulge in Teddy's shorts, massage'n intensely but gently while she talk'd to his manhood as if it were a warrior. "Oh so you think you can handle what Ms. Rita has to offer?" She ask'd, while ly'n between Teddy's legs, holding his 7 ½ inches of pleasure, suck'n it thru his shorts, holding eye contact with Teddy as he look'd down at her. "C'mon out of these shorts and let me teach you what I know."

Teddy came out of his shorts and Ms. Rita's eyes widen'd as if she had just been given a ten carat diamond ring. She grabb'd his thickness, massage'n and inspect'n it until she was completely satisfied with what she saw. Instantly, she took the head of his dick into her mouth, while look'n up at him to make sure he could see her bring him pleasure.

"Oh shit!" Teddy said as he ran his fingers thru Ms. Rita's hair.

Tickle'n the tip of his dick with the tip of her tongue, she tells Teddy how good he taste to her, then she show'd him that freaky side of her that she was dy'n to let out. Slow, fast, slow, fast, down the side of his shaft, back up to the head, then deep throat.

"You not gone cum for Ms. Rita?" She ask'd between slurps.

"Baby, that shit feels so good. "Teddy express'd.

"Mmmm, You taste good" She said as she seductively suck'd the head of his dick as if it were a super blow pop." But I gotta feel you inside me.

You got condoms?"

"Damn! They in the car?" Teddy said, look'n down at her, anxious to slide inside of her.

"Can I trust you inside me without a condom?"

"Can I trust you?"

Teddy ask'd, chuckling.

"I'm serious, You ain't gone cum all fast and shit are you?" She inquired with the sexiest smirk on her face." I'm tell'n you Teddy, my shit is like crack, You'll get a quick fix and be chase'n that same high forever."

"Well, let me git my first fix."

"Hi you want it"? Never mind, she crawl'd up and straddle'd him, she slid down on the throbb'n head of his dick. She realize'd that it had been a while since she had been enter'd. "Damn Teddy, my little shit is tight."

"Don't-chu run now." Teddy filled his hands with her ass cheeks, spreading her wide and slowly plunged deep inside of her.

"Mmmm-Teddy... That's my spot." She moan'd as Teddy continued to stretch her insides to fit his width and length. Teddy wasn't the biggest she'd had but he was definitely stretch'n her shit out. IN-OUT, IN-OUT, SLOW GRIND'N, LONG DICK'N..." Oh my GOD! TEDDY! TAKE IT- OUT SOME." He disregard'd her request as if she had given him an order to give her his all. Even though she was on top, Teddy was in full control. "Ssss...Mmm...uh-ahh, you all up in it. Oh shit Teddy! I'm cumm'n!"

Ms. Rita said as she let loose and began to ride Teddy like he was a wild bull with his nuts tied. She sat straight up on his dick and froze with both of her hands holding her up on his chest, nothing movin but her waist, gyrate'n in a circular motion, contract'n her muscles while her body released its love juices. "Oh my GOD!" She released as she collapsed onto Teddy's chest. Her soak'n wet pussy was hot and pulsating on Teddy's dick while he held her close with her face cuff'd in his neck. Teddy traced his finger tips down the crease of her back, chas'n sweat.

"You alright?" Teddy ask'd.

"Mmm Hmm." She mumbled.

Teddy laid there still, allow'n her a few minutes to gather herself while they exchanged throbb'n sensations.

"My turn." Teddy said, notice'n how strong the throbb'n sensation in her pussy had gott'n.

"Got-chu Baby, I can go all day. I told you I'm back'd up." Ms. Rita said as Teddy flipp'd her on her back. Slidin between her legs, she look'd at him and said "Handle Yo Bisni-ohh!" Before she could finish her approval, Teddy enter'd her wet pleasure island, goin deep. "Teddy! I'm gone git-chu" She pant'd, I'm so wet. You feel so good in me."

They began to talk dirty to each other.

"Tell me to fuck dis pussy."

"Ohhh! Fuck-dis-pussy!" She demand'd, as Teddy pick'd up the pace from slow dick'n her to a steady but not fast pound. "YESSSS! Dig in this pussy!"

"That's what I'm talk'n bout, take this dick."

"Fuck me Teddy! I'm gone nut-on this fat dick." The dirtier the talk got, the more intense the sex became.

"Ms. Rita!"

"Yes Teddy!"

"I'm bout to cum in dis pussy!"

"You wanna cum in this pussy sweetie?"

"Oh shit!"

"Put that nut where it belongs!" She said as Teddy was try'n to dig thru her womb.

"Here it cum! Dis good ass pussy!"

"I'm cumm'n too! Fuck ME TEDDY! IT'S – OH my god! It's yours! I feel it in my –oh shit TEDDY!

You feel dat nut baby?"

"OH SHIT RITA!"

Teddy yell'd as he began to release his built up love pressured juices.

"Teddy!          It's so hot!          DAMN!

This dick is good!      Fuck this pussy!"

She said while tear'n the flesh in his back as she dug her nails deep into his skin obtain'n multiple orgasms.

Once they both had completely empty'd their pleasure chambers, Teddy roll'd over on his side while Ms. Rita ly in his arms. Look'n into his eyes she said in a whisper rubb'n his curly fro." That was incredible. You made it worth the wait... And you didn't even taste this pussy." They shared a laugh as they got their breath back.

For the rest of the afternoon, they laid around feeding on each other sipp'n champagne, eat'n fruit and test'n each others stamina. In the end, Teddy's youth over road that horny, freaky shit she was talk'n. He put her in a submission position that put her down for the rest of the night til he return'd from the club at 4 am the next morn'n.

She told Teddy she want'd him doggy style. Teddy wasted no time and show'd her no pity. He had Ms. Rita grabb'n the sheets, runn'n and begg'n for a break until she gave in admitting she couldn't take no more and need'd some rest. She fell asleep instantly. Teddy clean'd her helpless body up and tuck'd her in the bed and that's where she stay'd sleep'n without any solid food until Teddy return'd.

After that night, they were both unsure of what was next to come of what they had created but only time would bring a manifestation of their lust fill'd, sinful day together.

## Chapter 15: Aggie Fest

After a lust fulfill'n Saturday & Sunday between Teddy and Ms. Rita, they put some time between the two of them because Ms. Rita didn't know how to deal with her emotions and feeln's for Teddy. For the follow'n two weeks, they only spoke at work and they spoke on the phone maybe 3 times.

It was Friday April 25th, Ms. Rita invited Teddy to lunch to try to explain the distance. Instead, she inform'd him that she was leavin going to Greensboro after work to spend the weekend with Iyana's aunt, her dad's sister. It was AGGIE FEST WEEKEND at NC A&T. Teddy really didn't care, he figured he'd hang out with his other chics, until he got to the club that night.

For once in a long time since Teddy had been work'n at Party Zone, he was on time, able to make the weekly meet'n Charlie has at 9:30, thirty minutes before the club open'd. Charlie and others jokingly congratulated him for his presence. Normally, by 9:30, cars would be settl'n in the park'n lot prepare'n to attack the line by 9:45. For some odd reason, the park'n lot look'd like a ghost town with the exception of the cars from the club employees and the few cars that pass'd thru here and there.

Once the meet'n was over at 10 and the club open'd, it was a mystery as to why there was nobody in line to party until Juan, Teddy's brother alert'd every one of the festivities in Greensboro at NC A&T. Immediately, Teddy thought back to his lunch with Ms. Rita.

"T-Rock, C'mere." His brother call'd him to the bar.

"Yeah?" Teddy answer'd as he approach'd him.

"If Charlie let us off early, we goin to Aggie Fest."

"Shiiit- les go, I'm ready."

"You got money?"

"What kinda fuck'n question is that?"

"Ah-ight, stick around cause I'm about to go let Charlie know that this shit is senseless to stay open waste'n electricity."

Soon as Juan left out of Charlie's officer, Charlie came out and paid everybody one night's pay for coming in, Juan had told Donnie his plan to hit Greensboro and Donnie was with it but he had some business to handle with Big Pin. They agreed to meet at Donnie's house in an hour. Everybody went their separate ways.

Juan ran the whole plan down to Teddy, "It's 10:30 now, we gone meet Donnie at 11:30, hit the road and git there by 12:45. We'll party tonight with Tim," Tim was Juan and Teddy's distant cousin that went to A&T. Then we'll go to the show tomorrow afternoon and leave afterwards to make it back here to work tomorrow night."

"That's cool. I'm wit it, follow me to the crib to drop off my car and pick up a few things." Pick'n up a few things consist'd of more money, 2 oz's of herbals and his best friend, Ms. BABY 380° ( a small hand held gun that fits in the palm of his hand), who he took to all major events.

As plann'd, Juan and Teddy made moves. They got to Donnie's house and wait'd over an hour past 11:30. Now they were an hour behind schedule and Donnie was still no where to be found. Frustration sat in as a new plan had come into play. They left going to Juan's palce which was suppose to be the last stop before hit'n the highway. Try'n to be loyal friends, they end'd up wait'n at Juan's till 3:30 for Donnie to call, no Donnie. Both had fall'n asleep wait'n, now it's fuck it.

"Donnie some bullshit. Les go!" Juan said as they gather'd their things and head'd for the car.

Teddy was simply ready to meet their new destination. He had been to Greensboro before, hang'n out with Tim but not no all out party shit.

Plus, he was in search of Ms. Rita to see what she really had goin on.

Finally, they hit the highway about 4:15, arrive'n in Greensboro exactly an hour later. Greensboro is approximately an hour and fifteen to twenty minutes away, give or take. Well in Juan's case, take the whole fifteen. He's drive'n his 89' Mustang 5.0 and he never does the speed limit, he tries to capture every bit of what's on the speedometer when he's on the highway and Teddy drove no differently.

As they approach'd the campus of A&T, you could literally smell the party in the atmosphere as leftover parties still linger'n around, as the town attempt'd to rest before the next day's festivities. Adrenaline begin to pump thru Teddy's body as they got closer to the campus, add'n to the leftover traffic. He had never seen anything like it. Trash was everywhere, Police were directing traffic and cars were park'd everywhere on the side of the roads and in people's lawns. By the time they reach'd the campus and found a park'n space near Scott Hall, the dorm Tim stay'd in, daylight was on its' way.

As they walk'd to the dorm, Teddy was in awe of how the campus look'd. Beer bottles, cans, paper and all types of debris was scatter'd everywhere. Entering the dorm, they clould hear music coming from multiple rooms. The hallway look'd like the yard. When they came to Tim's room, the door was crack'd. Juan enter'd first with

Teddy on his heels. It was dark and music from the radio station was play'n at a low volume. The little 12x13ft box space was fill'd pass capacity. There were two heads in one twin bed, one up top and one at the bottom fully dress'd.

Tim was in his bed alone and there was literally no walk'n space as Teddy and Juan step'd over bodies try'n to reach Tim's bed space. Once they got thru, Juan sat near Tim's chest and Teddy sat near his feat simultaneously. Tim jump'd up from his drunk'n slumber to notice his cousins. "Ahh-man, "Tim said as he focus'd in on Juan, "Boy, you miss'd it. You jus git'n here?" He ask'd in a groggy tone.

"Yeah, me & Ted." Juan respond'd.

Tim look'd down toward the bottom of the bed at Teddy look'n at him from under a blue Polo ball cap with the red man in the middle. "Whussup hot ass?" Tim ask'd his lil cousin.

"Man, ain't shit, ready to party." Teddy respond'd.

"Well, we gone do plenty of dat. You bring something for me?" Tim ask'd speak'n of the herbals Teddy was known for distributing. That's why Tim calls him "hot ass."

"Boy, you know I don't leave home without it." Teddy said.

"Well put Big Cuz on, Burn one!"

"It's in the car, we gotta step over all these niggas." Tim jump'd up, "Well les step ova these niggas den."

They all proceeded to step over the bodies lay'n from wall to wall as they head'd to the car. Tim gave them the rundown of the day's activities, Tell'n them about the actual Aggie Fest Concert behind the stadium that consist'd of performances by Allison Williams, Big Daddy Kane, N-Tice, and Barbara Whithers. Teddy add'd that he need'd to purchase an outfit for the concert. Being that Tim had to find them some tickets to the show, he decided to take them to Four Season's Mall and Teddy could shop then.

When they return'd to the room, Teddy grabb'd a cup and fill'd it with beer from the keg Tim had in the corner of the room. After he spark'd the joint and the aroma began to fill the room, the bodies that ly still in the middle of the floor began to resurrect one by one like the movie NIGHT OF THE LIVIN DEAD. Moments later, everybody was meet'n everybody, slapp'n five, blow'n guns from about four more joints that had been add'd and prepare'n to party this beautiful Saturday away.

It was 9:30 AM and they had several stops to make so they left the dorm in route to get everything take'n care of. Coming out of the park'n lot, next to the book store LUFORD, Juan took a left going toward Lindsay St. right after they pass'd

Cooper Hall, a blue 1990 Sundance convertible with 'Pump It HOTTIE' on the front bumper pass'd them blow'n the horn relentlessly.

At first, they didn't know who it was but the car stopp'd in the middle of the street. As Juan slow'd down, he noticed the two chics in the car motioning for him to meet in the park'n lot. Juan, whipp'd the 5.0 into the park'n lot and sped toward the Sundance. "Oh shit!" Juan said, Dat's Mocha and Porchia.

Donnie gone be mad at me cause I'm gone fuck Porchia tonight."

Juan and Mocha pull'd up to each others driver's windows. They park'd so close that neither of them could git out.

Both roll'd their windows down. "Hey Juan" Mocha said in her little flirtatious voice, "Lil SEXY Cuz!" Mocha yell'd out.

"Hey Lil Sexy Cuz!" Ms.Porchia greet'd, look'n pass Juan and Mocha.

Teddy didn't bother to speak, he jump'd out of the car and pimp'd over to Ms. Porchia's window. She greet'd him with a big smile, "What cha'll doin up here?"

"We just got here a few hours age to hang out with our cousin Tim.

Whussup wit-chall?" Teddy ask'd

"My sister go to school up here so we came up to be with her yesterday."

Teddy reach'd between Ms. Porchia's legs and grabb'd a bag.

"You been shopp'n?" He ask'd

"I just bought a BLACK BART T-shirt."

"Let me git dis."

"What do I get?" Ms. Porchia ask'd, being very flirtatious.

"Whut-chu want?" Teddy ask'd.

Ms. Porchia held her head out the window, look'n Teddy up and down and answer'd, "What do you think?"

Teddy laugh'd.

"Whats going on tonight Mr. Teddy?" She ask'd.

"All I know is we're going to some concert."

"That's this afternonn. What about tonight?" She inquired.

"Nothin that I know of." Teddy answer'd.

"Why, whussup?"

Ms. Porchia grabb'd a pen and a piece of paper, "Where you stay'n?"

"Wit Tim in Scott Hall, 3014 B."

"Here's my sister's #, call me and when we hook up tonight, You can get this t-shirt."

"Dat's a bet.  Mocha, y'all be careful."

"We gone try Lil Sexy Cuz."

"See ya later. "Ms, Porchia emphasized,

"TONIGHT."

"Ah-ight. Peace." Teddy said as he jogg'd back to the car.

They took off to handle their business, Juan look'd at the # in Teddy's hand and said, Donnie gone kill you."

Tim popp'd Teddy in the back of the head and said "Ya lil young hot ass still fuck'n nigga'z girls."

"Hell no!  She just wanna hangout. She gone git me a BLACK BART T-shirt and I'm gone give them some weed." Teddy lied.

They went on about their business, shopp'n for clothes, food and liquor. Teddy went to Dillards and purchased a short sleeve orange and white Polo shirt with some Polo jean shorts. He stopp'd thru Foot Locker's for a pair of all white Tretorn's with the gold stitch and Lim's for a pair of gold Versace shades and a bottle of Versace Blue Jean cologne.

Making it back to the dorm in time enough to shower and change, when they got to the stadium, N-Tice was perform'n. There was close to 20,000 people in attendance. As they moved toward the back of the crowd to set up their grill, Teddy look'd around in amazement at all the people. After they settled in, Teddy grabb'd two Guiness and left Tim, Juan and their friends as he took off in search of Ms. Rita.

"Keep yo hat ass outta trouble." Tim said.

Teddy waved as he took off into the crowd. There were chics everywhere as he manuever'd thru, exchange'n smiles and greetings with many. People were everywhere, sitt'n on quilts, blankets and lawn chairs. A lot of folks had tents. It was like being on a campground.

Everybody was enjoy'n the festivities.

Kwame' was next to perform. Teddy moved thru the crowd to the front of the stage where he stood throughout Kwame's performance. He began to make his way back to where Juan and Tim was cook'n at, to chill while Allison Williams peform'd. It was extremely crowded to be try'n to walk around, let alone look for someone but out of the blue, Teddy hears his name being call'd. He look'd around not know'n where the voice was comin from but the more he moved in the direction he was movin in, the voice got clear'r, "Teddy! Ova here."

They voice direct'd 20ft to the right, there she sat on a quilt with four other classy chics in their designer shades, Ms. Rita. "Come here Sweetie." She waved.

Teddy made his way over to their quilt, "Whus happen'n?" He ask'd stand'n over the five model look'n chics.

"What are you doin here?" Ms. Rita ask'd in amazement.

"Not expect'n ta run into you that's for sho." He said, as they all laugh'd.

"Well, here I am, sit down for a minute."

As Teddy sat on the quilt next to Ms. Rita, one of the chics ask'd, "Is this the cutey you left my brother for."

"Tish, Reka, Nik, Step, this is Teddy."

"Hi y'all doin?" Teddy ask'd.

Everybody exchange pleasantries.

"You drove up?" Ms. Rita ask'd.

"Nah, I rode with my brotha my cousin Tim go to school here."

"You talk'n about KAPPA Tim from Charlotte?" Step ask'd

"Yeeaaa." Teddy answer'd.

"Tell him, he could call somebody." Step said.

Step was extremely sexy. Tall, mixed look'n chic with long brown hair with gold streaks.

"I ain't never been to nothing like this before. "Teddy said.

"Are you enjoy'n yourself?" Ms.Rita ask'd.

"So far so good." Teddy said as he reach'd to pull the Guiness out of his pocket. He was hit from the side with a cloud of smoke. "I can smoke?" He ask'd.

"Only if you sharing." Nik retort'd.

Teddy pull'd out a Swisher Sweet cigar pack'd with weed and lit it.

"What is that?" Step ask'd

"Sssp… hold'n the smoke in," I roll mine in cigars. "Wheeeew."

Teddy said exhale'n the smoke from his lungs. He motion'd to pass the cigar to Step on the other side of Ms. Rita.

"Oh Rita, I know you ain't try'n to be prissy in front of your little cutey."

"Girl, you know they give us random drug test."

"One little pull ain't going to hurt shit." Step urged.

Ms. Rita took the cigar and took a few pulls and pass'd it.

Ms. Rita caught a quick buzz and began to whisper sexy obscenities in Teddy's ear while he laid back between her legs listen'n to Allison Williams. He burn'd one more with the chics and then told Ms. Rita he was going to catch up with Big Daddy Kane and Mr. C his DJ (Teddy had met them back in 89' at Weekends).  He made his way to the side where the artist were comin from. Kane made his way to the stage, he partied.

During his show, Teddy stood on the side kick'n it with N-Tice. N-Tice was a female MC from Greensboro. Halfway thru Kane's show, Teddy told N-Tice he look'd forward to see'n her later. She walk'd away as soon as Teddy turn'd to walk away, 'Ms. Baby 380' dropp'd down his leg from his waist. He tried not to look obvious but when he bent down to get her, somebody yell'd,

"He's got a gun!"

The whole crowd shift'd from one side to the other like a wave. Everybody began to run, trampling people sitt'n on the grass, and knock'n over grills burn'n people. It was tragic. Teddy blend'd in the crowd until he made his way back to Juan and Tim. The show end'd and they wait'd til the crowd calm'd and the ambulances had clear'd the way. They pack'd up and walk'd toward the dorm. All the way over there, a few people look'd at Teddy and whisper'd back and forth. When they reach'd the back park'n lot of Scott Hall, some dude call'd Tim to the side. Tim return'd cuss'n Teddy out.

"Yo hot ass always fuck'n something up!" Tim yell'd in Teddy's face.

"Whut da fuck you talk'n bout?" Teddy bark'd back.

"You know what the fuck I'm talk'n bout. Where's yo gun at?" Tim ask'd, mad as hell.

"Why?"

"All that shit out there was caused by You! Everybody was have'n fun! Why did you pull it out?"

"Nigga, I didn't! It slipp'd from my waist!"

"Why did you take it in the first place?"

"I take my shit every where I go!"

Tim walk'd away shakin his head in disgust. When they got back to Tim's dorm room, his neighbors left a message that his girlfriend Crystal got trampled and was at Wesley Long Hospital.

Tim want'd to fight Teddy but cousin or no cousin, Teddy would have pistol whipp'd Tim. So instead of arguing with him, Tim got Juan to take him to the hospital, leaving Teddy with his roommate Derrick and his homeboys from Richmond, VA. Teddy got so drunk that he pass'd out. When he woke up, it was 4:30AM. He forgot all about Ms. Rita until Derrick's homeboy told him a chic came by for him twice and when Juan came up from the strip he told Teddy that Ms. Porchia left a message that she would see him back in Charlotte.

Teddy was hung over and they were about to leave. Tim and Juan smoked a joint before they left.

"Tim, my fault cuz. Is Crystal alright?" Teddy ask'd.

"She's alright cuz. My fault for trip'n on you earlier. You have a goodtime?" Tim ask'd as he put his arm around Teddy's neck, "You welcome up here anytime."

"This shit was straight but I got too drunk drank'n them 40's of Old Gold." Teddy said.

They all said their good byes and Juan and Teddy hit the highway completing their 24 hour adventure.

## Chapter 16: The Hookup

A week went pass and Teddy hadn't heard from Ms. Rita. They saw each other in pass'n at work but no communication after that. Strangely, that didn't bother him, but what did, was that he miss'd Ms. Porchia in Greensboro.

The Sunday after Teddy and Juan got back from Greensboro, jealousy was in the air. Donnie told Juan that Charlie fired him and Teddy for not show'n up to work Saturday night. Neither of them cared but it was hard to believe since he end'd up close'n early just as they did the night before. Juan and Teddy knew Donnie would be upset but it wasn't their fault. After all, Donnie was the reason they didn't get there Friday night.

When Teddy got off from work Friday afternoon, he went to pick Mia up and went to his Mom's place in Earle Village. It had been a few weeks since his mom and Shan had seen Mia or Teddy and Teddy hadn't seen his niece Lekrell in a few weeks so it was definitely immediate family time.

This was Queen's weekend off and being that she rarely had time to spend with her children and grandchildren, she was beside herself. Queen cook'd Teddy and Shan's favorite Friday meal, fried flounder, slaw, pinto beans and fried cornbread. Teddy rent'd movies and sat back while Shan play'd with Lekrell and Mia til they were dead tired. Queen and Shan gave the babies their baths and put them to bed while Teddy fell asleep on the couch watch'n "Walk'n Tall."

Saturday afternoon after Queen had finish cook'n grits, eggs, leftover fish and biscuits, Teddy was laid back watch'n Eddie Murphy "Delirious" when his pager went off. It was Tiger wonder'n why he didn't show up at the club last night.

"Man, Donnie said Charlie fired us last week."

"Dat nigga just mad because Y'all left his big ass. Be yo ass at work tonight!" Tiger demand'd."

"And have my medication."

"Man I got Mia wit me for the weekend but I'll try my best."

"You do dat!" Tiger demanded.

"Ah-ight den. ONE!"

Teddy was glad he still had his job, he loved free money and work'n at the club for Charlie was free money.

For the rest of the day, he laid around rest'n and play'n with Mia and Lekrell. It was 9:30 and Queen had been call'd in to work also. Teddy ask'd Shan to watch Mia while he went to work and Shan agreed, as long as he put her to sleep before he left.

That threw Teddy off another hour.

Arriving at the club about 10:45, the club was super pack'd. When Teddy enter'd the club, Nina greet'd him with a huge smile, "Heey Neenah." Teddy spoke.

"Hey Boy! You betta not quit!" She demand'd.

"Nina, I never said I was quit'n. I heard I was fired."

"Ain't nobody fired You." She inform'd him as her whole expression change'd, "But you might be fired after tonight. I know I saw at least 5 of your girls come thru here, so be careful. Charlie said to tell you to hurry to your station when you got here."

"Thanks Nina." Teddy said with a wink and a smile before walk'n off.

Teddy knew that Nina's warn'n was real so he was try'n to hurry to the DJ booth before being spott'd, but he had to run to the bathroom first. As he came out of the bathroom, he turn'd the corner and ran dead into Ms. Porchia. "Oh Shit! Scuse me."

"Teddy!" Ms. Porchia said in surprise. "What happen'd to you last week?"

Teddy smiled and said," My fault. I got so drunk I pass'd out. Damn! You look good as fuck!" He compliment'd her on the red haulter top and tight blue jean skirt she had on.

'I'm glad you like it, I thought you would. "She said as she gave him that seductive look that says,

'I WANT YOU AND I KNOW YOU WANT ME TOO.'

"Yo, do me a favor?" Teddy ask'd as he held her hand try'n to get away. "Come to the DJ booth
at 11:30. I gotta go cause I'm late."

"Alright." She said as Teddy shot her wink and a smile. He rush'd off to the DJ booth, arriving there without run'n into any of his chics. Tiger had jokes, "So you finally decide to make it. Every chic you done smash'd in life is here tonight, include'n Shanta!" Tiger express'd with emphasis.

"Git the fuck outta here! Word?"

"Word! You'll see, they all done been by here. That's why Big Pin is guard'n the door."

Teddy look'd out to the dance floor and saw Shanta and her fass ass crew freak'n dudes on the sideline.

"Tiger, I'll be back!" Teddy said as he rush'd out the booth toward the other side of the dance floor. Makin it thru the heavy crowd, Teddy ran up on Shanta and watch'd as she went to bend over in front of the dude she was freak'n and came back up. Shanta noticed Teddy and froze. He montion'd for her as a child bein told what to do by her father, she immediately follow'd Teddy's lead. The guy she was freak'n was piss'd but it was a good thing he decide'd to keep his mouth shut because not only would Teddy have beat his ass, Tiger had sent Big Pin to follow Teddy in case anything popp'd off.

Taking Shanta into the back office, he blast'd her, "Bitch don't come to my job play'n games!

"Ain't nobody play'n! This is the first conversation we've had in months."

"And the last! Go home!"

"I ain't got no ride. I came here with China 'nem."

"C'mon, it's a cab outside. Here's $30.00."

## Chapter 17: First Date

Teddy hadn't been a Church goer since his youth but his mom made him promise to take Mia. She was the proud grandma and want'd to show her other grandchild off. So like promised, Tim, Mia, Shan, and Lekrell went to Church with Queen.

While they were there, Teddy's pager start'd vibrate'n. He thought it was Ms. Porchia but it was Shanta, so he stepp'd out to call her and before he could return her call, the pager went off again, this time it was Steve. Shanta was call'n to let Teddy know that she was wait'n on him to drop Mia off and Steve want'd him to come thru after Church.

Soon as Church was over, Teddy kiss'd Queen, Shan and Lekrell and they went their separate ways. He took Mia home and argued with Shanta about the previous night at the club. Then she attempt'd to throw herself at him ask'n him to let her suck his dick. All Teddy could do was laugh.

He kiss'd Mia and left.

Before he could make it to his grandparents' home, Ms. Porchia was page'n him. He arrived ten minutes later. Not want'n to seem as anxious as he was, he listen'd to what Steve want'd.

He want'd Teddy to hang out with him, Toya and Cherese. Teddy was hang'n out with Cherese on the strength of Steve. Cherese and Toya were roommates at Barber Scotia. They were cool but at the moment, Ms. Porchia had Teddy's attention.

"Man, I'm goin out with Ms. Porchia. That's her page'n me now."

Teddy grabb'd the phone and call'd her. She answer'd on the first ring. "Hello?"

"Yes, may I speak to Ms. Porchia?"

"This is she. Is this Lil Sexy Cuz?" She ask'd jokingly.

"Hi You?"

"I'm fine, how was Church?"

"It was Church. My thoughts was with You."

"I know. I've been want'n to call you all morn'n."

"Why didn't You?"

"I didn't want to seem like I didn't comprehend what time you told me to call."

"Well, here I am. Hi You want to do this?"

"Mocha is here, she wants to go."

"Who's drivin?"

"We can drive."

"Ah-ight, hold on." Teddy said as he click'd over to call Donnie on the three way. Before he click'd back over he ask'd Donnie to hang out with him, Ms. Porchia and Mocha. Donnie told him he didn't care. Teddy click'd Donnie on.

"Porchia!"

"I'm here."

"Can Y'all meet me at Donnie's? He's going with us."

"Yeah, what time?"

"Give me 30 minutes."

"Alright Baby. See You then."

"Ah-ight. Peace."

Teddy change'd his clothes and Steve dropp'd him off at Donnie's. When they got there, Mocha and Ms. Porchia were already there. Ms. Porchia had on some khaki shorts and the BLACK BART t-shirt she had purchased the week prior. Look'n good as fuck as usual. Teddy stay'd true to form, he wore Polo Sweat pants, a Polo t-shirt with a Polo headband and some brand new all white Air Force One's.

Ms. Porchia ran into his arms. They kiss'd. "Y'all ready?" Teddy ask'd.

"Where we goin?" Mocha ask'd.

"Les go to the Carnival at Freedom Mall." Teddy replied.

"That's cool." Mocha said.

"I'm wit it." Donnie agreed.

"Long as I'm with You." Ms. Porchia chimed in.

They all agreed and left. Teddy and Ms. Porchia sat in the back seat while Donnie rode shotgun. As they rode, Ms. Porchia filled Teddy in on her life and vice versa.

Her name is Porchia Janae Grier. She's a 18 year old senior in High School at Olympic. She was accept'd to attend college at NC A&T, NC Central and Norfolk State. She hadn't decided which school would accommodate her in the fall. Her father owns Grier's Dry Cleaners on Beatties Ford Rd.

She was raised in Hampshire Hills, one of the prominent middle/upper class black neighborhoods in Charlotte. Her financial background was secure. She was spoiled and use to getting her way. It was evident in her pursuit to obtain Teddy's heart. She had an illuminating smile and the sexiest alluring eyes that had Teddy caught up in her spell.

When they weren't talk'n, they were engaged in the most seductive form of intimacy outside of the actual sex…. itself. Kiss'n and mumbling between their lips.

They start'd out at Freedom Park. It was the usual Sunday afternoon ride thru crowd. Then they head'd to the Carnival. Once they had rode all the rides and play'd the games, they were walk'n to the car when Shanta and her cousins' pull'd into the park'n space beside Mocha's car. Before they could get in the car, Shanta, China, Mesha, and Nicole were getting out. Teddy and Ms. Porchia stood hand in hand nothing to hide. China's loud ass was the first one out of the car.

"Hey Teddy."

"Whut up?"

She in turn went on to speak to Donnie. China and Donnie are Timia's God parents.

The girls in Shanta's crew were moving out of the isle as Teddy, Donnie and Ms. Porchia was attempt'n to get into the passenger side of Mocha's car.

"Teddy," Shanta call'd out.

"What Shanta?" Teddy replied in a irritated tone, know'n what she want'd was of unimportance.

"Mia needs some sandals when you get a chance." She stated, to show Ms. Porchia and her cousins her power over him.

"Why You didn't tell me when I dropp'd her off?" He ask'd.

"I forgot."

"Shanta don't fuck wit me." Teddy said as he walk'd toward her diggin in his pocket and pull'n out a healthy wad of money. He damn near thru five $20.00 bills at her. "Don't spend her money out here!" He demand'd as he turn'd and walk'd back to the car know'n he had given her more than enough money for Mia's sandals and Shanta's outing with her crew.

During the whole exchange, Ms. Porchia stood by the car door watch'n as her soon to be man handle'd his business with authority. She then hopp'd into the back seat as Teddy follow'd and they left. They rode around the rest of the afternoon enjoy'n each others company being chauffuer'd by Mocha. The date end'd after they had dinner at Pizza Hut. On their way to Donnie's house, "Hold On" by EnVogue came on.

That was Ms. Porchia's song, she dedicated it to Teddy. When they arrived at

Donnie's, Donnie and Mocha got out of the car to excuse themselves from their obscene mushiness. Their behavior immediately went into overdrive. Teddy kiss'd her while caress'n her tender breast and manuever'n his heads down between her legs. "Mmmm." She moan'd at the touch of his fingers fiddling thru her shorts. Teddy could feel the heat coming from her pleasure grounds. Ms. Porchia reclined back and open'd her legs further to experience Teddy's more intimate affection. He unzipp'd her shorts and slid his hands into her panties to enable him to slip his finger into her extremely wet and slippery love canal. The heat became so intense that they were breath'n hard, pant'n, bite'n and suck'n each others lips until she came on his finger, leave'n his finger drinch'd in her love juices. "I want You in me now." She demand'd as Teddy was suck'n her bottom lip.

"Uuh-ahh." He said, "our first time won't be in no car."

"You got me so horny." She moan'd.

So he just stopp'd everything instantly. His hands came out of her panties, he back'd away from kiss'n her and push'd the seat up in front of him and open'd the door to get out. Ms. Porchia chased him as he got out fix'n her clothes. Teddy began to laugh. "Why You do that?" She ask'd as she trapp'd him against the car noticing his erection thru his sweat pants. She grabb'd a handful of his manhood sideways and demand'd,

"Let me have some!" She stated up in his face with her hand grasp'n him as if she was a threat.

Teddy look'd her in the eyes still laugh'n and said, "No, not tonight. I don't sleep with other dude's chics."

"Where did that come from?" She ask'd, while still hold'n his throbb'n manhood captive. "I know you want it." Ms. Porchia said shake'n his stiffness as evidence.

"I might do but I want it all to myself."

"You got me all to yourself."

"Porchia, you said you haven't seen dude since that night at the club. You never said Y'all broke up."

"How can I prove it?"

"That's up to you, I don't know. But when we take it there —"He grabb'd her crotch. "You will be mine." Teddy said.

He could tell she wasn't use to being denied but Teddy had to bring her into his world instead of enter'n hers.

"I'll write him tonight and express mail it tomorrow."

"Whatever." Teddy said as he held her close, "Whus da rush?"

"Ain't no rush, but you betta get rid of Ms. Rita and the rest of your flock too."

Teddy laugh'd and said, "You betta be worth it."
Mocha walk'd up, "P, You ready?" We got school in the morn'n, we gotta go."

"I guess so." She pout'd, "I don't want to leave my Baby."

"Lil Sexy, you need a ride?" Mocha ask'd.

"If that's not too much to ask. I'll give you some gas money."

"C'mon boy." Mocha respond'd. Teddy and Ms. Porchia rode in the back seat cuddlin while enjoy'n their new found romance.

Once they reach'd Teddy's aunt's place in Dalton Village, they stood outside the car as they discuss'd each other's schedule and the next time they'd see each other.

"I get out of school at 11." Ms. Porchia stated.

"I'll be here. I gotta go to school to get my school bus at 12:45."

"So I'll be here by 11:30."

"See ya tomarra." Teddy said as he kiss'd her and went into the apartment.

For the next few days, like clockwork, Ms. Porchia made her way to Teddy's arms by 11:30am and hung out with him for an hour before he had to return to work. She would return every evening after she got off from her part time job at Allstate and stay until 10 or 11.

Daily, she tried to break Teddy down and it was evident that he was getting weak. Every night, once she was gone, he experience what men call, "blue balls." That comes from holding an erection for a longtime and not being able to release. It causes tremendous pain in the testicles (the balls).

Thursday, May 8th, when Teddy pull'd his school bus in the circle and park'd, he noticed Ms. Porchia's Camry in front of his aunt's apartment. Something had to be wrong. She was never at his place that early.

As he approach'd the front door, he noticed Ms. Porchia sitt'n in the driver's seat with her head down. He immediately walk'd to her car door and tapp'd the window. She look'd up at him startled with tears in her eyes.

Teddy grabb'd the handle of the door as she unlock'd it and pull'd the door open. "Whus wrong?" He ask'd with sincere concern.

She pass'd him a letter that she had in her lap. It read:

*Porchia,*

*You is a bitch. You aint shit I been cheet you I fill sary fur you I wit lot a gurl. I gon fuk you up win I see you agin. You boyfried bet watch him bak. You hire.*

Teddy bust out laugh'n. "Whus dis baby?" He ask'd, as he pass'd her the letter, "I know that ain't what I think it is."

"It's the letter from Lamont."

"So why are You cry'n? I couldn't even read that shit. What is he doin in college? He's fuck'n illiterate!"
"You just don't understand."

"Well, C'mon Baby, les go in the house and You make me understand." Teddy said as he grabb'd her hand and assist'd her in getting out of the vehicle. "And why are You not at work?" He ask'd.

"I was too upset and I need'd my man." She said, let'n Teddy know that she had done her duty in make'n sure she was all his.

When they enter'd the apartment, Porchia sat on the love seat part of the sectional. "You want something ta drink?" Teddy ask'd walk'n into the kitchen connect'd to the livin room.

"I'm fine, I just want to lay in your arms."

Teddy grabb'd a Tropicana pink grapefruit juice when his little cousin RayShawn came runn'n into the house.

"Hey Porchia."

"Hey Shawn. Where you been?" Porchia ask'd.

"Down by my girlfriend's house."

RayShawn was 13. He stays home by himself til Teddy comes home every day at 4:30 or his mom comes home at 9:30 PM from drivin the city bus. He was order'd to stay in the house until an adult gets in but, RayShawn was hard head'd.

"If Jean knew yo ass was outside that'll be yo ass." Teddy said.

"C'mon Baby, les go upstairs."

Ms. Porchia hopp'd up and follow'd Teddy to his room. He closed the door behind them. She sat on the edge of the bed exposin her pink panties under her khaki skirt while Teddy sipp'd on his juice.

"So dude supposed to be mad?"

"I don't want to talk about him. I'm all Yours'." She said pull'n Teddy towards her by his waist.

"Why were you so upset?"

"He said some hurtful things and all I tried to do was be good to him."

"First of all, how did you even understand what da fuck he was say'n? That shit don't make no sense." Teddy said as Ms. Porchia just sat there listen'n "and two, how do you think he felt see'n you freak'n on the dance floor that night?"

She look up at him and said. "Teddy, I was just dance'n."

"Yeuh, but is that what I have to look forward to?  Look how bad they beat his ass. All over you. That was fuck'd up."

"So you tell'n me, you don't want me?"

"What if I am? Are you going to run back to this nigga that beat-cho ass?" Teddy inquired, test'n her sincerity.

"No, that's over.  Teddy, I'm in love with you and I've never ever had you inside of me." Ms. Porchia said with tears in her eyes. "You are all I think about. When I'm not here with You, I want to hear your voice.  All I want is You."

Ms. Porchia's statements hypnotized Teddy. He bent down towards her and they began to kiss as Ms. Porchia lean'd back on the bed with Teddy in between her legs while her skirt rose up to her waist. "Can I have what belongs to me?" Ms. Porchia ask'd as Teddy lift'd up and laid next to her. Caress'n her thighs, he rubb'd up to her pleasure spot, slid'n her panites to the side.

Before, she had the thin soft hairs lead'n to her paradise playground but this time, it was freshly shaved and smooth as a baby's ass. That turn'd Teddy on when he spread'd her inner lips and the moisture from her hot pussy soak'd his fingers. As he play'd inside of her pleasure pot with his fingers, he look'd at her in amazement of how wet she was.

"It's Your fault. Ssss. It feels good too. Mmmm. Come here." She said as she pull'd his fingers out of her and start'd reach'n for his button on his shorts.

Teddy stood up and dropp'd his shorts along with his boxer exposing all of his glory. Ms. Porchia's eyes widen'd as if to ask herself, WHAT HAVE I GOTTEN MYSELF INTO. Teddy crawl'd between her legs on his knees, he pull'd her wet pink panties off, and replace them with him. He held his shaft, teasing her pussy with the head of his dick using her love juices for lubrication.

"Mmmm, let me feel it." She demand'd.

Teddy intruded himself into Ms. Porchia's love canal only giving her the head. "Oh My God!" She yell'd as he slow dick'd her. "Ssss." She pant'd, "Ted-dy. Gimmie all of you. Umph — but take it slow — it's been a while." Teddy continued to extend himself inside of her as she moan'd, scratch'd and bit him. "This your pussy!" She said as tears stream'd down her face.

"You alright?" Teddy ask'd as he slowly slid in and out of her tight fitting vagina.

"Um hmm. Its' jus been so long."

Teddy extend'd himself as much as she could take and began to grind inside of her as she begg'd him not to stop. He push'd deeper and instantly, her insides exploded all over his thickness. Ms. Porchia grabb'd his back throw'n her legs up to her shoulders, inviting his full length and girth inside of her while she pull'd him to her for a lustful, gut wrench'n kiss. Teddy went from slow grind'n to long, hard steady strokes "Oh shit Teddy." She scream'd as the bed began to beat the wall, "This your pussy! This your pussy! It's Yours. Ittt's Yoours!!!"

"You like this dick?" Teddy ask'd.

"Ye-ye-yes! I love my dick! This my dick Teddy!"

"I like dis tight pussy."

The more Teddy talk'd dirty to her the more she threw it back at him until it was his turn to match one of her multiple orgasms. As he strongly plunged thru her and let off the first burst of fertilize'n punch, the warm fluid sent orgasmic chills thru Ms. Porchia. She join'd him in his orgasm. By the time the finishing deposit had ran thru her, she was cry'n uncontrollably, tell'n him she had never experienced nothing like that.

Teddy just ly inside her throbb'n and sweat'n until she had calm down. "I LOVE YOU TEDDY. Please don't ever leave me."

"I LOVE YOU TOO. I ain't goin nowhere Baby."

From this day forward, Teddy's life would never be the same.

## Chapter 18: Meet Da Parents

The next few weeks were magical between Teddy and Ms. Porchia. For the first time in Teddy's dealings with the opposite sex, he was using the "L" word. Ms. Porchia had Teddy's undivided attention. It wasn't the sex, she was the most inexperienced he'd ever had. She was different from what Teddy was use to and whatever it was, he loved it – he loved her.

Day for day they were together.   Ms. Porchia talk'd about Teddy to everybody who would listen. It was a week before graduation and she want'd her parents to meet the new love of her life. Teddy agree'd to the meet'n but he kept putting it off because he want'd the timing to be right. He really wasn't into meeting parents and outside of Shanta's, he never met his chic's parents.

Two weeks ago, Teddy's Aunt Jean total'd his car leaving him without transportation. He could have easily ran out and purchased another car but he was saving his money preparing for college so he decided to wait until he was about to leave to get another car. Ms. Porchia was currently all the transportation he need'd.

It was Friday, May 30th. As ususal Ms. Porchia met him at his place after work for dinner before he went to the club. After dinner, Ms. Porchia told Teddy she need'd to stop by her house before she dropp'd him off at work. Teddy refused. "I can't go over there like this. Drop me off at Kato's."

"Like what, you look fine." Ms. Porchia said.

Teddy want'd to make a good impression on her folks and he didn't feel that a Nike Flight 23 sweatsuit, Jordan's with a 20 inch herringbone and nugget earrings was a good impression. He had drug dealer written all over him. "Baby, you're fine. Trust me."

"Why can't we just wait?" He ask'd.

"Baby, I just got to let them know that I'll be in a little late. I'll only be a second."

"I'll sit in the car."

"No you won't. Stop being scared, they're going to love you like I do."

"Ah-ight, if you say so." He answer'd with an uneasy feel'n. Teddy hated being outside his comfort zone and Ms. Porchia had him head'd straight to UNCOMFORTABLE BLVD.

Pulling into her parent's driveway, Ms. Porchia could see the look of discontent in Teddy's face. "Cheer up Sweetheart, it's just my parents."

Her statement was so true but it still didn't change his mood, "Porchia, let's just get this over with." Teddy said as they got out of the car.

They enter'd the split level home from the side door, entering the kitchen. Connect'd to the kitchen was the dining area. From the dining area, you could either proceed to go downstairs to the family room and den, or you could go upstairs to the bedrooms. Left of the dining room, straight ahead was the foyer which lead straight to the front door and to the left was their immaculate living room which possess'd all white antique furniture with a pure white GRAND piano.

"Porr – shaaaah," an angelic voice from upstairs call'd out "is that you?"

"Yes Ma. Come here, I want you to meet Teddy." Teddy look'd at her with a firm stare, "You set me up."

Ms. Porchia just smiled, "You're ok." She said as Teddy stood in the dining room by the stairs waiting for the appearance of the lady of the house.

"Ma!"

"Porchia, I'm coming." Her mother stated as she made her way down the stairs.

As she materialized, Teddy noticed her slim frame and medium height. She possess'd a light mocha complexion and eyes like Droopy with bags beneath them like a drunk.  SO THAT'S THE PURPOSE OF THAT FULLY STOCK'D BAR IN THE FAMILY ROOM. Teddy thought to himself.

"Ma, this is Teddy." Ms. Porchia said with a smile introducing her new love interest.

"Hi Teddy, I'm Regina Grier." She said as she extend'd her hand to him, giving him a full once over.

"How are you?" Teddy ask'd in a fully mature voice.

"I'm fine. We've heard so much about you." She said with a smile.

"I hope it was all good things." Teddy said return'n the smile.

"It's all under investigation," Mrs. Grier retort'd with a smirk on her face as Porchia jogg'd upstairs. "So where are you from Teddy?" She ask'd as her whole demeanor changed to, 'WHAT DO YOU WANT WITH MY DAUGHTER?'

"Oh, I'm from Charlotte."

"I figured that, what neighborhood?" She ask'd, fiddle'n in the fridge. HERE WE GO, THE THIRD DEGREE.

Teddy thought to himself.

"I was raised in Earle Village."

"Earle Village!" She said sounding like an echo.

"Yes Ma'am, Earle Village but I'm staying with my aunt in Dalton Village until I leave for school."

"Oh, you're going to college?" She said with surprise in her voice.

"Yes Ma'am, FAMU on a band scholarship."

All of a sudden, a big Samoan wrestler look'n guy waddled down stairs in some terribly worn Fruit of a Loom briefs.

"Hey Teddy." The Samoan wrestling, nasty look'n dude spoke with his gut hang'n over the briefs as if he was overdue and ready to deliver anyday. "I'm Lyndell Grier, Porchia's daddy." Teddy in disbelief, held back his laughter, "Nice to meet you Mr. Grier."

"Did I hear you say you were going to FAMU?" He ask'd commenting on the conversation he came in on.

"Yes sir, I'll be leavin in July going to FAMU on a band scholarship."

Mrs. Grier interjected, "So you two shouldn't be focus'd on no serious relationship no time soon. School should be your priorities right now."

Teddy sensed her disapproval of him, as Ms. Porchia ran down stairs changing the subject.

"Daddy! Put on some clothes.

"She said in embarrassment from the sight of her old man. Ms. Porchia look'd more like her dad than she did her mother and it was obvious they were closer.

"Girl, this is my house." He said in his high pitch'd soprano voice. "If I want to walk around naked, that's my option."

"DA-DDY!"

Ms. Porchia said as she cuddle'd under Teddy's arms. "I'm taking my baby to work, I'll be back later."

What do you mean later Porchia?" Mrs. Grier ask'd.

"Before one, after twelve."

"Where do you work Teddy?" She ask'd.

"At this club call'd PARTY ZONE."

"I don't think we want our daughter hang'n out at such a place. That's where she was when she got jump'd on." Mrs. Grier retort'd.

"Ain't nobody gone put their hands on her but I'd rather her just drop me off." Teddy said in agreement with Mrs. Grier.

"First of all, I'm grown. I'm 18."

"Porchia, 18 isn't grown. Grown don't live at home." Her mom said sarcastically.

"Porchia, go have a good time and be safe. Don't stay out past one. You aren't that grown," her dad said as she kiss'd him right below his short curly fro on the corner of his forehead.

"Bye Daddy."

"Y'all take care Mr. & Mrs. Grier. It was nice meet'n you." Teddy said as he and Ms. Porchia proceed'd toward the door.

"OK Teddy." Mr. Grier respond'd.

"Uh huh." Mrs. Grier mumbled.

Riding down the street, Teddy was quiet and kinda reserved.

"What are you think'n?" Ms. Porchia ask'd as she grabb'd Teddy's hand and began to caress it.

"Nothing." He responded as he laid back listen'n to '911 is a joke' by Flava Flav.

A silence took over the car as Ms. Porchia turn'd the radio off.

"Talk to me." She whined.

"What do you want me to say?" He ask'd in a dry, disgust'd tone.

"Say anything."

Teddy sat silent look'n out the window for about 30 seconds.

"This ain't gone last long." He said.

"What!?! What's not going to last long?"

"Us"

"What do you mean?"

"I could feel the tension. Your mom won't allow us to be happy, You'll see."

"She's not like that."

Ms. Porchia couldn't convince Teddy otherwise. He knew that his heart and new love affair was in jeopardy but for now, his heart wouldn't allow him to turn away.

## Chapter 19: Graduation Night
## (June 6th, 1990)

It was the day of all days. Teddy was a year behind but he was finally about to walk across the stage and receive his diploma. The night before, his cousin Sam that play'd on the football team for Harding had a major graduation party. He attend'd the party with Tip and Donté. Donté was one of their high school friends from Queens, New York.

They all got so drunk and high, they all woke up in Donté's sister's car outside of Teddy's aunt's place at 7:30am. Graduation start'd an hour later.

Teddy was severely hung over. He was due to graduate at 8:30, he had to pick up his check and be at the Coliseum by 1:00 for Ms. Porchia's graduation. With the help of his aunt, he was on time for everything.

Before he made it to the Coliseum for Ms. Porchia's graduation, he stop'd by the Merchandise Mart right next door to pick up her graduation gift. Teddy dealt with a private distributor company called Diamonds In The Rough. The owner was Moroccan. Teddy met him thru Sasha a few years back. Saladeen loved doing business with Teddy because he always gave him ideas. Plus, Teddy purchased all his jewelry there. Saladeen did a class ring for Ms. Porchia that was 14K gold with a 2 carat diamond in the center with "I'll Always

Love You" going around the face with 19 on one side and 90 on the other. On the inside of the band read TEDDY – N – PORCHIA 4 LIFE. In a regular jewelry store, Teddy would have paid $5K or more but Saladeen done it as a gift and a favor for $900.00.

When Ms. Porchia walk'd across that stage, she heard her family cheer'n but her eyes follow'd to the man that loved her as she heard his voice yell'n, "I LOVE YOU PORCHIA."

"I LOVE YOU TOO!" She said as her eyes met his over 100 feet away, both waving and blowing kiss's.

Immediately after the ceremony was over, she hurried straight to Teddy's arms. They embraced each other. "Congratulations." "Congratulations to you." Teddy said.

"I'm sorry I couldn't stay to see you after your graduation." She explain'd.

"That's alright, I saw you act'n crazy with my Mom'nem when they call'd my name."

"You know you show'd out." Porchia said as she hit him in his chest. She was speak'n of the show he put on comin across the stage. Fly and a few other band members that were perform'n with the concert band play'd the intro to Keith Sweat's "How Deep Is Your Love" when Teddy's name was call'd, the crowd went crazy and Teddy walk'd across the stage with one hand up, point'n one finger up to the sky as if to be thank'n GOD for gett'n him here.

People that didn't even know who he was stood up and clapp'd. "You think you the shit." She said as he held and kiss'd her.

"You like it!" He said as he reach'd into his pocket.

"No, I –" She began to speak and stop'd as Teddy present'd the little black velvet box. "This for me?" She ask'd as she open'd it. Her mouth dropp'd when she discover'd the little treasure inside. She had tears in her eyes as she told him how gorgeous it was and how much she loved him.

"The next one will be an engagement ring. This is simply a promise ring." Teddy stated, "Baby, you gotta go get with your family and I got mo money to collect."

"What time we leave'n for Project Graduation?" She ask'd.

"Baby, I don't know because I think I gotta work at the club. I know I gotta go in. Just pick me up at 9." "I Love You. I got a big surprise for you tonight." Ms. Porchia said with a sneaky smile on her face.

"I Love You too. Tell yo parents I said Hi."

"I will." She said as Teddy popp'd her ass when she walk'd off.

Teddy rode around smoking cigars fill'd with weed all day feel'n himself until about 4:00 when the night before caught up with him. He caught up with Kato for a haircut (Kato was the best barber in Charlotte by far because he could literally draw pictures in your hair with the clippers). Before Teddy left the barber shop, Kato told him to meet him at the club by 10. Teddy left and went straight home and pass'd out. He slept until Ms. Porchia arrived at 9:30.

"Porchia, why are you so late?" He ask'd as he let her in.

"I call'd and paged you. I'm sorry. Baby, I knew you was in here sleep. Hurry up and shower.

You still gotta go by the club?" She ask'd.

"I sure do." Teddy respond'd as he jump'd into the shower.

It was 10 o'clock by the time they left. On the way to the club, Ms. Porchia stopp'd by Popeye's, their favorite spot to get them a 30 piece nugget, onion rings and biscuits. When she pull'd up in front of the club, it wasn't the normal crowd, in fact, it was a small crowd.

"I'll be right back."

"Try ta hurry up."

"Ah-ight Baby."

Teddy walk thru the door speak'n to Big Pin as usual.

"Congratulations Teddy!" Nina holla'd.

"Thanks Neenah. Where is everybody?"

"In there wait'n on you."

Steve, Kato, Juan, Donnie and Tim was all there crowd'd around the dance floor. They had a curtain separat'n the dance floor from the bar area. Charlie only did that when he was having a lock up. Soon as Teddy walk'd thru the curtains Tiger got on the mic." There go that sorry muthafucka. Ladies! Meet the youngest nigga in charge. He's the reason y'all here tonight. T-Rock git-cho ass to the middle of the dance floor. Congratulations Nigga!"

Two very attractive naked chics came and escort'd Teddy to the middle of the dance floor and sat him down in a chair. Six chics with all types of bodies took turns dance'n in front of him as close to 70 somethin dudes look'd on and toss'd one's, five's, ten's, twenty's and some hundreds.

The six chics danced around him in a circle to "Me So Horny" by 2 Live Crew while they dropp'd money in his lap. Even Charlie stood watch'n and cheer'n him on. The song was only about 5 minutes long but with Tiger back spin'n and restart'n it, it last for about 20 minutes. Teddy forgot all about Ms. Porchia until one of the bouncer alert'd Tiger that she was out at the bar piss'd.

"I ain't never seen a stripper make the money you just made without takin nothing off."

Tiger holla'd over the mic. "We love you Bwoy! Git cho money, git-cho shit, and git da hell out!"

All of the naked ladies cordially help'd Teddy gather all of the money from the floor as other dudes came by dropp'n more money and on his way out, Charlie gave him an envelope. When Teddy walk'd pass'd the curtain Ms. Porchia was sitt'n at the bar fume'n until she saw all that money he sat on the bar beside her. They sat there and ate their food. Ms. Porchia count'd out all the money on the bar. "Baby, do you know how much money this is?"

"No, what is it?"

"Six hundred and seventy three dollars."

"Is that all?" Teddy ask'd with his mouth full. He reach'd in his back pocket for the envelope Charlie gave him and pass'd that to her. "Whus in there." He ask'd her.

She pull'd out a wad and began to count. "Teddy, this is a lot of money." She said as she continued count'n. "Baby this is $800 not include'n the $673." She said, as if she wasn't use to see'n that kind a money at once. It was nothing to Teddy.   Just more to add to his stash.

Steve, Kato, Juan, Donnie and Tim came out to the bar not knowing he was still there.

"Congratulations Porchia. Let me see your ring." Kato demand'd, as Ms. Porchia held her hand out. "Yo son! I like dat! Ain't – chall going to Project Graduation?"

"Yeeaa, we bout ta leave now." Teddy said.

"Follow us to my brotha's crib in Tryon Forest, I left yo money down there." Donnie said.

"Les go, we late."

They all pour'd out of the club and Teddy drove Ms. Porchia to Donnie's brotha's crib. Donnie ran in the house and came back out with an envelope. Teddy had jump'd into the car with his brother, Kato, Steve and Tim to hit the joint they were pass'n around. He only hit it once and got out of the car.

By the time he walk'd back to Ms. Porchia's car, something wasn't right. He walk'd to the passenger window and told her, she need'd to drive. She could look in his face and tell that something was wrong so she slid into the driver's seat as he open'd the door to get in. He gave her yet, another envelope and extended the passenger seat back in recliner mode.

"What wrong?" She ask'd as she pull'd out of the apartment complex.

Everything was in slow motion. He replied, "I need something to drink."

When Ms. Porchia got to the top of Lamberth Dr., she took a right turn toward town and stopp'd a block down at a Kato gas station.

She got him a peach Nehi. He took one sip and pass'd out. Ms. Porchia was furious. Instead of driving all the way to Carowinds, she went and park'd at Freedom Park and sat in the car as Teddy came in and out. This continued until 5:15 Saturday morn'n.

When Teddy came to his senses completely, he noticed where he was and also noticed Ms. Porchia wasn't in the car. He reach'd under the seat for his .380 and immediately got out of the car to go find his woman.

Closing the car door, he yell'd, "PORR – SHAAH!"

She didn't respond so he proceed'd to search for her in the pitch black park. He walk'd past the first baseball field call'n her name and still no response. The next field was approximately 100 yards away, something told him to walk toward that field and as he approach'd the bleachers, he noticed something wrapp'd up in what look'd like a quilt.

"Porchia!" He call'd out.

"What Teddy." She said in a somber voice.

He walk'd over to her and wrapp'd his arms around her. "Baby, I'm Sorry." He said.

Ms. Porchia lean'd back into his arms, "I thought you were dead."

Teddy chuckled, "So why you didn't take me to the hospital?"

"You told me not to."

"Hi you gone listen to a half dead man?" He giggled, hugg'n her tighter. "Baby, that had to be Angel Dust cause I only took one pull."

"Well, maybe you need to quit smoking."

"Maybe I do. You know I'm gone make this up to you?"

"How?"

"We'll think of something."

Ms. Porchia stood up and turn'd to face Teddy, open'n the quilt to expose her naked body.

Teddy question'd her nakedness and she responded that she was prepared to make love to him when he came for her. They wasted no time, Teddy came out of his clothes and join'd her in nakedness as they made love in the quilt on the grass behind the bleachers until the sun came up.

## Chapter 20: First Fight

Relationships are most beautiful in their infant stages. Everything is so fresh and new. You adore the smallest things about each other. The phone calls are longer and the only person you notice in your eye sight is your lover.

Since graduation, the only job Teddy had was the club and his little QP a week weed hustle. Ms. Porchia was still part-time at Allstate as a customer service rep thru the week and she work'd at Belk's on the weekends. All in between time, they were inseparable.

This was totally new to Teddy. He was always on the go doing something. If he wasn't fuck'n chics Kato, Tiger and Steve sent his way, he was hang'n out with Fly, E, Tip, Donté and their other homeboy, Petey try'n to enter the music business. As of lately, he only had time for Ms. Porchia and Mia, the two women that ruled his heart.

It was a typical late summer Friday morning. Ms. Porchia had come to pick Teddy up and brought him back to her parent's home. No one was there besides the three day a week maid, a little older lady named Hatty. Hatty loved Teddy. She had known him since he was a kid. Hatty had a son name Jimmy that died of Sickle cell. Jimmy and Teddys' uncle Steve would almost everytime end up in the hospital at the same time and they became the best of friends in sickness. The last time she had seen Teddy was at Jimmy's funeral some five years ago.

She had heard his name ring'n throughout her employer's house but she had no idea it was him.

"Hey Baby!" Hatty said as her eyes register'd in that he was who he was.

"Hey Ms. Hatty!" Teddy said as they embraced each other.

"So, you're the Teddy I've been hear'n about."
"Yeup, this is my Teddy." Ms. Porchia said as she ran upstairs toward her bedroom.

Immediately, Hatty approach'd Teddy and told him to keep his guard up because the Grier's didn't think to highly of him. She told him to stand his ground at all times with them. She continued to do her chores and left shortly before midday.

Ms. Porchia's dad was at the cleaners and her mom work'd for WSOC TV as an associate producer, so they had the house to themselves. Ms. Porchia cook'd lunch for them. They had ribeye steak, baked potatoes and garden salad with vinegarette and creamy Italian dressing, and for dessert, each other. Their after lunch sex was so intense that Ms. Porchia fell asleep right where she left the stains of her last orgasms. With his dick enlarged between her ass cheeks and the back of her head rest'n in his chest, their bodies bond'd in rest until Teddy's pager went off disturb'n the peace and unity that they possess'd.

Teddy gently attempt'd to move without disturb'n Ms. Porchia but the peace they had captured in that moment came from a bond that couldn't be obtain'd alone so Ms. Porchia abruptly got up and made her way to the bathroom. Teddy, while check'n his pager, watch'd her naked ass sway from side to side as she pranced out arous'n Teddy. DAMN I LOVE THAT GIRL. Teddy thought as her presence escaped his vision.

Teddy pick'd up the phone to call Fly. He had paged three times. That was abnormal. While dial'n the number, Ms. Porchia came into the bed and wash'd their dried but still moist love juices from his pubic area. Teddy laid back enjoy'n the warm rag massage as he spoke with Fly.

"Whut-chu doin tonight?" Fly ask'd.

"Nuthin, the club probably gone be closed. You know Expressions is takin Charlie's business," Teddy said.

Expressions was a new night club that Charlie's old DJ start'd. It was right around the corner from Party Zone on North Tryon. Everybody had to check out the new spot and that was the topic of Fly's conversation.

"Les check it out, we ain't been out in over a month. Since you got wit Porchia, we don't ever hang out unless we practicing or got a show."

"I'm wit it. What time?" Teddy ask'd as Ms. Porchia left the room only to return momentarily with a rinsed, warm rag and a towel to finish what she start'd. Little did Teddy know, she was only eaves dropp'n. "I gotta pick up my rental by three and I'll be to pick you up after that. Dat's cool?" Teddy ask'd as Fly confirm'd and he hung up the phone.

Ly'n across Ms. Porchia's canopy style bed as she finish'd dry'n him off, Teddy got a stiff erection while she massaged his dick.

"Come here." Teddy demand'd feel'n horny as she stood over him.

"Where are you going tonight?" She ask'd in a distort'd tone.

Teddy smile'd at her question. "Come here." He said as he tugg'd at her arm.

"No!" She said as she pull'd away. "You're not fair." She explain'd, "You didn't ask me what I had plann'd".

Teddy sat up on the edge of the bed, erection weakening, "Porchia, I'm just hang'n out with Fly tonight –" He stopp'd in the middle of his explanation and paused, "Why am I even having to explain myself. I haven't been nowhere without you in the past month.

"Why is it a problem?"

"Ain't no problem!" She snapp'd back.

Teddy got real agitated real quick, jump'd up and start'd putt'n on his clothes. "Porchia take me home. I ain't wit dis shit!"

Ms. Porchia got in his face point'n her finger in his forehead, "You're selfish! You could have ask'd me if I had something plann'd first."

"I didn't have to ask you shit." He said as he tried to move from in front of her. All of a sudden, PAP! Was the sound of her open hand going across Teddy's light honey color'd red face. Teddy grabb'd her hand and wrapp'd his hand around her neck. "Bitch, you stupid?  Don't ever put-cho hand in my muthafuck'n face.  Whut da fuck wrong wit-chu?" He ask'd in an outrage, pushing her to the bed.

He grabb'd the phone and call'd a cab as she cried, begg'd and plead'd for his forgiveness. Teddy grabb'd his things and sat on the front porch until the cab came. He left not look'n back not know'n whether that was the end of their month and a half love affair.

## Chapter 21: Heartaches

It was the first half of the second week of July, Teddy hadn't heard from Ms. Porchia in two weeks. After their fight, Ms. Porchia tried to call Teddy several times but he never answer'd or return'd her calls until a week later. When he attempt'd to call, he was inform'd that she was out of the states in Frankfort Germany visit'n her aunt Helen. Teddy was miss'n her severely and he had only a week left before he was due to leave for college.

He sat in on a beautiful Saturday, depress'd, hang'n out with Mia and Lekrell. Mia was gett'n older and very attach'd to Teddy. She was now 8 months old and could detect the emotions of her surroundings. Normally, she would be all over the place when Teddy had her and Lekrell together, but this day, her mood was just as somber as her dad's. He laid back on the couch in his mom's livingroom watch'n Scarface on video tape while Mia ly on his chest. Teddy was miss'n Ms. Porchia severely, to the point he couldn't eat, sleep or socialize.

Teddy's mom was rest'n, gett'n ready for a double shift while his sister Shan sat on the back porch talk'n on the phone.

"Teddy, git da phone!" Shan yell'd.

Immediately, Mia peek'd her head up look'n into her daddy's face with a playful smile as if she knew the voice on the other end would make her daddy's day.

"Yeah." Teddy said as he put the receiver to his ear. There was an echo and then a pause.

"I miss You," the soft tender voice said from the other end.

"I'm so sorry for smack'n You, I LOVE YOU and can't stop think'n of You. Can I please see You when I get home Monday?" She said in a rush'd voice in hope of not being hung up on.

"Porchia?" Teddy respond'd inquisitively unsure.

"Who else You let smack You?" She ask'd.

"Why did You just up and leave the country without let'n me know?"

"I call'd You several times and You never call'd back."

He paused know'n it was his own fault.

"Do You still love me?" She ask'd.

"More than You'll ever know." Teddy said, acknowledging his true feeln's while Mia grabb'd at the phone, play'n in his face.

"Timia's there?" Porchia inquired, hearing her step-daughter's voice.

"Yeea, we hang'n out."

"Put the phone to her ear."

"Hold on." Teddy said as he put the phone to her ear. Timia listen'd for a second, "Heeey" She said, possibly repeat'n what she heard, "Da – da – da – da" She said as she bounced in her daddy's lap while hitt'n him in the chest.

Teddy took the phone from her ear. "I'm back."
"I can't wait to get back home to You." Ms. Porchia said.

"I can't wait til You get back either."

"You hear that?"

"What?" Teddy ask'd with sincere concern.

"My body call'n You."

Teddy giggled. "You got me."

"Teddy, I LOVE YOU so much. I gotta go, I'll call You before I get on my flight Monday."

"I LOVE YOU too. Be safe."

"Alright, I bought You some of this German beer and some vodka."

"What about"- She cut him off know'n what he was think'n.

"Don't even think about it Teddy. Even if I could, I wouldn't after what happen'd graduation night. I gotta go love. Love You."

"I LOVE You too."

"I'll see You Monday night at 10."

"Ah-ight."

Once Teddy was off the phone Mia could tell that her daddy was in better spirits and he could tell that she knew it. Teddy's heart was a little at ease but he was still think'n about bein away from Ms. Porchia and Mia for so long. He was going some twelve hours away and wouldn't return til after Thanksgiving from school. The marching band plays every weekend at every game. He had six days left before he left for school and not only did he have cold feet, his feet were frozen.

Upon Ms. Porchia's return, she let Teddy know that she was for sure she was going to A&T. Teddy express'd discomfort about going to FAMU.

The band was no longer important. His heart, Ms. Porchia possess'd.

It was July 23rd, two days before Teddy was scheduled to leave. He and Ms. Porchia was on the phone with the registrar's office. Teddy decided that if he couldn't get into A&T, he would sit out a semester instead of going all the way down to Florida being away from Ms. Porchia. He had enough money saved to pay his own tuition for a year without housing. However, the process was even more simple than that, he was eligible for financial aid. Instead of leaving going to Florida, he left Friday morning going to Greensboro to register for school. Everything went as well as to be expect'd. They couldn't guarantee housing but they would be able to let him know if his financial aid was approved within the month. Classes begin August 25th and he had to be back on the 11th for freshman orientation.

With $35,000.00 saved, Teddy was prepared to start the next phase of his life with the love of his life.

## Chapter 22: College Life

The first few weeks of school for Teddy was somewhat strenuous getting use to. He took a full load which meant he was in class from 8 in the morning til 7:50pm. Ms. Porchia was across the campus in Barbee Hall while Teddy was roommates in Scott Hall with his cousin Tim. Besides lunch and dinner occasionally, they had very little time for their so called relationship.

After a few weeks of school, Teddy had gotten into the swing of things and start'd to hangout a little bit.  His next door neighbor Rock was around town. Even though Tim was Teddy's roommate, he didn't have much time for him. Tim was a senior, that work'd at MCI in the customer service department and nurtured his relationship with his college sweetheart in his spare time, which meant, Teddy had to find his own way. That's where Rock came in, Rock took Teddy to massive parties. 2 – 6 parties were the things to do then. Spots like the Turtle Club, Hero's and gym jams. Ms. Porchia and Teddy barely saw each other unless it was time to mate.

While Ms. Porchia would take off every weekend going back to Charlotte to work her part time job at Belk's, Teddy stay'd in Greensboro enhancing his popularity unless he was going home to check on Mia.

Teddy and Rock were superb spades players, taking on several different teams in the dorm for money and capitalizing. Teddy and Rock as a spades team were mention'd at the Student Union. In the basement of the Student Union, the who's who of the camp that were skill'd in the game met daily to battle.

There were several good players to come thru the Union, but very few were exceptional. Teddy and Rock fit into that category and were being call'd out by a crew of upper classman that lived in a big white boarding house call'd "The Cave." These cats were the best at cheat'n not to lose. However, Teddy and Rock were great at winnin and beat'n the cheaters. Several teams tried and very few succeed'd in beating them which gain'd them popularity throughout the campus.

Teddy hated the campus life, so after first semester he moved off campus with a few guys from Red Springs NC.  Brad, Jon and Chris were a few of the cats Teddy met at the Student Union and became cool with.

Once a month, Teddy would go home to purchase his weed from Kato. He had several clients from campus and had to maintain his own habit until Kato was accused of murder and went to prison. Teddy was destroy'd at having his mentor and cousin bein taken away from him but it also left him having to deal with strangers to purchase his weed.

For a while he purchased at spots like Monroe's on Bessemer and on the hill off Lee Street. Ms. Porchia knew nothing about Teddy's dealing in street herbal distribution but she knew of his use. Teddy tried his best to keep his personal life and business separate. At first, he did a good job but the deeper he got, the more obvious it became.

Everything Teddy did was focus'd around Ms. Porchia and Mia, Ms. Porchia marveled at the popularity and reputation Teddy had earn'd himself. He was known by massive upper classmen but mostly by the women. The women befriend'd him and the dudes envied him. If You want''d to find him day to day, he was either in the arms of Ms. Porchia or in the presence of one of his many women friends.

Teddy was quick to make changes where they were need'd in his life and after the fall semester of daily classes Monday thru Friday from 8am to 7:50pm, he knew that was definitely a change that had to be made. At the beginning of the spring semester, Teddy made sure none of his classes began before noon on Mondays and no classes after Thursdays at noon. He was established in the in-crowd and throughout the spring, he was either throw'n a cookout or attend'n one that he had to supply the party favorites.

Other times, he was traveling going to different cats hometown partying. Half of the time, when he went to Charlotte, none of his family ever saw him unless he stop thru to see Mia and drop'd off some money.

Ms. Porchia only spent time with Teddy thru the week and nine times out of ten, Teddy was with a crew of chics. Nothing sexual, he look'd at it as business and network'n. They saw to it that Teddy knew everybody that was somebody, attended the major parties and was well-known to the masses. They all knew and loved Ms. Porchia and Ms. Porchia was very acquainted with them all.

In one year, Teddy found himself more established in the college circuit than 90% of the seniors. He was so caught up in the moment that he hadn't taken the proper time to get to know the so called love of his life.

Teddy handled his business on all levels; school, streets, and women, but he never prepared himself for Ms. Porchia and her family ties.

## Chapter 23: First Anniversary
## (May 8th, 1991)

Things had been moving so fast for Teddy and Ms. Porchia for the past year that it almost slipp'd Teddy's mind that it was their first anniversary.  In fact, it did.

It was the last day of school, Teddy and his roommate Brad went to clean out Ms. Porchia's dorm room. As Teddy reach'd for her 12 inch TV on the desk, he saw her calendar mark'd off on Friday, May 8th "Our 1st Anniversary/Last Day of School". Teddy thought to himself, "OH SHIT! TODAY IS OUR ANNIVERSARY"!

He finish'd pack'n all of her things into her Camry and his 300 ZT. They unload'd most of her things at Teddy's place in Carolina Circle and the rest at Ms. Porchia's sister's in Colonial Place across town.

Teddy left Ms. Porchia with her sister Kenya so that he could surprise her later that evening plus, Kenya was preparing for graduation Sunday. She was graduating from A&T and she had began to celebrate.

"Porchia, I got some business to take care of, what-chu got planned later?" Teddy ask'd nonchalantly, not indicating he was aware of their anniversary.

"I'll be her at Kenya's." She said, with a touch of disappointment in her tone.

"You wanna go get something to eat later or you want me to leave you some money for something?" Teddy ask'd, know'n the answer.

"I WANT YOU TO TAKE ME OUT TO DINNER! Thank You!

You got time for everybody else but me." She explain'd, as Teddy chuckled at her tone.

"Be ready by 6."

"No, you be here by 6!" She said with much attitude, as Teddy play'd along.

"C'mere" Teddy said as he grabb'd her, pulling her into his arms. "Whus wrong?" He ask'd, as he kiss'd her lips and she turn'd her head.

"You make me sick Teddy!" She said, hitting him in his chest.

"Every since you been out here, you don't pay me any attention. You came to A&T to be with me and I don't see you." She said, as she continued to vent. "If you aren't with Zita, Meka, Shine, or Mesha, you somewhere in Creek Bend gamblin with Steezo, Ant'no, Rod, and Slice. We never go out." She pout'd.

"Make some time for me. I didn't say much during the school but classes are over. Even Kenny been hear'n your name out here and we from Charlotte."

Teddy kiss'd her cheek as if to disregard every word she said, "Be ready at 6." He said as he let her go and turn'd to walk out the door.

"Teddy!" Kenya yell'd.

"Yeah!" Teddy answer'd.

"Come here before you leave."

Teddy back track'd and walk'd into the kitchen where Kenya stood on the telephone. Kenya was ok, so Teddy thought. She was tall, something like 5ft 10, light skin, red in tone with shoulder length brown hair and bouggie like her mom.

"Whussup?" Teddy ask'd

"Leave me something."

"Somethin like what?" Teddy ask'd, play'n stupid to her demand.

"Teddy, don't play. I know your whole crew. I've purchase from you and you didn't even know it thru Shine. Need I say more?"  She ask'd, with her lips pucker'd in the air.

Teddy kinda smiled at her statement and dropp'd a little less than a quarter bag on the table. "Congratulations." He said as he made his way back to the front door. "Be ready by 6." He said to Ms. Porchia sitt'n on the couch with the remote control, channel surf'n, stopp'n on "ALL MY CHILDREN."

"Whatever Teddy!" She said, as she suck'd her teeth and Teddy walk'd out the door.

FUCK! Teddy thought.

"I GOTTA GET TO THE MALL, FIND HER SOMETHIN, FIND A HOTEL ROOM AND GET CHANGED BY 5. I GOT 3 ½ HOURS."

His first stop was HECHT's in Friendly Shopp'n Center. He started look'n at rings but he gave her one for graduation last year. Then he look'd at some necklaces and bracelets. Nothing was appeal'n. He came to the watches and fell up on the ladies Gucci watches with the removable ring around the face with six different color replaceable rings for $275.00. PERFECT!

He thought, pulling out his brand new HECHT's charge card to charge Ms. Porchia's anniversary gift. He saw a gift basket with scent'd candles, peach boy wash, and all over body spray, he had to have. As the cashier pass'd him his bag and receipt, Teddy look'd at his Movado watch think'n, 'I'M ON SCHEDULE', when his pager went off. It was one of his many customers and he had forgot that it was Friday, one of his biggest days. Immediately, he went to a phone booth and call'd Shine. Shine and

Mesha were roommates in Forest Grove. Shine, Mesha, Zita, and Meka was responsible for him having so many customers, so he kept the bulk of his weed at their crib.

"Shine!" Teddy yell'd in a rush.

"Whut boy?"

"I need'ju."

"Whut?"

"Today is me and Porchia's first anniversary and my pager is blowing up. I'm try'n to get a room and spend the rest of the night with her ---" She cut him off.

"Boy bring me the pager.  But –chu gone pay me."

"I got-chu! But can you do me another favor?"
"Whuut Teddy?"

"I need to get a reservation at a hotel tonight."

"Boy, this is graduation weekend! You want a miracle! I'll call you back!" She said, hang'n up the phone without say'n bye.

Shine and Mesha were Teddy's heart. Shine and Teddy were closer. She would let him use her ear, sleep in her bed and they basically were boyfriend and girlfriend without the sex. Shine was from Mooresville. She was 5ft 8', high yellow with gorgeous features, slim with big titties and no ass at all.

Mesha, on the other hand was 5ft 5', with mocha chocolate skin, slim with a nice ass and long wavy hair. She resembled Pocohantas. She was from New Bern. Her and Teddy were the same age, two years younger than Shine. No matter what, they made sure Teddy was taken care of.

As Teddy rode down Wendover towards Highway 29, his pager went off. It was Shine. Instead of stopping to call, he went straight to her spot. Using his key, he let himself in.

"Shine!" Teddy yell'd as he entered the back door thru the kitchen.

"I'm back here in my room."

Teddy walk'd thru the living room and turn't the corner into her room to see her sitt'n on the edge of the bed naked, lotioning her body. "Damn Shine! Put them pillows up!" Speak'n of her big ass titties.

"Nigga, you act like you ain't seen these big sexy muthafuckas befo."

"Because, it's a surprise everytime." He said as she stood her slim frame up and walk'd to her dresser. "Shine, you would be a dime if you had a little bit-a-ass."

"This good ass pussy makes me a quarter Nigga! Here." She said as she passed him some info on a little piece of paper. "There wasn't anything else available so you gone spend some money on that girl tonight." She said, stand'n completely nude in front of Teddy as he stared at her freshly shaved kitten, stick'n out from between her thighs like a fist.

"Quit stare'n at my shit Nigga! You can't afford this."

She joked.

"Fuck you!" Teddy said.

"No, you fuck Porchia and I'll fuck my sugah daddy."

"Yo nasty ass. Whut is he 80?" Teddy said as she shot him the finger.

"Gimme the pager. I got two pounds here, if they come git all of this, fuck it, they have to wait til tomarra."

"Thank You Shine. I gotta go." He said as she slid on her thigh length satin robe givin him a hug.

"Have a good time." She said, following him to the back door.

It was 3:45 when Teddy got back to his place, he had 2 hours to get ready, shoot by the hotel and get to Ms. Porchia. Shine found him a suite downtown at the Sheraton Hotel on Elm St. for $150.00.

He want'd to slide thru and set it up before he brought Ms. Porchia there that evening.

He laid out his clothes. A tan linen Nautica outfit with some brown Cole Haan slippers. He accentuated the outfit wit his gold herringbone chain, Tag watch and his onyx and diamond pinky ring with the nugget bracelet to match the charm on his necklace.

Teddy, as a 20 year old adult had plenty of style and class. At 5ft7', he was chubby 185 pounds and the women loved his curly hair. His name fit him.  Times like tonight when he wasn't in his jeans, Timberlands or Nautica boots, Teddy would turn the lights out on most, with his flamboyant style of dress. He never had to compete for attention from the ladies because he possess'd a style of his own.

Pack'n a overnight bag  before he stepp'd out, he check'd himself in the mirror as he spray'd Nautica cologne high and low in front of him and walk'd thru it. Pleased with the results, he grabb'd his Versace shades with the rest of his things and was on his way.

He stopp'd by Harris Teeter to get some Moët for the hotel room. He also got some pink roses and some candles. Little did he know when he got to the suite, it had a Jacuzzi and a fully stock'd mini bar with all types of the mini bottles of liquor. In classic fashion, he filled the Champagne chess with ice, sat it by the Jacuzzi, went into the bedroom laid the roses on the bed with a card that read HAPPY 1ST ANNIVERSARY. I COULD NEVER FORGET MY 1ST ANNIVERSARY WITH MY 1ST LOVE. I LOVE YOU, YOUR TEDDY." Sitting right beside the roses was the box with her Gucci watch in it. He then set the candles throughout the suite.

It was 5:15 and everything was set. He had almost forgot to make the reservations at her favorite restaurant. He grabb'd the phone and call'd TK Tripps, set the reservation for 6:30 and ask'd them to bring out their 3x5 inch cake that they give for birthdays when they finish'd their dinner. They made a note by his reservations and now, Teddy was set.

He arrived back at Kenya's at 5:45. Ms. Porchia look'n at Teddy in awe, think'n, HE REMEMBER'D, until she ask'd "Why you dress'd up?"

"I got somewhere to go after we eat." Teddy answer'd.

"Teddy, you make me sick! I'm not going anywhere with you look'n like this. "She said, defiantly.

"Baby, you look fine." Teddy said as Ms. Porchia stood wear'n some shorts a cute top and some sandals. "C'mon."

"No! Let me change first. It won't take long, cause I'm not going nowhere with you look'n like this and where you going afterwards? I'm goin." She said as she rush'd into the room to change.

"Jus hurry up and don't be try'n to jump in the shower, you shoulda been wash dat pussy." Teddy said jokingly, knowing that she had already showered by her fresh scents he smelt when he walk'd in.

"Shut up! You know I keep my shit fresh!"

Teddy loved when Ms. Porchia talk'd dirty to him. She was a good girl but she had it in her to get guttah. Teddy loved that side of her. Just hearing her talk about her pussy turn't Teddy on.

Ms. Porchia came back to the living room wear'n a tan linen Chanel sundress with no panties and some Chanel high heel sandals look'n gorgeous. "Where we goin?" She ask'd as she walk'd up to Teddy kiss'n him on the cheek and grabb'n his hand to leave.

"Les jus go, befo we be late." He said, grabb'n her ass as they walk'd out the door. "Baby, you look good as fuck!" Teddy said, gawk'n at her body.

"Thank you. You don't look half bad yourself."

"Half bad? You look'd at me and ran to change." Teddy said chuckling as he open'd the passenger door.

"I can't lie, you-look-good-to-me." She said as she sat in the passenger seat. "Baby, what's todays date?" She ask'd before Teddy closed her door.

"Hell, I don't know." Teddy answer'd nonchalantly as he closed her door.

He got in on his side, look'd over at his gorgeous arm piece and kiss'd her before driving off. He sensed her unease of think'n that he had forgotten their day.

Arriving at the restaurant just in time, there was still a fifteen minute wait, so they kill'd the time at the bar. Teddy order'd for the both of them – strawberry daiquiri for her and Johnnie Walker Black Label on the rocks for him. As they sip'd their spirits, Teddy reveal'd how much of a difference she made in his life and that he was glad that he came to A&T instead of leaving her to go to Florida. Ms. Porchia express'd how proud she was of Teddy's 3.0 GPA and how he maintain'd thru the year. Their waitress took them to their booth and took their order.

Throughout the wait, they continued their conversation. Ms. Porchia told Teddy she was proud to be known throughout the campus as his lady. Teddy told her he wouldn't have it no other way. She then ask'd where were they going after dinner because she wasn't lett'n him out of her sight tonight because he look'd too good. Teddy told her to just enjoy the moment, then the waitress return'd with their meal. Ms. Porchia had grill'd steak and onions with grill'd shrimp, baked potato with sour cream and butter. Salads came with both meals. Teddy had barbecue beef ribs with the same side orders. She had tea and Teddy had water with a double shot of Johnnie Walker. They ate til they were full and just as plann'd, Teddy stated that he had somewhere to be and ask'd for the check.

"Teddy, I know you aren't about to jus drop me back off? That's not right!" She whisper'd, "So I gotta stay by myself tonight? Kenya is with J celebrating and you gone just drop me back off." She said, as the chipper little white chic came to the table with the miniature sheet cake and their bill.

"Mrs. Porchia Massey, it is with great honor that on behalf of myself and the staff here at TK Tripps, we would like to wish you and Mr. Massey a Happy Anniversary."

Ms. Porchia look'd at Teddy with her freshly manicured hands covering her face with tears in her eyes.

"HAPPY ANNIVERSARY LOVE." Teddy said, reach'n for her hand.

"I LOVE YOU TEDDY. I thought you forgot." She said as Teddy caught the tear runn'n down her face with his napkin.

"I Love You Too. Now cut this cake so we can go."

"Can I take it with me? I'm full." She stated, still in awe that he actually remember'd.

"That's fine cause I got somewhere to be." Teddy said, stick'n to the script.

The whole expression on her face changed. "You still dropp'n me off?" She ask'd in a puzzled tone.

"Yeea" Teddy said with a pause, "Sometime tomorra." He said with a huge smile. "Baby, will you spend the rest of the evening with me?" He romantically whisper'd.

"You make me sick." She said, digg'n her toes into his crotch under the table. "I wasn't going anywhere anyway." She said, rolling her sexy light brown eyes. "Happy Anniversary to you," Ms. Porchia said reach'n over the table to partake in tasting Teddy's lips.

Teddy paid the bill and left a nice tip for the waitress that so diligently assisted him in making their dinner a success. They rode down Wendover listen'n to Color Me Bad "I WANNA SEX YOU UP". Ms. Porchia loved that song and Teddy loved it from the scene in New Jack City.

"Baby, where are we goin?"

"On a rendezvous, just sit back and enjoy the ride."

The tape Teddy made had all of their favorite slow songs on it. When Laila Hathaway's "Heaven" came on, Ms. Porchia grabb'd Teddy's hand and didn't let go until they arrived at the Sheraton.

"This is the party that Kenya and J is coming to." Ms. Porchia said, think'n that Teddy was bring'n her to the A&T graduation party that was being held in the ballroom.

"Not this party."

"This is a private VIP party."

Ms. Porchia look'd at Teddy with a confused look. "So who's having it?"

"A couple of friends of mine. Just relax, you wit me." Teddy said as he got out of the car, making his way to her side to open her door being the gentleman he was.

They enter'd the hotel notice'n the party promoters sett'n up for the night's events. It was 8:15 and the party starts at 10 but Teddy's party would be well under way by 10. They hopp'd on the elevator to the top floor, and walk'd all the way to the end of the hallway. The corner room had two doors, the first door read SUITE 1020. Teddy pull'd out the key and enter'd the room. He left a peach incent burn'n when he left and the aroma was sweet and pleasant to the nasal passage when they return'd.

Ms. Porchia stood at the door as it closed behind her.

"This is beautiful!" She said in a whisper. "You did all of this for me?"

"Look at the Jacuzzi!"

Teddy sat down on the couch and began to roll a blunt. His weed in cigars had been given a name by Reggie Noble a-k-a Red Man.

"Why didn't you tell me so I could have brought a overnight bag?" She ask'd

"Then it wouldn't have been a surprise." He said as she sat on his lap.

Teddy lit the blunt and blew the smoke in her face. "I Love You Porchia." He said.

"I Love You Too Baby. You gone let me smoke with you?"

"Here, take one pull." Teddy said as he held the blunt to her lips. She took a nice pull and held it in.

Ms. Porchia knew Teddy didn't like for her to smoke but on special occasions that they were alone, he would permit it.

"I don't have anything to wear to bed, get into the Jacuzzi or nothing." She said.

"That's the point. You don't need NOTHING!" Teddy said as he slid his hand between her legs. "Damn! Somebody's wet." He said as he separated her lips below notice'n the warmth of her love juices flow'n.

"Mmm Baby, you know weed makes me horny." She said as she open'd her legs wider exposing her pleasure park.

Teddy was feel'n jus as horny or shall we say, freaky. He told her to lay back on the couch. She slid off of his lap into the corner of the couch as she was told with her legs spread wide, while Teddy slid down on his knee with his head and arms between her legs. This was uncharter'd territory for Teddy. Out of all the many women he had entertain'd sexually, not one could say that he ever orally attempted to please.

He began to play around her clit as she moan'd and pant'd. "I've never done this before." He said.

"Ssss. Done what?" She ask'd and Teddy kiss'd her clit. "Oh My God!" She scream'd as the sensation of his lips ran thru her spine leaving her back arch'd and her eyes open'd wide, confused by this new found pleasure that Teddy was embark'n on.

"That feel good?" Teddy ask'd.

Ms. Porchia gave off a sexy laugh, "Oh - yeah!"

"You have to tell me what to do." He said as he spread her lips and embraced her clit with his lips.

"TEDDY!" She scream'd.

Teddy was definitely a new comer but he had seen enough fuck flicks not to be green.

"Am I doing it right?" He ask'd as he gently suck'd on her highly sensitive body part.

"Yes!" She said as her head fell back look'n to the ceil'n and look'n back down at Teddy look'n up at her as her hands grilled the back of the couch and the armrest.

"Lick it." She demand''d in the sexiest voice ever imaginable.

Teddy took the tip of his tongue and stuck it in her honey hole, and with her thick creamy love juices on the tip of his tongue, he lick'd from her pussy to her clit.

"Like that?" He ask'd.

"Hell – yeah!" She moan'd with her head back in the crease of the couch.

He lick'd her again in the same fashion.

"Oh my God Teddy! Don't stop!"

DAMN SHE TASTE SWEET. Teddy thought to himself.

I CAN GIT USE TO THIS.

He repetitiously lick'd her clit like a thirsty dog drink'n water.

Ms. Porchia grabb'd the back of his head, "Ba – by – I – I – I'm – aaaa – bou – ta – cum." She said as she pant'd and began to jerk uncontrollably.

Teddy stopp'd lick'n her clit and began to gently suck on it. He noticed how hard it got and also the clear liquid substance leak'n from her pussy as she began to beg him to fuck her. As Teddy slid two fingers inside of her and continued to suck on her clit, Ms. Porchia found a rhythm and in seconds, she was cry'n out in pleasure. "This is your pussy! Gimmie my dick!"

Teddy's hand was snotty. He stopp'd and got up. He look'd at her and ask'd. "You ok?"

She couldn't answer, she was still gyrating on the couch and moan'n. Teddy was so turn'd on, it was like he was a kid that found a new toy.

He went into the room, wash'd his face and hands, then he lit the candles and began to take off his clothes. Ms Porchia came staggering in minutes later, fixin her hair.

"Baby, you were great!" She said before she noticed the pink roses. "Teddy, those are gorgeous!" She said as she jump'd her now naked body in the middle of the king size bed. She grabb'd the card and the gift box as Teddy stood observing and smoking a blunt. After reading the card she look'd up at Teddy and smiled say'n thank you, "Baby I'm still cumm'n". She said as she held the box up as if to say, FOR ME TOO? "Teddy, this is too much. That last gift took the cake." She said as she unwrapp'd the Gucci watch. "No – You – Didn't!" She crawl'd over to the edge of the bed and jump'd up into his arms and they shared a very sensual and intimate kiss.

"You know I love you, right?" Teddy ask'd.

"I know you do." She said as Teddy held her by her waist as their bodies united. "My turn." She said with a smirk on her face.

"Whut-chu mean yo turn?" Teddy ask'd.

"You taste me, I taste you." She replied as she lick'd and suck'd her way down to his dick. Grabbing his manhood with both hands. She began to caress it, then she went down the side of his shaft suck'n. She lick'd all the way back to the head and began to nibble at the pre-cum leak'n from his dick.

"Mmmm, Ssss, Shit! That feels good." Teddy released.

You done done this before, I see." He stated.

Ms. Porchia stopp'd in mid stride as she was about to enter his head into her mouth. "No! You are my first!
Why?"

"Dat shit felt too good."

"Nah. Yo girl (speak'n of Mocha) been given me lessons with blow pops and tonight, you my supersize blow pop.

Anyway, that was your first time and my pussy still nutt'n" She said as she look'd up at him and took the whole head of his pipe into her mouth.

"Got Damn Porchia!" Teddy moan'd.

"Ummm hmm." She moan'd as she look'd up at him bring'n ultimate pleasure. She suck'd him fast then slow, deep throat to head for twenty minutes, try'n to bring him to some pleasure he so wonderfully brought to her in the other room.

"Porchia" Teddy called.

"Huh" she respond'd with her mouth full of him.

"Baby, I want to cum in you."

"Umm" She groan'd as she pull'd him out of her mouth, "Well come here then". She said as she turn'd around and spread eagle on her knees with a serious arch in her back, gripp'n the comforter on the bed preparing for the pleasure and pain combination to take her to ecstacy.

Teddy grabb'd his pleasure pole by the base and smack'd Ms. Porchia's ass like swipe'n a credit card.

"Mmmm!" She moan'd as Teddy slid the head of his dick into her wetness. "Oh shit, Teddy!" She said, look'n back at Teddy as he dug deeper and deeper until she had consumed as much as she could.

"Ssss! Damn, this pussy so wet. "Teddy said as he slow grind'd her, feel'n every inch of her womanly insides.

"Mmmm... Because – it's – Yours." Ms. Porchia respond'd.

Her response got Teddy a little more excited as his rhythm became a little stronger and a little faster. "I want all of you in me tonight." She look'd back at him and said.

Teddy then pull'd out of her and turn'd her over on her back and pull'd her ass to the edge of the bed. Slowly, he began to give her all of him, inch by inch, throbb'n the whole way. By the time he had increased himself fully inside of her, her pussy began to contract, grabbing and fitting every inch of his dick like a glove. "Teddy." She moan'd, "Baby, I can't – stah- oh my God – cumm'n." Her panting and nonstop sensual screams brought a nonstop pounding. "Isss – Yours! Fuck me Teddy!"

"Oh shit!" Teddy said as he felt his love begin to flow down, "Porchia!"

"Cum in this pussy!" She demand'd. "I'm cumm'n too!"

As Teddy began to free himself, he dug into the top of her uterus and gave her short strokes as he spray'd her insides and she released her thick, snotty cum down the sides of his dick that sound'd like gas but were only small air pockets coming from her being completely fill'd during her release.

They both fell asleep in the same position they came in, sweat and cum everywhere and Teddy still enlarged inside of her pussy.

That night, Ms. Porchia graduated – from being the most inexperienced, to being the best lover by far, that Teddy ever had.

## Chapter 24: The Games Begin

Two months after school began in the fall semester of 91', Teddy and E went down to Livingstone College with Fly to open up for SWV. E attended NC Central, he caught a ride to Greensboro to hook up with Teddy.

Ms. Porchia had previously been complain'n about not spending no time with Teddy so he invited her to come and drive instead of him driving his car. Teddy and E had plann'd to go on down to Charlotte and get suites at the Residence Inn on N Tryon St. for the weekend. E was pick'n up his girl and his daughter that night, Teddy was pick'n up Mia and Lekrell Saturday afternoon.

Everything went according to plan, with the exception of E's daughter comin. Friday night was spent partying. They drank, smoke, and fuck'd the night away.

Saturday morning when Teddy got up, Ms. Porchia was walk'n thru the suite butt naked cook'n. Teddy was really feel'n himself as he started his morning with a joint.

"Baby, you ready for breakfast?" Ms. Porchia ask'd.

"It depends, if you are breakfast?"

"You didn't get enough last night?" She ask'd referring to the open buffet of pleasure pudding she served the night before. Ever since their anniversary, oral pleasure were a definite everytime intercourse was at hand.

"Please check your pager, it's been vibratin all morn'n."

"Ah-ight." Teddy said as he grabb'd his jeans from the floor check'n his pages, noticing Shanta had page'd.

"Hi long you been up and where you been?"

He ask'd as he pick'd up the phone to call Shanta.

"Why? I been up long enough to go shopp'n to make my man breakfast."

"So hi in the - ." "Shanta there?" Teddy ask'd as he held two conversations, one with Ms. Porchia and the other on the phone. Holding his finger up to Ms. Porchia as he paused, wait'n for Shanta to come to the phone. "Why da fuck you butt ass na - ."

"Whussup, you paged me?" He ask'd Shanta.

With attitude, Shanta ask'd, "What time you comin to git Mimi?"

"Why? Where da fuck you goin?" Teddy ask'd aggressively.

"Don't talk to her like that!" Ms. Porchia ordered in a low tone to a whisper.

"Teddy, why do we always have to go thru this."

She began to ask as Teddy cut her off.

"Look man –." He said, honoring Ms. Porchia's request. "Do you have a specific time you need me to be there?" He ask'd in a mild tone.

"Can you be here before 3?   And Ms. Queen call'd, she wants to take Mimi to church tomarra. I told her she would probably be with you."

"Ah-ight. Gimmie til 4 and I'll be there."

"Mimi will be here with moma if I'm gone. Are you taking her shopp'n?"

"Of course!"

"Please don't by no mo toys."

"Yeuh – right! Stop play'n! She's 1 ½ Shanta.

We taken her and Lekrell to Toy 'R Us."

"Who is we?"

"Me and Porchia."

"Porchia's with you?"          "Yeea…"

"Tell her I said hey."

"Baby, Shanta said hey."

"Hi you doin girl?" Ms. Porchia yell'd from the background.

Shanta and Ms. Porchia were finally on civil terms after a rocky start. "She chill'n." Teddy respond'd to Ms. Porchia.

"You need anything?" Teddy ask'd before getting off the phone.

Shanta only spoke of a few things Mia need'd around the house.

"I'll leave some money wit-cha mom to last a few weeks." He said as they said their goodbyes.

"Ni – why da fuck you cook'n butt ass naked and you don't have clothes on?" Teddy ask'd as he stood watch'n her from the room upstairs.

"Cause yo nasty as like to see me like this."

She said, as she glanced his way, know'n how to get a rise out of him. "Cum eat... Daddy." She ordered with a sexy smile as she put the pineapple juice on the dining table.

Teddy brushed his teeth and came down the stairs, dick swang'n. Ms. Porchia had cook'd Teddy's favorite; grits, eggs, turkey sausage, pancakes with strawberries and strawberry syrup with sliced cantaloupes.

"Can I have dessert with breakfast?" Teddy ask'd eye'n Ms. Porchia's mid/lower section.

"You nasty! Eat breakfast first."

"Me and Melanie thought it would be cool to go to the Jazz in the Park later since it's so nice outside, but it's up to you and E." Porchia stated, referr'n to E's girl.

"I'own care. I gotta pick up Mia & Lekrell by 4 or 4:30."

"So we can leave here n about 3 hours and hangout in the park for about 2 hours. Cool?"

Dat's cool." Teddy said.

They finish'd their breakfast and instantly turn'd their suite into a porn studio, lick'n, suck'n and fuck'n thru the whole spot til they collapsed on the floor in front of the fire place. As they laid cuddled in a ball of love, there was a knock at the door, "Who is it?" Teddy yell'd.

"Man, open da doe." E said with his slow, country drawl.

"Man, we naked! Hol up!" Teddy yell'd.

Ms. Porchia jump'd up and ran upstairs, dropp'n Teddy's jeans down.

"Baby, it's 1:15, I'm getting in the shower."

She said, closing the bathroom door behind her while Teddy answer'd the door in his jeans, no shirt.

"Whussup?" He said as he held the door open for E and Melanie to enter.

"Y'all worse than us." Melanie said.

"And y'all damn near live together in Greensboro." E add'd.

"Don't worry about hi we love each other. Sit-challs ass down somewhere while me and the wife git dress'd." Teddy order'd.

"Send something down to smoke Nigga."

Teddy ran upstairs, dropp'n a zip lock plastic bag full of weed down to E with a pack of Tampa Nuggets. "Roll 3." He said as he went into the bathroom to shower with Ms. Porchia. By 1:45, they were dress'd and on their way to the park. Freedom Park was pack'd, people everywhere. It was a Festival. Food booths everywhere; corn dog stands, elephant ear stands, icees, etc... They walk'd thru, sat, ate, smoked, and enjoyed the festivities while runn'n into high school classmates and friends. On the way leaving the park, they pass'd by Kenya and her boyfriend J, neither couple spoke.

As plann'd, they pick'd up Mia and Lekrell by 4:30. They shopp'd out at South Park, basically in Belk's. That's where Ms. Porchia work'd weekends in gift wrapp'n. She got 30% discount off every purchase. After shopping thru a few other stores, they took the girls to Toys 'R Us on South Blvd. and head'd back to the suites.

Arriving back at the suite about 7:15, Teddy ran thru the suite play'n with the girls while Ms. Porchia order pizza. Teddy was a good dad and uncle but Lekrell look'd at him as dad too. She never could pronounce Teddy correctly so consequently she called him Deddy which equal'd out to be Daddy. Mia 1 and Lekrell 3, they loved the time they spent with Teddy. In a lot of ways, Ms. Porchia envied Teddy's relationship with the girls but in her own way, she loved them also.

Teddy ran those girls raggedy until the pizza came. They fed them, gave them their baths, and watch'd TV with them until they went to sleep. Now it was grown up play time.

Ms. Porchia really had Teddy's nose wide open'd. It was something brand new. He loved the family orient she brought to his cipher. She completed him – so he thought.

As they laid cuddled up, Teddy fell asleep next to Ms. Porchia, honoring her value in his existence.

8:30 AM Sunday morning Teddy woke up to Mia sitt'n on his head and Lekrell yell'n. "De-ddy, De-ddy."

"Yes LaLa?" Teddy answer'd, pull'n Mia away from sitt'n up and down on his head.

"Here" Lekrell said, handing him his pager. "You pagah."

"Thank you mommy. You hungry?" Teddy ask'd as he sat up grabb'n his shorts while Ms. Porchia lay on the mattress that they slept on play'n with Mia.

"Yes." Lekrell answer'd in her soft proper tone.
"Da – I – hongey." Mia said as she look'd over her head at her daddy while Ms. Porchia changed her diaper.

Look'n at his pager, Teddy noticed his mom had paged him 911 five times from 7:15 to 8:15. He immediately grabb'd the phone to call her.

"Hey." Teddy said, "Whus wrong?"

"Where's Porchia?" She ask'd, being straight forward.

"She right here."

"I know, the Griers have been call'n here since last night, leavin messages. When I got home about a hour and a half ago, they had 15 messages on my machine. That's fuck'n ridiculous! And they were call'n when I walk'd in the door. Them people not gone worry me. Tell that girl that her dad said that he better see her before she leaves town and he knows she's still here. How? I – don't – know."

Teddy deliever'd the message to Ms. Porchia as she sat look'n like she got caught with her hand in the cookie jar.

"You got my granbabies wit-chu?"

"Yeuh, can't – chu hear'm?"

"Well, get them dress'd, I'm on my way to get them."

"Ah-ight. Love you."

"Love you too son.

Tell Porchia, I said she better call her family."

"I will Ma. Peace."

Teddy didn't know what the big deal was.

"Why yo people tripp'n?"

"Kenya's big mouth." She said as she got dress'd, "When we saw her leaving the park, she must have told my parents I was in town."

"So what is the problem?" Teddy ask'd, still confused.

"They just like to know where I am at all times."

"Git the fuck otta here!" Teddy said in disbelief.

"Where you goin? Just call them!"

"Baby, I'm gone run over there and come right back, I promise."

"Well, can you help me dress the girls right quick?

"Sure!" She said as she grabb'd Mia.

She help'd dress the babies and fed them the cantaloupe and strawberries that were left over.

"I'll be back in a few." She said as she kiss'd the girls, then kiss'd Teddy. "I Love You. Bye

Mia, bye La La." She said as she rush'd out the door.

In less than 15 minutes, Teddy's mom was there to pick up the girls. "Have my babies eat'n?" Queen ask'd.

"Gam Ma we ate shrawberries." Lekrell said.

"They ate some fruit – strawberries and canteloupes."

"Whus a matta gramma's baby?" Queen ask'd Mia as she sat in her car seat with her bottom lip poke'd out.

"Huh wont huh daddy." Lekrell said.

"Don't cry Mia, isss aw – wight."

Seconds later, Teddy was unstrap'n his daughter. By the time he could pick her up to his chest, she was cry'n like she had been bitten or pinch'd. That broke Teddy's heart. Mia was so attach'd to Teddy that she made it very hard for him to leave her unless she was asleep when he left. Queen somehow was able to calm Mia down so that they could leave, but now it was Teddy in tears. He hated being away from Mia. Before Queen and the girls left, Teddy gave his mom $500.00, a hundred for herself, a hundred for Lekrell, and three for his Mia.

Check out was at 11, there still wasn't a sign of Ms. Porchia. Teddy got a late check out which allow'd him to stay over until 6pm. E and Melanie check'd out at 11. One of E's homeboys that went to Central with him came thru. That was his ride back to school.

Teddy loved his blunts. He laid around the suite watch'n football, smoking and dosing off.

Waking up around 4:30 to his pager, think'n it was Ms. Porchia, he was piss'd off.

Instead of being Ms. Porchia, it was Fly. Teddy return'd his call. Luckily, Fly was in town and need'd some weed. When Fly came to cop, Teddy decided to ride to Salisbury and wait there and Ms. Porchia could pick him up on her way thru to Greensboro.

All throughout the day Teddy had been call'n Ms. Porchia's parent's house and receiving no answer. This last'd thru the night. To say he was worried was an understatement. He was check'n his pager to see if his battery was dead, call'n himself to make sure his coverage was straight and still no Ms. Porchia. The last effort he made to contact her was call'n her parents house at 11:30. Her mom answer'd, tell'n Teddy how disappointed they were in their decisions and actions.

Teddy stated that all he want'd to know was Porchia alright. Mrs. Grier informed him that she was back in school and her father warn'd her that if she continued to see him, he was back'n out on her tuition. Teddy found himself furious. Not at the fact of the tuition and her pop's threat but because Ms. Porchia left him ass out and didn't think enough of him to simply page him. He call'd her dorm room, when she answer'd he paused.

"Hello," the warm, sleepy voice answer'd. Still no response, "Hell-o?"

"Porchia," Teddy call'd out in low frustration.

"Oh hey, where are you?"

Teddy chuckled to cover his anger as he stood in Glover Hall, a girl's dorm at Livingston. "Where am I?" Where did you leave me at?"

"I came back by the room and they said you had check'd out."

"Porchia, don't make me cuss yo ass out! Check out was at 11am. I check'd out at 5:15pm. Why da fuck couldn't you call. I'm straight though. Fuck You!" Teddy spat thru the receiver as he smash'd it down on the hook.

His heart was hurt. Again, he found himself in uncharter'd territory. He'd never felt this way before. He was piss'd, hurt and confus'd and all he want'd to do was inflict the same pain on her.

So he began with where he was, Fly dated the baddest little short bowlegged chic on the dance squad. Teddy and Fly were at their room smoking and drink'n. Fly's girl, Tracy's roommate was after Teddy since the SWV show. Her name was Nivea. She had been basically throw'n herself at Teddy all night but the lack of know'n the whereabouts of Ms. Porchia had his whole existence under arrest. When Teddy walk'd back into the room, he was a totally different person. Fly hadn't seen this side of his friend since his high school days. Teddy sat on the bed with Niv, he whisper'd in her ear, she whisper'd in Tracy's ear and they stepp'd into the hallway.

Fly ask'd Teddy what was going on, Teddy told him he was gett'n ready to smash Niv. Fly didn't believe him until they return'd and Tracy told him to c'mon. Teddy told Fly he had to be at the train station by 9:20 and they left.

The only thing better than pussy is, new pussy. He stay'd up til 4am freak'n Niv. She was 5ft 6', chocolate, about a size 3-4 with a fat ass and bowlegs with some great pussy. Four nuts later, he was fast asleep. Tracy came in at 7:30 to her roommate givin head like she work'd for Sigmund Freud. That concluded Teddy's business in Salisbury. Fly dropp'd him off at 9:00.

Arriving in Greensboro by 10:20, Teddy caught a cab to his place to prepare for his afternoon classes. He had miss'd his two morning joints.

Leaving his last class at 5:50, Ms. Porchia walk'd up to him as he walk'd to his car.

"I'm sorry." The voice cry'd, traveling behind him. Say'n nothing, he walk'd faster to his car. "Teddy! Please talk to me? Things just got a little complicated."

Unlocking his car door, still refuse'n to look back, he replied very calmly, "Well, we don't want things to get complicated for little Ms. Porchia, do we?" He referenced as he threw his book bag in the back seat.
"Teddy, it's not like that."

"How the fuck is it then? You fuck'n left me and far as I'm concern'd, this game is over!" He express'd as he got into his car. He roll'd his window down and yell'd before he pull'd off. "When you grow up, look me up – Daddy's little girl! I got a daughter, I ain't got time to be pacify'n somebody elses." And he left her stand'n on the side of the street in tears.

## Chapter 25: Big Lies in 92

It was quite obvious that Teddy was no good at deal'n with relationship issues by the way he kept his distance from Ms. Porchia. Being a Pisces, his nature was to love inspite of conflict. Instead of conflicting with Ms. Porchia and his heart, he accept'd love from many different chics at the colleges and several local tenders.

Throughout the fall semester of 91', he rarely saw or spoke to Ms. Porchia unless they were in passing. They sexually interacted with each other whenever Ms. Porchia hormones spoke up. He couldn't deny his love for her but he also knew that if her parents want'd to play tug of war for her love, he would lose − it was apparent from her blatant disregard for him when they call'd or were in the vicinity.

Their birthdays were exactly a month away from each others. Hers was January 19th and his was February 19th. That month began a new chapter in their lives. They had put away their disagreements and Ms. Porchia decided that she didn't care what orders her parents gave or what they held over her head, she want'd to be with Teddy. So he thought.

Ms. Porchia had been work'n at Belk's in South Park Mall part time on weekends during school and full time during the summer for the past two years. She liked her job becasse she had a little inside illegal hustle. Belk's employees were entilled to a 30% discount throughout the store but every second and forth Saturday, they would open at 8 AM allow'n employees and their families to come in and purchase merchandise that was already on sale for an additional 50% - 70% off and regular merchandise 50% - 70% off.

Whereas, as a set of crystal coasters normally price'd at $150.00 on sale for half off regularly and on the 70% off table would run you $22.50. Ms. Porchia would purchase that item and take it back to a different Belk's and receive the total amount ($150.00) back for a refund. Belk's return policy was simply, have the merchandise and you could get a cash refund for the amount on the tag without a receipt as long as you had proper ID.

One day Teddy was in Belk's when Ms. Porchia was return'n some china and crystal coasters she had purchased, getting ready to move into her apartment in the summer. Teddy knew nothing about her hustle, he was simply there to purchase some clothes for Mia on her employee discount. Ms. Porchia went to Customer Service and present'd the merchandise, the cashier ask'd for her ID and Ms. Porchia remember'd that she had left it over her sun visor in the car.

The cashier told her, that's fine, we can use your husband's." Ms. Porchia ask'd Teddy did he have is license and in the blind he present'd his license to the cashier becoming a co-conspirator.

The cashier took his license, wrote down his info and gave him a full cash refund for the merchandise. Simple as that, no questions ask'd.

Fast forward to mid March of 92. Ms. Porchia had purchased a Dooney & Burke pocket book regularly priced at $325.00 for maybe $20.00. She was attempt'n to get her hustle off, when the cashier realized that the same pocket book had been out of stock for over a year after she had scann'd it, she told Ms. Porchia that they would have to send it back to the manufacturers and they would send her a check in the mail.

A month later, Ms. Porchia went to work as normal on a Saturday morning and was greet'd by the store security.

"Ms. Grier, could you please follow me?"

One of the middle aged white guards guided.

"Sure." Ms. Porchia answer'd in a puzzled tone as she follow'd the guards to a little office inside of the stock room where her boss Ms. Mildred and an older white guy in his 40's were waiting.

"Good morning Porchia." Ms. Mildred greet'd.
                    "Good morning."

"Porchia, this is Mr. Goldsmith. He's our store district manager and he as a few questions for you."

"Good morning Porchia." Mr. Goldsmith interject'd, "I'm going to keep this as brief as possible. On March 13th, you return'd a Dooney & Burke handbag that you purchased here at the employee's sale for $21.00. It was brought to our attention that you were attempt'n to get a refund for the regular ticketed price of the handbag. I also have several other receipts for your purchases that you've return'd and received full refunds – including one your boyfriend return'd for you. These are fraudulent charges.

However, Ms. Mildred ask'd that we simply terminate your employment. Here's your last paycheck, thank you for your services. Ms. Mildred, I'm done here." Mr. Goldsmith closed his folder and left the office.

Ms. Porchia sat look'n stunn'd, shock'd and embarrassed.

"Porchia, what were you think'n?" Ms. Mildred inquired. "I am so disappointed in you. I want'd to try to keep your job for you but instead I had to bust my ass to keep you from being arrest'd.

"I'm so sorry." Ms. Porchia express'd. "It just happen'd and I got carried away."

"I hope you let this be a lesson to you and you think before you do something stupid like that again."

Ms. Porchia left very confused. She immediately call'd Teddy to tell him about her brush with the law and losing her job. Teddy couldn't believe that she had it in her to attempt such a hustle. He chuckled as he realized how upset she really was.

"Porchia, you'll find another job. Don't worry about it. You betta be glad your ass didn't git arrest'd."

Teddy sarcastically sympathized with her.

"Should I tell my mom and let her call to see if she could get my job back?"

"Who da fuck is yo mom? You're grown!

Accept your mistake and find yo ass another job. Tsss." Teddy hiss'd. "Tell yo mom, that's the dumbest shit I've ever heard. I'm gone." Teddy said as he disconnect'd from her in disgust.

Instead of taking Teddy's advice, Ms. Porchia gave permission to Ms. Mildred to speak to her mom. Ms. Mildred tried to cover for Ms. Porchia by telling Mrs. Grier that Teddy had return'd the china and crystal coasters leading her to think that it was Teddy's fault that Ms. Porchia was fired. Going on to inform Mrs. Grier of an argument that took place in the parking lot between Teddy and Ms. Porchia and insinuated that Teddy was physically abusing her.

Teddy got wind of the situation when he call'd the Grier's home that evening to speak to Ms. Porchia.

Mr. & Mrs. Grier got on the phone together and Teddy sat quietly as they falsely accused him of everything from extor'n to trick'n Ms. Porchia. Once they were done, they didn't care to hear his side, they just hung up on him.

Thirty minutes later, Teddy got a call from an apologetic Ms. Porchia that he refused to accept.

As far as Teddy was concern'd, that was the straw that broke the camel's back.

"Aye look right, when you see me, go in the opposite direction. Lose my fuck'n #'s and grow the fuck up wit-cho childish simple ass!" Was whut Teddy had to say before he hung up on her.

By Wednesday, Ms. Porchia hadn't return'd back for classes after the weekend. Her roommates and suite mates were worried about her. Teddy ran into Tresa, her roommate while leaving the Student Union when she gave him the news. He couldn't fake like he didn't care, he simply told her, he would check into it when he got home.

Ironically, when he arrived home and began to listen to his answering machine, the last call was from his grandmother.

"Teddy, this is Mother. You need to call as soon as you get in. Queen and I need to speak with you about something very important."

Teddy immediately call'd his grandparents home. His mom had recently moved in with her parents to help out because they were getting older and her father's health had began to fail.

"Hello?" Queen answer'd the phone on the second ring.

"Ma! Whussup?"

"Hey Baby. Moma need you to come home for a few hours."

"When you talk'n bout, Friday?"

"No son, now."

"Whus wrong? I got to try and find out whus goin on with Porchia. I just found out she's miss'n and nobody has seen her since she left coming back to school Sunday. Is it an emergency?"

"Look. Just come on home and once we take care of this, I'll help you call around to find Porchia.

OK?"

"Ma, whut is it? Is it an emergency?"

"Yes – it is an emergency, but it's not detrimental.

"Please just come now."

"I'm on my way. See ya in a few." He said.

"Be careful. I Love You."

"I Love You Too."

Teddy wasted no time hitt'n 29S to 85S. From Groomstown Rd. to Statesville Rd, Teddy arrived in Charlotte in exactly 50 minutes flat but that was the norm. Pulling into his grandparent's driveway from the front driveway, he didn't see the surprise in the back yard.

As he got out of his car in front of the screen'd in patio, he was met by his mom and grandma.

"That don't make no earthly sense!" His grandma yell'd. "You gone kill somebody!"

"Whut Mother?" Teddy ask'd, know'n she was speak'n of his speeding.

"Boy, it takes us a hour and a half to drive to that place."

"That's cause y'all old." Teddy joked as he hugg'd his grandma.

"Come give yo moma some sugah Boy."

Queen order'd.

"All I want to know is whut's the emergency?"

Teddy ask'd as his uncle Steve came out. "Whussup Dad!?! Teddy ask'd his uncle in excitement.

"Ain't nothin, just got home from the hospital yesterday." Steve answer'd. Speak'n about his month and a half stay he had in Presbyterian Hospital, still suffer'n with Sickle Cell Anemia.

"You look good." Teddy compliment'd as they hugg'd.

"Porchia's in the house." Steve whisper'd a warn'n.

Teddy's whole expression change. Want'n to get back in his car and leave, he ask'd, "Whut's the emergency?"

"Son, we barely ever see you." Queen answer'd try'n to butter him up for what they had in store.

"Come on in the house." His grandmother order'd.

Teddy walk'd in side by side with Steve, cutt'n up like old times. Walk'n thru the kitchen to the den, he could smell her familiar scent. Soon as he walk'd thru the door of the den, there she sat on the sofa next to his grandfather's recliner with puffy swollen pink eyes.

"Whussup ole man?" Teddy spoke to his grand-pops.

"Hey son, look who's here." His grandpop's said being funny.

"Yeuh, I see." Teddy said, disregarding her presence while walk'n down the hallway to Steve's room, where he and Steve discuss'd a few things before being interrupt'd by Teddy's mom.

"Boy, Mother wants you in the living room." Queen advised.

Teddy look'd at Steve with that look as if to say, HELP. He went into the living room and stood there amongst his grandmother and Ms. Porchia sitting side by side on a pure white antique sofa that only special guest are allow'd to sit on.

"Teddy, I want you to listen to this baby." His grandmother said.

Mrs. Stacks really loved Ms. Porchia for her grandson. After all, the Stacks family was one in the same as the Griers.

Ms. Porchia began to apologize, cry and admit her wrong. She then plead'd with Teddy to take her back, stating that she would never turn her back on him again and profess'd her love for him over and over again.

Teddy gave in after a lot of begg'n and plead'n but let it be known that the games were over. Finally, they left together, Teddy follow'd her up the highway. She stay'd the night at his place while they had lustful make up sex.

All seem'd to be going too well until two months later. Ms. Porchia had moved into her new place with her roommate Neesy. They lived in a two bedroom apartment complex call'd North Winds. Teddy and Neesy's boyfriend Red had finish'd cook'n out on the grill. A good time was to be had on this Friday night. They made daiquiris and smok'd weed, listen'n to Dr. Dre's Chronic" album and play'n truth or dare. Everything was beautiful until Neesy ask'd Ms. Porshia on a truth, how old was she when she first gave oral sex? Ms. Porchia's alcohol induced truthful answer end'd what start'd out to be a good night. She answer'd, "17" after a pause for thought.

At first, her answer didn't register immediately until Neesy ask'd Ms. Porchia was she sure and she respond'd, "Yeuh, I was a junior –" and before she could finish, Teddy ask'd, "With who?" His tone must have jarr'd her memory causing her to try to cover up her unconscious truth because she answer'd in a unsure tone, "You".

Teddy spazz'd, "Bitch you ain't even know me you Jr year."

"But I – I – I." She stutter'd.

"I – ME ASS! Porchia, I'm through wit-cho lies and deceit. That was something you didn't even have to lie about. I knew that you were with dude for 2 years, I know you loved him so I knew it was possible but you lied that night of our anniversary. FOR NOTHIN! Man, I'm out! One thing after another. Whut next?" He ask'd as he gather'd his things to leave. "Latah Red." Was his last words before slamm'n the door.

Four months pass'd before they held another decent conversation because instead of Ms. Porchia just comin clean with the truth, she dismiss'd it with, she didn't remember whether she had or hadn't done it.

They ran into each other at A&T's homecoming. Teddy was high, tipsy and feel'n himself with his peeps when they stumbled into Ms. Porchia and a few of her girls. It was as if she had a root on him. "Hey Teddy." She greet'd him with a innocent smile. "You look'n good."

"Preshate it. Hi you been?" Teddy shot back.

"Could be betta, but whos' complain'n."

"I hear dat.   Aye, well y'all enjoy yourselves." Teddy said, with the intentions of makin it away without being allured into the beauty she was radiating. Ms. Porchia had her hair pull'd back in a ponytail under Teddy's black furry Kangol with some jeans fitt'n her endless curves, some black rider boots and a black w/white fur Sherlin jacket.

"Teddy, can I speak to you for a second?"

"Whussup?" He ask'd, as he approach'd her to the side while their individual friends conversed.

Look'n into his eyes as if to hypnotize him, she ask'd, "Did you love me?"

"Porchia, don't do this. I'm gone." He replied as he turn'd to walk away.

"No!" She demand'd as she grabb'd his arm.

"Answer my question, PLEASE!"

Turning to look at her, he explained, "Porchia, it's not a day that goes by that I don't think about you. Yes, I loved you and I always will, you were my first love but I ain't nobody's fool. It's always something with you."

"I know it seems that way but if you aren't seeing anybody, I need another chance. Neesy went home this weekend, come see me tonight, we'll just talk."

"I'll see. I ain't gone make no promises."

"I'll be there. I know you still got the key, use it – if you decide to come." Ms. Porchia said as she saunter'd away knowing that he would be by her side by the end of the night.

Just as the sun rises in the east and sets in the west, Teddy made his way to her side to cuddle in her nest, allow'n their relationship to move forward to another level. It was no secret that he sincerely loved and missed her. He was more than willing to give their love another chance. Even though he had plenty prospects to choose from, none of them could compete with Ms. Porchia for Teddy's heart and they all knew it.

## Chapter 26: Expect the Unxpect'd Part II

The beginning of 93' was very profitable for Teddy. He had began to not only hustle marijuana, Fleezo, and Ant'No had a coke connect that allow'd Teddy to supply them with weed in exchange for the coke. Ms. Porchia knew of Teddy's illegal dealings and she hated it, but she never said anything about it even though the word had made it to the streets of Charlotte that Teddy was one of the main marijuana distributors between Greensboro and Charlotte. Her parents had plenty to say but Ms. Porchia continued to rebel due to the fact that Teddy was supporting her and he assured her that he would drop out of school to pay her way if need be.

Mr. & Mrs. Grier constantly defamed Teddy's character from the rumors that surfaced about him. On one of Teddy's weekend runs to Charlotte, he discovered some disturb'n news of his own concern'n Mr. Grier. When Teddy arrived to deliver to one of his customers, they threw him the local and state section of the Charlotte Observer.

"What am I look'n for?" Teddy ask'd Alan. Teddy and Alan were good friends thru his man Donté.

"Yo peoples in dere."

"Who"?

"Yo fathah – in-law Nigga." He said with a chuckle.

Teddy open'd the inside of the paper to see the ad that read, "3 Kilos of cocaine found in cleaners." Was the sub-heading with a picture of "Mr. Self-Righteous", Lyndell Howard Grier himself. Teddy just smiled at his audacity.

Ms. Porchia was the last to find out. Teddy didn't want to tell her because he figured she already knew and was too embarrassed to talk about it but that wasn't the case at all.

By the middle of the following week, the news of Mr. Grier's arrest had land'd in Ms. Porchia's lap and she was damn near in shock. She brought the news up to Teddy and was sincerely disappoint'd to see that it was no surprise to him.

"How long have you known about this rumor?"

She ask'd in disbelief.

"What rumor?" Teddy shot back.

"Don't play dumb." She replied with a sarcastic smirk on her face." The rumor about my dad being arrest'd."

Teddy chuckled, "Hi you figure it's a rumor?"

"Because soon as Chasity told me after class this morning, I call'd home and he told me it was a rumor?"

"If you say so." Teddy paused, piss'd off that Mr. Grier has left Ms. Porchia in the blind like she was a kid. "What's a rumor Porchia?"

"The whole thing. There was no arrest and there was no cocaine."

"So you tell'n me Charlotte Observer prints bogus lies and stories?"

"What do you mean Charlotte Observer?"

"Porchia, it was in the newpaper last Friday, he got arrest'd Thursday afternoon."

"How do you know?" She question'd.

"Baby, I saw it and I got the article in the car." He explain'd with regret.

"So, you knew and didn't say shit?" She ask'd feel'n betray'd.

"Hold up!" Teddy demand'd in a challenging tone. "That shit ain't none – a – my business! I thought you knew and was too embarrass'd to talk about it. I felt like if I brought it up, you would have thought I was throw'n it in your face."

She immediately soften'd her tone and began to speak display'n her pain. "No, I didn't know. Chasity caught me after class and ask'd me, was daddy alright? I didn't know why he wouldn't be so I said, 'yeuh he's fine, why?' and she told me that her mom told her to make sure I was alright. I ask'd her why wouldn't I be and that's when she start'd talk'n about cocaine, arrest, and lawyers. So I stop'd her and ask'd who got caught with coke, got arrest'd and need'd a lawyer. That's when she told me what she knew.  You got the article?" She stop'd and ask'd.

Teddy hate'd being the one to confirm her nightmare. "Yeuh, it's out there." He answer'd, not want'n to really get involved.

"Will you get it for me please? I know he didn't just straight out lie to me?" She question'd out loud.

ISN'T THIS IRONIC? Teddy thought. "Yeuh, I'll go get it." He respond'd as he walk'd out of the door.

As Teddy return'd with the article, Ms. Porchia sat wait'n. Teddy gave her the article and sat across from her on the love seat. Soon as she read enough, she blurt'd out, "I can't believe he lied to me like that."

Humbly, Teddy replied, "I'm sorry he did that, but now you see how it feels to have somebody you love and trust lie to you. He probably want'd to protect you, that's all." He ration'd.

"Mmm Hmm." She mumbled, as she stared at the article with pain in her eyes. "I ain't no muthafuck'n chap to be protect'n! I'm 21 years old! If he fuck'd up, he fuck'd up! Don't try to lie about it! Coward!" She yell'd, as she express'd herself.

Teddy sat mad at Chasity, "Chasity talk too much!"
"Don't blame her, she was being a friend."

"A nosey friend! That's people's problems today, don't know how to tend to their own business."

Ms. Porchia and Chasity grew up together. They were neighbors and their families were close.

Ms. Porchia call'd home and blast'd everybody. Then she call'd Kenya and gave her a piece of her mind. From that day forward, she didn't care what they had to say about Teddy, she rebelled.

Soon as school end'd, Teddy's lease was up and he want'd his own place without roommates but Ms. Porchia had another idea. By June, Teddy had moved in with Ms. Porchia, Neesy and Red.

Red was younger than Teddy by five years but he was bout his business and Teddy loved that.

Plus, by him having Neesy that remind'd Teddy of himself back in the day with older chics. Red was a work'n dude but he would cop work from Teddy every now and then. He was from Greensboro – The Grove. Even though he was young, he held his own. Red had plenty of chics and when Ms. Porchia and Neesy wasn't around or took weekend trips home, he and Teddy turn'd into men whores. That last'd throughout the summer.

By the middle of September, Neesy had an announcement to make. Neesy and Red were expect'n a child in April.

When Neesy told Ms. Porchia and Teddy about her pregnancy, Ms. Porchia possessed a look of jealousy that was so obvious that Teddy and Neesy ask'd her was she alright. While Teddy was congratulating them, Ms. Porchia was off into a daze. Finally, she came out of lah – lah land and gave this half ass, "I'm happy for y'all."

That day was crazy for Teddy, Neesy and Red left that afternoon going to Neesy's hometown to tell her parents their news and Ms. Porchia attack'd Teddy as soon as they left. They began in the living room on the floor and ended up in their bedroom. Ms. Porchia back'd her ass up like it was a dump truck and dropp'd her snotty, wet load on Teddy's dick, using her vaginal muscles on him as if they were in a fucking wrestling match. This was the freakiest and horniest Teddy had ever experienced her and he was thoroughly enjoying it, until he felt himself about to release his love juices. "Oh − shit! Ssss. I'm − cumm'n." Teddy express'd as he began to throb inside of her.

Ms. Porchia look'd over her shoulder as Teddy felt her pussy contracting. "Baby, I'm − bout − ta − ssss − nut on − ssss − oh shit! Cumm in this pussy." She said as she took him all the way inside of her. As she began to nut and Teddy join'd her, Ms. Porchia began to beg in tears while they orgasm'd, "Nut in me! Baby, please nut in me! I want your child! This your pussy! Put your child inside me."

Ms. Porchia had never express'd her desire for a child before and Teddy was really confused. That orgasm was so incredible for Teddy that he continued without needing recovery time. He slid from under Ms. Porchia and began to pound her from behind doggy style until they reach'd yet another orgasm together. That one took the cake, they both pass'd out until later that evening.

Teddy never acknowledged Ms. Porchia's request to go half on a little one but for the next few weeks, Ms. Porchia continued to non-stop freak Teddy out of his mind.

The holidays began to come around. Teddy doesn't celebrate but they were inseperable. This was the closet they had been since they first got together 2 ½ years ago. Instead of going to Charlotte for Thanksgivin, they stay'd in Greensboro. Teddy display'd his cook'n skills for

Ms. Porchia by cook'n the complete Thanksgivin meal complete with homemade desserts.

It didn't stop there, they studied together, ate together, anybody on the outside look'n in would think that a wedding was in the making. Teddy handled his street business but he made sure to make it to Ms. Porchia's bed by 10:30 every night.

Ms. Porchia let it be known to her family that if Teddy wasn't invited, then she wouldn't be home for Christmas. He really didn't care to be around her family though, but on Christmas Day he and Timia went thru for a few hours. There was very little you could do to separate them. Teddy stay'd in a hotel room as he normally does when he comes to Charlotte.

Even though she spent all of the day and majority of the night with him, she end'd their Christmas vacation in Charlotte the day after.  Ms. Porchia was a teacher's aide and Teddy was self-employed so they spent every day leading up to New Years cuddling and eating. Anything Ms. Porchia ask'd for, if Teddy wasn't cook'n it, he was order'n it, if he wasn't order'n it, they were goin out to get it.

December 31st, early Thursday morning, Teddy and Ms. Porchia had just finish'd attack'n each other when Ms. Porchia jump'd out of bed runn'n to the bathroom. She gave up everything she had consumed the night before. Teddy rush'd to her side as she gripp'd the toilet like a drunk begg'n GOD to give'm another chance. They tried to figure out the cause, remembering everything they ate the night before.

Teddy fell asleep only to be awaken by Ms. Porchia on her knees cry'n and throw'n up at the toilet. He got dress'd and help'd Ms. Porchia clean up and get dress'd and took her straight to the MOSE'S CONE HOSPITAL ER. She regurgitated the whole way there in a bag. Once she was being seen, the nurse took her vitals and also the bag of her guts to be test'd. The nurse ask'd the last time she had her menses. Ms. Porchia explain'd that she had been irregular since she had tumors removed from her ovaries a year ago.

The nurse took a urine sample and ask'd her what was the last thing she ate before she left the two of them in the room. Ms. Porchia continued to throw up as they wait'd. When Teddy wasn't by her side rubb'n her head and back, he was going thru the cabinets and drawers. Finally, the Dr. enter'd after about 40 minutes. Doc was tall, slim, white cat with wire rim glasses hang'n on his nose. He was in his late 40's, early 50's with his sunroof back (he had no hair in the middle of his head).

"Ms. Porchia Grier, I'm Dr. Weiten. We ran some test and you don't have food poisoning but you are a couple of months pregnant." He look'd over his glasses with a smile.

"Congratulations."

"I think I'm going to be sick." Teddy stated, holding his stomach.

"I take it you're the father." Doc said, reach'n out to shake Teddy's hand.

Teddy stood speechless in lah – lah land as Ms. Porchia did at the news of Neesy's pregnancy while shaking Doc's hand.

"Yes he is." Ms. Porchia answer'd the Dr.'s question for Teddy.

"Oh – yes Sir Doc. Pardon my manors."

"Don't worry. You look like you just saw a ghost. Are you ok Mr. _____ "Massey".

Teddy Massey. I'm alright, just a little shock'd that's all."

"Well mommy to be, I'm prescribing you a little something for the nausea. Morning sickness is to be expect'd and it could last throughout the day for the next few weeks but what you need to do is see an obstetrician for some thorough prenatal care. I don't see no need to keep you here, so you're free to go.

Take it easy pop's." The Dr. joked as he released Ms. Porchia.

Teddy assist'd gently the woman carrying his next child to the car. He couldn't believe what had just taken place. As they drove home, hand in hand, Teddy start'd to put it all together. THAT'S WHY I'M HOME AND IN THE BED BY 10:30 OR 11 EVERYNIGHT. He thought. I HOPE IT'S A BOY!" ALLAH, just let it be healthy." He silently pray'd.

At that moment, Teddy's love for Ms. Porchia reach'd a whole nother plateau.

"When are you tell'n your parents?"

"I'm not in no rush." She respond'd but soon as they walk'd in the door, she call'd Teddy's mom and grandma. They are all close, they couldn't wait to spoil her.

The day before Ms. Porchia's 22nd birthday, January 18th she went to her first Dr's appointment. Teddy was right by her side. They did a ultrasound to find out how far along she was and to find out when she was due. July 15th was her due date and she was well on her way thru a healthy pregnancy.

Although Ms. Porchia was content with her parents not knowing, Teddy began to notice that she was avoiding them. It was February 19th, Teddy's 23rd born day. He did the math and realized what she had done. Before she told her parents about the baby, she want'd to be far enough along that an abortion was out of the question. Teddy told her she had to stop avoid'n them and let them know. He also offer'd to talk to them by himself.

At this point, Ms. Porchia only cared about Teddy and their unborn child. Instead of going to her parents or ever speak'n to them personally, she told them on their answer'n machine.

In no time flat, all hell broke loose.

The Griers were try'n to set up all kinds of meetings and Ms. Porchia had rebell'd and refused to be a part of any meeting.  As far as she was concern'd, the only meet'n that need to be held was the meet'n about her baby shower and she didn't need to be there.

The Grier's contact'd Ms. Queen and ask'd her to talk Teddy into meeting with them ASAP. Teddy agree'd but on his time which was a month later.

When Teddy arrived, he could tell that they were desperate about whatever it was they want'd because they were unusually cordial, offer'n drinks, food and small talk. After Teddy denied all offers, Mr. Grier in his feminine soprano voice cut thru the chase. "Teddy, when is my daughter due?"

"In July." Teddy answer'd in short.

His answer startled the odd couple as he could tell by their expressions.

"Y'all aren't ready for a child together. You already have Timia, how are you going to provide for another child?"

"WHOA! That's all y'all call'd me over here for, to question me about how I'm going to take care of my children. With all due respect Mr. & Mrs. Grier, I don't only take care of my daughter, but I take care of yours too while I pay my own way thru college." Teddy calmly explain'd.

His answer cut like a knife so Mr. Grier out of anger, lash'd out, "I got $10,000 right here, right now for you if you ask Porchia to have an abortion. And if she does, we won't ever try to come between y'all again."

"First of all, I don't want or need your money. Second she's too far along."

"I have a place that goes up to six months."

"Aye look right." Teddy said as he sat up, "Y'all some sick folks. But I tellya what I'mma do." He stood up, "keep ya money, I'm gone run your generous offer across your daughter. If she accepts, I'll be back for the money and you can have her back too, but make it $20,000 for my pain and anguish. If she doesn't accept, y'all leave us alone to raise our child together. This meet'n is finish'd. I'll let myself out." Teddy taunted as he walk'd towards the door.

"Y'all have a nice day."

Soon as he got into his car and began to drive down Cove Creek, he pick'd up his cell phone and call'd Ms. Porchia. He told her word for word what was said and they both had a good laugh. Ms. Porchia told him that he should have taken the money and told them that he tried.

They laugh'd some more at their uncouth audacity.

## Chapter 27:  A Life 4 A Life

Pregnancy had a radiant effect on Ms. Porchia's already gorgeous skin tone and she wore her pregnancy well. Teddy had her spoil'd. He dropp'd out of school to be at her every beck and call. Their love was self-evident.

On this rainy April spring day, Ms. Porchia and Teddy had a Dr.'s appointment to see what the gender of their child to come would be. They had several discussions of whether or not they want'd to know in advance but since Teddy's uncle Steve had it in his head that it was a boy from day one, that really ignited curiosity in Ms. Porchia.

As they enter'd their Dr.'s office, there were several expectant mothers wait'n with their significant others, a few with friends for support and a few sat by themselves. Teddy vow'd to be by Ms. Porchia's side from beginning to end.

They sign'd in and took a seat. Moments later, the receptionist call'd Ms. Porchia for a urine sample.  Just as she sat comfortably in Teddy's arms, the nurse enter'd the waiting room with her chart.

"Ms. Porchia Grier," she call'd. "Follow me."

Ms. Porchia and Teddy stood hand in hand and follow'd the short, petite, African American, mid 30ish lady. Quite noticeably, they could see her perfectly, round derriere and wide spread hips as she switched from side to side escorting them to their room. TEDDY BETTA NOT BE WATCH'N HER ASS, Ms. Porchia thought. DAMN, SHE GOT A PHAT ASS! Teddy thought as Ms. Porchia squeezed his hand as if she heard his thoughts.

"Right this way." She said, pointing into the little room. "I need you to strip down to the gown right there on the bed and the Dr. will be in soon." She inform'd, as she left closing the door.

Teddy sat in the chair beside the bed as Ms. Porchia undress'd, put on the gown and sat awaiting her obstetrician. Minutes late, Dr. Barnes enter'd the room.

"Good morning." He greet'd, with a smile. "So we're doing your monthly exam and checking to see if the little one will be 'daddy's little girl' or 'moma's boy'. He said as he look'd thru her chart.

"How's everything going Porchia?"

"We're fine, jus gett'n big."

"You haven't seen nothing yet. How's Dad?" He ask'd, Teddy.

"Long as they're alright Doc, I'm great. Every night she has to have Breyer's butter pecan ice cream with a Mc'Donald's apple pie."

"Oh, it gets worst, trust me. Porchia I need you to lay back and put your feet in the stirrups. "He said as he rolled around on the roller stool grabb'n rubber gloves. "I have to check the placenta."

Dr. Barnes was older, maybe early 60's with a short greyish fro display'n his Indian and African roots. He stood about 6ft2' with a medium to heavy build. His hands were the size of a quarterback, Teddy noticed as he slid his hands in the gloves preparing to insert two to three of his huge fingers into Ms. Porchias' vagina.

Teddy respect'd Dr. Barnes and his job but that didn't stop him from dislike'n another man touch'n his woman. He attempt'd to read a book while Dr. Barnes did his examination but he couldn't help notice'n Ms. Porchia frown'n face as Doc enter'd her. DOC, IF I THOUGHT YOU WAS ENJOY'N YOSELF, I WOULD FUCK YOU UP! were Teddy's thoughts before being interrupt'd.

"Porchia, everything looks good. The nurse will be in to do your ultra sound and I'll see you in my office before you leave." Dr. Barnes said, interrupt'n Teddy's torturous thoughts.

"Thank you Dr. Barnes." Ms. Porchia said as he walk'd out of the room.

Less than five minutes later, the same nurse that lead them to the room enter'd to do the ultrasound.  She put on her rubber gloves, grabb'n a clean folded sheet and put it across Ms. Porchia's waist and pull'd her gown up to her breast exposing her stomach and began to massage it with a flat face, short hand held wand. The wand was connect'd to a computer like screen that display'd static look'n images that she described all the body parts of the fetus and also allow'd them to hear the baby's heartbeat. Her diagnosis was, they were having a girl. Ms. Porchia was so excited, while Teddy was happy but hopin for a boy. He already had two girls.

Once they were home, Teddy call'd Steve to tell him that his prediction was off and inform'd him that they were having a girl. Steve was in the hospital raise'n hell, tell'n them the Dr. didn't know shit. Teddy gave Ms. Porchia the phone and left the room while they argued back and forth.

Two days later, Steve call'd back to let Teddy know that he was going home Saturday morning. Teddy wasn't home but when he enter'd the door, Ms. Porchia order'd him to get the phone. "Teddy, it's Steve. Tell your crazy uncle that we're having a girl." She said as she pass'd him the cordless.

"Boy, whussup?" Teddy inquired.

"Maaan, jus ready to go to da crib. You comin home this weekend?"

"Yeea, iss Spring Fest so we comin down to party."

"Jus bring my usual." Steve order'd, speak'n of his usual weed request.

"Ah-ight, I'm gone try to git there early enough to pick you up from the hospital. I'll let — chu know."

"Ah-ight. Tell Porchia I said take care of my nephew."

"I will. Take care." Teddy said, hanging up the phone, chuckling at Steve and Ms. Porchia's feud. "Bay-bee, Steve said, take care of his nephew." He joked.

"You laugh'n, but you believe him and you was there."

"That's between ya'll. Me and my baby ain't got nothing to do with all that, we jus try'n to be healthy."

"WHATEVA!" She yell'd.

Saturday morning April 30th, Teddy was on the phone with his mom discuss'n his trip to Charlotte. Teddy told his mom he was getting up so that he could get on the highway because he was pick'n Steve up from the hospital.

"Ma, call Steve's room on 3-way for me."

"Boy,  Steve probably gone already."

"Jus call'm Ma, I told him I would pick him up if he was still there when I got in town. I'll be there in a hour 30 minutes."

"Hold on boy, you git on my nerves. You can't never jus talk to yo Moma."

"Jus call'm." Teddy order'd jokingly.

She click'd over and dail'd the #, when she return'd, the line was busy.

"Teddy, the line busy baby." She said as she dismiss'd the other line. "I'll call'm back in a minute."

They continued to talk for a few minutes while she continued to call periodically only to receive busy signals.

"Ma, I'm gone. I'll see you later today. Tell Steve I'll be there by 12."

"Hold on baby, my other line is beep'n." She add'd, before click'n over to the other line. Moments later, she return to the other line cry'n uncontrollably. "Teddy, he's dead! Oh my GOD – my brother is dead!" She wail'd.

Teddy's heart began to beat severly fast as he listen'd to his mom in mourn'n. "Who Moma!?! Teddy ask'd.

## "ST – ST – STEE – VIE!"

Teddy was no more good. Ms. Porchia grabb'd the phone to find out why Teddy was cry'n so uncontrollably scream'n "Nooo, nooo, noooh." Ms. Porchia immediately got off of the phone and went to comfort Teddy as she held his head in her bosom. She hated see'n her man so lost and weak in spirit. As she rock'd back and forth trying to alleviate some of his pain, her own tears fell as she felt her own pain of losing Steve.

At that moment, Ms. Porchia and their unborn child became Teddy's whole world. Steve was more than Teddy's uncle, he was in alottaways like his Pop's but more like his brother. Teddy was never really close to Queen because she always show'd favoritism to Shan and as adults, Shan and Teddy were at best – enemies. Steve and Teddy were the critically acclaim'd Black Sheeps of their family.

Steve's death did something damaging to Teddy. After the initial shock of his death, Teddy never shed'd another tear. He didn't attend the wake, he knew that their family would find a way to embarrass the dead so he held his own personal celebration of his life with a few friends that he knew loved Steve and he loved them.

At the funeral, Teddy sat on the front row with his grandparents and Steve's stepson Ricky minus Ms. Porchia. Her mom's graduation was at the same time as Steve's funeral and in classic fashion, Mrs. Grier made a big issue out of Ms. Porchia not being in attendance. Teddy left it up to her to decide which one was of more importance and resent'd her for not being there to support him and giving her farewell to Steve considering how close they were.

Not even a month later, Mrs. Grier and Kenya organized her baby shower. It was pink and yellow. Teddy had began to distance himself from Ms. Prochia and her family. He had took on a full-time job at Advanced Home Care delivering hospital equipment and medication to Hospice patients.

Teddy had moved Ms. Porchia from North Winds to Aspen Woods. After Neesy had her baby, the lease was up so they all went their separate ways. Since Teddy was rarely at home and the Dr. had put Ms. Porchia on bed rest, she ask'd Chasity to move in. Chasity was cool. She fuck 90% of Teddy's friends that start'd out with Steve.

July 15th came and went and still no baby. She had her by-weekly Dr.'s appointment on August 10th, Dr. Barnes assured them that if she made it to her next appointment, he would induce labor. Every since her initial due date, Teddy had been makin Ms. Porchia walk two plus miles a day.

The following week, Teddy had got fifty pounds of chocolate tie in. He had his honey Jap wait'n on twenty. Biggie Smalls was in town perform'n at club DYH. That Friday afternoon, Mat from Manhattan was having a cookout for Biggie at his spot. Teddy was Mat's main man. They threw parties together and he purchased tree's from Teddy.

At the cookout, Teddy got a hold of Biggie's demo before Ready To Die debut'd. "GIMME DA LOOT" had Teddy so open'd that he didn't even stay for the party at DYH. He went to pick up Fly at his girlfriend's spot and they hit 85 South goin to Charlotte to git some of dat loot Biggie was speak'n of. By the time Teddy and Fly got there and check'd into a suite at the Embassy to set up shop, Chasity call'd say'n Ms. Porchia was in labor.

When Jap arrived, Donté, Fly, and Teddy were extremely high but Teddy had to get right back on the highway. He left the suite to Donté and Jap. Teddy and Fly hit the highway arriving at the Women's Hospital in Greensboro in exactly one hour just to find out that it was a false alarm.

Aug. 22nd after Ms. Porchia's by-week'ly appointment, as promised, Dr. Barnes admitted Ms. Porchia to the maternity ward. He immediately broke her water. She was in labor for 27 hour before she began to have complications. They baby's heartbeat began to decrease. Dr. Barnes order'd an immediate cesarean section.

Ms. Porchia was rush'd to the operating room. Teddy scrubb'd up and follow'd with his camcorder in hand prepared to film his daughter's entry to the world. Hours prior, Ms. Porchia got an epidural shot that had her numb from the waist down. Everybody was extremely worried. Mrs. Grier arrived right before they took Ms. Porchia back. Some people don't get it, she came in giving orders until the nurses inform'd her that she couldn't be in the delivery room and if she continued to give them a hard time, she would be ask'd to leave.

Approximately 15 minutes later, Ms. Porchia gave birth to a 9 pound 13 ounce baby man. He was huge! The nurses clean'd the baby up and grabb'd the camcorder as Teddy cut the umbilical cord. Teddy was the happiest dad. With all the excitement and disbelief, Teddy took his son to meet his mommy.

"Tell mommy hi Nu-Nu." Teddy told his son.

Exhausted from the intense labor, Ms. Porchia spoke to her son. "Hey there. You almost kill't mommy." She said as she blink'd, releasing a tear, "If only your uncle Steve were here to see you."

The nurse instruct'd Teddy to follow her to the nursery. Teddy carried his son passing Mrs. Grier on the way to the nursery.

"Can I please see? That's my grandchild." Mrs. Grier ask'd and before Teddy could respond, the nurse intervened.

"Sorry ma'am, not now."

As bad as Teddy wont'd to keep walk'n, being the proud father, he stopp'd and uncover'd his face for a quick second allow'n Mrs. Grier a peak at her grandson. Once they were inside the nursery, they weigh'd, measured and wash'd him. They also gave him his shots which piss'd Teddy off that he had to stand by and watch them hurt his newborn son.

Teddy left to go change clothes and call his family and friends. When he return'd, Steezo, Ant'No, and Shine met him back at the hospital with "IT'S A BOY" cigars. Kenya was also there with her mom. Ms. Porchia was breast feeding their bundle of joy when Mrs. Grier stated that they should name him after Mr. Grier. Teddy disregard'd her "REQUEST" with a joke of his own, "If he wants a son to carry his name, yall betta git ta work."

Everybody in the room laugh'd with the exception of Mrs. Grier and Kenya. Ms. Porchia had just finish'd feeding him and pass'd him to Teddy. Teddy sat analyzing and adoring his son, noticing certain specifics they shared like, his curly hair, wide nose and features they didn't share, like his greenish grey eyes. He could have easily be mistaken for a white baby, that's how bright he was.

Ms. Porchia took a turn for the worst two days later. Right after they named him (Teddy

Bernard Massey) and Teddy sign'd his birth certificate, they began to take Ms. Porchia's vitals before releasing her when they realized she had a fever of 102.3 and her blood pressure was extremely high. They decided to keep her and run some test. Due to her carrying him over the term, his weight was too big for her frame which push'd her intestines back causing her to retain fluids that would normally pass with child birth. Ms. Porchia end up staying in the hospital for two more weeks. Lil Teddy was released after a week to Big Teddy. He had to go purchase all new clothes for his son due to the assumption he was a girl. Teddy took him home in a Dallas Cowboys onesie.

Queen came to town to assist with Lil Teddy so that Big Teddy could stay at the hospital with Ms. Porchia. Finally, the swelling went down and they were able to go home and be a family.

.

## Chapter 28: Issues

Lil Teddy brought life full circle for his dad. Teddy made it to a point to spoil Lil Teddy and Ms. Porchia. After Lil Teddy was born, Teddy made sure Timia came up at least once or twice a month and most of the summer. It was important to Teddy that his children were raised together.

Due to Ms. Porchia complication, Teddy end'd up losing his job while being home caring for her and Lil Teddy but he compensated by increasing his customers and promoting parties.

Increasing customers meant meet'n new people. One of Teddy's main business associates in Charlotte (Allan) introduced him to one of his loyal customers (Rob). Allan made the connection because he couldn't fill his orders. Teddy and Rob had done severe business throughout '94. Rob was one of Teddy's most lucrative customers. Not because he had money to purchase but because he was link'd to plenty of real live dope boys that loved to purchase plenty trees and with Teddy's prices, it wasn't half bad being a middle man. Come to find out, Rob was Lamont's bestfriend. Lamont, Ms. Porchia's ex.

Five days before Teddy's 24th birthday, Rob pop's up in Greensboro with his brotha-in-law wanting 10 pounds. Rob had access to call Ms. Porchia's house being that they knew each other.

He called her house because Teddy had left his cell phone, he only used it on weekends and when he was handling business. It was neither, so he left it home on the charger and carried his burn out phone.

Teddy was at one of his home girls crib in Mallard Lakes getting his hair braided when Ms. Porchia page'd him. When he return'd her call, she gave him the # to where Rob was call'n from. Teddy hit Rob to see what his business was. He told Rob to meet him close to his crib.

Even though Rob knew Ms. Porchia, and Teddy knew his every where-about, Teddy still never allow'd him to their place. Since Rob was in town to purchase 10 lbs, he told Teddy to throw him 10 and he would come back Friday with the loot. Instead of sending 10, Teddy ask'd Rob would it be cool if he cop'd a ride back with him and his brotha-in-law cause he had some extra business in the QC and he'd make it worth his wild. Rob didn't hesitate on that deal, but wonder'd why Teddy didn't drive.

Teddy had just re'ed up. He took 30 pounds and 4 ½ ounces of coke. Ant'no and Teddy's man Price had a crib in Forest Grove that was a gold mine. Being that Steezo and Ant'No was from Brooklyn, they named the money spot in Forest Grove "FORT GREEN" after Fort Green Projects up top. They in turn call'd their crew the "FORT GREEN FAM." Before Teddy left town, he got Rob to take him by the Fort to pick up one of his girls for protection. Protection meaning Stacy, Ms. 380 or Shine, Baby 9. He chose Shine and hit the highway.

There was always more money to be made in his hometown than he initially came for, that's why he load'd up on this two day trip. It was a brisk Wednesday night. When they arrived in town, Teddy told Rob to take him to get a hotel. Rob insist'd that he stay at his place. For some odd reason, Teddy had a little trust in Rob. Not enough to allow him to his home but enough to drive him around and post up at his spot.

Teddy had a plan lay low at Rob's allow'n a few cats to come thru Wednesday night. Thursday afternoon, take 5 pounds over to his home girl's spot in Parker Heights. Theresa sold break downs for him. Then Friday morning, take Mia some money and balloons by her school and hit the highway by early noon.

Wednesday night, Teddy sat at Rob's spot gambling with Rob and a few of his homeboys that came thru to purchase. Tunk and spades were the games. Outside of gett'n rid of the bulk of the trees he came with, Teddy had made a small fortune. He was feel'n himself. Teddy always kept a fifth of Corvoursier at all times with him and since Steve's death, he had acquired an extreme coke habit. Smokin trees, snort'n poweder, shot'n liquor straight from the bottle and chunk'n was the nights starter festivities.

Rob got a call then pull'd Teddy to the front room to ask him did he mind if Lamont came thru, he want'd weed and coke. Teddy didn't give a fuck but he sober'd up a bit and made sure Shine was cock'd and by his side. Fifteen minutes later, Lamont arrived with yet another big ass football play'er look'n nigga. Rob and Lamont play'd football together at Olympic, Teddy's guess was, most of these lame ass jock dudes play'd together in high school.

After Teddy did his business with Lamont, the tough guy with him want'd to try his luck at the tunk table. From the looks of things, he was the one with the change because soon as he sat at the table, he act'd like $50.00 a hand was pennies until Teddy told him to call the pot. Everybody was enjoy'n themselves before MR. BIG STUFF arrived.

"Two hunnit a hand." Mr. Big Stuff propos'd.

"Fuck it!" Teddy said, place'n two hundred in the middle of the table and another two on the side.
         "Two on high spade."

Rob's brotha-in-law stay'd in the game but the other cat excused himself, let'n them know that their taste was too expensive for him.

Mr. Big Stuff and Kev (Rob's brotha-in-law) stack fifty's and hundreds on top of Teddy's while the others watch'd from the side line. You would have thought Teddy had a rabbit in his pocket, out of seven games, he won five. Two tunk hands, a 49 off the deal and 2 drops, winning four of the side bets. When Teddy didn't win, Kev did.

Teddy wasn't talk'n shit, taunt'n or nothing, he had on his game face. Mr. Big Stuff kept makin little sly comments throughout the games that Teddy simply ignored. Mind you, everybody in the spot is at least 6ft2 except Teddy and Kev. Kev was about 5ft10. Teddy excused himself to the half bath right next to the kitchen where they were gambling at. Mr. Big Stuff's back was to the bathroom door. While Teddy was relieving himself, he could her Mr. Big Stuff's mouth.

"Fuck dat bitch ass nigga! Everytime he kiss that bitch, he suck'n my nigga's dick." You could hear Rob and Lamont try'n to shut dude up. "Rob, you remember when the coach caught dat bitch suck'n Mont's dick in the locker room? Ni this sucka fa love ass nigga got a baby by dat bitch."

A good night just turn'd bad. Teddy pull'd Shine out, click'd the safely off just in case dude was wait'n for him on the other side of the door. Rob was tell'n dude to leave while Lamont was plead'n with him to come on when Teddy open'd the bathroom door.

Mr. Big Stuff simply underestimated Teddy because when Teddy came out, he was still seat'd with his back to the bathroom door. As his body shift'd to the right in his chair, turning to face

Teddy, he was met up close and personal by Shine coming at approximately 30 mph. POW!!!! The gun went off as it slamm'd against his nose. Blood splash'd everywhere and huge bodies duck'd, jump'd and leap'd to the floor as Mr. Big Stuff's limber body collapsed onto the kitchen table. Teddy still as calm as if nothing happen'd.

"Whut-chall niggas all in the flo for?" Teddy calmly ask'd, "Yo Lamont man, git-cha dude bafo he bleed to death."

Mr. Big Stuff laid face first on the table top in a puddle of his blood dripp'n to the floor, totally out.

"Is he dead?" Lamont ask'd in a humble tone.
"I ain't shoot da nigga. Da gun just went off when I hit'm cause I was hold'n the trigga. Somebody git me da fuck outta here." Teddy said nonchalantly.

"C'mon T, I got-chu. Les go!" Kev said as everybody began movement except Teddy's victim.

Kev and Rob help Teddy gather everything quickly as possible before the cops came because Milton Rd. apartments was known to Keep the Police cruise'n thru. Teddy got everything including the six pounds Mr. Big Stuff had already paid for. On his way out the door, Teddy caught eye to eye contact with Lamont sending him a telepathic message, I'M GONE KILL YOU AND YO MAN.

"Teddy, I didn't have nothing to do with that." Rob shot.

"Well, hi he know all my business Lamont?" Teddy sent a lip cock smirk." I'mma see ya." He said, as he shot him a wink and walk'd out.

"T, call me when you git where you goin." Rob shout'd. Teddy didn't respond. He follow'd Kev to his car in a hurry noticing Rob's neighbors peek'n out of windows. As they pull'd out of the complex, they rode pass fly'n police cars with their sirens full blast turn'n off of the Plaza onto Milton Rd. Kev was smart, he turn'd down Cove Creek and end'd up on N. Tryon St. next to the bowl'n alley.

"Kev, you can just take me to get a room." Teddy said as his mind raced between Ms. Porchia's lies and whether that stray bullet hit somebody in the next apartment or something.

Teddy decided to stay at the Hilton in University Place. Riding down N. Tryon toward University Place, he was quiet and reserved as he stared out the window with his arm rest'n on the door and his forehead rest'n between his thumb and his fingers, feel'n betray'd. Betray'd by Ms. Porchia for lying and by Rob for putt'n his business out.

"T, you straight ova there?" Kev inquired with concern in his tone.

"I'm straight. It's always somethin."

"Well let me be the first to tell you, you handle'd yo bizzniss. If it had been me, I'd probably be face'n a life sentence. Pon is a big ass knuckle head that ain't never grow up. He pussy. He only tried you cause you smaller and believe it or not, he ain't got no straighten'n.

Kev was older, mid 30's, from North Charlotte. He knew the game all too well but had escaped it. Now he was married to Rob's older sister, had 3 kids, work'd at Coca Cola and hustled a little weed at his job and throughout his old neighborhood.

"Man, niggas gossip like ho's. Why Rob put my business out there? Whut part-a-da game is dat?"

"T, niggas be envious and jealous of shit dey can't figure out. You doin it! I respect the fact that you didn't take niggas to yo crib. That says a lot about you. Fuck what dem niggas talk about. When it comes time to cop, you da connect. Fuck dem niggas, keep doing whut-chu doin."

Teddy mainly listen'd as they pull'd into the park'n lot of the hotel. He ran in, paid for his room and came back.

"Kev, I got a extra six pounds you can have back here." Teddy said with a chuckle.

"Whut-chu want fo'em?"

"Dem you."
"Whut-chu mean dey me?"

"On da house nigga. Purchase 10 git 6 free. A Teddy one time special."

"Nah Boy, I pay my way. Whut-chu want back?" Kev was a G. Teddy knew he wasn't taken'm for free.

"Bring me $1,800.00." Teddy told him, know'n that he would take that deal

"I'll see you tamarra. You gone be here?"

"Yeea, I'm pretty sure. Here's my pager #."

Teddy said as he hand'd him a business card.
"You want Rob to know where you at?"

"I'll probably call him tamarra cause I need a ride back Friday. Jus keep it to yoself where I'm at."

"I can dig it. Git-chu some rest."

"Pre-shate it Kev.

PEACE."

Teddy close his car door and went to his room. His first order of business was to call Ms. Porchia.

When he told her what happen'd, he could hear her snifflin. He sarcastically ask'd her did she still not remember. She sobb'd uncontrollably until Teddy scream'd, "Fuck You!" in the phone and hung up on her.

He contact'd Teresa, let'n her know what time he was coming to drop and pick up. She alert'd him that her kids had chicken pox and she couldn't do it but she had somebody that she could get to do it.

The next day about 4:20pm, Teddy call'd Teresa to see who she had set up for him. It turn'd out to be this young 19 year old chic name Diane that use to ride Teddy's school bus. She has always been around Teresa when Teddy comes to hang out and smoke or make a drop.

However, Teddy never like'd her fass ass. She had a two year old daughter and thought that made her grown. To top it off, she was a stripper. Teresa had a hard time convincing Teddy but it was either her or nobody. He finally agreed.

"Tell her to be at-cho crib and ready in an hour."

Teddy call'd Rob to come get him. Rob was there in no time, ready to redeem himself, think'n he had lost Teddy as a connect. Rob gave him the run down on Pon on their way to Teresa's. He also assured Teddy that he never discuss'd him with Lamont and that Lamont's source was Mr. & Mrs. Grier whom he stays in contact with. That info did Teddy's heart good because he was planning to teach Rob a lesson in loyalty.

They got to Teresa's spot about 5:30. Diane ask'd Teddy what all he need'd broke down and bagg'd up. He told her, a pound in dimes – one in quarters – one in halfs, ounces and Q P's. She ask'd him to go pick up her roommate Shanna so that she could help her and she wouldn't be late for work.

They rush'd to State St. to pick up Shanna and shot them to the room. Teddy gave them orders and told them he'd be back by 9:30. He took the rest of his work and went to Alan's spot in Cedar Green. Sitt'n at Alan's gambling, all the rest of the coke and weed Teddy had was gone.

By 9:45, they were back in the room and Diane and Shanna had finished everything and was gett'n out of the shower. The whole room smelt like a big weed forest, now it smell like a Victoria's Secret display counter.

Teddy told the chics thank you and pull'd out the money he won the night before play'n Pon and Kev. When he attempt'd to give her $600.00, Diane told Teddy she wasn't for hire and when he needed her to just call from then on out. She also gave him $1,800.00 that Kev dropp'd off. Teddy realized that a page he disregard'd earlier was Kev. Right then he felt bad about all the times he had cursed her out.

Diane and Shanna pranced thru the room in their stripper thongs and bras getting ready for work. Teddy was at the table counting money while Rob was being mesmerized at the half naked figures that pranced around in front of him.

"Goddamn!" Rob express'd as he count'd his money. "Whut I got to pay to keep yall here?"

Immediately, Teddy's head came up out of his count to see what Rob was think'n bout when he observed Shanna's healthy, round petite ass bend'n over to retrieve something out of her bag and Diane standing back on her bowlegs looking in the mirror paying homage to the beauty of her charcoal skin as she pull'd her shoulder length silky hair back into a ponytail.

"Whut-chu work'n wit?" Diane ask'd as she glanced over out the corner of her eye through the mirror at Rob count'n his change.

Teddy intervened. "Whateva it takes." Sitt'n in front of stacks of 20's, 50's and 100's equaling out to be a little over $20,000.

"Teddy, there is no charge for you but he gone pay to play."

"Di, if one stay both-a-yall gone stay so I'm gone pay too. Whut-chu normally make on a Thursday night?" Teddy ask'd.

Both girls answer'd almost simultaneously "Close to five hundred."

"Well, here's fourteen hundred. Git naked." Teddy said as he lean'd back in the chair under the light toss'n a stack on to the bed next to Shanna, signify'n.

Shanna gather'd the money stack, count'd it and split it. "Di, whu-chu gone do?" Shanna ask'd with a smile. "Gimmie my cut! That's what Di gone do." Diane implied, look'n back over her shoulder.

Shanna gave Diane 8 and kept 6 without a single complaint.

"Who got i-d?" Teddy ask'd.

"I do' Diane respond'd.

"Here's a fifty, go pay for the room next door."

Diane slid into her swear pants and a t-shirt with some flip flops and walk'd out switch'n her bowlegg'd ass uncontrollably.

Teddy paid for the girls and the room, holding firm to his word when he told Rob he was going to look out. Rob had already got off for the week, but so did Teddy. He got a free $1,800 plus $4,700 from gambling the night before.

Shanna want'd Teddy bad. She cut the clock radio on and start'd teasing Teddy, biting at his crotch until shot got a rise, then she turn'd around and sat in his lap while Rob watch'd her put on her show for Teddy.

When Diane return'd with the other room key to see Shanna straddling Teddy, she stated, "Bitch, you got me fuck'd up. Yo room next doe."

Shanna smiled at Teddy as if to say, SORRY" then got up and pull'd Rob by the hand lead'n him next door.

Teddy wasn't mad, that was a win-win situation. Diane wasted no time show'n Teddy her gratitude. Her brain game was priceless. Once she was done and ready for some personal gratification, she put a condom in her mouth and used her mouth to apply it. She straddled Teddy in the chair he sat in, fuck'n him stupid. Orgasm after orgasm. She was so good, Teddy could barely tell he had on a condom. He pick'd her up while still enlarged inside of her and placed her on her back on the edge of the bed. She purr'd like a kitten, pant'd and softly moan'd while gasp'n for air as Teddy released all of his pain, frustration and pleasure that was built up for Ms. Porchia.

In the heat of the moment, he collapsed on top of her with his mouth to her ear and exhaled, "Damn Porchia!"

"I – hope – that's – a – com – pliment." Diane replied out of breath.

Teddy just laid there, still inside of her bout to lose his mind while she continued contracting her vaginal muscles, creating another explosive orgasm for herself causing a chain reaction that left Teddy pound'n, digg'n and long stroke'n the pitts of her vagina until he was thrust'n her so hard and deep that the condom was misplaced inside of her. Teddy removed himself from Diane's sex garden to notice while plow'n the grounds he lost his glove.

"Where's the condom?" She ask'd as she observed their inner fluids combined and dripp'n from Teddy's manhood.

"Shit if I know! I thought I had it on."

"Find it Teddy!" Diane demand'd toss'n her legs up and open.

Teddy began to search, digg'n deep inside of her as she continued to get off. Needless to say, the deeper he dug, the further back he had to be push'n it because he never found it.

The next morn'n when Diane went to the bathroom, the condom mysteriously appear'd. She began to curse and taunt until Teddy woke up. He calm'd her down with his calm apology, tell'n her that he got her off digg'n so far inside of her look'n for it. They all shower'd, dress'd and check'd out.

Teddy was ready to get back to Greensboro and begin his celebration. They start'd by dropp'n Diane and Shanna off at their crib on the State St. On the way to Parker Heights, they took Tuckaseegee to Ashley Rd. After going across Freedom Dr., they came to the stop light at I-85 Access Rd. across from the IHOP at Freedom Mall.

When the light changed, Rob went thru the light and took an abrupt right turn into the park'n lot of the Amoco gas station. Teddy thought that he almost past and just quickly whipp'd into the drive way. He jump'd out to go pay for the gas not taking note to what was about to take place.

Leaving out of the store, Teddy saw 3 cop cars surround'n Rob in his mustang and two cops watch'n him come from the store. Soon as Teddy saw a way out another cop car pull'd in to cut off his path. The officer straight ahead motioned for Teddy to come his way and Teddy follow'd his instructions.

They took Rob to the Police cruiser and sat him in the front seat while they instruct'd Teddy to sit in the passenger seat of Rob's car. While Teddy sat there, he stuck all of his money into the inside pocket of the leather jacket he wore. The inside pocket had a hole in it that lead to the inner lining, which held all of Teddy's money secure.

The cops return'd to the passenger side and told Teddy to step away from the vehicle. Teddy did as told and when he did, the cop when straight up under the seat to the gun then he popp'd the trunk and went straight to the bag that held the pound of dimes in it. Luckily for Teddy he had left Diane with the other 4 pounds but from what he had just witness'd, Rob was snitch'n so when the cop question'd Teddy, he claim'd everything. They immediately search'd him, by-pass'n all of his money, handcuff'd and placed him in a separate Police car from Rob.

After reading Teddy his rights, the cop went back thru Rob's car thoroughly. While Teddy sat there, he heard the officer call in his charges; possession w/intent to sell and deliver marijuana and carrying a conceal'd firearm.

They then call'd off Rob's charges; driving while license are revoked, fictious tags, expired inspection sticker and wreckless driving. THIS DICKHEAD, Teddy thought AND HE SNITCH'D ME OUT. HO ASS NIGGA! I SHOULDA SHOT EVERYBODY IN DAT NIGGA'S CRIB THE OTHER NIGHT. EXCEPT FOR DAT NIGGA KEV. DAT'S A REAL NIGGA. DAMN WHY DID I FUCK WIT DIS LAME? I COULD HAVE RODE THE TRAIN BACK. MY FIRST DRUG CHARGE. Teddy's mind was race'n a mile a minute. I HOPE ALTON IS IN TOWN.

Finally, the officer came and ran Teddy in. He process'd in two hours and soon as they brought him down to use the phone, this time he made it into the cell. When he call'd Alton, he was already out front bail'n someone out.

"Teddy, say no more, you out. I'll see you in less than 15."
"Thanks AL."

"Don't mention it. See ya in 13 minutes." Alton joked.

Teddy chuckled at his count down and look'd at his Swiss Army watch.

Alton was so punctual, those 13 minutes was bogus, try 10 minutes and they were call'n "Teddy Massey! ONE WAY". The officer call'd grant'n Teddy his freedom. Alton was wait'n out front to give Teddy a ride.
Between February 95 and February 96, Teddy caught two more marijuana charges in Charlotte and a gun charge in Greensboro. Teddy was now officially in the game.

Rob continued try'n to contact Teddy after their release until Teddy changed every number he had and moved Ms. Porchia and Lil Teddy once again. Teddy had a decision to make, either discontinue his ties to Rob for his dishonor or bring him to his death for violating the code.

Lil Teddy made plenty of his father's life changing decisions for him. Teddy's decision to attempt to make his relationship with Ms. Porchia successful

was totally attributed to his life hero, his lil man
Teddy
                                                    Jr.

## Chapter 29: Ride or Die Chic

Throughout 95 going into 96, Teddy's love for Ms. Porchia increased tremendously but his respect and trust in her decreased tremendously due to her constant deceit and lies. The motherly love she show'd Lil Teddy was out of this world. Her love for Lil Teddy created a love within Teddy for her that was undeniable. However, the wedge between them remain'd every since that altercation with Lamont and Pon.

When Teddy arrived back in Greensboro after that terrible trip to Charlotte, he couldn't look at Ms. Porchia, he only want'd to deliver her the same pain she had served him. She tried to get Teddy to talk to her but he only avoided her, only find'n time for his son when he was in her presence.

Teddy's birthday was the following Sunday and he hadn't spoke to her since his return Friday night. Ms. Porchia attempt'd to celebrate his birthday with gifts from his son and Timia but Teddy was unbreakable. The first thing he said to her was, "I'm not like you, I refuse to deceive and lie to you. I fuck'd my little homegirl Diane Thursday night".

She instantly broke into tears, "Don't leave me Teddy!" She sobbed, "I'm sorry! I – Love – You!

I promise I won't lie to you no more. I was scared." She wail'd.

Ms. Porchia's plea broke Teddy's heart. He instantly forgave her and they made up with dinner in front of their fireplace with some exclusive hot make up sex. She never thought twice about his confession of sex with Diane. Never so much as question'd whether he was still seeing her or not. Ms. Porchia had come to realize how much Teddy valued her.

Their bond became so tight. Two months later, April 30th, the first anniversary of Teddy's uncle Steve's death, Teresa contact'd Teddy to tell him that Diane was pregnant and the baby was his. She said Diane was scared to tell him so she deliver'd the news. Teddy wasted no time tell'n Ms. Porchia. Her response was, "She just want some money. Tell her to have the baby and we'll have a blood test. If it's yours, we'll take care of it. If not, she knows the rest".

She was sincerely supportive. Even after Diane gave birth November 4th to Teddy's twin, his youngest child. A 6 pound 2 ounce baby doll named Timari Jaron Massey. That earn'd her a lot of her respect back in Teddy's eyes.

Life moved forward. Steezo, Teddy, Ant'No and Price continued to add on to their "Fort Green Fam". The most notable was the team of chics that went all out for the fam. Nisha and Jay was from Gastonia a-k-a Gas House; Mo, Dee, Talita, and Nicole went to Bennett College – that was the

Maryland crew. Shyah, Rish, Tay, and Mesha was from New Bern and Teddy's bestfriend Net from Kings Mtn.

Together, they ate together, got money together and play'd together.

Everybody in the Fort had their separate hustles but they all came together to reup.

Price and Ant'No were the only two on the lease and actually livin at the Fort. Price met Ant'No thru Teddy. Price was a Q-Dog from Raleigh. He and Teddy met thru a mutual friend name Slice their sophomore year and became real close. Price was a only child try'n to get his degree, but he hustled trees on the side and work'd as a bartender at a club call'd Elm City. Price let Ant'No move in with him straight out of prison on the strength of Teddy. The Fort start'd out as a low key weed spot but within a months time the Fort was gross'n $45,000.00 a week. They distributed weed, coke and hard. The members of the Fort used it for a stash spot for weapons, money, and drugs.

Teddy and two business partners open'd a urban clothing store, the first of its kind in the area. You had Underground Flavaz II on Randleman Rd. but they specialized in t-shirts, mix'd tapes and cds. Urban Touch was located on Bessemer. They sold such urban name brands as; DADA, MECCA, SHABAAZ BRO., HELLY HANSEN, VERSO, PERASUCCO, MAURICE MALONE, PHAT FARM and several other not so familiar brands. They sold the Durango style boots, shades, leather coats etc...

Diesel and C were the visible partners in the store. Teddy was in the streets, very seldom coming thru the store. They hired Diesel's sister Tammy, Ms. Porchia, Arnessa and Nesha to work in the store. At the same time, Teddy and C had a janitorial franchise they purchased thru Jani-King in Charlotte. Teddy was the visible partner making sure they had adequate help to clean their higher pay'n companies.

Every Sunday night was family night at a club call'd "Pure Passions" for the Fort Green Fam. "Pure Passions" was a strip club that the Fort used thru the week for a meet'n place. On Sunday's, "Pure Passions" would have Ladies Lockup from 8pm til 11pm then open the doors to the dudes to join the hot and horny chics til 3am.

Teddy, Steezo, Price, Ant'No and the rest of the Fort were of the celebrities of "Pure Passions". They never arrived before 2am on Sunday's. Ms. Paula ran "Pure Passions" and she loved the members of the Fort. Anytime they enter'd the club after 2, Ms. Paula made sure they had their typical 6 bottles of Mo, a case of Heinekens and Teddy's bottle of Corvoursier.

Throughout all Teddy's adventures, Ms. Porchia support'd her man. Even when Alton (Teddy's bondsman – Ms. Porchia's cousin) inform'd her that he had a inside source that the

FED's were watch'n Teddy. Alton's inside source was himself. His brother-in-law had just been convict'd after being found guilty of racketeer'n, traffick'n heroin and extortion. Alton had his hands in on the heroin and did some coke business with Teddy.

It was the last Thursday in July of 96', Teddy, Diesel and C went to Raleigh to the "Up In Smoke" tour feature'n the Fugees, Tribe Call'd Quest, Nas, Busta Rhymes, and Cypress Hill. It was held at the Walnut Creek Amphi Theater outside. The concert began at 5 o'clock. By 5:30, it was completely rain'd out. So severe that nobody attempt'd to run for shelter, being that the only shelter available was the bathroom and your own vehicle.

An outdoor event of this magnitude held over 20,000 people and only 2,500 were under the tent with the stage. Teddy, Diesel and C were amongst the soak and wet, but that didn't stop a good time. About an hour or two into the show, Teddy's pager start'd going off. It was Ant'No with the 911 emergency code. They left their cell phones in the car because they weren't allow'd in.

For fifteen minutes, Ant'No page'd back to back. Teddy knew something bad had happen'd because Diesel and C's pagers began to go off. It really hit Teddy when Ms. Porchia began to page relentlessly with 911. Something had to be wrong because everybody that was paging knew where they were. They stopp'd by the Fort before they hit the highway to try and get the whole Fam to roll.

The show end'd about 10:30. They had hell find'n the car in the rain but soon as they did, all three of them immediately got on their phones.

Teddy call'd Ms. Porchia, Diesel call'd his sister and C call'd his girl.

"Porchia, whut da fuck?" Teddy animatedly ask'd.

Meanwhile, C and Diesel made contact too.

"Baby, the Fort got bust'd a little while ago." Ms. Porchia stress'd.

Receiving the info about the same time, they all began to rant.

"Whut da fuck?"

"Oh shit!"

"Dat's fuck'd up!"

Ms. Porchia knew the full scoop. As she spoke, Teddy listen'd mad as fuck about the loss he had taken; 9 ounces of coke, 15 pounds, $8k, a twelve gauage and a .45 automatic. Ant'No and Price wasn't home when it happen'd. This dude name Fatz from Gastonia was hold'n the Fort down. Steezo was there and so was Nisha, Joy, Tay,

Lita, Nikki, Shyah and Mesha. Fatz and Steezo were arrest'd and all the chics were taken down for question'n. Fatz and Steezo were charged with 50 pounds, 25 ounces of coke, 65 assort'd guns and $30k.

Steezo, never hustled at the Fort, he only slid thru to either drop off, pick up or hang out. He was only hang'n out with Fatz and the chics when the bust took place. Fatz was the only one there hustling – he shoulda took all the charges.

While they were in question'n, Detective Gray, the Detective assign'd to the case pull'd out pictures of Price and  Ant'No coming and going from the Fort, Teddy with Lil Teddy being pick'd up by Ms. Porchia, C, Diesel and several other chics coming thru on the regular and also pictures of the whole Fort Green Fam partying at Pure Passions.

The chics were released and told to stick around because they may need information from them. Fatz was also released. Steezo wore all the charges. However, Nisha and Joy immediately got in touch with Teddy to confirm that Alton had already warn'd Teddy of. They said Det. Gray was mostly pointing out the pictures of Teddy, Price, Ant'No and Steez.

Teddy was out on bail, facing time for pending weed charge in Charlotte with violations of probation in both Charlotte and Greensboro. His next court date was in March of 97. Teddy's plan was to lay low, back out of the streetz, continue to run the janitorial service and eat off of the money he had already stack'd.

In December of 96', a week before Christmas, C had a package knock'd off in Louisiana coming from Texas. C's driver brought the ATF's DEA's and FED's back to C's crib in Greensboro.

C was a cool ass, low key college geek that had school and book smarts. He was from Goldsboro. His family was middle class citizens. C was so smart til he was stupid. He had graduated from A&T with the class of 95' but he never attend'd the school of hard knocks. He was about as street smart as Erkell but he had connect's in the weed game. When his driver got hit with the 100 pounds, he cut an immediate deal to give up C. C was so greedy and grimy on the low, his driver was a customer he literally stole from Teddy. To top it off, Teddy met dude thru "Go Figure".

Teddy, C and Diesel had just open'd Urban Woman in the same shopping strip with Urban Touch. Both stores were freshly stock'd, ready for the holidays and New Year. The day after C's arrest, the FED's padlock'd both stores. Teddy and Diesel had no way of recoup'n none of the $150k they had come together with to open the new store.

Meanwhile, Alton had hired Teddy a new attorney to represent him with the state charges he was facing. He basically just got a favor for a favor from the Federal Attorney Jesse Wellington that was representing him. Jesse knew that the FED's were trying to tie Teddy into their case with Alton and his brothers so he went before the prosecutor and got all of Teddy's charges consolidated into one with the term of 6-8 months active. March 19, 1997 10 days after Biggie's death, Teddy left to do his first ever bid. When he left, he had a little over $11k left. His only concern was that Ms. Porchia and Lil Teddy would be ok.

With 6 -8 months ahead of him, Teddy began his little stretch on a dolo mission. Ms. Porchia kept his account straight but he didn't allow no one to come see him except Queen for the first three months. It made his time easier for him but harder on Ms. Porchia because even though Teddy was attempt'n to protect her, she felt that he should have allow'd her to be there for him day for day.

## Chapter 30: Meet Poison

Three months before Teddy was released, he was sent to a camp call'd Umstead in Butner NC, about an hour straight up 85N. Ms. Porchia, Lil Teddy and several of the chics from his escort service came every week like clockwork.

Teddy's life had severely changed in the 90 days prior to arriving at Umstead. He met a brother named Shabaaz that was from his projects. Shabaaz took Teddy under his wing introducing him to AL-Islam. It was totally different from what Teddy had been initially taught about Islam. Instead of lessons, he was introduced to the Qu'ran. He took his Shahadah and had began to structure his life with the five daily prayers.

However, arriving at Umstead took him back to his old ways. He own'd card games, canteens and several pornography books that he rent'd out. To him, he was living the life. Every visit, he sent Ms. Porchia home with five hundred to a thousand dollars.

Ms. Porchia received her degree in Special Education  from A&T that May. Teddy purchased her a brand new Dodge Stratus with the money he had left over before he got lock'd up. After being introduced to AL-Islam, he decided that he was going to marry Ms. Porchia approximately a year after his release but he was planning to get his own place first, attempt to finish his last year in school and purchase them a home.

Instead, she insist'd that he come back home to her and Lil Teddy. He allow'd his heart and emotions to rule his rational think'n by forsaking all of his vows to ALLAH by going straight back home to her. His thoughts was that he owed her that much for holding him down.

Once Teddy was home, Ms. Porchia promised him a beach trip that they postponed til 6 months later. They decided to go on the day of Kenya's wedding. Kenya was due to get married on April 25th.

Teddy began working for a Heat'n and Air conditioning company two weeks after his release. His boss was his main coke customer before he went to Prison. He gave Teddy a bogus title in the company such as "Clean Up Inspector". All he did daily from 8am to 7pm was drive around with a quarter or half of cook rock while his boss smoked in between jobs. Every Friday he cash'd a check for $2500.00.

That last'd from September 30th til January 2nd 1998 when Teddy's class's began at Guilford Tech Community College. He continued to work for the Heating and Air Conditioning Company but only work'n weekends.

His whole view on life had changed. Even though he was still hustling coke, he didn't see it as deal'n. To him, he was work'n and providing for his children and soon to be wife. Steezo was lock'd up and had been 3 months after Teddy left.  Ant'No was still hustling weed which result'd in Teddy deal'n with one of Steezo's old connects. Beno was cool but he want'd Teddy to get more from him than a quarter or a half every day or every other day but Teddy didn't want to get into it as he was before he left.

His main goal was to simply save his money to put a down payment on a home by August. He only spent money on bills and clothes. All he did was go to school and work. The rest of his time was spent with Lil Teddy and Ms. Porchia when she wasn't work'n. She had a salary job with Adavanced Home Care, the same company Teddy work'd for when she was carry'n Lil Teddy.

One afternoon, Teddy had gotten in early from class when the phone rang.

"Hello?"

"Teddy where's Porchia?"

"Hi you doin Mr. Grier?" Porchia's at work." Teddy respond'd wondering why he ask'd that dumb ass question.

"Mmmm Hmmm" He groan'd, "Whut are you doin answer'n my phone?" Mr. Grier ask'd.

Teddy paused, confused and offend'd, he shot back, "why are you call'n my crib?"

"Your crib? I pay rent, lights and phone at yo crib!" He retort'd, "Tell Porchia I call'd." CLICK! He slamm'd the phone down in his ear.

Teddy was furious, things didn't add up. How was it that he and Mr. Grier were pay'n the bills. Ms. Porchia dismiss'd it say'n, Mr. Grier just said that because he didn't want Teddy living there with her but it wasn't his choice. Teddy let it go knowing that he didn't like him anyway, so he left it at that.

On Friday April 24th, Ms. Porchia, Teddy and their son left Greensboro head'd to Charlotte in preparation for Kenya's big day. Soon as they arrived, Ms. Porchia took Teddy to rent a car. They were driving the rental to the beach after the wedding and since Teddy reach'd town so early, he figured he'd make some extra change at his breakdown spot. After renting a convertible Chrysler LeBaron, they went their separate ways.

Teddy went to surprise Mia at her school by having lunch with her. In the middle of his lunch date with his Princess, he got a page from Ms. Porchia, she need'd him to watch Lil Teddy and her little cousin from Germany while she went to the hairdresser. It was 10:45am when he left Huntingtowne Farm Elementary School. He met Ms. Porchia at the beauty salon about five after 11.

After pick'n up the little guys, Teddy took them to get their cuts at Anderton's on Statesville Rd. Teddy's barber Rich was the best barber in Charlotte. His client's included several Hornet players and the majority of the influx ballers. Beyond the barber shop, he took the boys to Celebration Station to kill time. By 2:30pm he met Ms. Porchia back at the beauty salon. Ms. Porchia approach'd Teddy and the boys look'n so good, that Teddy grabb'd her by the waist pulling her into his embrace. "C'mere wit-cho sexy ass." Teddy said, kiss'n her. "I love yo hair."

"You like it?" She ask'd, blush'n as she ran her fingers thru her spiral curls.

"I can't wait til we get to the beach tamarra." Teddy express'd with that sparkle in his eyes. "I'm gone fuck this up." He said as he ran his fingers thru her hair.

"Boy, you nasty. I gotta go, I'm late as it is. You know I need you to watch your son during the rehearsal tonight at the Church."

"That's no problem, I'll be there."

"I'll call you about 6 so you can meet me. Love Me?" She ask'd with a sexy smile as their lips and tongues intertwined.

"No question." Teddy replied releasing her lips. "I'll see ya latah, Nu-Nu!" Teddy yell'd out to Lil Teddy. "I don't wanna hear no bad report on you."

"Yes Dad." Lil Teddy respond'd.

"Who's my hero?"

"I am Daddy. Love You."

"Love You too Nu-Nu. PEACE."

"PEACE OUT DAD!" Lil Teddy yell'd as they went their separate ways.

Teddy left to go pick up Donté, his right hand man. Out of all of his class mates, Donté was his closest friend. They became extremely close when Tip left and went back to Chicago. Teddy never rode around with dudes but whenever he was in town or partying, Donté was his sidekick. Donté was the quiet type, with not much to say if he didn't know you. That's why Teddy had him as his gun man. They were never the trouble type. It was real simple with these two, get money, have fun and fuck whores.

Once he got with Donté, they head'd straight to the breakdown spot, The Master's Inn on Independence. Ms. Porchia's cousin L'Roy had introduced Teddy to this cat name BUTT-NAKED. BUTT-NAKED kept a room at that motel. He was a go getta. If he never told you he smoke, you'd never know it. He got the name BUTT-NAKED because he was known to be in the motel room wit a bad ass bitch, butt naked in some Timberlands, but he was mostly known for his hustle. Anything you want'd, BUTT-NAKED could get it, any dope you had, he could get rid of it.

When Teddy and Donté arrived, Butt-Naked was stand'n on the balcony of the motel in some boxer shorts with the smiley faces on it and a fresh pair of wheat Tim's cuss'n one of his broads out until he saw Teddy pull in.

"Bitch, I made You!" Butt Naked yell'd, "Hi you gone tell me, you done? I own you. I tell you who put dick in yo nasty ass pussy."

Soon as he saw Teddy, he flipp'd, "NEPHEW!" He yell'd out to Teddy. "Come on up. I'm jus putt'n out some trash. Bitch, you leave, don't come yo ass back!"

Teddy and Donté laugh'd at the sight of BUTT-NAKED in his boxers and Tims but they were glad to see he at least had on some boxers.

BUTT-NAKED loved to see Teddy comin because he knew he had the best work around and the best prices. He immediately got dress'd and prepared to make a million. BUTT-NAKED was what they call a SMOKAH, he wasn't a junky. A junky had no morals, all they want'd to do is get high. A smokah dress's to their own desire, keep themselves up and provides for themselves. BUTT-NAKED was a TOMMY HILFIGER King. He stay'd fresh.

"Nephew, what we work'n wit?" He ask'd as Teddy and Donté sat on the extra freshly made up bed.

"I just brought down a ounce. I only got til about 5 and then I'll be back latah on ta git rid of the rest."

"Nephew, you came at the perfect time. I just got paid, I got $600.00 but this cracka down the side walk got a stash and he just bought me some kind bud down here. So jus sit back and chill, smoke on this bud while I make us rich."

Teddy and Donté sat there long enough to smoke a blunt and make $600.00 off of a quarter. Teddy left BUTT-NAKED a quarter and they took off. He still had to pick up his Maury Gators that went with the Armani linen suit he was wear'n to the wedd'n and get his nails done.

By the time they return'd at 5:15, two hours later, BUTT-NAKED had another $600.00 wait'n. They sat there smoke'n kind bud and turn'n crack to bread. Before he knew it, time had gotten past him. Teddy check'd his pager and cell phone, it was 10 after 7 and no sign of Ms. Porchia. He attempt'd to call her phone but got the voicemail so he paged her. Receiving no response. They stay'd at the spot til every bit of the work was gone, leaving about 9:40pm. Teddy attempt'd to call her phone and pager again and still received no answer.

Frustration began to set in. Instead of wait'n on her to call back, they went to Champagne's Strip Club for some drinks.

About 12:30am when they left the club, Teddy tried gett'n in touch with her again. When she never return'd his calls, Teddy call'd her parents home. Mrs. Grier answer'd tell'n Teddy that Ms. Porchia wasn't there and she hadn't seen her since the rehearsal dinner and they were currently tryn' to find Lil Teddy. That did it, Teddy was vex'd with Ms.

Porchia. Little did he know, Mrs. Grier was play'n him but it was Ms. Porchia's fault. If she keeps her word and contact him before the rehearsal, everything works out fine.

Teddy was too wired to sleep. He and Donté sat up in the Summerfield Suites, smoking weed, drank'n liquor and watch'n movies until 6:00am. After call'n Ms. Porchia's cell phone, he wasted no time call'n back to her parent's home.

"Hello?" Mr. Grier answer'd in his high pitch'd feminie voice.

"Sorry to be call'n so early but is Porchia there Mr. Grier?"

"Yes Teddy, hold on a sec."

Teddy held while he call'd Ms. Porchia to the phone. He attempt'd to self talk to himself so that he didn't lose it.

"Hello?" She answer'd half sleep.

"Where's Teddy?" Teddy ask'd sternly.

"He's with my cousin. What's wrong?"

"Where's your cell phone and pager?"

"I left them in my car. I was with Kenya."

"Porchia, you never leave your pager, what the fuck is going on?"

"What do you mean, I forgot it."

"You forgot it, hm? What happen'd to you call'n –" Teddy was interrupt'd by Mr. Grier pick'n up the phone.

"Porchia, Jeanae and Graceland call'd. I thought Teddy was with them. Your mother said nobody has located him yet."

Ms. Porchia smacks her lips. "Let me call you back."

"What da fuck you mean call me back? Where's my son?" He lost it. "Everytime you get around yo people you lose focus. Hi da fuck you don't know where yo child is wit-cho stupid ass?"

"I – I – I" She stutter'd as Teddy cut her off.
"All you had to do was call me to watch him like you said you would do. You got 15 minutes to fine my child before I get there." Teddy threaten'd as he slam'd the hotel phone down.

He hung up the phone, brush'd his teeth and raced to the other side of town. Ms. Porchia met him at the side door, very apologetic but still had no answers as to where Lil Teddy was. Teddy was furious and talk'n loud in these peoples house at 7:00 in the morning. His voice carried so loud til he had woke up everybody in the house including Lil Teddy. He had been asleep the whole time in the guest room next to the den. Lil Teddy immediately ran to Teddy's arms. Teddy question'd him about who brought him home. He told him he rode with Ma Lois. Ma Lois is Ms. Porchia's God mother. Lil Teddy is a very independent child. The adults were so intoxicated and caught up into the festivities that Lil Teddy got off to himself to watch TV and fell asleep.

Although Teddy was glad to see his son, he was still furious with Ms. Porchia about her carelessness and neglect to keep their plans. After waking the entire Grier family, guest and all, Teddy left outraged with Ms. Porchia. He was so outraged that he skipp'd the wedding. Ms. Porchia's blatant disregard for everything around her including her own child when she enter'd the presence of her family ate at Teddy.  It left him not wanting to even be in the presence of her or her family. FUCK A WEDD'N! Was his thoughts.

About 3 o'clock that afternoon, Teddy received a call from his mom. Queen was as upset with Teddy as he was with Ms. Porchia. Queen attend'd the wedding in the blind not knowing the drama that surround'd this supposedly happy event. She explain'd to Teddy that after the ceremony, Ms. Porchia rush'd  to her side and broke down cry'n, while her whole family stood observing and consoling her as she explain'd that morning's events.

Queen express'd how out of place she felt as everybody look'd on at her like she had given birth to the aniti-Christ. Ms. Porchia's behavior ate at Teddy's existence. He immediately call'd to inquire about her lack of tact. Queen ask'd him to be nice, so he approach'd the conversation in a calm state, consider'n her nosey aunt from Germany was eavesdropp'n and Ms. Porchia was carrying a jazzy tone that Teddy had never experienced. Teddy felt himself about to lose control so he put all the drama aside and ask'd her what time were they leaving for the beach.

"I'm not going to the beach. I'm not leaving here until tomorrow, going back to Greensboro."

"What!?! Porchia stop play'n, we been plann'd this trip for the longest."

"Well, plans are off, you can go, I'm not!" Ms. Porchia lash'd out. The phone went completely silent.

Disappoint'd, Teddy respond'd in a humble, calm tone, "Dat's cool, jus get Teddy ready. I'll take him and Mia with me."

"My child is stay'n with me. Take your daughter, Teddy's not going either."

At that point, all bets were off. Teddy was never the aggressive  type  until he was push'd to the limit and at that moment, she had him caged in and a demon was comin out. "Bitch – who da fuck you thank you talk'n to? You got me fuck'd up! I tell ya whut, I'm on my way back to da Boro, you got exactly 3 hours to meet me back there with my son or I'll kill everything that moves in that house except him." Teddy yell'd in the phone before disconnect'n.

"PRETTY POISON has struck again!" Donté joked, "MS. PRETTY POISON PORCHIA GRIER! Do you actually think she's going to meet-chu there?" Donté ask'd as he pass'd a freshly lit blunt to Teddy.

Teddy hit the blunt and exhaled, "Wheeew…Two thangs you don't fuck with – my children and my money. If she's PRETTY POISON? I'm da ugly antidote. That bitch would have came out better havin a baby by satan. I'm torcher Xang!" He yell'd, furious at her audacity.

The sad fact of the matter was that nobody had proof of Teddy's torcher antics but there were several rumor's float'n thru Charlotte and surround'n areas of his heinous acts towards the few that dared to try him.

Teddy paid for the suite for an extra night, leaving Donté to relax the rest of the day while he got on the highway. Riding up the highway, he blast'd the soundtrack to JAY-Z's STREETZ IS WATCH'N. As his anger settled, the pain set in. Teddy's gut told him that Ms. Porchia would not be show'n up.

Upon his arrival to the empty apartment, he immediately began to pack his things. Once everything was in the rental, he went back inside to wait just in case she decided to show up. The lack of sleep and the adrenaline rush from the past day had taken it's toll on him as he fell asleep in the living room while the TV watch'd him.

When he awoke to the dark empty apartment, he call'd two of his closest chics, Nisha and Joy. Nisha and Joy loved Teddy to death. They were the two that inform'd him of Det. Gray's nonstop interest in his where abouts when the Fort got bust'd. And they were also the two that introduced him to the PIMP game as an alternative hustle. Both chics were slim and exotic look'n enough to be super models but their under 5ft3' heights would destroy that dream.

Joy being the thicker of the two was closer to Teddy and would do anything he practically ask'd of her. He told her what had taken place and she immediately offer'd him to stay with them. They lived in a two bedroom spot in Valley Ridge Apts. Which meant, he would be sleep'n on the couch when he was there but quiet as kept, Joy would never allow that to happen.

Before leaving to take his things to his new spot, he call'd Beno and alert'd him of the preceding. Teddy had saved well over $15,000.00 break'n down quarters and halfs posing as a Clean Up Inspector for Luke's Southeastern Heat'n and Air. Beno was ecstatic that Teddy had finally decided to step his game up. He knew of Teddy's earning potential before he did his miniature bid. He told Teddy to meet him at their usual spot, Spoon's Pool hall and Billiards. They met and talk'd and Beno alert'd Teddy that he could fill any order he need'd, but stop play'n and get something that would hold him off for a minute. In Teddy's mind, 9 ounces was sufficient until he went straight to Luke's place down Randleman Rd. In less than an hour, Teddy was $13,500.00 dollars richer and already in need of reup.

Beno only charged him $5,500.00 so that was a $8,000.00 profit. Luke call'd a few of his buddies up and took every thing Teddy had in one whop. Teddy had just met with Beno at 8:30 and by 9:30, he was try'n to get back at him. Beno didn't hesitate to brush Teddy off, his thoughts, THIS NIGG IN ONE DAY WENT FROM A OUNCE TO A QUARTER BRICK AND IT'S GONE WITHIN AN HOUR? HELL NO SON, SOMETHIN AIN'T RIGHT! "Aye Yo T-Biz, do you. I'm on my way out the area. I'll contact you when I return."

Teddy sensed his fear and chuckled but respect'd his caution. Still, he had to get more work and get back to BUTT-NAKED. His mind was on making a serious amount of money in a short time span.

Without a second thought, Teddy hit the highway head'd back to the Queen City. On his way down, he contact'd his younger cousin L-A. L-A was a walk'n gold mine. He got in the dope game on the low. Teddy had no idea he was even in the streets until his name popp'd up and they ran into each other. They both had their own connects but if one didn't have, the other would supply. L-A opt'd to meet at Bailey Billiards on Albemarle Rd. in an hour.

By 11 o'clock, L-A walk'd into the Pool hall dripp'n in jewelry to assist his cousin. L-A was on his last leg and basically dropp'd what he had on Teddy for a little of nothing. He gave him a big eight for $1,500.00 and Teddy left. That was all he need'd. He took BUTT-NAKED a ounce and went back to the suite where he had left Donté. Donté was tied up with one of his many situations when Teddy arrived. He knew what it was and just laugh'd when he saw Teddy walk in.

Ms. Porchia had officially created a monster and the wrath that Teddy was about to bring as a hustler and single black man would be spoken about for generations to come.

## Chapter 31: Poison Strikes

Sunday afternoon after the fiasco the day before. Teddy was at the Master Inn with Butt-Naked try'n to plan his next move when his mom paged him 911. He call'd her no sooner than he read the number. She inform'd him that Ms. Porchia had taken out a warrant for 'Communicating A Threat', and she want'd him to turn himself in. At first, he was totally against it, but he realized that he couldn't have a warrant over his head with the mission he was on.

He tied up all of his business, contact'd his new bondsman (an old school mate) and turn'd himself in. This took place at 5pm. He had plann'd to be out by 9 or 10 the same night but little did he know, they hold you without a bond until the next day for 'Communicating A Threat' and 48 hours for actual 'Assault on A Female'. Teddy was there for the duration. Once he was dress'd out and in a pod, he call'd Queen. She inform'd him that Ms. Porchia had call'd and said she wasn't pursuing the charges.

Teddy told Queen that the magistrate told him that Ms. Porchia could show up in court to his first appearance and have the charges dismiss'd.

Queen immediately call'd Ms. Porchia on 3-way to inform her and Ms. Porchia assured her that she would meet her there. She lied, she didn't show up. That left Teddy to have to post bond.

His new bondsman was nothing like Alton. Teddy miss'd Alton. The FED's came down with secret indictments against him and his brothers and put them away for life. Teddy had already paid the bondsman a $1,000.00 down payment with an agreement to pay the rest immediately after he was out. Instead of making Teddy a priority, Teddy sat in the county jail 4 extra hours because he had pilot lessons in South Carolina.

Once Teddy was out, he hook'd back up with Donté at his spot. His mind was in overdrive. He had a set goal of the amount of money he was seek'n to obtain and in a certain amount of time. First things first, a job. Teddy contact'd this cat name Tarik that was the regional manager   for all of the Willies Records from Va to Ga. Tarik lived down the sidewalk from Teddy and Ms. Porchia in Greensboro. He ask'd Teddy which Willies did he want to work at and Teddy chose the Willies on Beatties Ford Rd.   He start'd immediately.

Donté and his siser Gena offer'd Teddy a place to stay til he got situated. Day by day Teddy attempt'd to contact Ms. Porchia so that he could see Lil Teddy. Everyday that pass'd made the pain worse. He hired an attorney to represent his domestic case. His attorney (Oscar Forté) recommended Teddy go thru counseling due to the nature of his crime. He sent him to United Way Family services so that when his case went to court he would already have a head start and have a report from the counselor to present to the judge.

Teddy had vengeance in his heart for Ms. Porchia, the sweetest revenge, "SUCCESS". Willies Records was his haven. Daily, he sat in Willies servin harrd, soft and trees. Once weekly, he saw his counselor. David Sumter was his name. He was a cool, young counselor. Teddy felt comfortable confiding in David and David admired Teddy's devotion to his children and Ms. Porchia. They were basically the same age, David may have been 3-4 years Teddy's senior.

As the weeks roll'd by, Teddy continued his mission. It had been a month since he had been in the presence of Ms. Porchia or in her arms. He was focus'd on his goal. Instead of purchasing a car straight out, he stay'd in new rentals.

Two days after he had been rear end'd on his way to work, Teddy enter'd the Charlotte Police Dept. to get a Police report. Approach'n the counter from the long line, Teddy was greet'd by a super attractive sister that stood 5ft6', about 162 pounds, petite/full figured with vicious curves. She had a bronze, brown skin complexion and her hair was in a doobie wrap.

"Next" she alert'd in a soft sexy alto voice as Teddy approach'd her. "How may I help you sir?" She ask'd with a thick New York accent.

"Yes, I was in a accident two days ago and I need the Police report." Teddy said handing her the report # and his license. She grabb'd his hand as she was grabb'n his info and her soft touch sent waves straight thru to the center of Teddy's nervous center. As she walk'd away, Teddy's eyes follow'd every sway of her hips from left to right in the brown, yellow and gold color'd rayon fitt'n skirt. When she return'd lust linger'd in Teddy's eyes.

"Here you are Mr. Massey."

"Thank You." Teddy obliged, "Es-cuse me?" He inquired in a low tone, "You mind me ask'n your name?"

"It's Peaches Sweetie." She replied with a smile.

"Ms. Peaches, what time do you leave for lunch?"

"I had an early one Mr. Massey. I have some catch'n up to do here."

"Could I leave you my # and you give me the pleasure of taking you to lunch sometime?"

She blush'd at Teddy's invite. "What is it cutey?" She ask'd in the most flirtatious tone.

Teddy gave her the # and shot her the signature wink and saunter'd off.

Ms. Peaches watch'd Teddy stroll off with an air of confidence and a helluva swagger.

Two days later, Teddy got a strange page '355-100-9718-411'. He was in a rush on his way out the door to run some errans before he had to be at work. Grabb'n his cell, he dial the #.

"Police Dept., Pamela Deas speak'n, how may I direct your call?"

"Um – did someone page Teddy Massey?"

"Yes someone did Mr. Massey. Ms. Peaches would like to know if you're available for lunch today?"

The strange melodic voice ask'd.

"Funny." He chuckled, "How are you?"

"I'm fine and you?"

"I'm better now that I know you didn't throw my # away."

"Why would I do something like that?"

"Good question, how bout we chop it up over lunch?"

"I'm game, I go in about 20 minutes."

"I'll call you from the park'n lot. I'm in a wine color'd Cherokee."

"Alright Sweetie. Peace."

Teddy made two stops and was downtown at the Police Station by 5 til 12, ten minutes ahead of time. Ms. Peaches was walk'n out to the parking lot in less than 2 minutes of Teddy's call. She was in a cream linen pants outfit look'n business casual and very classy, her hair in her signature doobie wrap, walk'n with a radiant glow.

"Hello Mr." She greet'd as she enter'd the passenger seat of the air condition fill'd SUV.

"Hi you Miss Lady?" Teddy ask'd in his somewhat country sophisticated drawl.

"I like this Teddy, and it smells good in here too." She express'd.

"Why thank you. This is just a rental and the fragrance is sweet mango."

"No Sweetie, not the mango, the underlying scent." She said, speak'n of the left over weed scent that sat under the scent of the mango.

"Damn you can smell that?" He ask'd with concern.

"Yes Teddy. That's fine, you're ok." She answered.

They had lunch at Sonny's bar-be-cue down Monroe Rd. As they sat and enjoy'd their lunch, she had the chicken while Teddy enjoyed his favorite, the chopp'd beef. Teddy was taken by her presence. She exuded such class with the flamboyant sex appeal of Chaka Khan. She reveal'd she was 36 years old and from Brooklyn. Her and her ex-husband moved to North Carolina to raise their son who at the time was 16.

Upon their separation, Ms. Peaches left her son to be raised into manhood by his father. Teddy really fell for her when she reveal'd that she was Muslim and had full knowledge of self.

After getting to know each other a little over lunch, Teddy took her back to work with a promise to call later on. Ms. Peaches reach'd over the armrest, gave Teddy the most sensual kiss on the cheek with a promise of a lot more later on.

Later that night at work, Teddy found himself think'n about Ms. Peaches in the midst of his troublesome thoughts of Ms. Porchia and Lil Teddy. Business at Willies was slow and the only customers that came thru were the ones Teddy was servin. It was like that Monday thru Thursday. When Teddy's customers came thru, they automatically purchased Cd's or something out of the store. As he escort'd one customer to the door, he was greet'd by one of Willies customers. This wasn't just any customer, this chic was the thickest. Passing Teddy as she enter'd, they caught eye contact.

"Can I help you?" Teddy ask'd.

"Sure," She said as she walk'd to the NEW RELEASE section.

"Well, what can I help you with?" Teddy ask'd as he approach'd her from behind noticing her super round ass. She had the type of ass that resembled a basketball. This sister was healthy in all the right places, big ass, thick thighs and nice hips with a flat stomach.

"Do y'all have that "So Anxious' single by Ginuwine?"

"Here you go." Teddy pull'd the cd for her, "whut are you so anxious for?" He ask'd while he got his flirt on.

"Anxious for whateva." She said look'n Teddy up and down.

"Can you handle that?"

"Handle what?" Teddy ask'd with a chuckle as he observed her smooth caramel complexion and 5ft4' frame. "Are you always this aggressive?"

"You start'd it." She replied rubb'n her fingers thru her short blond cut. "You been watch'n my ass the whole time I've been in here and I been watch'n yo ass too." She said with a sexy smirk. "How old are you little boy?" She ask'd while follow'n Teddy to the cash register. He cover'd his ass and they both share a good laugh.

"The name is Teddy little old lady and old enough to rock da boat." He turn'd and replied as he laid the cd on the counter and walk'd behind her. She return'd the favor covering her ass.

Yeuh, right! I'm Stacy."

"Nice to meet-cha. You from around here?"

"I'm from Statesville but I live on Bradford."

THAT EXPLAINS THAT COUNTRY THICKNESS. Teddy thought. "You live wit-cho man?" Teddy inquired.

"Hell no!    Y'all too complicated. I'm 34 and independent. No man, no kids, just me and my nieces and nephews."

"You really is old." He joked.

"Nah cutey, just experienced. How young are you?"

"I'm 27, is that too young?" Teddy ask'd, still flirt'n.

"Nah, that's trainable." She said, smile'n as she pass'd him a business card.

"So you're a beautician?"

"A good lover too."

"We'll have to see about that." Teddy said as he thump'd the card.

She said her goodbyes and left. Teddy was beginn'n to realize that the best way to get over one woman is the companionship of many.

The next day he had an appointment with his counselor. He inform'd David of his encounters with the new chics. Dave encouraged the interaction. "Sitt'n around wait'n on Porchia to return isn't going to bring her back. Explore your options."

After meet'n with Dave, Teddy thoroughly explored his options with Ms. Peaches and Stacy the whole weekend. Being more comfortable with Ms. Peaches, she got the bulk of his time. Plus, Stacy was a workaholic.

## Chapter 32: Meet Poison

Exactly 2 months had pass'd, still no Ms. Porchia. It was the last Sunday in June. Teddy had a court day first thing Monday morning at 9:00am. He and Ms. Peaches both woke up late from a late night. They were extremely rush'd but Teddy was able to get her  to work on time, find parking and get to court on time.

The courtroom was pack'd as he enter'd. He scour'd the room for a seat while search'n for Ms. Porchia. His heart was beat'n a mile a minute anticipating seeing her even though she told his mom she wasn't coming to court. In his mind, he always expect'd the opposite of everything she did. Instead of seeing Ms. Porchia, he saw Queen four rows up waving for him. She was still in her all white nurse's outfit. No sooner than Teddy sat down and began to converse with Queen, Teddy saw his attorney talk'n to the DA. As Oscar walk'd behind the DA motion'n for Teddy to come up, the DA call'd their docket #.

"Judge, hear comes case #98CRS 100297, Grier vs Massey." The DA call'd out.

"What do we have?"

"Well Judge, on April 25, 1998, the defendant Teddy Massey allegedly threaten'd to kill everybody in the offendent's parents home.  However, the offendent Ms. Porchia Grier is not in the courtroom. Mr. Massey's attorney, Mr. Forté is present with his client. Mr. Forté has alert'd me that Mr. Massey is currently in counseling and he has a report on Mr. Massey's evaluation." The DA said as he approach'd the bench with Teddy's evaluation. The judge took the papers handed to him and began to review them.

"Mr. Massey please stand." The judge order'd. Teddy rose and stood beside the DA's table front and center of the Judge with Mr. Forté by his side. "I see you're currently in counseling. I commend you for  taking the initiative to correct the problem before it actually became a problem and being that Ms. Massey isn't here, I'm dismissing all charges."

"Thank You Your Honor." Teddy said with a half a smile.

"Mr. Massey, continue your treatment. It will only be beneficial to you. Even I see a shrink." The little white man said look'n over his glasses at Teddy.

Teddy and Queen left the courtoom together. The whole process took about 40 minutes. He took his mom to her car before takin off to meet Donté.

"She call'd the house last night and talk'd to mother while I was at work." Queen said as Teddy pull'd up to her car.

"Who?"

"Porchia Boy!"

"Whut she say?" Teddy ask'd.

"Mother said she just want'd to know were we alright and had we heard from you. You know mother don't know nothing so she didn't tell her nothing."

"Good!"

"Boy, you can sit there like you don't care all you want. Mama know better."

"I jus wanna see Nu-Nu."

"Boy, whatever. Give Moma some sugah. I gotta go. Call me latah."

"Ah-ight Ma. Peace."

Teddy and Queen went their separate ways. Teddy drove off wondering what exactly did Ms. Porchia want and why didn't she call him. Dismiss'n his thoughts of her, Teddy shot to the Master's Inn to meet Donté at BUTT-NAKED's.

Upon complete'n his business, Teddy head'd downtown to Simmon's Soulfood restaurant to get Ms. Peaches some lunch before he had to be at work. He was really into Ms. Peaches but he was more into himself and guarding his heart. That was what he liked most about her and Stacy, they didn't pressure him. He saw them when he saw them and they both made themselves available at his request. For that, they got flowers and lunch delivered to their jobs and several other perks that came with being involved with an all out hustlah.

In the past 2 months, Teddy had flourish'd into a full fledge street monster on some real live gentleman shit. His counselor Dave was partly responsible for his new level of intelligence and assist'n him on how to deal with his anger when it comes to family, friends and business. Everything he was learn'n up until this point was about to be test'd.

On his way to work leaving Ms. Peaches, Teddy was sitt'n at a stop light on Beatties Ford Rd. that intersected at LaSalle St. listen'n to "Love For Free" by Rell, off of the Streetz Is Watch'n cd when he happen to notice the kid sitt'n in the back seat of this silver 88 Jaguar. The – kid was irate sitt'n in his car seat behind the driver's seat kick'n and point'n at Teddy. When he look'd, he noticed the car, then pull'd up to look at the driver and his heart dropp'd. Wish'n he hadn't seen her, they caught eye contact. Ms. Porchia's eyes got wide as half dollar coins. They both dropp'd their windows.

"Pull over at KFC." Ms. Porchia yell'd.

Teddy nodd'd and pull'd thru the light roll'n up his window. He pull'd into the park'n lot of KFC and park'd, Ms. Porchia follow'd. Before he could get out of the rental, Lil Teddy was stand'n at the window of the Camry tugg'n at the door. Teddy unlock'd his door and Lil Teddy pull'd the latch open anxious to get to his dad. "DA-DDY!" He yell'd as he jumped into Teddy's lap.

"Hey Nu-Nu!" Teddy said embracing his son. "I miss'd you boy!"

"I miss'd you too Daddy. I'm going with you." He spoke excitedly.

Teddy just smiled and held his son absorbing all of his loving energy. Ms. Porchia stood to the side watch'n the reunion of her son and his dad.

"Hi you?" Teddy ask'd as he look'd up at the woman who was in charge of his heartaches.

"I'm good. You?" She inquired look'n away break'n the eye contact.

Ms. Porchia was a weakness to Teddy.

"I'm fine now." He said look'n down at Lil Teddy in his lap.

DAMN, THIS BITCH LOOK GOOD AS FUCK! Teddy thought as his eyes scour'd her from head to toe. Ms. Porchia had on some DKNY white jean shorts with a yellow DKNY tee shirt.

"You look'n good." She express'd as Teddy step'd out of the car putting Lil Teddy down allow'n Ms. Porchia to take note of his 15 pound lighter frame dress'd in grey Polo Sweats with an all white Polo tee shirt with the blue man set off with a fresh pair of all white Air Force ones, jewelry pieces sparkling. "Can I have a hug?" She ask'd.

Teddy step'd towards her extending his arms open as Ms. Porchia fell into his embrace.

"Umph, you smell good! Whutz that?"

"Polo sport."

"Let me let-chu go. I can't take that. You smell too good."

Letting her go, he acknowledge'd the erection in his sweats by grabb'n his crotch expose'n the width and length of his manhood brought on by Ms. Porchia's touch.

"Somebody miss'd me." Ms. Porchia look'd and smiled. "Where were you goin?"

"DADDY can I go with you?" Lil Teddy ask'd tugg'n at Teddy's arm.

"Nu-Nu, I'm on my way to work after I get me something to eat. Y'all in a rush?" Teddy ask'd hope'n they would have lunch with him.

"Not really, where do you work?"

"Next door at Willies. C'mon" Teddy answer'd grabb'n Lil Teddy's hand and walk'n toward the side door of KFC as Ms. Porchia follow'd.

Teddy order'd his typical 18 piece hot wings and Lil Teddy's original recipe chicken legs. Ms. Porchia just want'd a Pepsi. After they complete'd their order, they took a seat in the corner booth. Lil Teddy was eat'n and talk'n a mile a minute, tell'n Teddy everywhere he had been. Teddy became overwhelm'd in his emotions and before he knew it, he was in tears – just happy to see his son. His appetite vacated him as he struggled to hold his composure. He had never been as close to anyone as he was to his little man and being away from him for the past two months, not hearing his voice, ate at Teddy's existence. He was just happy to see his son and listen'n to him express how much he miss'd him also.

"Daddy, I'm going with you and we're going to see Mia and Mari."

"Teddy, your Daddy's gotta go to work.

Maybe we can see him tomorrow."

"Nooo, Mommy. I'm going with Daddy, right Dad?" Lil Teddy said look'n for confirmation from a torn Teddy. Teddy sat try'n to hide the tears from his son with his head down. "Mommy, my

daddy is cry'n. I can't leave him. It's alright Daddy."
Lil Teddy said very proper rubb'n Teddy's back.

"I'm alright Nu-Nu" Teddy said with a
chuckle. "I'm just glad to see you." "Me too Daddy.

Mommy, are you glad to see my daddy?"

"Yes Teddy, Mommy is."

"Well, you can go with us." Lil Teddy said.

"We gotta let Daddy go to work and we'll
call him later and maybe we can go to the park
tomorrow."

They wrapp'd up everything there and
went their separate ways. Teddy and Ms. Porchia
discuss'd a few issues. He even told her he was
dating a few chics. She admitt'd and apologized for
what she had done. By 6:00pm, Ms. Porchia and Lil
Teddy was at Willies check'n on Teddy. Teddy's
heart ached to be with his family. He was a totally
different person. His first love and his son, the love
of his life was all that matter'd to him.

The next day, they hung out at Freedom
Park. Teddy was off from work. It was a beautiful
summer Tuesday afternoon. They fed the ducks
while Lil Teddy ran wild. Ms. Porchia and Teddy
play'd and flirt'd relentlessly as if they were a new
couple. On the train, Lil Teddy pretend'd to be the
conductor while Teddy and Ms. Porchia got off a
quickie. She sat on his lap riding him cowboy style,
which was her intent. That's why she show'd up in

a stretch GAP skirt with no panties. Grind'n back and forth, they both climax'd together. Classic make up sex. Ms. Porchia's mission was to claim what was hers. Teddy was a sucka for love when it came to Ms. Porchia.

That was simply an appetizer for the weekend. They plann'd a weekend rendezvous up in Greensboro. That Friday before Teddy left, he had an appointment with his counselor. They hadn't met since the court date Monday past. For some reason David took a liking to Teddy. He respect'd his compassion for his children. The topic of discussion was, runn'n into Ms. Porchia after court.

"So how did that make you feel seeing her and Lil Teddy for the first time in two months?" He inquired, pry'n into Teddy's thoughts.

"Excited – nervous – still angry but see'n Lil Teddy had me a little emotional. He was just as excited." Teddy chuckled, "he was talk'n a mile a minute. Daddy this, daddy that."

"Porchia – what was her response?"

"Almost like nothing had happen'd. Glad to see me."

"That's what we can't allow to happen. Something has happen'd, a lot of something has happen'd and what you can't do is allow her to sweep it under the rug. She has to be held accountable for her role in all of this also. This is a family service. You can't be a family alone. She too needs to come in and speak with someone. You guys have a not so pretty history. There are still unanswer'd questions that need to be answer'd on her behalf. Are you catch'n my drift?"

He ask'd Teddy in search of confirmation, swiveling side to side in his roller chair thump'n an ink pen against his lip while Teddy attentively listen'd and consummed everything he was say'n. "Please move with caution Teddy. You've made too much progress to back track and lose it. I tell ya what —." He said while reach'n for one of his business cards. "Ask her to set an appointment. Explain to her your intense sessions we've had deal'n with your anger. Do not just pick up where you all left off. That's a disaster waiting to happen.

If you want your family back or you are considering getting intimately involved with Porchia again, I advise you to get her in here first. You have issues and so does she.

You're making the necessary moves to correct yours while she's living the illusion that it's all you. Her deceit, lies, her lack of authority when it comes to her parents getting into you guys business.  All of these issues and plenty more need answers. One thing about family counseling is, you can't heal half of the problem, its all or nothing. If she doesn't agree to come in, I advise you to reconsider dealing with her on any level outside of your son.  In the long run, she'll use him as leverage over you again as she just did. She know you are weak for your son and she also knows how much you love her. It's so detrimentally obvious but I'm challenging you to stand up for you. In the long run, you'll be glad you did."

Teddy took everything David said to heart, not tell'n him of the plans he had to be with her this weekend. However, he knew that everything David said was true.

Things went as plann'd. They stay'd at AmeriSuites off of Wendover Avenue. Teddy had somewhat shunn'd their intimacy, showing the majority of his attention to his son. Ms. Porchia sensed something was wrong while they were pool side watch'n Lil Teddy swim.

Teddy's demeanor was distant when it came to her. As she began to inquire, he exposed his concerns tell'n her he couldn't afford to be hurt again as she had just done. She in turn ask'd him what could she do to prove that it would never happen again. Teddy pass'd her the card and told her that they couldn't be together if she didn't get counseling also. She immediately agreed to it with continued apologies. That turn'd their weekend into an all out sex/fuck/love fest.

## Chapter 33: Moving On

After a sex fill'd makeup weekend in Greensboro, they return'd back to Charlotte to their separate lives. Ms. Porchia made an appointment to see a counselor at the Family Services that she never made it to. Teddy being the intellectual street dude he was, he continued his counseling, continued his mission to get rich and continued his relations with Ms. Peaches, Stacy and Ms. Porchia.

No matter how much Ms. Porchia spoke about getting back together. Teddy denied her and kept his other affairs up in her face because she wouldn't go to counseling. So, Ms. Peaches was #1. Instead of break'n down and going to get counseling, Ms. Prochia used the only leverage she had – Lil Teddy.

By the end of July, Ms. Porchia had grown tired of being back with her parents and not being able to be with Teddy whenever she want'd to be. It was no secret that his wealth had severly increased and he was becoming a major topic. In an attempt to prove to herself how much pull she had with Teddy, she told him she want'd to attend grad school at T in the fall. Teddy ask'd her what did she need. She explain'd that she could get financial aid to cover her classes but she need'd a place to live. Teddy agreed to provide that. He got her another spot in North Winds.

As bad as he want'd to start over with Ms. Porchia, he remember'd every word of advice David had given him. He was single and lovin it. As long as Ms. Porchia denied counseling, he denied their relationships.

Being that Ms. Porchia had a place in Greensboro, Teddy pick'd up a part time job work'n at Foot Locker's under Price. Steezo had just got out of Prison for those charges at the FORT and the whole crew was beginn'n to formulate once again.

It was the end of October, Ant'NO was coming home after serving 5 months for parole violation. Everybody got jobs. It was a new day. If they were going to hustle, they were going to have jobs. The FORT GREEN FAM had matured. Steezo was now married with seeds, Ant'NO lived with his girl and even though Teddy wasn't with Ms. Porchia, he basically lived there.

Teddy had a nice 7 month run. He was sitt'n on $75,000.00. He was no longer hustling coke, it was back to weed. Beno, Teddy's coke connect shut down shop when the FED's lock'd up his little brother. Teddy was content with just push'n trees.

For Christmas, he purchased a 99' Montero Sport truck fresh off the lot for $28,000. Before it was ever seen on the streets, Teddy put another $10K in it. He had a homeboy that work'd for NORTHEASTERN AUTOBODY REPAIRS – John put some 20 inch Enkei Spiders on it with the Tonka toy Toyo tires. He install'd the Sony Playstation and DVD system with Alpine TV Headrest, 5000 watt kicker amp with 3 – 12 inch kicker solo batteries for the 20 disc cd changer and the viper alarm with remote start.

The FORT GREEN FAM was beginn'n to make some major moves in the streetz again. Teddy and Steezo began to promote parties, bring'n a lot of artist to town while attempt'n to put Ant'NO's album together. They were doing everything as a family. On Sundays they would come together at Ms. Porchia's with their wives and children. Teddy would take turns cook'n with Ant'NO.  Ant'NO gets down but, Teddy would make Yo moma call her moma giving him high praise on his cook'n skills.

After a while, Teddy grew tired of front'n like everything was everything between him and Ms. Porchia. She was satisfied with the way things were and wasn't think'n about no counseling.  Ms. Porchia thought she had work'd her magic but all the while, Teddy was really phase'n her out. He was pay'n her rent so he had all access but at 28, Teddy was ready to start his family. He had hoped it would be with Ms. Porchia but she was up to her old tricks. No matter how much Teddy stress'd her going to get counseling, she would entertain it momentarily to shut him up, but no progress.

Meanwhile, Steezo had got a new coke connect and the FAM was eat'n. Teddy had hook'd up with Net to do an Entertainment company call'd BLACK MONEY ENTERTAINMENT. Teddy was in charge of the Def Jam Street Team out in Greensboro, Winston, and Raleigh, which made it easy for them to promote parties with artist.

BLACK MONEY didn't really focus on artist, they had production teams that consist of producers, writers and artist. PLATINUM THOUGHTS was the big ticket. There were 3 producers, Dre, Vex and Teddy. Vex was a chic that was blood raw with the beats. They did all the introductions for the 102 JAMZ personalities.

In February of 99', BLACK MONEY had a talent search competition at the Howard Johnson's ballroom on High Point Rd. They were in search of a heavy spit'n MC, a girl group, a guy group and a solo male and female artist.

At the registration, this young lady approach'd Teddy inquiring about the fees and requirements. She stood 6ft1' and she was gorgeous. She possess'd model qualities but she was a little too thick for the model scene. Her skin was milk chocolate smooth, she had chinky eyes and the sexiest lips.

As soon as the young lady and Teddy began to converse, the flirting began. She introduced herself as Tinara. Teddy shook her hand and introduced himself. There wasn't anything bashful about this sister, she went straight in for the kill.

"Mr. Teddy, I was considering enter'n your competition but, if I can have You I've already won."

"Tinara, I'm a grown man, why You got me in here blush'n. I ain't use to bein chose, I do the choosin."

"Is that right? Well, You are the chosen one." Tinara said with the sexiest smile.

"Ok, so You chose me. You came down here to audition, please give me a sample."

"A sample?" She ask'd and began to sang, not sing, sang Debra Cox "How Did You Get Here."

Tinara's angelic voice melt'd Teddy's whole existence. For the rest of the evening, he sat in converstation with Tinara to the side. She help'd to judge the rest of the talent. Tinara was 21 and from Philly. Her family had moved down to Winston Salem. She was currently a college student at Winston Salem State and very talent'd. After the initial flirting, they left that where it was and continued their converstion on a business, intellectual level. The attraction was automatic but they were both content getting to know each other and viewing personal goals.

While they were still engulf'd in each other, a 16 year old cat named Manifest brought the house down. He was a rapper. Tinara and Teddy both agreed that the young dude was the winner of the contest hands down since Tinara had been removed from the competition.

Nett, DJ Polo, Capital J, Teddy and Tinara all concluded that Manifest had won 1st place. He was award'd $500.00 and unlimited free studio time at Obia Studios with the producers of choice.

Tinara and Teddy exchanged info and promised to contact each other when they could find time away from their individual dead end relationships.

## Chapter 34: New Beginning

Things between Teddy and Ms. Porchia were completely on hold. He still stay'd over occasionally for the sake of Lil Teddy but other than that, all he did was pay rent and take care of his son.

By the end of April, Teddy and Tinara were in full fledge relationship. He moved her into her own place. She was like his right hand man. Tinara was by his side at all times. She respect'd and loved his hustle. The only time they were apart was when drugs were involved or he was stay'n at Ms. Porchia's.

So far, 99' was very prosperous for the founding members of The FORT. Everybody was eat'n. It was a Tuesday night in early August, Steezo call'd Teddy's cell phone to alert him of an emergency meet'n at Spoon's Pool hall. Teddy was always late. Not intentionally but simply because everything had to be right which meant triple check'n everything before makin a move. He hated forget'n something.

When he arrived at Spoon's, it was unusually crowd'd for a Tuesday night. Everybody was there – Steezo, Price, Ant'NO, Nett, Joy, Diesel, C, Shine and other FORT members. Soon as Teddy walk'd in, he was greet'd by the town ballers. He greet'd Mina (the bartender) and she gave him his usual (a double shot of Corvousier), then he made his way to the end of the bar where Steezo and the rest of the FORT was post'd shoot'n pool.

"Whut up son?" Steezo said as he and Teddy dapp'd each other.

"T-DADDY!' Joy yell'd as she ran up to embrace him.

"Whus goin on wit-chall? Whus the occasion? I ain't seen half You mu-fuckas in months. Whus the deal?" Teddy inquired.

"We celebrate'n wit P." Ant'No said. "He leavin tamarra son."

"P, where the fuck You goin? Nigga"

"Foot Lockers gave me my store. I gotta leave tamarr. I'm movin to Florida."

"Git da fuck outta here!"

"Word up son, that's why we all here." Ant'NO add'd in.

"T, come ova here son. Les shoot da one, we need to poli for a second." Steezo said.

Teddy grabb'd his drink and pool stick. Him and Steezo began to shoot pool.

"Yo son, the Fam need You to take that trip with P to the F – L – A."

"For what?" Teddy ask'd look'n puzzled.

"First of all, P ain't got no license. He needs You to drive him down there. Plus, You work for Foot Locker and You can get P's back while he gets settled in and check da spot out because the Fam bout to expand." Steezo explain'd.

Teddy's mind began to run a mile a minute. "So Y'all want me to just pick up and dip in less than 24 hours?" Teddy ask'd in disbelief.

"Yo T, iss You and me baby." Price said as he wrapp'd his arm around Teddy's neck. "You knew I was in managers train'n. We plan'd this remember?"

"We plan'd for me to work under You when You got-cho own sto. We ain't plan to jus up and run to Florida without warn'n. Nigga I got kids and a new bitch, I don't even have time for goodbyes."

"Yo son," Steezo interject'd. "You stay on the road more than any of us. There's no need for goodbyes. Anytime You need to get here, You get here."

"Whut difference does it make that P don't have license if we drivin both whips?" Teddy ask'd.

"We not driving both whips, jus mine. You can leave Yours out here. Nigga, open Yo mind to new beginnings. We grown, les go get this money. You got my back?" P ask'd.

Teddy look'd at P, glanced at Steezo and Ant'NO, "Man, fuck it! I'm wit it." He said after takin a deep breath.

Soon as Teddy agreed, it was like a major celebration for a member becoming a made man In the MOB. Teddy didn't see the big deal. Steezo told Mina to give everybody with The FORT what they're drink'n and made a toast to new beginnings.

Teddy and Steezo were off to the side talk'n privately. It amazed Teddy how much thought and preparation Steezo had put into this move in less than a few hours. He had it all set up, Nett was handling all of the Black Money affairs Ant'NO would handle all of Teddy's street affairs and Steezo himself would keep his currency straight. The whole move wasn't to be handled as a move, it was all business and that's how Teddy present'd it to Tinara and Ms. Porchia.

Once everything was etch'd in stone, Teddy left for Winston to be with Tinara for the night. On the way out there, he call'd Ms. Porchia and told her that he was leavin town on business for a few weeks and he would be by there tomorrow before he left.

Tinara understood his moves but she didn't necessarily like them. Teddy smash'd her all night, leaving her on a high note the next morning. They were set to leave by 3pm.

Teddy arrived back at Ms. Porchia's by 9:15 that Wednesday morning. She cook'd breakfast, his favorite, salmon patties, grits and eggs with fruit salad. It was actions as such that made Teddy wish he could marry her. He play'd around with Lil Teddy for a couple of hours, explain to him that he was going out of town for a while and pack'd his things. Lil Teddy fell asleep and Ms. Porchia got freaky.

Sitt'n in her living room in just a t-shirt, she press'd play on the VCR to watch the fuck flick that was in. Try'n not to pay her any attention while pack'n, he heard her moans coming in from the living room. At first, his will power and the session with Tinara the night before increased his strength until he walk'd pass her to the kitchen and heard how wet and juicy she had gotten herself.

"Can I taste You before You leave?" She ask'd in a begg'n typed seductive voice. "My pussy so hot. C'mere. Let me suck U while I play wit this pussy?"

Totally distracted and try'n to hold on to what little strength he had, Teddy responded, "Porchia, You see I'm busy".

"It won't take long. Please. Soon as I put it in my mouth, I know I'm gone nut. Please. Jus come here."

Teddy stopp'd, look'd over at Ms. Porchia's legs widely spread'd apart, notice'n her please'n herself and also notice'n his super hard erection he now possess'd. He hated the power she had over him but that was one emotion he would have to deal with later. He walk'd over to the couch she was sitt'n on and stood in front of her, as she aggressively grabb'd at his sweats, pull'n his dick out.

"Hell yeuh, my baby always git up for me." She said, speak'n of Teddy's super hard dick while she slowly engulf'd him inside her mouth while she masterbated. "M – m – mmm" She moan'd. "You – taste good. Lemme suck this dick wit my pussy." She said as she maul'd and slurp'd on his pre-cum.

"Why can't I resist – You?" Teddy ask'd.

"Because – this Yo pus-sy. You made it good like this. Mmmm – You know iss good." She said lay'n back on the couch invite'n Teddy inside of her.

Dropp'n to his knees, Teddy pull'd her by her waist to the edge of the couch. Entering her was all it took, Ms. Porchia nutt'd everywhere. Her pussy muscles contract'd relentlessly as Teddy slowly enter'd deeper and deeper into her womb.

"Ohh! Fuck me!" She moan'd. "Isss been so long." She purr'd, and pant'd. Teddy wasted no more time, he got a slow steady pace to where he could feel her insides getting wetter and wetter. Every stroke, he could see streaks of her snotty love juices on his dick. Ms. Porchia praised Teddy for how he was able to keep her cumm'n nonstop.

For the next 40 minutes, they went from the couch to floor, from doggy style to missionary, sweat'n and talk'n obscenely nasty to each other until Ms. Porcha was cry'n real tears in the middle of the grand finale orgasm that they shared together.

Teddy left her lay'n in the middle of the living room floor to go shower and continue pack'n. GOT DAMN! THAT BITCH GOT THE BEST PUSSY IN THE WORLD! Teddy thought to himself as he walk'd away.

After he got out the shower and got dress'd, he got everything ready and relax'd on the same couch he and Ms. Porchia had began their sexcapde. Ms. Porchia had shower'd and come to join him, ly'n in his arms. They had a decent conversation. Ms. Porchia told him that she respect'd everything he was doing and she was going to do her part to assure that they were a family.

He didn't really believe her but he really hoped that she would handle her end of the deal so that they could eventually be a family. They both fell asleep on the couch talk'n. Lil Teddy woke them up about 1:30. Teddy sat down with his son to let him know that he was leaving town for a while but he would be back for his birthday in a few weeks.

By 2:30, the whole FORT GREEN FAM was at Ms. Porchia's as if they were sending them away to Prison. All business was tied up. Ant'NO came to take Teddy's Montero and put it up. Ms. Porchia stood by noticing the structure and the code that Teddy lived by. Steez and Ant'NO assured Teddy that Ms. Porchia and Lil Teddy would be fine. Ant'NO pull'd Teddy to the side to let him know if Tinara need'd anything to have her call and he'd take care of it.

A little over 12 hours later they arrived in Cocoa FL. Check'n into their hotel. The place they would call home for the next two months. After check'n in at the Ramada Inn on highway 26, Teddy and P opt'd to unpack the next day. They enter'd there room, took showers, smoked a blunt, laid back and relax'd try'n to unwind from their road trip. P flipp'd thru the channels on the TV while Teddy call'd back up north to let everybody know that they arrived safely.

Price was ask'd to take that particular store on Merrit Island for more than one reason. The first being, the manager walk'd out leaving the stock room entrance door open'd and they got clean'd out. The second being that, this particular Foot Locker's is in the main mall in this area and only averages $5,000.00 on a weekday and close to

$50,000.00 weekly. Price was next in line to get a store and with his experience, Venator had confidence in his ability.

Price pull'd extra strings to get them to send Teddy with him but being that it was all done on such short notice, they made it possible so that Price would have qualified assistance.

The first week was strenuous and intensly hectic. They had to do a complete overhaul – restock, evaluate their strengths and weaknesses and touch basis with each individual employee to get a better understanding of what was needed. Price put Teddy in charge of stock.

Teddy was use to purchasing all of his Timberlands and Air Force Ones from Foot Lockers and this store didn't have not one pair. He had his work cut out for him. Timberlands, Air Force Ones and Jordans were the top sellers in the stores up in NC and it was important to set that same trend down there in order to be successful.

Daily, they left for work by 8AM and return'd no earlier than 1AM. For the first two weeks, all they did was work, eat, work, sleep, work and work. Teddy and Tinara had their first argument because she was missing him and didn't know what he was doing. She knew that he was work'n but she wasn't use to his new work schedule. He barely had time to have a decent conversation with her. Ms. Porchia on the other hand was being understand'n and supportive. She accept'd the once a week phone call and didn't complain.

Two days before Teddy was due back in NC to record with the new artist Manifest and for Lil Teddy's birthday, Teddy call'd Tinara's phone and some dude answer'd. The dude said he had the wrong #. That same night when he call'd, she rush'd off the phone. Teddy sensed something strange.

He flew into town for four days. His first night back in town, he had a session in Winston at Infinite Recordings on the corner of 5th & Trade down from the bus station. When his flight arrived, Ant'NO pick'd him up in his Montero at the Greensboro Airport.  Ant'NO fill'd him in on the last few weeks. He gave Teddy $5K and two ounce of hydro. Teddy dropp'd him off and hit 40 west to Winston.

After getting the session started with Manifest, Teddy's gut told him to call Tinara. When he call'd, she tried to rush off the phone again but he stopp'd her when he told her he was on his way over.

"Where You at?" Tinara ask'd frantically.

"I'm at the studio, I'm on my way."

"Baby, stay there. I'm comin over there." She said, rush'n.

"Tinara, whus goin on?"

"I'll explain when I get there. I promise."

"If You ain't here in 10 minutes, I'm comin." Teddy said before pushn the "END" button on his cell.

10 minutes later, Tinara pops up with tears in her eyes, apologizing and explain'n. She told Teddy she had got lonely and let her ex come over, one thing led to another and now he won't leave. Teddy told her he forgave her and respect'd her honesty but he want'd that nigga out of his spot before he left town.

The next three days was spent with Lil Teddy, Mia and Mari celebrating Lil Teddy's 5th birthday. Teddy and Ms. Porchia paraded as a couple at Chucky Cheeze after Teddy show'd up in dramatic fashion escort'd by Joy, Shine, Mesha, Kim, and Sari. Ms. Porchia's parents and grandparents were in attendance as well as the members of The FORT. Everybody had a ball, Teddy enjoy'd his children and friends while he was home the past four days but, it was time to get back to business.

When Teddy arrived back in Florida, it was back to work non-stop. For the next month Teddy and Price went all in to raise the standards of their store. Their weekly profit was up by 75% which were the results of their hard work and no play.

Price got cool with the head security guard of the Mall, Reese. Reese was the countriest New Yorker You ever met but he was cool. He always told Price and Teddy that he was going to take them out on the town but they would always be too busy. This particular Friday night, Reese caught them at work early and told them he want'd them to meet his chic's sister and cousin. Teddy wasn't with it but Price talk'd him into it.

They closed the store on time and left right after – something they hadn't done since they had been there. They got to the hotel, shower'd and changed. By 10:20, Reese was there to pick them up. Before arriving at the chic's spot, Reese stop'd by the Package Store and they all got a pint of their liquor of choice.

Meeting new chics was always a hobby and favorite pass time for Teddy. He was infatuated with the hunt. Even if it was just meet'n on a platonic level, women were very intriguing to him and it was always a pleasure to be around them. What made this so different was because they were the first chics they had interacted with in the area outside of work and Teddy going to the beauty salon to get his hair braid'd and nails manicured.

Reese warn'd that it was always 3 – 10 broads at this spot at any given time. When they arrived it was only 3 present, Trisha – Reese's chic, her sister Treace and her cousin Keava. Keava immediately went after P.  She wasted no time let'n him know that all he had to do was ask and she would deliver.

In general, they were fun chics. Trisha was the more talkative one. She was country thick like Stacy, cute with 3 bottom gold teeth. They were at her place. Trisha was cool in Teddy's eyes but she ask'd him a million and one questions like she was a reporter. At 25, she seemed to have herself together, being a good mom to her five year old son.

Keava was a flirtatious, 5ft2' cutie that remind you of Regina King in Boyz In The Hood. Throughout the night as they play'd cards, Keava and Price flirt'd relentlessly. Keava was a year younger than Trish. Treace was the baby of the group. She was 19 and had just graduated from high school. On the low, she was like the moma of their crew. Even though she drank and smoke weed, she was quiet and extremely lady like. Treace look'd like a 15 pound lighter version of Kim from the Parkers.

Teddy enjoy'd himself hang'n out with some new chics, while P went on to score, Teddy and Treace teamed up to beat Reese and Trish in spades. Half way thru their game, P and Keava went to Trisha's son's room. After the game, Trisha and Reese excused themselves to also indulge in adult activities. Treace was about to leave, when she ask'd Teddy was he going to be ok. He ask'd her for a ride back to the hotel. Right next to the hotel was a Waffle House. He told her to drop him off there or she could join him. She chose to join him say'n she didn't want him to eat alone.

They enjoy'd their meal. Treace talk'd more in Teddy's company privately than she did all night long, but still very cautious and reserved. Although Teddy thought she was attractive and vice versa, there were no immediate sparks fly'n. She offer'd to pay the bill and that turn't Teddy on but he refused her offer. It was about 1:23 AM when they pull'd in front of the hotel room. She ask'd Teddy what was he about to do. I KNOW THIS LITTLE YOUNG THANG AIN'T TRY'N ME. He thought. I WILL END HER WHOLE CAREER, BUT SHE DO GOT A FAT ASS AND SOME SEXY ASS LIPS.

"Probly smoke a blunt and watch a pay per view movie."

"You want some company?" She ask'd.

"Come on in."

She join'd him. When they enter'd the room, the hotel phone light was blink'n and Teddy's cell phone had 11 miss'd calls. Teddy always left his phone on the charger and used it only when necessary.

"You can have a seat anywhere." Teddy said as he sat on the bed near the hotel phone to check the messages. He enter'd the code to retrieve the messages and began to listen. The first message  was from Tinara earlier tell'n Teddy,

Ant'NO had given her the rent money and she need'd money to get her car serviced. The next call was also from earlier, Ms. Porchia just want'd to let him know she was think'n about him. Stacy call'd with a similar message. Nett call'd to let him know that Manifest completed 3 songs and 102 JAMZ was play'n it in rotation. And the last call was from Ms. Porchia.

"Teddy! Who do you think You are? You tell'n me to get counsel'n and when I call You, the front desk clerk suppose to be sending me to the voice mail but I get your message. Fuck You! I don't care if we aren't together per say, You got too many bitches! You got too many bitches! You pay'n rents and GOD know what else. NIgga, You need more counsel'n. I got-cho heart remember that!" CLICK!

Teddy was furious. He grabb'd his cell phone to return Ms. Porchia call. He took a deep breath.
"You alright?" Treace ask'd.

"Yeeh, I'm straight. A little baby moma drama." He said as he pull'd out a plastic bag fill'd with some of Florida's exotic marijuana call'd 'Crypt'. "Roll'n a blunt." He said, throw'n her the bag and a blunt as he dial'd Ms. Porchia's #.

Ms. Porchia answer'd in a groggy tone.

"Sorry I woke You." Teddy said in a calm demeanor.

"What Teddy?"

"Why all the drama on the voice mail?" He ask'd.

"I don't have time for this, I'm sleep."

"Look, I'm not try'n to argue with You. In fact, You know I want to be with you."

"Whateva Teddy" She said interrupt'n him. "I thought things were gett'n better between us."

"That's the problem, You doin too much think'n and not enough action. All You got to do is see a counselor and we can make moves."

"Teddy fuck You, I don't need counsel'n, You do! Go get some more and be with your other whores." She said as she disconnect'd.

Teddy threw the phone on the other bed beside Treace.

"I take it that was baby moma?" Treace said with a candid smile.

"One of'em."

"You love her."

"Yeeh, but sometimes love ain't enough."

"I wouldn't know." She said look'n back over her shoulder with a sexy smile.

"I wish I didn't know."

"Here." She said pass'n the blunt. "What movie we watch'n?" She ask'd as she scann'd the choices.

"Pick one. It don't matter to me."

"I'ma pic something that will take your mind off of your issues."

She chose a XXX-rated flick and came over to the bed beside Teddy. They laid back talk'n and tripp'n off of the flick and like clockwork, one thing lead to another. Teddy felt guilty for the combination of pleasure and pain he brought to Treace's existence. She withstood the frustration Ms. Porchia caused, anxiety caused from the job and his built up horniness.

Treace was good for Teddy, she kept him young. Throughout the rest of the year, she hungout with him. Right before Thanksgiving, she help'd decorate the townhome Teddy and Price began to purchase. If she wasn't at Teddy's, he was at her place hang'n out with her and her mom. She was a breath of fresh air to Teddy. "No stress" was her motto.

Even when Teddy went to NC for a few days on business, she knew he was takin care of his extracurricular activities with his prior acquaintences but she never let that become an issue when they were together. Teddy call'd her his T – N – T (Tender N Train'n).

Right after the beginning of the new millennium, January 10, 2000 Ant'NO was found dead in his apartment in Georgetown Manor. Teddy and Price was devasted. From that moment on, Teddy's life would never be the same.

## Chapter 35: Betrayal


Attending Ant'No's funeral was about virtually impossible for Teddy and Price because somebody had to run the store. Teddy left going back to NC as soon as he got the news. After the autopsy was complete, Steezo and Teddy paid to have his body flown back to Brooklyn. It took a week to finalize all of the funeral arrangements.

Steezo and Teddy took it extremely hard. They sat up in East New York with Ant'NO's family try'n to make sense of the whole thing. Teddy vow'd not to rest until there were answers to this atrocity and somebody was pay'n the price for Ant'NO's death but for right now, all they knew was that he was robb'd and murder'd at his place early Saturday morning January 10, 2000.

Ms. Porchia, Nika (Steezo wife), Isha (Ant'No's wife) and the rest of the FORT arrived two days before the funeral. Price was able to get a flight in and back out the same day of the funeral.

After all the precedings, Steezo and Teddy held a meet'n with the whole FORT GREEN FAM concern'n their street investigation. Ms. Porchia stuck by Teddy's side like a trooper. She knew he was hurt and even though they had issues, she attempt'd to help him deal with the pain.

Before Price left going back to Florida, he and Teddy talk'd concern'n Teddy's return. Teddy let him know that he need'd time, it was a good possibility he wouldn't be return'n and he might need him for an alibi so keep him on the payroll. Price understood and he want'd more than anything answers to Ant'No's murder.

A week later back in Greensboro, Teddy was handling business as usual. Very few knew he was back in town. Most of his days was spent in the studio with Manifest.  As of lately, he had regain'd the passion for the music. On the average, he was dropp'n 10 beats a day and Manifest was assault'n each track as if he was the government leading the attack on terrorism.

This particular night, Teddy had just left the studio. It was 12:15AM, hunger pains was riddling thru his body so he decided to run thru Jake's Diner on High Point Rd. While he wait'd for his order, one of Teddy's good friends, Deloris walk'd in. Deloris use to work in their clothing store.

"Hey Teddy." Deloris said as they embraced each other.

"Whussup Lady? Hi You been?" Teddy said holding her by her waist.

"Everything is everything. I'm sorry about Ant, that shit was fuck'd up."

"Yeeh it was." Teddy replied with disgust in his face.

"I saw Porchia a few weeks back at The Rib Shack. Y'all still together?"

"Dee, You know how dat goes. That's Lil Teddy's mom, I'm gone always love her but I don't know if we will ever be together again."

"Ant'NO didn't tell You about the shit that went down that night at The Shack?" Deloris ask'd in amazement.

"Nah, what shit and when?" Teddy ask'd.

"It was the Friday before X-mas. Ant'NO was up in The Shack popp'n bottles like he do and when I came back up front from the dance floor, he was in Porchia's face cuss'n her ass out like a dog, Dat nigga Angelo pull'd Porchia back and Ant'NO push'd him. The bouncers came thru and stood between'em. They escort'd Angelo out and Porchia was with him."
                "Yeeh, dat nigga!"

"Remember, we was beef'n wit dem niggas when we had the spot in Forest Grove?"

"I know.  Everybody said dat nigga Lay-Lay that popp'd up on the scene with dat little young nigga Baby D was the one who shot Angelo and You set it up."

Deloris inform'd.

"Git da fuck outta here!" Teddy said in suspense. "I didn't know dem lil wild niggaz. Shiit, dem lil muthafuckaz had us watch'n our back. I heard when  Angelo got shot, it was a robbery gone bad."

"Exactly! Set up by You! That's what the word was and still is."

"So dat nigga Angelo was with Porchia at The Rib Shack and had beef wit Ant'NO?"

"I'm surprised You didn't know because when I heard about Ant, that's the first thing I thought about."  Deloris express'd.

"Dee, stay in touch Baby, You ain't seen me, You feel me?"

"You know I got'cho back Nigga."

Teddy left a $20 bill on the counter with the food he order'd and left. The information Deloris just threw on him destroy'd his appetite.

I KNOW KARMA AIN'T CAME TO BITE MY ASS LIKE THIS. Teddy thought as he drove to Steezo's. ALLAH, WHAT IS GOING ON? He ask'd his LORD. His mind began to drop back to the events that Deloris had brought to mind. HOW COULD ANYBODY KNOW THAT LAY-LAY AND BABY D WAS WITH ME? THE ONLY PERSON WHO KNEW WAS

PORCHIA. NOBODY FROM THE FORT EVEN KNEW. I KNOW THIS BITCH AIN'T BATTIN FOR ANOTHA TEAM.

Teddy's thoughts ran rapid. He pull'd into the park'n space in front of Steezo's condo and call'd him on the cell phone.

"Yo, You sleep?" Teddy ask'd when Steezo answer'd.
"Nah son, I just got in."

"I'm outside. Come out, we need to poli for a sec."
"Ah-ight son, I'm on my way."

Teddy sat wait'n while he listen'd to his Jucy Pear cd.

"Whut up son?" Steezo ask'd as he jump'd into the passenger side.

"Did Ant tell You he had beef wit Angelo at the Shack a few weeks back?"

"Yeeh, but that shit was dead'd. Ant'NO said he shouldn't have got into that because that was Porchia's business."

"Why da fuck! Y'all niggaz ain't said shit? You know we was beef'n wit dem ho as niggaz a while back."

"Son, we was a lil nuts then. Niggaz is eat'n now. Angelo, Poncho and that nigga Rico cop work from me."

"Soo You gone disregard them niggaz cause they cop'n work? Since ,when did some shit like that ever matter?" Teddy ask'd in a rage. "Niggaz git'n soft or what? Did you know that them niggaz think I had Lay-Lay and Baby D shoot dat nigga Angelo?"

"Yo son, that's why we put the plan together for you to go to Florida wit P. We been knew dat shit! I knew if we told You, You would have never left. That shit was old news but fresh beef. Nigga, we was protect'n You!"

"Fuck dat! Dat nigga fuck'n wit my baby mom's and Y'all niggas ain't say shit?"

"Yo son, Yo attention been on Tinara, what difference did it make?"

"Dat bitch was with me in NY for Ant's funeral when I could have had my woman wit me. I fuck'd dat bitch!  Ain't no tell'n what da fuck! Got me fuck'n behind this nigga!"

"Calm down son!"

"Easy for You to say. I betchu dat nigga had something to do with Ant's death!" He vent'd. "Yo, I'm gone."

"Yo son, I got-chu. Jus calm down. Ain't no need in jump'n the gun. We gone let this shit die down and let the streetz talk cause they always do.

By da way, when the last time You spoke to Lay-Lay and Baby D?" Steezo retort'd as he open the door and got out, insinuating he knew the truth.

Teddy more vex'd than he was on the way over. He was initially going back to Ms. Porchia's but he need'd to think so he went to Tinara's. From there, he put his plan together.

As the days toll'd pass, Teddy went on like everything was cool. Daily, he met with Deloris for information. Being around Ms. Porchia made his skin crawl. He question'd Steezo's loyalty and wonder'd could he have been a part of this bullshit.

Two weeks later, Deloris had Rico's address. That was a start. Teddy began to follow Rico. He brought Donté, Jap and Fly to town with 3 of Fly's baddest broads that danced at Club Champagne in Charlotte. Teddy stay'd in contact with Nett concern'n the Entertainment Company and being that she was so sexy, she was always down to be the bait to catch a snake mix'd into their crowd.

Teddy was gett'n everything in motion for the upcoming weekend. It was one of Greensboro's all out party weekends and this was the weekend he would get answers. OutKast, Ludacris, and Fabolous was in town. Steezo was host'n the Grown & Sexy After-Party. Deloris told Teddy that she saw Angelo and Ms. Porchia in the mall park'n lot talk'n and she has one of her girls going out with Angelo that Friday night.

"Teddy, I don't know if he's fuck'n Porchia or not but they definitely got something going on. I know You got something plann'd, everybody is going to be at Steezo's party Friday night and You already know them niggas will be out there ball'n."

"Yeuh, I do have a plan but who You got goin out wit dat nigga?"

"Silatia."

"Deloris, You know I want dat pussy and You got her tied in with this shit."

"Fuck You Teddy, I wish You would fuck Silatia. I'll kill dat bitch. You been hold'n me off for the longest because of Porchia and You thank I'm jus gone move out the way and let-chall be together?

Nigga, you got me fuck'd up. I'm on Yo team goin all out, please don't play me."

"It was a joke, DAMN! Stay focus'd Dee. I can't fuck You, we too close. That might fuck shit up."

"Whuteva Teddy. I gotta go. Keep me post'd."
Dee said as they disconnect'd.

Silatia was a bad bitch and very few could speak of being in her presence let alone her bed. Simply put, her and Stacy Dash could have been twins. She was a designer Queen. If it wasn't top of the line fashion, she wasn't caught in it. Deloris was the same as far as fashion went but she look'd like a short thick Thelma from Good Times. She was super dedicated and loyal to Teddy. She was one of those types that would hold on til the end because she believed in Your dream and saw the potential.

Being that Deloris had put Silatia on Angelo, Teddy told Fly he didn't need the four broads but they might want to stay and party – Teddy's treat, and he might need them for back up.

Teddy's plan was officially set. If Angelo didn't have anything to do with Ant'NO's death, it would simply be an all out message to the Triad that anybody that thought about beef'n with Ant'NO was in danger, including Ms. Porchia.

Friday afternoon, Teddy told Steezo, Ms. Porchia and everybody that wasn't apart of his plan that he had to fly back to Florida. Steezo dropp'd him off at the airport and Donté was there to pick him up.

The after party was being held at the Sheraton at Four Season's Mall in the Executive Ballroom. Teddy, Deloris, Nett and Fly were all using Motorola's new 2-way pagers. Teddy and Donté were outside in Donté's rental car wait'n. Fly sent the message thru 2-way that Rico was in deep conversation with Shayla. Shayla was the stunnah out of all the broads Fly brought.

Approximately 2 ½ hours later, the action began.

ANGELO AND SILATIA  ARE IN FRONT OF ME HEAD'N TO HIS CAR.
TOUCH "D"

Was the first e-mail Teddy received from Deloris.

SHAYLA AND RICO IS MAKIN MOVES. OUT!

"Fly" Guy

Was the next e-mail he received.

I'M IN MY CAR BEHIND Y'ALL T-DADDY.

FISH "NETT"

Was the e-mail NETT sent and blink'd her head lights for confirmation.

EVERYBODY PLAY YO POSITIONS AND MEET BACK AT THE ROOM. STAY IN TOUCH.

TE – DDY

Was the e-mail Teddy sent to everybody.

Teddy got out the car and Nett met him a car behind Angelo's Range Rover, while Jap and Deloris sat at Rico's Expedition. Teddy was glad they left before the party end'd because instead of having to follow these niggaz, they could take them in the park'n deck.

DEE, YOU DRIVE AND LET JAP HOLD THE PISTOL TO DAT NIGGA'Z MELLON IN THE BACK SEAT.
TE – DDY

THEY GIT'N OFF DA ELEVATOR

TOUCH "D"

Angelo was good and tipsy as he approach'd his whip gripp'n Silatia's ass.

"Hey Angelo." Nett spoke walk'n towards them.
"Nett, whus happen'n Shawty?" He inquired as she approach'd.

"Nigga, You know You look'n good." She exaggerated.

"Thanks Shawty." He said as she divert'd his attention allow'n Teddy to sneak up behind him, knock'n him out with the butt of a .45 cal.

Silatia grabb'd his car keys, hit the alarm and unlock'd the doors. Nett jump'd in the driver's seat while Teddy threw Angelo in the back seat, and Silatia rode shot gun. Meanwhile, Shayla and Rico got in the Expedition and she began to give him head while he lay back in the driver's seat. Rico was tipsy himself. Jap jump'd in the backseat of his unlock'd car door, getting the drop on him. Shayla jump'd in the back seat with Jap while Deloris open'd the driver's door order'n Rico to cross over the console.

"I can't believe I got caught slipp'n." Rico said pull'n up his Jil Sanders custom cut slacks.

"Shut-cho bitch ass up and git in Yo seat belt." Jap order'd putt'n the gun to his head. "Shayla, get out and check the dash board and under both seats for pistols."

Deloris pull'd out a 9mm from the console, while Shayla confiscated a .38 snub nose revolver from under the seat. "Here, call T-Rock." Jap said, giving Shayla his cell. She got Teddy on the phone.

"Tell'm we right behind them. Go to the spot.

"Deloris, why You doin –"

"Nigga shut da fuck up! I'll bang yo ass right here." Jap yell'd lower'n the gun from his head to his left knee and firing. POW!!!

"OH SHIT!!! Please don't kill me Joe!"

"Ni shut da fuck up and concentrate on the burn."

They rode out to a spot call'd Midway on the outskirts of Winston. This spot was country, no street lights, simply mad woods. Teddy stood outside of a barn in the middle of no where direct'n Deloris where to park.  She park'd on the side of the barn. Teddy approach'd the side where Rico cop pleas know'n that his life was near to an end.

"Teddy, it wasn't me Man." He said cry'n. "Lo done dat dumb ass shit. I told his ass."

"Don't worry, I might let—chu kill dat nigga for gett'n You caught up in this bull shit. But fa now git-cho ass out." Teddy chuckled. "I knew it was ya'll!"
"I can't move!" He cried. "Dat mufucka shot my knee out wit dat big ass shit!" He spat.

"You shot da nigga?" Teddy ask'd laugh'n at Jap.

"Da nigga talk too got damn much, like now." Teddy crack'd up laugh'n.

"Teddy, You stupid." Deloris said laugh'n while Shayla join'd in laugh'n at how impatient Jap was. "I didn't know what to think when Jap shot dis nigga. Meat fly'n every – got – damn where."

Deloris add'd to the humor.

Teddy help'd Rico out of his SUV and into the barn to the shameful sight of Angelo sitt'n butt naked cover'd in his own feces.

"Git naked Rico!" Teddy instruct'd as he let him go falling to his knees in pain.

Donté, Fly, Jap, Nett, Deloris and Teddy all stood aim'n guns at Angelo and Rico as if they were a fire'n squad.
"Rico, speak!"

Teddy order'd, "Whut happen'd to Ant'NO?"

"Angelo kill'd dat nigga."

"Rico, You's a bitch!" Angelo Yell'd. "They gone kill us You stupid mutha fucka, have some dignity!"

"Angelo befo this night is ova, You gone be a bitch too. Jus wait." Teddy chuckled as he dial'd a # on Angelo's cell. "Right now Yo baby mom's got dick in her ass and mouth. Remember Lay – Lay and Baby D? Here." Teddy toss'd him his phone.

"ANGELO, You stupid muthafucka! What have You done?"

She scream'd in the phone. "I hate – chu! I hate – chu! Die Slow!" his baby mom's lash'd out.

"Yeuh, I kill'd that nigga Joe! And I fuck'd that bitch Porchia.

She paid me to kill yo ass but-chu got me first. I'll see You in hell Fuck boy!" Angelo said as tears fell from his eyes.

"Shayla, suck Rico's dick for me. I'm not gone kill You niggaz but my nigga Lay – Lay got instructins to kill Yo daughter and that bitch Tione if You niggas don't follow these instructions. Is that nigga hard Shayla?" Teddy ask'd.

"He ready."

"Rico fuck dat bitch ass for git'n You into this bullshit and I'm only gon tell You once.  Nett hit dem niggaz." Teddy order'd.

Rico crawled over on his good knee and pull'd in behind Angelo.

"Teddy, You sick Fuck!" Angelo yell'd as Rico enter'd his rectum cover'd in shit.

Nett took a syringe filled with battery acid and inject'd it into Angelo's forearm. She then took another syringe and inject'd battery acid into Rico's ass. Shortly after both injections, they both fell to their death.

They left them where they lay, leaving both of their SUV's outside the barn.

As they rode down the highway, Teddy was deep in thought. THAT BITCH PAID THAT NIGGA TO KILL ME AND ANT'NO. DAMN ANT'NO, I HOPE YOU CAN REST IN PEACE NOW, ONE LOVE FAM. ALLAH, PLEASE FORGIVE MY SINS. Teddy silently prayed.

Teddy rode back with Donté, Nett, Deloris and Silatia in the Durango Donté rent'd. Instead of going back to Greensboro, they dropp'd Teddy off at Tinara's. He stay'd up all night try'n to figure out what to do with Ms. Porchia. Love is a strange energy, it takes up the same space as hate at times. It has the power to leave You as empty as a human corpse without a soul.

The next day, Teddy call'd to check on Ms. Porchia. She spoke so kind, warm and gentle. Lil Teddy was in Charlotte with Kenya and her husband for the weekend. Teddy end'd the phone call tell'n her she was on his mind while walk'n into her apartment as a surprise.

"Boy, You are always up to something." Porchia said with a smile.

"So are You." Teddy said, putting down a gallon size milk jug fill'd with gasoline.

"How was Your trip? I thought You was comin back Monday." She said, reach'n out to hug him.

Right then, Teddy snapp'd, "Porchia, don't touch me. In fact, don't – chu ever touch me again. I hate – chu Bitch!"

"Whu – Whut did I –"

"Bitch, you know whut – chu did. Dat nigga dead and You next." Teddy said before he sucka punch'd her, knock'n her out.

Teddy tied her up, gagg'd her and drench'd her in gas. He was totally out of control, experiencing temporary insanity. Lucky for him, he left the apartment. While he was gone, he came back to. Ms. Porchia had effectively ran a perfectly sane, intelligent brother crazy.

Teddy show'd back up at Ms. Porchia's apartment with no recollect of what he had done earlier. He rush'd to untie Ms. Porchia ask'n her who tied her up. She fell into his arms cry'n. Teddy kept ask'n her who did it, who did it and she never gave an answer, she just cried. Teddy clean'd her up, giving her a bath. Then he ask'd her did she want him to call the Police. She sensed something was terribly wrong but she also knew that she could do time for conspiring to kill Ant'NO. Teddy express'd to her that he didn't like what they had become. She was the mother of his first and only son and truly loved her. Ms. Porchia was so scared, when Teddy fell asleep, she went forward with call'n the Police. She told them everything he said and did. He was arrest'd and not given a bond.

By Monday, Angelo and Rico's bodies were found by some kids play'n in the area. They charged Teddy with two counts of Pre Meditated First Degree Murders, Kidnapping and Assault Inflicting Serious bodily Harm.

Teddy got his wish, the news reporters reported their deaths exactly as they were found. The Prosecutor had no witnesses so Teddy went to trial and was found guilty of two counts of Manslaughter, Kidnpping and Assault with intent. Ms. Porchia took the stand against Teddy in his trial. Teddy still loved her so much that he disregard'd the fact that she paid Angelo to kill Ant'NO, not to mention, snitch'n wasn't in his blood line.

He was found guilty on all charges and sentence to 11 – 14 years. His attorney request'd an appeal but by the time the smoke clears, he'll have done over 5 years in DOC.

## Chapter 36: Something to Nothing
## (Understanding Equality Born)

Sitting in the Guilford County Jail waiting to go to prison, Teddy found out that Ms. Porchia bought a brand new M3 BMW convertible. A week later, Shine was out at the Flea Market on 29 when she ran into Ms. Porchia out there sell'n all Teddy's clothes, shoes, jewelry, and studio equipment. He still had $35K, 17 ounces of raw cocaine and 50 pounds of weed at her apartment. Ms. Porchia never offered him a dime of his own money to assist him with his attorney fees or nothing. That's why he ended up with a Public Defender, Steezo, Donté, Fly and Jap basically disowned him. Teddy didn't sweat it because he knew that he didn't have a life sentence and the day would come that his vengeance would be felt by all. SUCCESS!

Ms. Porchia had done her best to run Teddy literally insane but nothing ate at him like when the sheriff served him the papers saying that she was changing Lil Teddy's last name from Massey to Grier.

From that moment on Teddy was a empty shell. His mentality was too strong to fold but his heart had reach'd its fate.  Later that night when the officers made their rounds, Teddy was found lay'n face down in the floor. Not answer'n to their call, the officers' popp'd his door and ran to his rescue. He still had a faint pulse. They rush'd him to Mose's Cone Hospital where he stay'd for two weeks recovering from a massive heart attack.

Instead of releasing him back to the county, DOC came to take him to Central Prison for processing.

Teddy's whole existence had changed before his face in less than a solid year. Starting out, Queen, Tinara, Treace and Nett was Teddy's only supporters. Tinara supplied all the visits while Queen, Treace and Nett sent money. Treace would come to town once a month from Florida to visit.

After Teddy's heart attack, his heart turn'd cold and all he cared about was his children and revenge. He didn't care to trust the women in his corner. As far as he was concern'd, they would all eventually turn on him as Ms. Porchia did.

As he began his travels thru the penal system, he had a big homie named Veteran Black from North Charlotte that he would walk and talk with. Vet Black was a real live gangsta. He lived by the code and always tried to give Teddy some sound advice. Teddy respect'd Vet Black because he didn't pull any punches, he was a solid dude. Teddy would confide in Vet about his situations, legal and personal. Vet kept Teddy's thoughts on even grounds – always encouraging him to do the right things and not to get caught up in the system. Teddy was 31 at the time and Vet was 37.

Throughout the time he was at ACI, they maintain'd a brotherly relationship. Vet was the influence that Teddy needed to focus on his calling.

Teddy realized quickly that eventually he would end up doing his time alone. If his appeal didn't come thru, he was look'n at a decade away from what he call'd family and friends. The adage "Out of sight, out of mind," slowly became a reality. Most of his time was spent studying different sects of Islam such as AL-Islam and The Morrish Science Temple of America while taking all kinds of college classes to further his education. It all play'd a part in Teddy's future revenge on his past love and so call'd family members. It also kept him focus'd and out of trouble.

After 2 ½ years at ACI, Teddy was transferred to PCI for some more college courses. Fresh off the bus, he runs directly into his first blood and mentor, Kato. Their reunion was epic, K was proud of the man Teddy had become and Teddy was proud to see that K was still holding his head up and stay'n strong.

In 92' Kato was falsely accused and convicted of first degree murder. He was given life plus 20 years. Teddy never kept contact with K after he was convicted but he had it in his mind that once he was rich, he was going to hire the best in the business to fight his conviction. K was innocent and Teddy knew it, but before he could reach fortune and fame, he reach'd his cousin face to face on common ground. K was still a boss and he was still big cuz, the class act that bred the true swag that Teddy possess'd.

Running into K really did Teddy some good. He dropp'd plenty jewels on Teddy to carry him thru his bid such as, he told him to always stand on his own, don't depend on nothing from the outside and to focus on creating currency from within.

Nothing in DOC was consistent except the time. Three years had pass'd already it was 2005. Just when Teddy thought things were looking up, he found out his appeal was denied. Throughout the past 3 years, Ms. Porchia would periodically send him pictures of Lil Teddy, write or except a phone call or two but never a visit. Teddy miss'd his son so much til it actually hurt and almost cost him his life but the sad part was that he never stop loving Ms. Porchia.

In August of 05, Ms. Porchia married a Police Officer who was moonlight'n as a Reverend. Anybody that knew Teddy and knew Ms. Porchia knew that she did that for security purposes. Teddy still loved her dearly but what he didn't know was that she never stopp'd loving him either. Hell, she had to see him daily thru his son. Although she knew her actions were wrong, she had done too much wrong to atone so she lived within her hell she had created not realizing that she was only hurting her child.

Teddy's philosophy was, Ms. Porchia didn't want to see him and her husband's coward ass was glad. Even he knew he could never have her as Teddy did. Everything that her husband loved most about her was qualities that Teddy embedded in her. 11 years is 11 years and it was evident that Teddy made her but like Jay – Z once said, "once a good girl is gone bad, she's gone forever." Teddy felt that if her husband was a real man, no matter how she felt about the child's father, Mr. Reverend would make sure that child sees his father. Only a coward would stand by and let the woman dictate the relationship.

Why make the child suffer, especially if the child's father wants to be apart of the childs life.

THAT'S WHY, THE SO CALLED BLACK FAMILY IS IN DISARRAY NOW. TOO MANY FATHERS ARE LOCKED AWAY AND TOO MANY WOMEN ARE USING THEIR CHILDRED FOR REVENGE. DAMN, WILLY LYNCH WINS AGAIN. BUT I'M CHANGING THE ENDING TO MY STORY, TEDDY WINS. He thought.

By the beginning of 2006, Tinara had completely phased out, Treace was miss'n in action and Queen, bless her heart was holding on by a thread. Her health had began to fail before Teddy left, giving her consistent up and down problems with diabetes. In June of 2006, the thread popp'd, leaving Teddy to mourn the loss of his old Earth. Queen died.

No one was by his side to whether the storm. Tinara had moved on with her life deal'n with any local joker that seem'd to be interest'd and Treace was nowhere to be found. Teddy's so –

call'd immediate family show'd no sympathy or concern for him. Had he not been stable in his faith, he would have more than likely committed suicide. So many people had depend'd on him in the past and now that he need'd some simple encouragement, none of those same people were there for support. His strength came from within and a new mission began.

Islam was his path, hip hop was his culture and Hov being his favorite MC made his mottos simply, "I WILL NOT LOSE!"

## Chapter 37: Rebirth   (Understanding God)

January 2007, Teddy transferred back to ACI from the mountains. He had no idea why they sent him back to this particular institution but he was kinda excited because he knew that he would get to see Vet Black once again. Plus, he knew this old head cat there named Bull City that was vicious with the law work. He tutored Teddy on his appeal, lett'n him know that his appellate attorney was jack'n him off. Teddy had pure confidence in Bull City's skills and as soon as they met up, Bull City immediately went to work on his MAR.

Meanwhile, running into Bull City was refreshing, but he also ran into the disappointment of Vet Black not being there. Vet, stay'n true to form, he had the pressure on the Mexicans and ACI was Little Mexico. The majority of the Mexican and Spanish guys on state was housed at ACI.

After running into the disappointment of Vet not being on deck, he ran into some of the real catz he had pull'd the last 6 years of his bid with, his Muslim brothas; Bilal a-k-a Crowe. Bilal was as thorough as they came. He was a native legend in the streetz of Greensboro. Teddy knew of Crowe before ever being graced by his presence. As Muslims, they shared common views and as men they shared the same street morals "No snitch'n, no homo, and fuck love. Love being a useless emotion that real men could do without. Respect plus fear, equal'd TRUE LOVE". With their definition of love, it was never a verbal thing, it was all action lead by RESPECT and when deal'n with either of them, RESPECT was automatically manifested. They were renegade Muslims, true to the word Muslims. They didn't believe in the division and sects of Islam. The Holy Qu'ran of Mecca was their road map, the Circle Seven was their compass and they dared not let man dictate their strive. Teddy loved Crowe more than he did his blood relatives. Their bond was etch'd in the book of life.

There was also Yasin a-k-a Bishop, a very spiritual and knowledgeable brother that Teddy saw as being a profound Spiritual Advisor one day (his very own with the wisdom and understanding he possess'd).

There was SABOOR a-k-a AKAFELLA, the coolest Muslim ever. He and Teddy had plans to set up Eateries throughout Charlotte and surrounding areas. Akafella was a helluva baker.

The other Bilal a-k-a Big Aki, he was from Charlotte. The brother had humility out of this world, with a quiet demeanor. When he spoke, Teddy was all ears because they came from the same back ground but he was older. He always provided Teddy with sound advice for life in general.

Teddy surrounded himself around the sincere brothers such as; Rashaad a-k-a Clint, Waheed from Greensboro, Malik Maynard, Na'im from Shelby, Nasir Ramadan, Nazir a-k-a Freddie

Leach and last but not least Brother Jamal a-k-a Jesus. That was Teddy's biggest brother. "LOVE IN, LOVE OUT WITHOUT A DOUBT," that was there bond.  Jamal was Teddy's all purpose brother. His go to for whatever.

That was just his Muslim brothers. When he began his bid, Teddy decided that he was done with the music business and his new mission was to establish mad businesses. However, music was his talent and it had began to beat him in the face. While in the mountains, he ran into his youngest daughter's cousin, Ty a-k-a Yung Factz. He was an MC. Not a rapper, a MC. Teddy and Ty were roommates. They would stay up late writing songs together. Ty was a real talent. He wasn't just an MC, he could produce and write R&B. Together, they came up wit NEXT COAST ENTERTAINMENT. North Carolina music "Da Carolina Way." Teddy just look'd at it as something to do to pass time but little did he know, it was a manifestation that would come to pass.

Walk'n thru the chow hall his first day back at ACI, he was strollin thru with his main man KO from Greensboro being acknowledged by all the catz and strays he had left behind 2 years ago when he heard a familiar voice yell, "TR!"

Teddy paid it no attention immediately because he had just pass'd his little homie Tony Robinson and spoke, they could have been call'n him, Teddy thought. No one on state ever address'd him as TR, they didn't know TR, THE REAL. And only Kato knew T-Rock.

Suddenly the voice got closer, "So TR, You gone just ignore ole Mani."

To Teddy's surprise when he turn'd around, it was his youg artist Manifest, all grown up. "Git da fuck outta here!" Teddy said while embracing his protége, "Nigga, I thought I'd be seeing You on Rap City or some shit by now."

"TR man, I heard about-cho- shit and that fuck'd me up. I thought I was gone git a deal fuck'n wit-chu but right after You got lock'd, I went on a robbin spree. DJ Polo caught me out there and hook'd me up MC'n for HOT 92.7 in Charlotte."

"Yeeh, I caught-chu on there a few years ago." Teddy interject'd.

"Yo TR, I was doin my thang. And Polo had me MC'n at CJ's on Thursday nights. I never forgot about-chu. So many labels offer'd me deals but I remember'd what we had plann'd and I didn't want to get fuck'd, plus I was facin this time. TR ENT. Is still THE REAL." Manifest emphasized as they dapp'd each other.

"TR was then, NEXT COAST is now."

"Whus Next Coast TR?" Manifest ask'd in an exaggerated tone.

"It's a movement. We still The Real but Next Coast is Carolina music da Carolina way."

"Whateva it is You cook'n, I'm eat'n. I know how You git down but check it out, I got another artist You gone love. His name is Vegas. TR, he's hot! You gone love'm."

Runn'n into Manifest was just another sign. Coming off of the loss of his mom, Teddy need'd new things to focus on. He put together a team of warriors to set the stage for The Next Coast Movement. Mani was the franchise, Factz and Vegas was the team and BIGG was assistant GM and player while Teddy own'd the team, handled the business and coach'n. Teddy's Moorish brother Trigg had his own company. "THUG COMMITTEE" which was Next Coast's brother. Trigg and Teddy both came from Charlotte. He rep'd McAuthur Ave. off Statesville Ave. They believed in each others vision and it was a fact that they both were a part of the other.

This young cat from Brooklyn name NaQuan was also an ally. He had his shit together. His company was Blue Diamond Entertainment. Nate had a "eat squad", a team of hyena MC's and he was bout dat change and lots of it. Nate, Latt, Rock, Booty and Rhino was sure to leave their mark in the hip hop game runn'n thru  NC, and Teddy put together a promotion team to rep "BLACK MONEY" promotions. These hooligans were pure thorough – breds. The Co- O MONEY STACKAZ; Hasan "da gambler", Doobie, Grier,

Gator, Flay, U-CONN, PRETTY, Mike P and Teddy's brothers OD and K-Lo. These were the hustlas hitt'n the streetz of Charlotte to take over one by one every year until the year 2015.

Tate, KP, Goob, Ty-Ty, Big Joe and T-Man were Teddy's Tre-4 representers. Sincere, Ace, Mo, Sid, Ghost and Big AL was rep'n for the Gas House. Dexter a-k-a Lil Raleigh, Chic, Mack and Will was rep'n the team in Raleigh. Frog, Speedy, Throw Back, Jake and Carlos had Asheville on smash. Tyson a-k-a "Bun B", Dee, Rocky, Booty and Charlie Black had Salisbury sewed up. Big Yel-lock and Black rep'd Burlington. Lazy a-k-a The Asian Sensation, Tigar "STYLES" and Squirll rep'n Concord.

The Greensboro team was the ultimate. Teddy's Muslim brother Bilal a-k-a Crowe and SELF a-k-a JIM JR was the head of the Next Coast/Black Money team out there. Solo, Insane, Dominic and T-Payne were on hand to help the team capture the green in the boro. Plus Lil Fanatic, but he was also a Next Coast heavy spitter.

Money was to be had and Teddy had the ultimate vision to capture it and put a permanent face to the hip-hop/music scene in NC. Again, revenge was his driving force. He had so many avenues he could have attack'd but first things first was his freedom.

While Teddy was in the mountains, TREACE found him on the internet and they began to correspond again. She express'd that she thought it was fuck'd up that he didn't reach out to her when Queen died. Treace and Queen had gotten rather close when Treace use to come to town to visit Teddy.

Teddy noticed that over the years, Treace had severely matured. She was no longer his T-N-T, she was a grown lady. She came to town two times within a month and on her second visit, she proposed. After being transfer'd back to ACI, Treace set up their wedd'n plans. On March 14, 2007, they were married. In Teddy's eyes, no woman could have his heart like Ms. Porchia did but Treace's loyalty earn'd her a first lady spot by the crown'd president of NC.

Treace's focus was to get Teddy a good attorney to get him out of Prison A-SAP. During her search, Teddy used his creative talents to write 2 books (Driven By Drugs and Sexually Motivated).

It started as an experiment and something to do to pass time at first, but once Driven By Drugs was complete, Teddy met this brother name Inf (short for Infinite). Inf was years younger than Teddy but his intellect spoke volumes. He and Teddy came across each other, when Teddy noticed Inf post'n up daily at a table writing rigorously. Teddy observed a book he had on the table call'd "How To Succeed In  the Publishing Game" by Vickie Stringer of Triple Crown Publishing. When Teddy approach'd him, Inf was such a peaceful brother. Teddy had been observing his swagger. He knew the brother had business about himself and once they began to communicate, Teddy's perception proved once again to be sufficient.

Inf was a Muslim, a Moor, Pisces, a philosopher and a young soul with old wisdom. He was Teddy's A-Alike. They bonded instantly. Inf took that writing shit to another level. Teddy simply want'd to sell a story, but Inf was your favorite author's favorite author. The brother had a talent to make reading a book like watch'n a movie, he paint'd a very vivd picture.   Inf read Driven By Drugs and began to tutor Teddy in different aspects of literary arts. Teddy took it all in and laid down a best seller in Sexually Motivated.

In the course of 8 months, Treace had been beat'n out of thousands of dollars by two different attorneys. Teddy was patient and continued to presevere knowing that he was destined to win.

In April of 2008, Teddy ran into a Muslim brother by name of Ze'Shawn. Ze'Shawn read Driven By Drugs and express'd to Teddy that he should be striving for publishing. Teddy agreed, tell'n him that he need'd a typist. Ze'Shawn was on his way home within the next month and offer'd to assist Teddy in getting the ball rolling for him. True to form, when Ze'Shawn got home, he assist'd Teddy til the very end. From getting his book publish'd to getting him a real attorney.

Christmas Eve of 2008, Teddy was finally released from Prision on a technicality in his case. Treace and Ze'Shawn pick'd Teddy up at the Prison in a limo. Teddy had received a $50K advance for the publishing of DBD and SM with royalties. He was sitting on $125,000.00. Teddy wasted no time stay'n in the states. Ze'Shawn had done the research and found Teddy a Brownstown overseas in Amsterdam.

Nobody knew he was home outside of his wife, Nett and Ze'Shawn. It was now time for Teddy to set vengeance in motion. Success was not to be denied and with the capital he had accumulated, success and revenge on the world was a guarantee.

## Chapter 38: Success Is Revenge

The day of Teddy's release, he and Treace left for Amsterdam. Teddy had so many business ventures to pursue but he wanted to leave the States in order to plan his take over. He had exactly 2 years to prepare for Manifest and Biggs arrivals home from prison.

Teddy knew in order to succeed, he need'd a good attorney on his team so he stay'd in contact with the lawyer Ze'Shawn hired to handle Teddy's case. Phil Dunst was a cocky short jaw that knew his shit. He was the man You want'd on Your team in a criminal case. Other areas of the law, he could direct You in the right path. Teddy inform'd Phil that he needed an all purpose attorney with a vast knowledge of all sects of the law.

Phil introduced Teddy to a young Asian and Black attorney named Lori Mills. Lori was gorgeous. At 5ft3, 120 pounds, she was a bombshell. She was a short Kimora Lee with more curves. Her eyes were flirtatious and business all in one. Lori had just completed the bar and Phil was her mentor. She had been a intern at Phil's law firm and Phil told her he would see to it that her career flourish'd.

After the introduction over a conference call'd between Teddy, Phil, Lori, Nett and Ze'Shawn, a formal meet'n was scheduled to take place in Amsterdam the following week. Teddy was financially stable and preparing to take his life and success to another level. His days were spent stress free, making love to his wife and making beats in his basement studio.  At a time where Lil Wayne, T-Pain, DJ Khalid and the Florida Boyz was runn'n the hip hop scene, Teddy knew that in order to put North Carolina in the forefront of the world of hip hop, it was going to take a proper plan, methodically mapp'd out. That was the reason for the overseas move. He didn't want Next Coast to look or sound like anything You had ever heard or seen.

When Ze'Shawn, Lori and Nett arrived, Teddy had mapp'd out a time line of the events that would take place leading up to the release of The Next Coast Family. First and foremost, he want'd an office for Next Coast downtown Charlotte or close. Ze'Shawn already had that cover'd. He was due to speak to the realtors that own'd the Cameron Brown building down on McDowell St. The office space was in the corner, one side facing uptown and the other side facing I-277 (Brookshire Freeway).

The space was approximately 1500 square ft. consisting of four offices and receptionist space in the center. Ze'Shawn also inform'd Teddy that they had a secluded storage space in the basement level of the building that they were willing to throw in for an extra $250.00 a month that he could use for a studio. Teddy told Nett and Lori to assist Ze'Shawn in getting the office set up and he want'd each of them to set up their own personal offices there. Nett was totally responsible for decorating Teddy's office. Ze'Shawn help'd with the state of the art electronics. That office space would serve as the home base for NEXT COAST ENTERTAINMENT. In the meet'n, Teddy inform'd his team that they weren't rich yet, but they were financially stable. Letting Nett and Lori know the other money making ventures he had on the stove such as; NEW CASH APPARAL, Exotic Import'd Fabrics and his new ear drive-in movie theatres. Ze'Shawn's mission was to simply trick out the studio with the state of the art equipment and find an engineer.

Within a two month period of time, Teddy had put together a gorilla business proposal for STACKZ ENTERPRISES and had accumulated over $2 million in grants and loans. He was now prepared to put his dreams in motion.

On Teddy's 38th birthday, Treace surprised him with the news that they were expect'n. The baby was due October 12th on Lekrell's birthday, but she gave birth to a 6 pound 9 ounces beautiful baby girl on October 28th (Steve's birthday). They named her Queen Ti'mony Massey.

In the spring of 2010, Nett and Lori had come together with a designer team and manufacturers to start the mass production of New Cash Apparal. The line was due out in the fall of 2011 right after Manifest's release which was

July 1$^{st}$ and the demos would be ready by the last week in June.

Teddy had began the Next Coast Promotions with Vegas who was released 2 months before he got out. Whenever Teddy was in town recording with Vegas, they wore the FREE MANIFEST, FREE BIGGZ, FREE FACTZ, and FREE FANATIC  t-shirts with the artist picture on the front and the NEXT COAST emblem on the back with the artist release date. Vegas was hott! He had the street banger "Ride Wit Me" produced by Teddy under his alias NECESSARY, and he had the hottest mix tape to hit the East Coast in ages.

Teddy was ready to put the heat behind Vegas and get the ball roll'n with the Next Coast Movement but Vegas want'd to wait until the whole fam was together before he  made that step. He was content being a feature artist on other people's joints. At the moment, NaQuan's Crime Family and BLUE DIAMOND had the game on smash. Teddy and Vegas kept it grimey. Everybody want'd Vegas on their tracks and everybody want'd Blue Diamond, nobody got their time of day.

Teddy's niece Lekrell was kill'n the R&B game and she had heard that Teddy was out but had no proof. Teddy kept tabs on Lekrell and Timia from afar. Nett made sure that they received a monthly check from STACKZ ENTERPRISES but Teddy felt that his coming out EXTRAVAGANZA was going to be the first time he has been sight'd in 11 years.

That was due to take placeTHANKSGIVING weekend 2011 on a Saturday night to celebrate BIGGZ coming home and formally introducing Next Coast to the world.

Money was piling in. Teddy was ready for war. His import'd fabrics had become the leading import between the US and Africa, importing such fabrics as, tiger and lion skins, elephant skin, lion fur, zebra and leopard skin ect…He had also taken part in the diamond exchange, importing different color diamonds and marketing the first ever seen two tone diamonds.

Life as Teddy knew it was at its' turning point. Success was at hand and he was staying true to Islam. His mission was to put ALLAH'S name in bright lights, recapture the love of his son and help get his fam that was still incarcarated free.

Infinite came home in August of 2010. He released a book entitled "NEXT TO NOTHING" that received high reviews from New York Times, Oprah's book club, Essence magazine and USA Today. He and Teddy went on a book signing tour together throughout Europe promoting their new releases that last'd a month and a half.

2010 was a milestone in Teddy's life and business. He assist'd Nett and Lori in starting their Marketing firm. BLACK MONEY MARKETING. They came up with all kinds of new innovative concepts to reinvent deadend companies, while still working full time for NEXT COAST and STACKZ ENTERPRISES.

Lori had made more money in six months then she had estimated making in 2 years.

June 26, 2011, Teddy had just arrived in town to set up shop for Mani's release. He had purchased a condo on Lake Norman. Everything he had done in the past 2 years had been a stepping stone for the mission that was at hand. Teddy had yet to purchase a car in the states.

When he visted, he always cop'd a rental but he figured now was just as good a time as ever. He went to Land Rover of Charlotte down Independence Blvd. Teddy was consider'n the new 2011 Range but he was never the type to do what everybody else was doing so he purchased a construction yellow 2011 Land Rover fully equipt'd with Navigational/DVD system and all the extra trimmings.

Everything was set for Mani's arrival. For the next few days, Teddy met with DJ's at WPEG and 102 JAMZ. He did a couple of different NEXT COAST advertisements. He met with Danny, the technician Ze'Shawn had hired to handle all sessions at BOONDOX Recordings. That was the name of the studio.

July 1st finally came. Teddy was outside the Prison at 8:00 sharp in a stretch Hummer limo. Their reunion was monumental. After Mani was released, he stepp'd to his freedom while the left behind prisoners applauded, congratulated and bid'd him a farwell.

"TR, you been work'n CHAMP! You ready?" Mani ask'd with excitement in his voice.

"The question is, are you ready? All of this is for You CHAMP." Teddy said with a smile. "Vegas said to git at'm when You get settled."

Look'n at the time before gett'n in, Mani ask'd, "So this is what it's like to be a franchise baller for NEXT COAST?"

"Nigga, You more than just a baller, You got ownership in the team You play for. Chunk or die!"

"We chunk'n!" Mani reiterated.

As the limo pull'd out of the park'n lot, Teddy ask'd Mani what he want'd to do first.

"Git me some food and drop me off at the studio. In fact, take me to the studio and order me some food from there."

"Dat's what it is, but we gone go by the office first. I need You to meet the staff."

They arrived back in Charlotte by 10:40. Mani was dressed in Gucci head to toe, his cornrolls were fresh and his swaggah was on 10. Entering the NEXT COAST office, Teddy introduced Mani to Raya the receptionist but Mani wasn't pay'n any attention to nothing but the music that was coming thru the surround sound speakers throughout the office.

"TR, who is that?"

"Where?"

"That track! Stop play'n." He said with a straight face.

"That ain't shit, just something I was play'n with last night. That's nothing, I got the exclusives at the studio. Jus relax, I got-chu. Raya, ring Nett, Lori, and Ze'Shawn and tell them to meet in my office in five minutes."

"No problem Teddy. K-LO, OD, Self, Crowe, Hi-C and Capone call'd earlier. I made calls for them and they said to let You know that they got their money early."

"Preciate that Raya." Teddy said as he and Mani advanced to his office.

Mani was amazed at the décor of the whole office. All the furniture was by Coach, state of the art computer systems ect... NEXT COAST murals taint'd the walls and was embroidered in the backs of every chair, sofa and or couch. Teddy's office was equipt'd with a 64 inch plasma wall TV, an entertainment system, an aquarium with exotic  fish swimming in luxury and an oil painting of the NEXT COAST FAM. As Mani rant'd and raved over Teddy's taste, NETT, LORI, and Ze'Shawn enter'd, all holding gifts.

"Manifest, this is Nett." Teddy introduced as Nett stepp'd forward.

"Nice to meet-chu face to face finally." Nett said, shaking his hand and passing hima a bag full of the latest electronics from Nextel.

"This for me?"

"Yeup, we gotta be able to stay in contact with You. Your Blackberry is fully charged and You got two new batteries."

"Thank You Nett."

"You're more than welcome." Nett said as she sat at the chair in front of Teddy's desk.

"Manifest, this is Lori."

With the most seductive look, Lori stepp'd forward in Mani's direction, reach'd her hand out to greet him, "Nice to meet You Mr. Mani." She said as he grabb'd her hand pull'n it to his lips.

"The pleasure is all mine." Mani said flirt'n back with her. Handing him uh envelope with

$20,000.00 in it with a NEXT COAST black card with it.

"I'm Your attorney, I'm here to assure You get rich and stay rich."

"Maybe we can do lunch or something?" Mani inquired.

"Who knows?" Lori answer'd in the most seductive tone.

"Not on my time Mani. You know the rules."

Teddy said jokingly speak'n of the 'No Employee Relationships' rule from TR ENT. "Mani, this is Ze'Shawn." Teddy introduced as they all calm'd down from the laugh Teddy had provided.

"Whut'z up Mani? Good to finally meet You, I've heard so much about you. I guess You already know that You are the sole reason for all of this." Ze'Shawn said as he pass'd him 3 crush velvet black jewelry boxes.

"Whus this?" Mani ask, open'n the biggest box noticing the NEXT COAST iced out platinum chain and charm. The other boxes had the match'n bracelet and watch. "Thanks Champ, this shit is crazy!"

Once Teddy was done introduce'n everybody, Mani was anxious to get to the studio. Teddy told him to c'mon and Mani follow'd him to the elevator. Teddy stuck a key in at the bottom of the #1 on the elevator panel. When the elevator door open, they got off into another office that had BOONDOX RECORDINGS pos'd above the NEXT COAST mural with pictures of Mani, Biggz, Vegas, Factz and Fanatic.

"TR, whut's this?"

"Your office Champ. C'mon, let me show You around." The first room was a mini kitchen with a microwave and fully stock'd refrigerator. The next room was the relax room with a recliner and a sofa with a big screen TV. The next room was the recording studio with the booth.

"Danny, whussup? This is Manifest." Danny was a 37 year old smoked out engineering genius.

"Dude, you got some killer tunes. I've been going thru'm, mix'n certain ones down. Ready to party?"

He ask'd Mani after address'n Teddy.

"Born ready." Manifest said, laugh'n at Danny.

"Ted dude, I know You brought me a gift from Your home?"

Danny ask'd speak'n of the exotic Amsterdam buds.

"Yeeh, I did." Teddy said reach'n into his pocket and pull'n out a bag of some light, light greenish purple buds, dropp'n about a quarter on the table. "Yall be careful."

"TR, I want dat track that was play'n in the office upstairs."

"Danny got'chu. I'll be upstairs. If You git something finish'd today, we'll debut it tonight on WPEG on the top 5 and on the 10 o'clock bomb on 102 JAMZ."

"Set it up then, cause that joint gone be done within the hour."

"Take Yo time, I don't need no rush job."

"Dude, he's safe right here with me and me spinach." Danny said with a wink, imitating Popeye.

Teddy left to handle more business. He sat in his office taking calls from his Muslim brother AZIZ a-k-a Tony Montana and Julius. Both of them were Charlotte natives. Julius wasn't Muslim, he was like an uncle to Teddy. Teddy had Lori looking into their cases, preparing to get them both new trials. N the mist of handling those issues, Raya beep'd in say'n Danny want'd him to run down ASAP. Teddy hurried back to the studio wondering what could be wrong but it was the total opposite, Mani completely recorde'd a anthem call'd "Touch Sump'n" over that beat he heard in the office.

"Whussup?" Teddy ask'd as he enter'd the room.

"Dude! He's genius!" Danny express'd. "Listen to this!" He said as he play'd it back.

Teddy couldn't believe his ears.

"Yo, git'chu some rest. We hitt'n the highway tonight."

"Fuck rest! We gitt'n ready to record allday til You ready to go."

"Let Vegas know to be here by 5:00. I'm call'n Nate. NEXT COAST and BLUE DIAMOND is bum rush'n at least two radio stations tonight."

"It don't matter to me, les do it. I'm home now Baby."

"Danny send that song to my e-mail and to Lori's e-mail now."

Lori immediately uploaded it to her computer sending a copy to the Library of Congress for copyrights. Teddy sent the song via e-mail to all the radio station contacts. By 3:20, WPEG was advertising NEXT COAST & BLUE DIAMOND would be takin over the radio station from 6pm to 8pm.

Everybody met at the Next Coast office for this one night test run promotional set. Nate slid thru in his Carolina metallic blue Mercedes Benz

CLK with Ms. Porchia's cousin LeRoy ridin shot gun and "the Hyenas" follow'd in 2 Range Rogers. Teddy, Mani, Vegas and Ze'Shawn were load'n up in the same stretch Hummer from earlier. Nate wouldn't dare be out done so they call'd back out to Queen City Limousines and Custom Rides.

Fifteen minutes later, an all black stretch Escalade pull'd in follow'd by an all black stretch F-650. Teddy supplied each limo with the purp he brought in town. Everybody was iced out in blue diamonds. The words BLUE DIAMOND was iced out in flawless Carolina blue diamonds while the back ground diamonds in NEXT COAST emblem were the same color'd blue diamonds. Nate, LeRoy, Latt, Ice, Booty, Rocky and Crime Family was self stackers and it was obvious that these two teams were destine to kill the game.

Charlotte was taken by storm. By the time they were leavin, all the callers want'd to know where NEXT COAST and BLUE DIAMOND were partying at on that Friday night. Nate and Teddy inform'd everybody that BLUE DIAMOND was perform'n 4th of July at the WESTIN hotel and NEXT COAST would be in the build'n as special guests. They got an identical response in Greensboro which confirm'd the movement.

NEXT COAST dropp'd "Touch Sump'n" independently, scoring the #1 ringtone in the country. In no time, every major label was look'n to distribute NEXT COAST. DEF JAM had the best offer overall.

Teddy dropp'd the Next Coast compilation "CHUNK'N" to hold off the wolves until Biggz and Factz were released. With the help of BLUE DIAMOND artist and THUG COMMITTEE, the compilation debut'd at #1 on the billboards top 40 albums with 3 of the songs in the top 3 single spots. All of the artist involved were the top featured artist of 2011, putting all eyes on North Carolina.

Finally, Biggz was home. He got out the week of Thanksgiving. Teddy had become known for recording and debut'n the same day. Biggz came straight out and record'd "Heaven on 22's" with Mani, Vegas and Trigg from THUG COMMITTEE and Nate from BLUE DIAMOND. Next Coast couldn't do no wrong. Biggz joint debut'd #1, #1 ringtone and #1 video on 106 & Park for a month strong. Biggz follow'd Mani's footprints to instant success.

The Next Coast compilation top'd off at 5 million records sold while Manifest sold 3 ½ million, Vegas sold 2 million and had movie roles being offer'd to him. Biggz sold 1.5 million and was still climb'n. He was Co CEO of NEXT COAST and NEW CASH APPARAL. Everybody was rich and Yung Factz had just come home.

At the NEXT COAST/BLUE DIAMOND THANKSGIVING EXTRAVAGANZA, Teddy's neice Lekrell show'd up with her entourage that consist'd of Teddy's daughter Timia and 10 others.

They posted up in the VIP. When Teddy took the stage to thank everybody for their support the past year and introduced himself along with the full NEXT COAST & BLUE DIAMOND artist, staff and supporters, Lekrell and Timia made their way to the stage.

As Teddy walk'd back stage sparkling like the star he was, Nett told him he had guests. At first sight, he thought to himself, I'M MARRIED, I DON'T HAVE TIME FOR GROUPIES. The 5ft6 curvacious chocolate drop, dipp'd in an all black Chanel fitt'n thigh length dress with the match'n stilettos cover'd in a full length black and white chinchilla approach'd Teddy bring'n a severe ice blizzard his way look'n piss'd.
          "Can I help You ladies?"

"Can You help us?" The other chic ask'd as they both laugh'd like Teddy had told a joke. Little moma had on a brown and tan Coogie dress, stand'n about 5ft8 in stilettos with a 3 quarter length tan mink on, draped in modest jewels. "TEDDY MASSEY!" The young lady spat with attitude, right leg out front, stand'n back on her left leg with her left hand on her hip.

"That's me." Teddy said look'n at Nett who stood beside him smirk'n with a 'I can't believe You don't know' look.

"Teddy, this Lekrell and Timia Massey." Nett said look'n like 'You in some shit now'.

Teddy's girls had grown up. Lekrell was 24 and Timia was 22. Seeing them brought pain to Teddy's memory of the late nights' stay'n up while he was in prison attempt'n to write his first book "DRIVEN BY DRUGS" while Officer Sears and Misenheimer cut him slack because he was driven by the need to provide for them.

They were disappoint'd in Teddy that he had been out long enough to have taken over the hip hop industry under their noses and the fact that he didn't know who they were. They all hung out together catch'n up on things.

Timia cuss'd out one of Teddy's business partners CeCe. CeCe was a ex stick up kid turn entrepreneur. Teddy liked CeCe because in a lot of ways, he reminded him of himself. CeCe and Mia had a fling but he didn't inform her that he was married. CeCe was feel'n Mia but she would stand second to no other woman especially not play'n the mistress role. Teddy taught her better and Teddy loved CeCe and his family.

Mia and Lekrell promised Teddy they would keep his secret low if he took them to see their little sister in Amsterdam. He agreed and told them he want to remain a ghost to all who forgot about him when he was in prison. They thank'd him for the monthly checks. Even though Lekrell had her own career. She stay'd up under Teddy and his team while Timia moved into the condo Teddy had on Lake Norman and travel'd with him everywhere as his personal assistance.

In 2011 alone, Teddy's worth shot to $75 million — most of which came thru STACKZ ENTERPRISES along with the diamond exchange and New Cash Apparal.

Yung Factz came home to money but nothing he had earn'd. NEXT COAST Compilation album "CHUNK'N Pt. 2 was going to be his coming out project with the single "AND 1" featuring MANI, VEGAS, BIGGZ and Teddy's new artist BEST KEPT "SHHH". This project was due out in the first quarter of 2012. "AND 1", the song and video was dropp'n February 21st, 2012.

AND 1 street team was tour'n with this 17 year old young kid from N.O. that they named Y.O, short for "Yung Official". He was the top recruit coming out of high school in 2013 and hadn't decided where he would be attending college that fall.

Lori and Nett thought it would be cool to feature the AND 1 street team in Yung Factz video since Y.O was the talk of the country. By January 15th, Lori had the deal confirm'd. Teddy did the treatment and would be directing the video that was due to be shot at the Time Warner Cable Bobcat's Arena start'n February 17th during ALLSTAR WEEKEND.

At this point, Teddy's swagger was completely out of control. He purchased a penthouse suite in the newly built Trump Towers downtown Charlotte for his wife Treace and baby girl Ti'mony. He rode around Charlotte in a platinum 2012 Aston Martin DBS in the hottest fashions but as of lately, he was display'n his personal line Timeer Aziz that was currently in developmental stages with his personal designer team and manufacturers. He brought out a few pieces here and there to get a rise out of his peers while using Timia and Lekrell to catch the eyes of the ladies in the Timpt'n Lady's line. Platinum and Titanium were his metals of choice to carry his two tone diamonds.

Everything he touch'd was an instant success and he often chuckled under his breath at how he came from the bottom of the barrel and rose to the top.

Arriving at the Bobcat's arena at 6:30am Friday, February 17th to start the video shoot for "AND1", Teddy saunter'd thru the arena text messaging several individuals on his Voyager touchscreen phone by Verizon. Hiding his eyes behind a pair of BVLGARI big face gold frames with canary yellow fade lenses, he was drapp'd in TRUE RELIGION head to toe; black jeans with the TRUE RELIGION cream sweater w/black trim accent'd with a pair of brown and tan Prada loafers, sparkling with his NEXT COAST jewels.

Teddy held on hour and a half meet'n with the camera man, sett'n the stage for this eventful day. By 6pm they were going to be open'n the Arena to the public to be a part of the 2 ½ day filming of the video shoot. Being that it was the NBA ALLSTAR WEEKEND, they decided to go with the same theme, holding different events for the kids and showing the actual ALLSTAR events on the big screen.

They also got live performances by the NEXT COAST ALLSTARZ featuring Y.O and the AND 1 ALLSTARZ.

Entering the midday, the whole NEXT COAST/BLUE DIAMONDS/THUG COMMITTEE Fam had arrived. Teddy had Infinite by his side assist'n and coach'n him in his directorial debut. Thru all the excitement and chaos, Teddy walk'd thru stress free as if he was in his element, poised for the challenge. No matter who approach'd him and in what manner they came, Teddy was cool and calm and will'n to assist.

All the artist were off gett'n prepared for their scenes, basically scattered about. Biggz and Teddy were to the side discuss'n a marketing scheme for Yung Factz first single from his debut album. Factz, Best Kept, Vegas and others were sign'n autographs for the some odd hundred fans that arrived early. Manifest sat in the locker room getting his hair corn roll'd by Timia while WPEG interview'd him and Y.O.

After the interview, Y.O told Manifest that he was a big fan and he still had "Touch Sump'n" on his ringtone. While they talk'd and chatt'd, Y.O reveal'd that he was from NC and he was feel'n the NEXT COAST movement. Mani ask'd him what part of NC was he from and Y.O respond'd, "I was born in Greensboro but my mom and dad is from here. My grandma on my mom side lives here and I have two sisters on my dad's side here in Charlotte.

"Who is Your mom and dad?" Mani ask'd out of curiosity.

"My mom name is Porchia."

"Porcha Troutman. That's her married name, she's a Grier and my dad is a Massey."

"Who Yo daddy Y-O?" Timia inquired as she view'd his 6ft2 frame. He was high yellow with grey eyes and low cut wavy hair.

"He's lock'd up.

His name Teddy."

Timia's eyes got big, "Do You remember your oldest sister?" She inquired.

"Yeuh, her name is Timia." Y-O responded, "I haven't seen her since I was five or six."

Timia and Manifest bust out laugh'n, Timia cover'd her mouth with both of her hands. "Yo real name is Teddy Myson Massey!"

She blurt'd out.

"Hi You know my real name? My last name is Grier."

"I know, Yo moma changed it boy! I'm Timia!" She said runn'n over to embrace her over grown little brother.

"Mimi?" Y-O ask'd unsure.

"Boy, give me a hug!" She demand'd as they embraced "Hi You been? We miss'd You."

"Mimi, how's dad?" He inquired with sincerity.

"He's good. We all been miss'n You."

Timia told him, hold'n back the surprise of their dad being released and the fact that he was the head figure behind NEXT COAST.

Before Timia continued to do Mani's hair, she whisper'd in his ear. "Text message my daddy and tell him to come in here, it's an emergency."

Lil Teddy told Timia that his mom was there for the shoot as they talk'd and caught up on the times lost.

"Teddy, you fass just like Yo daddy, I saw You watch'n my ass while You was talk'n to Manifest." Mia told him.

They all laugh'd.

"Shiiid, I ain't know who You was." Y-O said, "I'm a star, I saw You check'n me out the corner of Your eye too."

"You betta watch out for these ho's out here try'n to git a free ride and boy, AIDS is real!" Mia scold'd her little brother right before the door to the locker room open'd.

"MANI!" Teddy yell'd frantically for his main man, "Where You at?"

"Right here!" Mani call'd out.

Teddy walk'd around the corner to where Timia was doing Manifest's hair. "Whut's the emergency?" He ask'd, show'n the first sign of frustration for the day.

"The AND1 star want'd to meet'chu." Manifest said as Y-O look'd with confusion on his face. "Y-O, this is the owner of NEXT COAST, NECESSARY."

Teddy stepp'd to Y-O extending his hand out to give him a pound "Peace lil bru, I can't say I've seen your fame but I've heard a lot about-chu here lately. I just wanna know hi You tour'n wit deeze guys and You're still in school?" Teddy inquired as an OF concern'd about the young dude's education.

"I have a tutor 3 days out the week." Y-O answer'd.

"You do know talent without education is like shoes with no strings, You can never tie it up."

Y-O didn't know whether to keep it on some street shit or to answer in a humble adult to child manor. "Yes sir, my mom wouldn't allow me to play if my GPA was under a 3.0." He answer'd observing Teddy's street/business swagger.

"Damn, jus because I encourage You to stay in school, I'm sir now?" Teddy ask'd jokingly, as they all laugh'd including Y-O. "Nah, but seriously, You are the best in the country right now on some LeBron James shit and You're only a Jr. I got a son Your age and I only pray that he puts his education first."

Manifest and Timia sat back and let them talk without informing either of them who the other one was.

"Shiiid, wit a pop's like You, he probably on some Lil Romeo shit." Y-O inquired.

"I couldn't say, I haven't seen him since he was six. He's with his mom and her husband." Teddy inform'd Yung Official.

"My situation is a lot like Yours, I haven't seen my dad since I was six and I'm jus see'n my sister for the first time right now since then." Y-O said point'n at Mia.

"Whose Yo sista Champ?" Teddy inquired look'n at Mia in suspense while Mia and Mani look'd back smile'n and hunch'n their shoulders.

"Timia." Y-O emphasized.

"How is that?" Teddy ask'd chuckle'n at this absurb allegation.

"We got the same dad, he's in prison somewhere out here. Our dad was into the music business back before he went to prison.

He loved this type of shit."

As Y-O spoke, Teddy listen'd and began to observe Y-O closely looking into his eyes.

"Mia!" Teddy call'd out as he look'd in her direction, confused.

"Whut-chu want me to say, that's my little brother." She said look'n at him as she pucker'd her lips to the left side.

"Mia, this Yo boyfriend?" Y-O ask'd.

"That's my daughter."

"Dad, that's Lil Teddy!" Mia inform'd him.

Teddy look'd Y-O up and down in disbelief. "Nu-Nu?"

Teddy call'd out in a unsure tone.

"Mia, this our pop's?"

"Boy, who else call You Nu-Nu? Please don't'chall git all mushy, les jus party." Timia said.

"Yo Y-O, me and TR was lock'd up together and all he use to talk about is You." Manifest told him as they both stood in disbelief.

"I can't lie, I don't know WHAT to say. Hi You been?" Teddy ask'd his son in a uncertain tone.

"I'm fine. I can't believe this is really y'all!

Daddy You rich! I been read'n about Y'all in the XXL.

So you NECESSARY?"

"And You Y-O?" they both inquired of their alias's, laugh'n at each other. "Boy give Yo ole man a hug." Lil Teddy tower'd over Teddy's 5 foot 8 frame embracing him and jokingly rubb'n his pop's waves.
"I LOVE YOU MAN."

"I Love You too Daa. What happen'd to the corn rolls?"
"Nu-Nu, I got tired of'em."

"You still wear'n the part down the middle."

"I see You still wear'n Yours too."

"That's my trademark." Lil Teddy said with pride.
"Daa, hi long You been out?"

"3 ½ years but I went into hiding to stack my bread and get ready for now.

Where's Yo mom's?"

In the arena, courtside, C'mon!"

"Hol up, is her husband out there?"

"Nah, jus her. C'mon Daa!" Lil Teddy said with excitement in his voice.

"We got to hurry up because we go to get ready to film Your first scene with the NEXT COAST ALLSTARS."

"Ok, it won't take long."

Teddy follow'd his proud son while he talk'd a mile a minute enter'n the arena walk'n down courtside. Teddy's heart was beat'n so fast, he had to take a deep breath. As he released, he spott'd her off to the side bobb'n her head to Mani's new single "Kuntry Fried and KRISPY," wear'n one of the NEXT COAST ALLSTARZ jerseys. She wore Lil Teddy's jersey, the #23. Not for Jordan or LeBron, that was Lil Teddy's birth day. Walking up to where she was sitting Lil Teddy walk'd up cheezin like, LOOK WHO I'M WIT.

"Ma," Lil Teddy called out to get her attention. "This man want'd to meet'chu." He said look'n at Teddy.

"Whussup Porchia?" Teddy inquired, look'n at her mouth drop open in shock.

"Hey Teddy, what are You doing here?" She ask'd nervously,   "I thought You were gett'n out next year."

"Nah, I got out 3 years ago."

"Ma, my daddy owns NEXT COAST. This his company."

"Oh really?" Ms. Porchia question'd.

"Yeuh, I took the money from my two book sells and put this all together." Teddy respond'd, think'n to himself, SO THIS IS WHAT REVENGE FEELS LIKE.

"You look'n good. I almost didn't know who You was." Ms. Porchia stated, "You still got expensive taste."

"It is what it is. You look'n good as usual. How's the married life?" Teddy shot at her.

Mocking Teddy's answer, she responded, "It is what it is.

How's Your marriage?"

"Wondeful! I got a beautiful 2 year old daughter. I jus moved them in a Penthouse suite up in the new Trump Towers around the corner. Y'all have to come by after this."

"Can I stay the night?" Lil Teddy ask'd.

"You are welcome anywhere I am. That's between You and Your mom." Teddy said.

"Well, I'm leaving with You and Mia." Lil Teddy respond'd as if what he says goes.

"Porchia, please come by and meet my family. You're welcome to stay also." Teddy invited her humbly.

"My mom is expect'n us but there's probably no way I'm going to be able to separate him from You. He's been talk'n about this video shoot since he first heard about it and now to know that You are behind it all?

Teddy, You gone be with Your dad the rest of the weekend?" Ms. Porchia ask'd.

"Probably the rest of the year."

THIS NIGGA LOOK'N GOOD, SMELL'N GOOD AND HE'S RICH! WHAT THE FUCK WAS I THINK'N? Ms. Porchia thought to herself as Teddy and his son conversed. DAMN, I STILL LOVE THIS SEXY ASS BITCH. I WONDER IF THE PUSSY IS STILL GOOD AS I LEFT IT?

Teddy thought as Lil Teddy spoke with his mom.

"Nu-Nu, we gotta get this show on the road.

You ready?"

"Les do it."

"Porchia, don't go nowhere, I want'chu for a cameo."

"Only if I can have a hug."

Teddy couldn't resist. He extended his arms towards her. Ms. Porchia jump'd into his arms as they both held each other tight.

"Teddy, I'm Sorry." She whisper'd

"No need to be." Teddy whisper'd back, hating that he still loved her but happy he overcame her.

Teddy was the happiest he'd been since before Ms. Porchia took Lil Teddy from him 11 years ago. He took Lil Teddy around to everybody introducing him. They were inseparable. Lil Teddy observed every move his dad made and was very cooperative. They all had a ball doing the video. Lil Teddy from that moment on, stay'd with Teddy.

The "AND 1" song and video went straight to #1. Manifest won a Grammy for BEST NEW ARTIST. NEXT COAST/BLACK MONEY had a prosperous                                         year.

## Chapter 39: Poison In Poison Out

When the summer arrived, Ms. Porchia and her husband separated. Somewhere in her twist'd mind, she thought that she could get Teddy back.

Teddy took care of Ms. Porchia and all of his other children's moms. He purchased several houses, several cars and didn't stop until all of his children knew where he was and were receiving a chunk of his earnings monthly.

He established several NON PROFIT organizations, two state of the art Community Centers – one in Charlotte and the other in Greensboro. Monthly donations went to all the Masjids throughout NC.

North Carolina was finally at the forefront of the Entertainment Industry period. Inf was named the best-selling author of the year for "NEXT TO NOTHING." New Line Cinema ink'd a deal for Inf to Executive Produce and direct the movie. Inf sign'd NEXT COAST to do the sound track for the flick.

For Lil Teddy's 18th birthday, August 23rd, Teddy purchased his son a brand new Jaguar XF. He threw him a 18th birthday party at the WESTIN HOTEL fill'd with stars. Little Teddy was a star in his own right. He was well except'd throughout the industry without Teddy. Basketball was his meal ticket but he knew that he could give up basketball and work for any of his dad's many companies and ventures. With BLACK MONEY PROMOTIONS alone, it grosses at least $1.5 million every time they sponsor'd a party. BLACK MONEY had promoters in every major city throughout the Carolinas. Which meant, if there was a party in Charlotte there was one in Greensboro, Winston, Salisbury ect...that same night.

NEW YEARS 2013 was around the corner. NEXT COAST, BLUE DIAMOND and THUG COMMITTEE was sponsoring and host'n the New Years 2013 BASH at the Convention Center. They were having a $5 million ball drop at 12AM with a special performance by the NEXT COAST ALLSTARZ.

Blue Diamond was doing the first half of the bash from 10pm to 12am and they were due in LA to host a party out there with a performance. Thug Committee was taking over hosting after 12. Teddy and the whole Next Coast family was bring'n in the New Year at Teddy's Penthouse with their families, then the artist were leaving to perform at the Bash.

Everybody was having a ball at Teddy's. Family, drinks, and a major celebration for the year's accomplishments. After the New Year came in, it was time to get dressed. The event was a GROWN & SEXY black and white New Years Bash. Teddy wore DOLCE & GABBANA black and white slacks and vest with a white fedora to match the black and white chinchilla, black Maury gators with

D&G shades, accentuated with Tiffany diamond cufflinks, his 2 carat two tone black and white diamond earrings, his 10 carat NEXT COAST watch and a 10 carat diamond bezel bracelet set off with his crystal and platinum cane.

While Teddy was getting dress'd he got a text message from Ms. Porchia at the Bash ask'n were NEXT COAST perform'n and request'n a call back if possible. Teddy return'd the call. She inform'd him that BLUE DIAMOND had just left, Trigg was not host'n and he has the crowd think'n that NEXT COAST was on the WEST COAST. He told her they were due on stage within the hour. Ms. Porchia told Teddy that the party was sold out and people were still crowd'd around the red carpet out front.

"We'll be out there in about 20 minutes. Meet me out front." Teddy order'd.

"Is Teddy comin?" She ask'd, speak'n of Lil Teddy.

"I doubt it, he's with some chic he met thru Mia.

Why?"

"I was jus wonder'n. I'll see You when You get here."

"Ah-ight Lady. Peace."

Teddy really appreciated the friendship he had built with Ms. Porchia finally.

Once everybody was ready, Teddy sent for the stretch all black Navigator limo. Arriving in front of the red carpet, Yung Factz stepp'd out in all black Louis Vuitton head to toe, BEST KEPT wore Armani, BIGGS rock'd a custom tailor'd Valentino suit with Gucci shoes while MANIFEST twist'd the game in a all suede black Timeer Aziz suit with the all black suede Aldo Brué shoes. Teddy was the last to grace the red carpet. The crowd outside went crazy. As they walk'd toward the entrance, Ms. Porchia call'd out to Teddy. When he spott'd her, he direct'd security to let her thru. Ms. Porchia saunter'd to his side in an all black Prada ass grabb'n, thigh length dress with the Prada Stillettoes and a Timpt'n Lady mink.

Teddy text'd Trigg to let him know that NEXT COAST was back stage. Trigg introduced Teddy.

'"QUEEN CITY, for the past 2 years this individual I'm about to bring out has been responsible for bring'n You all 'Touch Sump'n', 'Ride Wit Me', 'Heaven on 22's', 'AND 1' and the current street anthem "Kuntry Fried And Krispy'. Without further due, here he is, NEXT COAST's own, NES – SA – SSAA – RY." Teddy pimp'd out on to the stage and the crowd went completely out of their minds.

"CHARLOTTE, NEXT COAST!" Teddy yell'd in the microphone "HAPPY NEW YEAR QUEEN CITY!" He paused to let the crowd calm down. "How can this be a NEXT COAST/BLUE DIAMOND/THUG COMMITTEE New Years Bash without NEXT COAST? Before we go any further, we gone pay some homage to all that play'd a part in Next Coast makin it this far.

ALLAHU – AKBAR!"

The crowd repeat'd his chant as he continued. "Yo, Next Coast as a family would like to thank our co horts; NaQuan and Blue Diamond, TRIGGA the RILLA and THUG COMMITTEE, my main man INF, PRINCE Ze'Shawn, all of You – Y'all are NEXT COAST and we love Y'all. Befo we step on dis shit, I personally want to thank WPEG and everybody there that work'd so diligently with us to get this good music to Y'all. And last but not least, my family. Y'all ready?" Teddy ask'd as the crowd went retarded.

The lights went off and individually each MC greet'd the crowd.

"NEXT COAST! Y'all ready to go all in with Mr. Everything?" Mani ask'd.

"Oh! Oh! Big Chunks is present Charr – lotte!" Biggz express.

"Y'all know it ain't fair Queen City. Factz is here QC." Factz taunt'd the crowd.

"Shhh … Shhh … FaVREEEL, BEST KEPT is here. I'm back home Yall. Shhh. Don't tell nobody." Best Kept whisper'd.

The 808 dropp'd and the crowd knew what it was, Mani, Biggz, Factz and Best Kept saunter'd onto the stage, and Yell'd into the mic's "I bee's" and point'd the mics to the crowd for their participation and they gave it up "Kuntry, fried, and Kris-py/high and I'm tip-sy/my swag is jus too risky so leave it alone/ Cause I bee's Kuntry fried and Kris-py/high and I'm tip-sy/this chic is leavin with me so git da hell on."

Teddy stood backs stage with Ms. Porchia while the Next Coast ALLSTARZ set the party off in overdrive. Just when they thought it was over, Vegas popp'd up and took it up another 5 notches.

"Teddy, You've really outdone Yourself. Whut'z next?" Ms. Porchia ask'd.

"Home. Bed. I haven't spent no time with my wife in weeks."

"Don't hate me for what I'm about to ask You." She said with regret.

"Porchia, I could never hate'chu."

"Well, just don't think less of me then." She said with a smirk.

"What is it? Spit it out."

She began to blush as she ask'd, "Will You spend the night with me?"

Teddy's mind ran a mile a minute before he answer'd.

"Where?"

"I got a suite at The WESTIN around the corner."

"Les go."

Teddy text'd Mani tell'n him he was out and not to call the Penthouse, lett'n him know the limo was wait'n on them when they got ready. From there, Teddy and Ms. Porchia left out, walk'd around the corner and the Hotel was directly across the street.

They arrived in the suite about 2:15AM. Ms. Porchia had thoroughly plan'd this. The suite had a fully stock'd mini bar with 2 bottles of Crystal, a Jacuzzi in the bedroom and fresh exotic fruits.

Teddy sat on the bed and watch'd Ms. Porchia walk over to fill up the Jacuzzi, while he rolled him a joint. After turn'n the water on, Ms. Porchia kick'd off her stilettos dropp'n 3 inches in height and brought Teddy a bottle of Champagne with two glasses to the bed. PORCHIA, YOU ARE GORGEOUS AS FUCK BUT I CAN'T FUCK YOU. Teddy thought.

They chatt'd until she cut off the water in the Jacuzzi. Teddy popp'd the bottle, pour'd two glasses, pass'd Ms. Porchia her glass and lit the joint. Ms. Porchia made a toast to a New Year and Teddy's success while sitting in his lap. She initiated a kiss that Teddy thought he want'd. Not only did he think he want'd it, but so did the erection he possessed. The kiss got very intense. Ms. Porchia stood up and slid off her juicy wet in the center thongs and sat back next to Teddy unbutton'n his vest and shirt exposing all of his prison tattoos.

"Damn, I miss'd You Teddy. My pussy throbb'n right now want'n You." She said in a seductive tone, grabb'n Teddy's fully erected dick. "Let me taste my dick. Iss been too long. He could never fuck me or love me like You."

Teddy was fine until she began to talk. He stood up and walk'd to the nightstand grabb'n the half bottle of Crystal, while Ms. Porchia slid out of her Prada dress exposing her flawless naked body and ly'n across the king size bed. Teddy walk'd close to the bed with his shirt hang'n open and still half tuck'd in his pants, took a sip of the Champagne from the gold bottle and stood there look'n at Ms. Porchia's beauty, despising her existence.

"Cum git whus Yours Teddy." She said as she slid her two fingers between her soak'n wet pussy lips display'n the contractions inside her vaginal walls.

Teddy began to seductively pour Champagne between her leggs as she pant'd and moan'd. Moving up to her navel – still pour'n the Champagne, she began to bring herself to an orgasm while masterbating.  All off a sudden, Teddy went from seductively pour'n the Champagne between her teenage perky tits to pour'n it in her face aggressively about to drown her, empty'n the bottle.

"Bitch, You think I jus forgot about the bullshit You did? I ought to kill Yo stupid ass now. Fuck You wit a A – I – D –S dick and die slow bitch? I let – chu live when I coulda murder'd You." Teddy rant'd as Ms. Porchia sat up naked on her elbow in the wet bed stunn'd at the sudden turn of events.

"Bitch, I lost my momma while I was gone!

You changed my son's last name and kept him away from me for 11 whole years. Man FUCK YOU! You miserable BITCH! I hate that I can't hate-chu but the love I have for You will stay right here with me." Teddy shout'd as he grabb'd his belong'ns and start'd for the door as he turned to face her before walk'n out, "I've loved You since day one and I will forever love You but I would never consider intimacy with You again. I LOVE

YOU PORCHIA." Teddy said as he shut the door behind him.

His build'n was 2 blocks up. He walk'd and shed tears at the sight of Ms. Porchia's tears and disbelief. HOW COULD A MAN ACHIEVE ALL HIS PERSONAL GOALS AND SUCCESS AND STILL BE SO UNHAPPY?

Teddy question'd himself as he walk'd.

When he arrived home, he shower'd, check'd every room for all his children. Everybody was present so he advanced to the master bedroom where his wife Treace ly wait'n. They made love the remainder of the morning and fell asleep around 5:30AM.

Teddy was woke up to a phone call at 11:30AM from the manager at the WESTIN HOTEL. He told Teddy that he had an extreme emergency concern'n a Mrs. Porchia Grier Troutman and his # was left for a contact. Teddy jump'd up and rush down to the hotel. As he enter'd the lobby, he could tell that something real bad had taken place. Cop cars were everywhere and so were ambulances and fire trucks.

Approach'n the desk, Teddy ask'd for the manager. He immediately came to the desk introducing himself. Mr. Lasko told Teddy that Ms. Porchia's body was found float'n in the Jacuzzi filled with blood that morning. She had cut her wrist and bled to death. Teddy's breath left him momentarily. Mr, Lasko and two officers caught him before he pass'd out sitting him down on the couch in the lobby. "Are You ok, Mr. Massey?" The officer ask'd.

"She left You a letter. That's how we knew to contact You."

Mr. Lasko inform'd as he pass'd the note.

Teddy unfold'd the letter and began to read.

*Dear Teddy,*

*If You are reading this, then please accept my apology for all the pain I've ever caused You. I never knew love until I got to know You. Love is what I know You have for me and our child. I apologize that I didn't possess that same kind of love. If I had, I would have never kept Y'all apart for so long.*

*Little Teddy is your son in every sense of the word. He has always loved You and I use to endure his resentment toward me. I loved You too but I was so caught up in my own bullshit that I could never truly express it.*

*Teddy, if I know You like I know You, then please forgive me for the pain and burden I'm currently inflicting on You and our son. In my own selfishness, I couldn't bear to live knowing that I'm Your first and only love and I kill'd the chance to ever experience that love again. Little Teddy barely wants to be around me since Y'all reunited. Your wife is a beautiful woman. When I see her and your daughter, I realize that my life is over. I know that you will help our son pick up the pieces.*

*Your GOD – ALLAH has bless'd You and for*

*that, I will rest in peace know'n that Little*

*Teddy is in the best of care.*


*I LOVE YOU TEDDY.*


*YOUR 1ST & ONLY LOVE OF THIS LIFETIME,*


*PORCHIA*


*P.S. Teach our son to be himself and love*

*himself.*


*4EVER AND A DAY,*


*YOUR PRETTY POISIN*

## AUTHORS BIOGRAPHY

## FOR ABDUL WAJIB TIMEER AZIZ

Abdul Wajib Timeer Aziz was born on October 17, 1971 in Charlotte, NC, where he and his siblings were raised in a single parent home by their mother. In his earlier years, he attended First Ward ES, Ranson Jr. High, and Harding High. Abdul had harsh but respectable learning experiences during his childhood. Abdul was inspired to write his first book by Ronald "Manifest" Winchester and Vicky Stringer, who is the author of "Dirty Red". "Pretty PoiSIN" is 85% realistic that is based on experiences that occurred in Abdul and people that surround him lives. The title of the book came from his son's mother, who was gorgeous but she had everyone fooled with her innocent beauty. The hardest part of writing "Pretty PoiSIN" was rewriting it over. In order to grasp the message in this book, readers will have to read it to find out. He considers his work as an URBAN EXXXPERIENCE.

Currently, Abdul enjoys spending time with his children Javel, Bernard, and Deon who are 25, 19, and 18. His hobbies are reading, traveling, shopping, and listening to the ocean. Favorite foods are salad and salmon. Favorite music is Hip-Hop and Alternative. One day he would love to visit the City of Mecca, for the Holy

Pilgrimage. His role model is Prophet Muhammad (SWA), and his mentor is Blake Karrington. His motto is "Network'n with each other to empower each other" which came from his NEXT COAST NETWORK'N GROUP. Favorite quotes are "The choices You make today is the life You live tomorrow" and "Boys play games, Men handle business".

Abdul Wajib Timeer Aziz would like to thank all his family and friends, especially Eureka Wiggins, Twanna Glover, Christina Johnson, Tiffany Huggins, Sherry Carrothers, CEA, Blake Karrington Presents, Marcus Massey, Dumar Hemingway and last but not least his dad Raymond Carrothers for helping him along

the way to getting "Pretty PoiSIN" published.
When people look back at his life, he want
them to remember him as a servant of ALLAH
that gave freely of himself to assist others.
The proudest moment of his life are his
children because they are the RIGHTS he
made in his life.

Abdul Wajib Timeer Aziz is currently working
on putting a Radio Tour together for his artists
that were on his soundtrack. His advice to
aspiring writers, is to expand, challenge
yourself and your peers to enhance in this
genre.

## Synopsis

Teddy is above and beyond the stereotypical young black male. School is an obstacle to be defeated and the plush life is a goal to be achieved. He is a born leader that's loved by many although the opposite sex is his greatest pitfall. Teddy is plagued by his past, the streets, and the love of his life Ms. Porchia. With the juggling of school, the streets, and Ms. Porchia parents he is covered around a brick wall that stands to divide the love between him and his son. Could prison, the loss of his loved ones, and his dignity as a man paint an ugly reality that turns out to be "Pretty PoiSIN?"

For Copies of Pretty PoiSIN and Manuscript Submissions:

Contact OhsoNecessary @ 704 968-5255

# ORDER OTHER URBAN FICTION TITLES

### Pretty PoiSin  $19.95

Teddy is plagued by his past, the streets, and the love of his life Porchia. With the juggling of school, the streets, and Porchia parents he is covered around a brick wall that stands to divide the love between him and his son. Could prison, the loss of his loved ones, and his dignity as a man paint an ugly reality that turns out to be "Pretty PoiSIN?"

### Country BOY   $14.95

Country boy is a fast-paced, action packed urban drama set in the dirty south. The story takes you away from the bright lights of the big cities. Where drug deals take place on city blocks and Street corners, to the backwoods, dirt roads and trap houses of the south.

### God Forgives: The Street's Don't   $14.95

Tired of living the life of a convict and petty hustler, Sanchez (Chez) Viles pieces together a crew of vicious and hungry hustlers and wages war against all who have set up shop in his city. No one outside of his crew is safe from the death and destruction that ensues, and it isn't long before the streets bow to his will.

### Mafietta: Rise of a Female Boss   $16.95

Mafietta follows Clarke, a woman tired of bankrolling her suitors, entertaining a man she normally wouldn't consider - a man from the underworld. Their perfect love story falls apart when a tragic turn of events forces Clarke to run the family business. When a good girl turns mafia queen, she is forced to choose between the love she's always wanted and a lifestyle she's grown to hate

Abdul Wajib Timeer Aziz          Pretty PoiSIN  503

Please circle your selection below:

| | |
|---|---|
| Pretty PoiSin | 19.95+5.95 (shipping and handling) |
| Country Boys | 14.95 + 5.95 shipping and handling) |
| God Forgives: The Streets Don't | 14.95 + 5.95 (shipping and handling) |
| Mafietta: Rise of a Female Boss | 16.95 + 5.95 (shipping and handling) |
| | |
| Total Amount Enclosed | $_____ |

Please submit payments Order Forms
(Leave Money Orders Blank) to:

Ohso Necessary
c/o Flowers By Lois
2624 Statesville Ave.
Charlotte, NC  28206

Include all information needed to ensure proper
delivery. Books will be delivered in 6-8 weeks.

Made in the USA
Columbia, SC
03 June 2022

61241505R00302